PENGUIN BOOKS

# IT ENDS HERE

Heidi Perks is the *Sunday Times* bestselling author of *Now You See Her*, which was a Richard and Judy Book Club pick, *Come Back for Me*, *Three Perfect Liars*, *The Whispers*, *The Other Guest*, *The Last Resort* and *Someone Is Lying*. *It Ends Here* is her eighth novel. Heidi is a voracious reader of crime and thrillers and is fascinated by the darker side of our closest relationships. Heidi lives in Bournemouth with her husband and two children.

*Praise for Heidi Perks*

'I was gripped from the very first page' **Claire Douglas**

'Slick, gripping and compelling' **Lisa Jewell**

'Kept me up late into the night . . .' **Lucy Clarke**

'Terrifically suspenseful and intriguing' **Liz Nugent**

'Whip-smart twists' **Chris Whitaker**

'Beautifully written' **Gilly Macmillan**

*Also by Heidi Perks*

Now You See Her
Come Back for Me
Three Perfect Liars
The Whispers
The Other Guest
The Last Resort
Someone Is Lying

# IT ENDS HERE

## HEIDI PERKS

PENGUIN BOOKS

PENGUIN BOOKS

UK | USA | Canada | Ireland | Australia
India | New Zealand | South Africa

Penguin Books is part of the Penguin Random House group of companies whose addresses can be found at global.penguinrandomhouse.com

Penguin Random House UK,
One Embassy Gardens, 8 Viaduct Gardens, London SW11 7BW

penguin.co.uk

First published 2026

001

Copyright © Heidi Perks, 2026

The moral right of the author has been asserted

No part of this book may be used or reproduced in any manner for the purpose of training artificial intelligence technologies or systems. In accordance with Article 4(3) of the DSM Directive 2019/790, Penguin Random House expressly reserves this work from the text and data mining exception.

Set in 10.4/15pt Palatino LT Pro
Typeset by Six Red Marbles UK, Thetford, Norfolk

Printed and bound in Great Britain by Clays Ltd, Elcograf S.p.A.

The authorised representative in the EEA is Penguin Random House Ireland, Morrison Chambers, 32 Nassau Street, Dublin D02 YH68

A CIP catalogue record for this book is available from the British Library

ISBN: 978–1–804–94648–0

Penguin Random House is committed to a sustainable future for our business, our readers and our planet. This book is made from Forest Stewardship Council® certified paper.

For Nelle

Who has been on this journey with me for ten years

## Monday morning, 7.26 a.m.

*A huddle of bodies fills one tight space and the scent of fear churns around the room. It has heightened since the gunshot and the piercing scream. Now no one knows what to say or do.*

*Maybe the gun will go off again. Perhaps this time aimed at someone's head.*

*I think about how you don't know what is happening to me right now. That you will be going about your day as normal, no clue anything is out of place in the world. I try not to imagine what you are doing because the thought is enough to break me. But somehow, I can't stop myself.*

*I wonder what will happen when they tell you: what they will say, how you will react. I'm not even sure whether anyone on the outside knows we are here, a bunch of early-morning customers in a coffee shop on the marina. You have to drive or walk down a long road to get here and there was no one else about when I arrived this morning.*

*But maybe someone heard the gunshot. It is only a matter of time before the police are called and they tell you I am being held hostage. And – oh God – the idea of that is unbearable: the thought of your pain the moment you realise my life is in danger.*

*But I need to focus on what's happening inside this room.*

*We've been in here for no more than eight minutes and the walls are already closing in. The air is thick with dread and it's making my head throb.*

*There is one small window that looks out onto the back of the building, but the sunlight doesn't reach it, which means the only light comes from a bare bulb hanging from the centre of the ceiling. Storage boxes are shoved to one side, but they aren't sturdy enough to sit on and so everybody is on the floor, which, judging by the dirt, hasn't been swept in a while.*

*I don't know who it was that screamed a minute or so earlier, but someone told them to shush and since then it has been deathly silent. I wonder if everyone is asking themselves,* Why us? What did we do to deserve this?

*Every time I close my eyes I picture your face and, for the briefest of moments, it makes me feel calm before an overwhelming surge of terror comes over me and I wonder if I will ever see you again.*

*Love is all that counts in the end. That's all it comes down to when you strip everything else away. You hear about people on their deathbeds, don't you? How they say it doesn't matter what you accumulate or how successful you are in your job, because when it comes to the end, it is only ever about the people you love and who loved you in return.*

*If I walk out of here, I am going to tell you again how much I love you. I just want the chance to say it once more. But that feels a stretch away, out of my grasp and out of my control.*

*The sound of the gunshot still pounds through my ears, reverberating inside my skull. I have never heard anything so terrifying.*

*Someone is bound to know we are in here now; I am certain of that. Help will be on its way. I can sense every one of us waiting, expecting the doors to be broken down any moment.*

*But the minutes tick by and no one comes.*

*And so, everyone keeps wondering what will happen next as they look at me for an answer I can't give, because I don't know either.*

*What I do know is that when the police find you and tell you I am being held hostage, you will fear the worst. You will imagine me hurt, or dead. But your thoughts won't turn any darker than that; it won't cross your mind for one second that I could be the one holding the gun.*

*I hadn't wanted anyone to know we are here. But there was so much noise and panic in the room, and I wanted it to stop. Pulling the trigger was a mistake, and now everything has changed. I wish you could tell me what I should do, even though it is already too late.*

# Detective Inspector Aaron Field
## 07.30 hours

'What's with the traffic today?' Aaron moans as he pushes through the doors of Southampton Central police station.

'I don't know,' Kelly replies as she strides quicker to keep up with him. 'Can you hold the doors?' she adds as the lift arrives. 'It's not easy keeping up with you with this, you know.' She gestures to her bump with a sweep of her hand.

'Sorry.' Aaron holds the doors back for her. 'It's taken me forty minutes to get here already. How are you doing anyway? Not long now, is it?'

'Six more weeks till my due date. Five till I get out of this place.' She laughs, but Aaron knows how much she loves her job and most definitely isn't counting down the days till she leaves. Kelly Holden has had two babies already and, each time, has been desperate to get back to work.

The doors close and the lift takes them to the second floor, where he holds them open again for her to go first. 'Did you have a good weekend?' he asks as the boom of his boss's voice erupts from where he is standing in his office doorway. 'Field?' he is calling.

'Sir?' Aaron answers.

'Just the man.' He stands where he is, one outstretched arm holding his door open, knowing it won't take long for Aaron to relent and walk over to him. 'There's been a report of a supposed gunshot from inside a café on the Isle of Wight,' he says when the DI is closer.

'A gunshot?'

'Called in at 7.26 by a Franklin Henderson, boat owner at Port Marina in Newport. Says he heard it coming from inside The Boatyard café. All quiet now and the café is shuttered up.'

'And we're sure it's a gunshot?' he asks his superintendent, who's already beginning to retreat into his office.

'No. We're not sure,' comes the reply. 'It's a bleeding coffee shop on the Isle of Wight, but I want you to check it out and get me an answer by 8.30.'

'Will do, sir,' Aaron says as the door closes, and Kelly, who's been hovering nearby, shrugs at him.

'What do you make of it?' she says as they walk over to their desks. Kelly sits down in her chair, unwrapping a bagel to sink her teeth into. Aaron watches as sauce oozes out of it and drips onto the detective constable's desk.

'I don't know,' he says. 'What is that place, The Boatyard, have you heard of it?'

Kelly nods, wiping sauce from her chin. He doesn't understand how anyone can care as little as she does about what she looks like when she eats, but he also kind of likes that about her. Despite the fact she's fifteen years younger than him, Aaron and his wife get together for dinner with her and her husband every six months.

They've become friends, in as much as he is with anyone he works with.

'We went there for lunch last summer with the kids,' she tells him. 'It was lovely. Shabby-chic café with a really cool vibe to it. They do art classes out the back apparently, and they had a craft fair on when we went. Don't know what it's like in the winter though,' she adds. 'We visited on a hot day in July, not a cold one in March.'

'The last time I went over to the Isle of Wight for fun was when my own kids were young. Ten years ago, I reckon. Now the wife prefers white sandy beaches with waiters who deliver her piña coladas every half-hour.'

'Don't we all?' Kelly jokes. 'This guy must be mistaken, surely. I don't see anyone walking into The Boatyard with a gun.'

'Yeah, no doubt.' Aaron leans forward and taps on his keyboard, pulling up the contact details for the nearest Field Intelligence Officers in the area. 'I'll get a couple of the guys to go down and check it out,' he says. 'I can't imagine anyone's got hold of a gun and started shooting the early-morning customers. Jesus, it's only just half-seven.'

'People still go out for coffee or breakfast, you know,' Kelly says. 'Just because you have every meal at your desk.'

He laughs. 'I went out for dinner last night. Anniversary,' he adds, glancing at her surprised expression. 'Twenty-seven years, can you believe? We got married at twenty-four. Both our parents thought we were too young.'

'You proved them wrong.' She smiles as she tucks back into her bagel. 'Though I don't understand how she still puts up with you.'

'Yeah, I think I agree with you there,' Aaron says, searching his computer for a Field Intelligence Officer and locating one near to Newport. He dials the FIO's number from his mobile.

'DI Field,' he says, introducing himself, as a man on the other end picks up. 'Any chance a couple of you can pop down to Port Marina and see what's going on? Report of a gunshot, inside the café down there. The Boatyard,' he clarifies. 'Maybe nothing but I need you to take a look and report back.'

'Sure. We'll head there now. Who called it in?'

'Someone called Franklin Henderson, one of the boat owners. Talk to him and get a feel for if he really heard what he says he did or if he could have been mistaken. Perhaps it was a car backfiring.'

'Or perhaps he's just some nutter,' the FIO adds.

'Exactly,' Aaron murmurs before hanging up. He's had enough calls like this over the years, excited members of the public imagining they've heard a shooting when it's nothing more than fireworks.

Eleven minutes pass before he hears from the FIO again. 'What's going on?' Aaron asks as he wanders back towards his desk, one hand wrapped around a cup of coffee.

'All a bit quiet,' the FIO says. 'Shutters down at the front of The Boatyard. Can't see anyone inside. No one else has come in since we've been here, and the car park is almost empty. Just two cars at the front that don't belong to your caller.' Aaron imagines them, a hundred yards back, watching the place through binoculars.

'You manage to speak to Henderson then?'

'I did. Says he knows what he heard. Ex-military apparently.'

'Is he?' Aaron asks curiously, as he puts his coffee down and slides onto his chair. Cradling his phone under his chin, he opens the computer and starts a search for Franklin Henderson. An ex-military man shouldn't be mistaken about gunfire.

'Says he saw a girl he knows called Jennie Hogan opening the café at 7 a.m., and then at least four other customers have gone in since. None of them together.'

'At least?'

'There's a back door. He wouldn't have seen anyone entering that way. And he didn't see any of them leave.'

'What do you make of him?'

'He's given me a full description of all five people he saw going in. Very detailed, like he's been watching the place himself for some reason. I don't know,' the FIO goes on. 'He's convinced, but I'm not sure I am. There's nothing to go on. Nothing that tells us either way whether there's anything untoward happening or not. But this guy Henderson?' The FIO pauses. 'Yeah, well, something about him feels off.'

'In what way?'

'Like he's on edge. But nothing I can really put my finger on.'

Aaron rubs a hand over his chin. 'Talk me through the place. What's the building like?'

'Main double doors at the front facing the water where there are tables and chairs outside all tied up, for the winter, I assume,' the FIO tells him. 'Can't see inside, the doors and windows are shuttered up. Round the side, there's another door leading onto a small car park, apparently reserved for staff. There's a Mini parked up there, which Henderson says belongs to Jennie Hogan. Another entrance at the back. All shut up too. Windows all along the front, shutters pulled down on every one.'

'But he's seen people going in? And this Jennie Hogan must still be inside?' Aaron says. He grabs a notepad and asks the FIO for the descriptions of the people Franklin Henderson has supposedly seen, making notes on what he's told.

'Jennie Hogan, a woman in her mid- to late thirties, who Henderson apparently knows because she has worked there for the last seven years. Lives with her grandmother nearby in Newport. She's the only one he recognised.

'Then a young female in running gear,' the FIO presses on. 'Wearing a woollen hat. Bright multi-coloured shiny leggings, orange zip-up top and dark sunglasses. Henderson assumes she was out for a jog and dipped into The Boatyard for coffee. Says they get a few runners who occasionally do that.

'Next up a male, looked to be in his early to mid-forties, close-cut hair, wearing a blazer and trousers. Flashy-looking type according to Henderson, says he looks like he had money. Arrived in a black BMW that's parked in the main car park at the front. Could be interested in buying the marina as the place is apparently up for sale.'

Aaron nods silently as he scribbles.

'Another female, no determinable age but Henderson guesses she's in her forties. Blonde hair, cropped into a very short style, wearing a long black puffa-type coat that came down to her calves with jeans underneath. Arrived from round the back of the building and seemed to have got down to the marina on foot.

'Finally, another male who Henderson thinks he recognises from TV or similar, but can't identify. Tall with facial hair and short wavy dark hair. Pulled up in a very shiny blue Audi TT, the only other vehicle in the main car park.'

'And the witness says he heard one gunshot?' Aaron asks.

'Yep. Followed by a scream.'

'Have you got his number?' Aaron says, making a note of it when the FIO reads out the digits. 'VRNs?' he asks now, jotting down the vehicle registration numbers of the Mini, the black BMW and the Audi TT as the FIO reels them off. They account for three of the people, two of them must have walked there, as the FIO suggests, or been dropped off.

'Anything else?'

'That's it.'

'And could the witness have missed anyone?'

'He says not if they went through the front, but the back—'

'Yeah, yeah,' Aaron says. 'He can't see that entrance.'

'Apparently, he was sat on his boat the whole time since Jennie Hogan opened up. Watching the place by the sound of it,' the FIO adds, a hint of sarcasm in his tone.

Aaron thanks him as he ends the call, agreeing that Franklin Henderson has been surprisingly helpful. Maybe too much so? He wouldn't be surprised to find the ex-military guy does this kind of thing on a regular basis.

Kelly leans to one side to peer at him round the edge of her computer, raising her eyebrows in a question.

'No idea,' he admits. Gun crime is rare in the UK, even more so on the Isle of Wight. Things like that just don't happen over there. 'But we have one name and two vehicle registrations, so let's track them down.'

# Ede

Ede Hogan picks up the duster and flicks it over the numerous photo frames that sit on her mantelpiece and sideboard surfaces. She has too many, she really should sort them, remove some maybe that are from years back, but she cannot bear the idea of it. Where would she even start?

She blows out a breath as she pauses in front of a photograph of her daughter and picks it up, wiping a smear of something undefinable off the glass with her finger. Her girl, her only child. Ede will go to her grave wondering how, if she'd done things differently, their lives might have turned out better. She blames herself, as any good mother would, for the mistakes her daughter made, the wrong choices that led her down paths too deep and too dark. Before long, it was too late for Ede to help her daughter turn her life around: Shona died when she was only thirty-eight.

She was far too young, and the situation was only made worse by the fact she left behind a daughter of her own. No nineteen-year-old should have to bury their mother like Jennie did. It was such an impressionable age, but then Shona's mistakes had impacted Jennie throughout the girl's entire childhood.

Ede had stepped in every time. Ever since Jennie was born, she was the sober presence needed when a child's only parent was a non-functioning alcoholic. Yet, despite how hard she tried to support them both, she will always question herself as a mother, and as a grandmother. She still beats herself up over how she handled things when Shona was alive. Could she have controlled her better? Did she seek the right treatment for her? *Enough* treatment for her?

There is plenty of guilt to consume you when you're related to an alcoholic, and plenty of people to tell Ede that, at the end of the day, there was nothing she could have done to save Shona. But Ede still wishes she'd been given a second chance, and then she might have proved them all wrong.

She carefully places the photo down with a sigh and moves on to a cheerier one of Jennie. There are many of her beloved granddaughter, now thirty-nine and such a different character to her mother. Where the last twenty years have gone, Ede can't fathom. Sometimes she wonders if it's the mundanity of their lives that makes it feel like they've passed in a flash. There hasn't been any of the travel and excitement, graduation celebrations or promotions like she'd hoped for Jennie. Her granddaughter has led a very quiet and unassuming life, and one Ede often forces herself not to describe as dull.

She stares at the picture before her. In it, Jennie is maybe ten or eleven and is wrapped in a knitted cardigan that Ede had made for her, despite the fact it was summer. On the tip of her nose is a splodge of red from where it had burnt in the sun. She was a gawky kid, even Ede could see that, but it didn't help that Jennie was told so by her own mother too.

Now, the landline trills, swiftly pulling Ede out of the past. It is a place she has been living in too much recently, since the present no longer offers any comfort and the window to the future has started to shrink.

She is always telling Jennie not to dwell in the past, spouting lines like they have come from a self-help book. 'You need to recognise what happened, you should never dismiss it, but don't let it shape you,' she has told her granddaughter. 'Live in the present, Jennie, but always have dreams for your future.'

'You're such a wise granny,' Jennie has often laughed in return, likely only half-listening and certainly not taking her seriously, which upsets Ede because she wants her to know the truth of the words even though they do sound comically poetic.

'No, I am anything but wise,' Ede has told her. 'I just want you to have it all. Learn from my mistakes.'

As she answers the phone where it sits at the end of the dresser, she knows that, nearing the age of forty, Jennie hasn't achieved any of the things Ede had in mind for her. Her granddaughter might plead she is happy but Ede doesn't see how she can be, with a life that is small and pretty uninteresting and no one but a seventy-eight year old for company.

Ede also knows there is only one person who calls her on her landline now, and that's her neighbour.

'How are you doing, Edith?' Marjorie's voice booms down the line.

'It's 7.30,' Ede says. 'How do you know I wasn't asleep?'

'I didn't. But you aren't, are you?'

'No.' She sighs. 'I don't sleep past 5.30 anymore.'

'You have things on your mind?'

Ede laughs. 'Of course. I have plenty of things on my mind. That's a stupid question.'

'I just meant, is it that or is there something else, a more physical reason, waking you up? Are you needing to get up for the toilet, for instance?'

'No more than usual, but I'm not discussing my toilet habits over the phone with you,' Ede retorts. 'Who knows who might be listening in.'

'I don't think anyone would be interested in our conversations,' her neighbour says. 'There's more going on in the world than your bladder.'

'Tell me about it,' Ede sighs.

'So, what are you worrying over?'

'Nothing new,' she says. 'Jennie mostly.' *I just don't know how she will cope*, is what Ede really wants to say.

'You're thinking ahead of yourself again.'

'I have no choice. I don't have that far ahead to think anymore,' Ede murmurs as she drops her duster and wanders through to the kitchen where she puts the kettle on and slumps down into a chair.

The washing-up from last night is still sitting on the draining board. She is sure Jennie had said she would do it before she went to bed, but then Ede had gone upstairs, her head in a blur following the words tossed between them throughout the evening. Both of them were left hurt and wondering how they'd got to that point, but then the topic of death can bring out the strongest of emotions, Ede finds.

'Jennie shuts it out like it isn't happening,' she says now, as tears dampen her eyes. Ede has been more prone to crying these days. 'I don't know what she's going to do when I'm gone.'

'Ede, my dear, she will cope perfectly fine. Jennie is forty next year. She's not a child.'

'She's still a child to me,' Ede mutters.

'Well, maybe that's the problem.'

'You don't have kids, Marjorie,' Ede snaps. 'You have no idea what it's like. You still worry about them, no matter how old they are.' She runs a finger around in circles on the surface of the table. 'Would you like to come over for a coffee?' she asks, hopeful and in sudden need of company. 'Jennie isn't here. She went off for an early start at the café this morning. She's doing an extra shift.'

'Do you need the money?' her neighbour queries, blunt as always, but they have lived next door to each other for so many years that they don't beat around the bush.

'She doesn't have to do it,' Ede tuts. 'But you know that for whatever reason she likes it there.' Though how can she be working in a café and living with her grandmother? She leans back in the hard chair, feeling it press into a spine that is already throbbing. It makes her wince.

Her and Jennie's lives have merged, she realises now. There are pieces of both of them in this home and it cracks Ede's heart a little to notice it with such fondness. To imagine the day when it will be just Jennie living here.

The tapestry she has hanging on the wall in the hallway – one her own mother had made – would look out of place anywhere other than in an old lady's house, but Jennie doesn't mind it. Ede's recliner stands in one corner of the living room, ready to push her upright at the touch of a trigger, then pull her back down into it again.

Meanwhile Jennie has bought cushions from online websites with names Ede doesn't recognise and chosen the Farrow & Ball paint for the wall behind the fireplace, in a shade called Lamp Room Gray when Ede would have opted for something a little more lilac. They blend in the communal areas, their bedrooms the only reminders that there is a whole missing generation between them.

'I told her I was going to sell some of my bedroom furniture the other day.'

'Oh, sweet Jesus, Edith.'

'I was trying to be practical. And I didn't mean get rid of anything she uses or sees every day.' Her mind drifts back to the pictures in the hallway. 'Jennie yelled at me to stop trying to box my life up.' At the time Ede had thought it such an apt way of putting it, but afterwards she couldn't get the picture of herself lying in a box out of her head.

'Just stop this talk, will you? I'm coming over,' Marjorie says, 'for that coffee, in case you'd already forgotten.'

Ede smiles. 'I hadn't,' she says as she pulls her mobile phone out of her cardigan pocket and thinks she will send a message to Jennie.

She hangs up the landline phone and types out *What would you like for tea tonight?* Ede glances at the message before she sends it and considers what a stubborn old fool she is when what she really wants to say to Jennie is that she is sorry.

# Rosa

Rosa Williams finishes her early-morning yoga class at 7.30 on Monday mornings, just as the sun starts to seep through the large sash windows of the room she rents in the old Victorian building. It is perched on top of a hill, and she can see the estuary and miles of Isle of Wight countryside from it. Rosa has to admit, it's one hell of a way to start the week.

Her clients are all chatting, sitting in a small circle while she offers the pot of Egyptian chamomile tea she made earlier. She passes around blue china mugs painted in various designs that she has picked up from charity shops and car boots over the years.

Rosa has always been a collector; as a child, filling scrapbooks with postcards of places she had been to and lining shelves with shells and stones from beaches she'd visited. As a teen, plastering bedroom walls ceiling to floor in tiny cut-out pictures of her latest band fads; and as an adult, with the charms she's accrued over the years hanging from the silver bracelets laced around her wrists.

Despite the tidiness of their home, she still squirrels away knick-knacks she's bought over the years. Suitcases filled with memories from her childhood are tucked away in the loft, hidden from Daniel who doesn't understand her need to hang on to anything.

When they moved house two years ago, he told her it was a chance to sort through it all. 'You could halve the stuff you need to take with you,' he said. 'And even then, halve it again.'

'But why would I?' she'd said then, genuinely dumbfounded.

He had laughed and cupped a hand under her chin, holding her face to his as he kissed her on the lips. 'I love you, Mrs Willams-to-be,' he'd said, because that was what she was back then. 'Keep anything you want.'

She and Daniel had met in a park, twelve years ago when he was still a wannabe writer, detesting every minute of his work for an online news site.

In contrast, Rosa, at twenty-two, was a newly qualified yoga teacher and loving life. She had found where she wanted to be and ignored friends who suggested that because she was only part-time it wasn't a proper job. Meanwhile they were burning themselves out in artificially lit offices, striving for promotions that would demand even more from them.

Daniel was sitting on one end of a bench, taking a phone call that became heated and ended with him hanging up. She sat at the other end, a coffee in hand and a rolled-up yoga mat across her knees. He'd turned to her and said, 'Sorry. I'm ruining your morning.'

'Don't be daft.' She smiled. 'Boss not happy?'

'Boss is never happy.' He smiled back but his eyes were heavy.

'What do you do?' she had asked him, and a conversation started that would end up lasting an hour and a half, because neither of them wanted to end it, for fear it might be their only one.

But a week and many more conversations later, Daniel was standing in her living room, gaping at her bookshelves and open-face IKEA cupboards. 'I don't get it but I kind of love it,' he told her, looking at her earnestly. 'It's like I can see exactly who you are.'

'And who are you, Daniel Williams?' she had asked.

He had smiled in return.

'Who are you?' she said again, a little more curiously this time, because he was nothing like the men she had dated in the past. Daniel was tall, with floppy hair and glasses, handsome in a studious way and so much more serious than anyone else she knew, and yet she was already falling for this man she didn't really know.

'I think I know what I'm *going* to be,' he told her. 'And that's happy.'

And Rosa had smiled, because, more than anything else, she liked the idea of that.

Two years later, they moved into a cottage in Bembridge on the east coast of the island, Rosa arriving in a large Luton van, followed by her dad in another, while Daniel had managed to fit his minimal belongings into the back of his car. Ten years on and their living space encompasses the things they've collected together, and Rosa can no longer see how she could separate them if she tried.

'I saw Daniel on TV last Monday,' one of her ladies says to her now as she fills her cup with tea. 'He looked very handsome, talking about his latest book.'

Rosa laughs, feeling the heat in her cheeks. This is the way the conversation will go now and it will fill up the next half an hour before they leave. 'He spoke so eloquently and came over very well. I thought you said he was nervous?' the lady asks.

'He was,' Rosa admits. 'He didn't want to do it. Daniel's never done anything like that before. I had to force him to.' She still can't believe how resistant her husband was to the idea when he has always spoken about wanting more out of his career.

Daniel's wasn't an overnight writing success, though to many it appeared that way when his debut novel did so well. 'If overnight means six years,' he would often say, making a joke of it. In reality, the rejections and torn-up manuscripts, and nights spent asking himself if he should just give up, had taken their toll. Now he is five books on and, with every new release, pushes himself to do better, to sell more copies, to *be more.*

'It's a big thing,' another member of the class joins in. 'He was so interesting. Although my son now thinks he doesn't have to bother with school to be a success.'

'Hmm,' Rosa says. 'Daniel didn't do well in his GCSEs and so he has this belief that education isn't the be-all and end-all. I've told him he should go into schools and talk about his books, but that maybe he needs to change his messaging if he does that!'

The woman laughs. 'He wasn't that bad. It's good to hear stories like his. How people can become successful when they don't give up.'

'No, Daniel certainly didn't give up,' Rosa says proudly,

because she *is* proud of her husband who was wallowing in his self-described failures when she met him, rejection letters pinned to the walls of the bedroom in his parents' house where he still lived.

He tells Rosa it's because of her that he made it in the end, and he writes as much in each of his books. *My beautiful wife, I would never have managed this without you*, he acknowledged in the first, and she thinks this is partly true if only for the fact she encouraged him to keep going. *Don't we make a good team?* he said in the second. Every dedication touches her heart in ways only he's ever been able to.

'I've read all his books,' another woman says to her now.

'That's kind of you.'

'Do you think he'll sign them for me?'

'Of course, Daniel loves doing anything like that.'

The class member smiles. 'I'll bring them in next week.'

'Maybe I'll ask him to come along if you'd all like to meet him,' Rosa suggests, and the women light up at the idea of her semi-famous author husband, who they all seem to think is pretty fit, coming to one of her yoga classes.

He'll jump at the chance of coming with her; he hates her walking here at 5.30 a.m. when it's still dark outside. He insists she must drive, or offers to drive her himself, but she refuses unless it's torrential rain.

Rosa sees beauty in the early mornings when the hills are rolling in mist, and the sun is only beginning to show itself. It is a kind of peace that can't be found anywhere else. But Daniel sees bleakness and fears his wife will get mugged or worse. He imagines hearing she has been found dead in a ditch.

For as long as she has known him, he has worried about everything and anything. His worst-case scenarios are what make him such a good crime writer, or perhaps his terrifying plots are what fuel them. She isn't certain which came first.

Finally, they are all ready to leave, and Rosa hangs back at the door as she waits to say goodbye to her ladies and tell them she looks forward to seeing them next week.

She will be home and in the shower by 8, eating breakfast with her husband half an hour later. *Hopefully anyway*, she thinks, because it depends on Daniel, and if he is even awake yet considering how late he was working last night. She had crept out of bed at 5 a.m. this morning and hadn't disturbed him.

Her husband's writing has taken up more and more of his time over the years since they first met. He throws himself so wholeheartedly into it that, whenever he is in the middle of a project, there is little room left for Rosa. She doesn't mind, not really, because this is all she wanted for him. She hoped he would find the life he wanted to be living, like she had. And, for Daniel, that has always been writing.

But there are times like now, when his head is buried in his laptop, when Rosa has no choice but to wait patiently for him to come out the other side.

Maybe this morning she will take him breakfast in bed. She will make his favourite, eggs Benedict, from a recipe her mother gave her. She will brew a pot of coffee and force him to eat and talk to her before he locks himself away in his office for the rest of the day.

They were sniping at each other last night, both irritable at the end of what had become a working weekend for him. He had shut himself away since Friday evening and Rosa was left to her own devices, reading books that weren't about crime, making Easter baskets for her nieces who are visiting from Scotland in two weeks' time.

The orange light of his desk lamp was glowing through the glass doors of his office when she went past at 9 o'clock on her way to bed, reminding her that their worlds are out of sync. He is a night owl, and she is an early riser. He didn't crawl into bed until gone midnight last night. He's not usually so absorbed in his work as to be tapping away on a manuscript at that hour.

'What's he working on now?' the last of her ladies says to her on the way out.

'I never know what Daniel's writing till he's finished.'

'Really?'

Rosa nods. 'He doesn't share anything with me until he's got a first draft done.' She smiles, not wanting to get into the fact it's that he doesn't feel he is good enough. Daniel hates revealing his work, even to her, until every word on the page is perfect. 'He tells me that this is the one though,' she says in a whisper like she is passing on a secret. 'He seems really excited about it.'

Rosa had questioned what Daniel meant by 'the one' because his five books so far have been highly successful as far as she is concerned.

He had made the *Sunday Times* Bestsellers List with his latest, and has sold over a million copies in total. He is famous on the Isle of Wight – at least, they recognise his name if not his face.

As soon as the last lady is gone, she locks up the studio and walks the twenty minutes back to their house, hoping Daniel is still in bed and hasn't already holed himself up in his office with a bowl of cornflakes.

Their house sits in the countryside in the middle of the island because this is where Rosa had always wanted to be, surrounded by rolling hills. After eight years of living in Bembridge, where they were five minutes' walk from the harbour, they sold their cottage to give her a slice of her dream.

Now, as she walks up the lane, she wonders if she is as happy here as she'd hoped she would be. In many ways, she misses their little cottage where they were surrounded by neighbours and had a friendly pub nearby. She misses the days when Daniel would sit in front of the fire with her in the evenings, sharing a bottle of wine while they talked about plans for things like getting a dog and starting a family.

She turns into the driveway and frowns when she notices her husband's Audi isn't there. Letting herself in the front door, Rosa calls out Daniel's name, peering into his office, but he's clearly not at home.

She sighs, sends him a text to ask where he is, assuming he has found somewhere else to write today for whatever reason, and realises how disappointed she is that her husband isn't there.

## Detective Inspector Aaron Field
### 07.45 hours

Aaron makes a search for the Port Marina on his computer and takes a note of its owners: two male business partners living in Dorset. As Franklin Henderson had mentioned, they have the place up for sale. Aaron finds contact details for both and tries their numbers, leaving messages when neither man picks up.

'What's the news?' his boss asks as he appears behind Aaron and glances over his shoulder. The superintendent looks harassed this morning, though that's nothing unusual.

'I'm not certain yet, sir. I have two FIOs at the marina, they've spoken to the caller, and we're tracing two vehicles in the car park.'

His boss nods absently, already moving past, his mind clearly somewhere else. He is giving off vibes that he doesn't believe this to be anything serious, but then Aaron can rarely second-guess him anymore.

He inhales a deep breath through his nose as he expands an image of the marina on his screen. Whatever the boss thinks, Aaron needs to find out for sure, but as he studies the picture he feels too removed to form any proper judgement from where he sits in a station on the mainland.

'I have an address for Jennie Hogan,' Kelly calls out from her desk opposite his. 'And her mobile number is going straight to voicemail.'

He looks up. 'Of course, there could be a reasonable explanation for that: she might have turned it off as she went into work.'

'And we have the registered owners of the vehicles. The Audi TT belongs to a Daniel Williams who lives in Newport. The BMW to a Jacob Hamilton, home address is London, Wimbledon to be precise,' she tells him as another call comes through from the Field Intelligence Officer at the marina.

'We saw some movement behind one of the shutters at the front,' he tells Aaron. 'Otherwise, the place is still shuttered up.'

Aaron glances over his computer at Kelly. 'We can't get hold of either Daniel Williams or Jacob Hamilton either,' she is saying to him. 'Both of them have their phones switched off too.'

Aaron's stomach tightens as he looks at his watch. A gunshot was heard nineteen minutes ago, there are at least five people inside the café as far as they know. The place is locked down, shutters pulled over every window, and *three* of the people inside have mobiles that are switched off. Whatever this is, something here isn't right.

'Hostage situation?' he says, more to himself than anyone else.

'Could be,' the FIO replies. 'Hard to tell.'

There are two most dangerous times in any hostage situation. One is when you send in firearms, but the second is right at the start. Meaning now, if he's correct in his assumption.

If no one has been shot yet, then the shooter doesn't necessarily want to kill anyone. But, of course, they don't know that this is the case. If this *is* a hostage situation, Aaron can't say for certain there isn't already a dead body inside The Boatyard.

'What's the story around the marina?' he asks the FIO. 'Who else has turned up?'

'No one else here yet, other than us and your witness, Henderson.'

'Okay, remove him from the area but don't let him go. I'll want to talk to him.' Aaron pauses. 'A strange place to hold people hostage though, don't you think?' he says as he peers at the images of The Boatyard on his screen.

'Maybe,' the FIO agrees. 'How do you want us to proceed?'

'What are the roads in and out like?' Aaron asks, as he leans forward and grabs his mouse, enlarging the map of the marina.

'One road in.' The FIO confirms what Aaron can see in the image.

He isn't familiar with Newport, but the aerial image shows that Port Marina sits at the end of the River Medina, south of the better-known Cowes. It berths about fifty to sixty vessels as far as he can make out with his minimal boating knowledge. The picture shows a car park to the east, presumably where the Audi TT and the BMW are parked, and then a building that must be The Boatyard. Behind this is a small, enclosed area, which is possibly the second parking lot where they have found the Mini this morning. He asks the FIO to talk him through the area, just to confirm he is right.

At the back of The Boatyard is the one long road the FIO has mentioned and all around is a sea of green hills and fields. That road and the river are the only two ways of getting to the marina unless you're on foot.

He plays over the little information he has: the fact the witness is ex-military, the place being locked up, and *three* phones turned off. It is this that drives him to make the call. 'Okay,' Aaron says. 'We're treating this as a hostage.

'Kelly, get officers to the three known addresses,' he tells her as she nods in agreement. 'Find out what we can, but for God's sake, I don't want family members worrying at this point. Not until we have some idea what the hell's going on here.'

Flashes enter his head; fears that he could be jumping in on a situation that isn't even happening. But what he fears more is doing nothing, only to find out it is.

Now, he needs to set a number of things in motion; speak to the Tactical Firearms Commander, update his boss, talk to a hostage negotiator.

'We're going to need to get a roadblock in place,' he says. 'Stop people from walking or driving down to the marina. Sooner or later, someone's going to want their boat, if not pay a visit to the café. And get onto the marine unit too so they can stop people coming into the harbour by boat.' He squeezes his eyes shut and presses his fingertips against the lids. 'And I want access to any CCTV,' he adds, praying he's making the right call and this isn't all too much on what little information they have. If it is, he'll cross that bridge when he comes to it.

# Liv

Liv Hamilton picks at her croissant, pulling a tiny piece off it and rolling it around in her fingers rather than putting it into her mouth. She isn't hungry, and if she weren't here, meeting her best friend for breakfast, she would have skipped it altogether.

'You're not eating that?' Katy says, her own mouth full of a large chunk of sourdough toast.

Liv sighs. 'It's too early for me.' It isn't even 8 a.m. yet, they had met at 7.30 before either of them had to get to work. 7.30 on a Monday morning isn't a good time to be eating. She usually grabs something like a porridge pot that she'll eat at her desk, and that's rarely before 10. But finding time to see friends who have kids now is becoming more impossible and Liv has to grasp the opportunity whenever she can.

'You don't feel ill?'

'No, I don't.' Liv pushes the plate away from her. She has been feeling *off* lately, but she doesn't want to think too much about that now.

'I'm glad we didn't go to that posh place you suggested then,' Katy says, clicking her fingers, searching for the name of it. 'Though the menu looked divine.'

Liv laughs. 'It does. I want to try it at some point. Maybe we could go for dinner?' she asks hopefully.

''Course.' Katy nods. 'Only you know what it's like.' She shrugs, forgetting that Liv doesn't know what it's like. 'Every evening the girls have a different club after school and I seem to spend all my time just driving from one place to another, usually in totally opposite directions. By the time I've fed them and got them into bed, the last thing I want to do is go out again.' She pauses, eventually, but it's too late. 'Sorry, Liv. Listen to me rattling on.'

'It's fine.' Liv waves a hand.

'No. It's not fine. Forget the kids, of course I want to go out for dinner with you.'

'You're busy, I get it.' Liv smiles, trying to show it doesn't matter, it isn't a big deal. She tells herself the idea of rushing about after little people sounds like hell. And it's true, her friends look permanently knackered. Katy has certainly aged since motherhood; she is always pointing out the lines that crack into her forehead and often sits at a table with her jeans undone. But Liv wouldn't care. She'd *like* to worry about C-section scars and be drained by the exhaustion of having a child who won't sleep.

Last night she had to tolerate dinner at her parents' sprawling house in Chelsea in the company of her two sisters, their husbands, and the four nieces and nephews she has between them. Each time conversation steered off in another direction, someone found a way to bring it back to the children.

At least this was how it seemed to her. It's how it always

seems. And the meal dragged on for ever: four courses, cheese at the end. Her father is a stickler for fine dining, even when it is only family present. She grew up in a household with too much pomp and, while her sisters have become mini versions of their mother, Liv hates every aspect of it.

'I've had to get two cleaners now,' her elder sister had sighed as she'd sliced into a creamy brie she was offering her three year old. As if this was a hardship for her. It was at this point Liv made her excuses and got up to leave. She didn't even have Jacob with her for moral support. The evening would have been much more bearable if her husband had been by her side, giving her a nudge and a wink, making her laugh at her father's expense when they were out of the room.

But Jacob had left home at 5 p.m. last night, for a meeting on the south coast this morning, and while Liv had asked him to stay, for her, he'd been adamant that he couldn't. She knew there was nothing she could say that would make him agree to leave the house at 5.30 a.m. on a Monday morning and drive down to the coast then because Jacob was not, and never would be, an early riser. Neither, for that matter, was she.

Liv stifles a yawn as Katy raises her eyebrows.

'This . . . what you're wearing today,' her friend gestures to her top admiringly, 'it's gorgeous.'

'Thank you.' Liv tugs at the green silk shirt. 'I treated myself.' She shrugs. 'I haven't bought anything for ages.'

Katy laughs. 'I'm sure that's not true. And anyway, why not? It's your money, you can do whatever the hell you want with it.'

Liv smiles and drops her gaze. Her world is a far cry from Katy's.

'So,' her friend says, with another mouthful forked in, 'how's Jacob? And marriage in general?'

Surprisingly, Liv feels a flush burning her cheeks. She tries to ignore Katy's stare. 'What?' her friend asks.

Liv frowns, shakes her head. 'Nothing. What do you mean?'

Katy shrugs, eying her friend's face. 'I don't know . . . I have the feeling there's something you're not telling me.'

'Of course not.' Liv makes a face and turns back to the food in front of her that she really doesn't want.

She hears Katy chewing as she watches her intently but eventually her friend says, 'Go on then. Make me jealous with all the wonderful dates you must be going on. Did you go to see *Moulin Rouge*?'

'We did. It was okay.'

Katy puts down her cutlery with a sigh. 'Will you just tell me what's going on?'

Liv turns and looks out the window, onto the already busy Russell Street in Covent Garden. They say London never sleeps and Liv thinks they're right. She's always loved living in the city and has never really wondered about moving anywhere else. Until recently, that is, when she's started to have dreams of getting away from everyone and moving somewhere more isolated, just her and Jacob.

It doesn't even have to be that far. Surrey would mean he could still get into work easily enough. She'd take the chance to give up work and do something different. It's not as if they need the money anyway. Liv fell into a job she isn't particularly interested in, but she's over the hump of her mid-thirties now and life could look so different for them.

Jacob isn't keen though. He wants to stay in London, for now anyway. 'What's the point in moving?' her husband says. 'We don't need a big, rambling house in the middle of nowhere.' He likes to be in the centre of everything, surrounded by the buzz and bright lights of the city.

And anyway, moving house won't solve their problems. They'll still have the same issue in Surrey. A different county isn't going to magically produce a baby.

'Is it Jacob?'

'No, of course not. Jacob's fine. He had to leave for work last night though,' Liv says, trying to change the subject. 'He had a meeting down south, so I don't suppose he'll be back till late.'

'You know, I still don't understand how you two can work together in the same office. Doesn't it drive you mad?'

'I like us working together. It's not as if we sit on the same floor. Some days I don't even see him. Anyway, I worked with him before we dated,' Liv says. 'Or *for* him, rather. I know no different.'

They crossed that forbidden line not long after Liv joined the company. 'Don't date the boss,' one of the girls had said casually to her while showing Liv the ropes.

'Does everyone?' she'd joked.

'I think everyone would like to.' The other girl smirked. They had stopped outside his office and Liv peeked in, almost audibly gasping when she caught sight of Jacob. He had looked up and grinned then, and though she didn't believe in love at first sight, she conceded there was an immediate lust. It was hard not to feel anything for a man who looked like Jacob. Just the kind of guy she had always been into: stubble that was verging on being a beard, blue eyes, dark blond hair and a kick of aftershave. He was leaning back in his chair, twirling a pen between his fingers. Open-collared white shirt and a blue suit. He *knew* he was good-looking. There was no way he couldn't.

Jacob assured her he hadn't been out with anyone else in the office. She wasn't sure she believed him but has never found out anything to the contrary. Besides, their relationship took off in an instant. They were engaged after a year, and married within three, trying for a baby soon after, though that was five years ago now.

Perhaps Jacob is right about not moving out of London. They don't need a bigger house than they already have. Liv watches her parents rattle around in a house that is far too big for them, a status symbol of a mansion with rooms they don't even use, her mother flitting ghostlike through them, always watching Liv's father with a suspicious eye. Never happy. Or she wasn't until he retired and they started spending half the year on holiday instead. 'Be careful about the type of man you go for,' she had once warned Liv. It was her first veiled admission that all was not good in her own marriage. 'Don't go for anyone with too much power. You can never trust them.'

Liv loves her father, but she would hate to be with anyone like him. Jacob might mirror him in his drive and ambition and his love of nice things, but that is where the similarities end. Her husband's attentiveness isn't something she's ever seen in her parents' marriage. And besides, Jacob doesn't have the money her mother warned her about, that comes from Liv's family. As far as she's concerned, the balance of power in their relationship is just right.

'Liv,' Katy urges as she leans across the table, 'I've lost you again and I know you. Something's on your mind.'

Liv studies her friend's face. One she knows so well since they met when they were only seven. 'I think I might be pregnant.'

'What?' Katy laughs, pulling back as she clamps a hand over her mouth. 'Are you freaking kidding me? I thought it was going to be something awful. Liv, why haven't you said anything? That's wonderful news.'

She nods, numbly. Of course it is, if it is *real*. It is the news they've been waiting and hoping for. It is everything she's ever wanted.

'Have you done a test?'

She shakes her head. 'I can't bring myself to.'

'God, why not?' Katy shrieks.

'Because what if I'm not?'

Katy frowns and reaches for Liv's hand. 'Do it. If you're not then you'll deal with it, just like you always do. But what if you are?' she squeals as she squeezes her friend's fingers.

'I've got one in my bag.' Liv pulls her black tote nearer and rests her hand on the packet she's been carrying around with her for the past week since the date of her period came and went. But she has been in this position before. And so, she tells herself, it doesn't mean anything. In a way it has helped that Jacob hasn't been on top of her dates this month and hasn't even asked her once if her period has started like he normally would. Liv has been trying not to think about that.

'Do it now. I demand it,' Katy says, excitedly. 'Drink your water and go to the loo.'

'I don't know.' It's easy for her friend to get excited when she won't ever understand the low Liv will sink into if she's not pregnant.

'I do. Come on, Liv. Imagine telling him tonight.'

Liv smiles then. She has already played out how she would tell Jacob. She wants to wrap up the test and give it to him like a present. She won't say anything, she just wants to see the expression in his eyes. Finally, everything he has been dreaming of will come true.

'Okay!' she says, getting caught up in the excitement herself now, wondering why she hasn't done it sooner, because she does actually feel different this time. 'Okay. Oh my God, I'm doing this!' She laughs as she gets up and grabs her bag, leaving Katy waiting for her at the table.

## Detective Inspector Aaron Field
### 08.05 hours

Aaron mutters to himself as he continues to stare at the image of the marina on his screen. 'I need to be able to see this place for myself,' he says. Field Intelligence can give him all the intel he needs, and Aaron could easily run the case from Southampton with blueprints of The Boatyard to help him. But still, he feels too distanced from it. 'Can you get hold of ferry times for me?' he asks Kelly. 'From Southampton and Lymington, whichever is soonest.'

He has dealt with a few hostage situations before, but they were all over and done with quickly. Usually involving drugs, gangs, people known to the police already. So far, not one of them has been conducted by a man with a gun waltzing into a café in broad daylight and holding up the waitress and several customers, who were most likely in the middle of enjoying their breakfast.

Since he came off the call with the FIO he's spoken to the hostage negotiator on duty, who happens to be based in Southampton too, and has briefed her about what little they know. In a moment Sarah Connelly had the landline number for The Boatyard and the negotiating team started trying to make contact, but as yet no one is picking up. And still not one of the three mobiles they have numbers for has been switched on again either.

Aaron has also briefed Tactical Firearms. They are the ones who will be making the decisions about how best to react, gathering intel on the situation inside the building and figuring out the tactics needed to preserve the lives of the people inside: if and when they need to send in armed officers.

Preservation of life overrides every decision or piece of information-gathering Aaron and any of his team makes from now on. He is sure he must be right, and the five people Franklin Henderson watched walking into the building this morning are inside it now against their will. And so, Aaron tries to ignore the splinters of doubt that lodge under his skin. This is a crime in action. They will dig in regardless. One wrong step could cost a life.

This is what makes a hostage scenario different from dealing with other crimes. They won't be rushing to send anyone inside because, as soon as you do that, you raise the stakes, and right now all they can hope is that every one of the hostages is still alive. A gun has been fired and someone could be badly injured. Or, worse, dead. All Aaron can do is call the right shots.

'There's a ferry from Lymington at 9 a.m.,' Kelly tells him. 'Forty-minute crossing and a twenty-minute drive the other side to the marina. You could be there for 10.'

Two hours from now. Anything could happen in two hours.

'You'd have to leave in ten minutes if you're going to make it though. And officers have been sent to all three addresses logged on the VRNs,' she adds.

Aaron nods in response. It will be good to get details from family members about at least three of the potential hostages. 'The other two that Henderson has seen going in, the two women who haven't been accounted for,' he says, 'how would they have got there?' He stares at the aerial image of the marina again with its road that snakes down to the harbour nowhere near anywhere else.

'I guess they walked there,' Kelly says, pointing out the only obvious answer.

'But why do that when there's a car park right there?'

'Some people do like to walk,' she says with a roll of her eyes. 'Early-morning stroll, joggers, dog walkers . . . though the witness didn't mention anything about dogs.'

'Hmm.' Aaron picks up his phone and taps out the number the FIO gave him for Franklin Henderson. He wants to talk directly to the only witness they have.

'Detective Inspector Aaron Field,' he introduces himself when Henderson answers. 'I'm aware you've gone through some of this with one of my officers, but I'd like to ask you some questions.'

'Of course.'

'Could you tell me where you were this morning when you heard the gunshot?'

'On my boat,' he says. 'The other side of the bridge.'

Aaron zooms in on a still image of boats lining the waterside, across the bridge from The Boatyard. 'What time did you get there?'

'6.30,' Franklin Henderson says without hesitation.

'That's early. It would still have been dark out.'

'Sunrise was 6.22,' he clarifies.

'But still . . .' Aaron mutters. 'Early for the second week of March. Do you always take your boat out at that time?'

'Not at all. I like to get here before anyone else arrives. No one else around – it's the best time of day. I make myself a cup of tea and have a bacon sandwich in peace.'

'Sounds idyllic,' Aaron concurs, thinking of the way he sat in rush-hour traffic as he'd crawled through the city this morning. 'But you say Jennie Hogan opens up the restaurant at 7 a.m.?' he asks.

'Not every morning. Sometimes it doesn't open till 9, other times even later. But this morning she opened at 7.'

'Is that unusual?'

'Not really. They seem to open The Boatyard whenever they want in the winter months. You can never tell.'

'And is it up to her?'

'No, I doubt it. I'm sure she does what she's told by the manager.'

'Do you know Jennie personally?'

'Yes. I know her. She's worked there for seven years, maybe even more than that,' he says, repeating what Aaron has already learnt. 'She lives nearby with her grandmother. Is anyone coming down here?' Henderson asks. 'Other than two scruffy men, who I have to say don't look like they're in the force, no one else has even turned up yet. I heard a *gunshot*. I assume you're taking that seriously. I do know what I heard.'

'We are taking it seriously,' Aaron confirms. 'And I am coming over, but I'm based in Southampton.'

'And there's no one on the island who can run the case?' Henderson asks. 'Someone could already be dead.'

'At this stage we don't suspect that to be the case,' Aaron says, moving him on. 'I believe you saw four other people besides Jennie enter the building.'

'I did.'

'I need you to go through what you saw with me again, with timings as best as you can and the order they went in.'

They still don't know who and what they are dealing with, how many shooters there are even. They can't presume it is just the one. They can't presume anything when they don't know why whoever is responsible has chosen this place to walk into with a gun and take a load of customers hostage. Why so early on a Monday morning? What is it they want? Why aren't they communicating with them?

'The woman in the jogging wear went in at just after 7,' Henderson is telling him. He is factual and succinct as he relays the detail Aaron already knows. For reasons unknown to Aaron, this witness kept a mental note of every one of the people who entered the café that morning, and according to him, nothing stood out about the way they acted or the clothes they were wearing. Each of them, it appears, was coming in for a coffee or breakfast; two of them had possibly been out walking or running. The man in a suit could have been there for business. These are all assumptions right now, but highly probable ones.

'And have you seen anyone else in the marina at all?'

'Not a soul before your two turned up.'

'Is it normal for that number of people to go in so early for coffee?'

'It can be. It's a popular place. Not always but it didn't seem strange.'

Aaron blows out a breath as he checks his watch and grabs his keys from the desk, standing and switching off his computer. He needs to leave if he's going to make the ferry.

'So as far as you have seen there are five people inside,' he says.

'As far as I have seen,' Henderson clarifies. 'But anyone could have got in through the back.'

He is right, of course, as they already know. Someone could already have been inside. Anyone could have entered the café in advance if they had wanted to. Waiting for these unsuspecting people, ready to ruin their day and possibly their lives. He needs to see what CCTV The Boatyard has that can be remotely accessed.

'It's too quiet and still in there,' Henderson is saying. 'I'm telling you, this isn't right. If no one else is going to do anything, I've a mind to go in there myself.'

'No,' Aaron says firmly. 'That's a very bad idea, Mr Henderson.'

'Jennie doesn't deserve this.'

*I'm sure none of them do*, Aaron thinks, but instead he says: 'Are you and Ms Hogan friends?'

There is a pause before Henderson answers, 'Yes, I suppose we are.'

'I really can promise you we are doing everything possible to ensure her safety. The best thing you can do for her right now is let us do our jobs.'

'I'm not going anywhere,' he says. 'Your man here is pushing me up the road, but I'm not leaving the area.'

'That's fine,' Aaron says. 'We can't make you. One more thing. Do either of these names mean anything to you? Daniel Williams or Jacob Hamilton?'

Another pause before Henderson answers. 'No,' he says eventually.

'You're sure?'

'I am.'

'Okay, well, thanks for your time, Mr Henderson. I'll be in contact again soon, please keep your phone on you.'

He hangs up, wondering what to make of Franklin Henderson and his attention to detail as he watched everyone arriving at The Boatyard this morning. Is it nothing more than luck that he happened to be in the right place at the right time?

'What are you going to do?' Kelly asks him as Aaron looks over his shoulder to see his boss is back in his office. Kelly is waving her wrist in the air, pointing to her watch. He really needs to leave now or he won't make the ferry.

Aaron sighs. He doesn't want to run this case reliant on second-hand intel and images on a screen. Staying stuck in Southampton means that's exactly what he'd be doing. He walks over and taps on the door of the superintendent's office, pushing it open when he's beckoned in.

'Sir, I believe we have a hostage situation at the marina,' he says, filling him in on what little he knows so far.

His boss raises his eyebrows as he taps a pen on his desk, waiting.

'And I need to go there.'

'To the Isle of Wight?' his boss asks. 'You can run it from here.'

'I know I can, but I'll do a better job there. And I need to leave now if I'm going to make the next ferry.' Aaron already knows he's cutting it tight.

'By the time you get there it could all be over, Field,' his boss points out.

'It's a risk I'm prepared to take.'

Firearms officers won't be rushing in before they have made contact with the people inside the café. That will only happen the moment they determine it is necessary, and until then, as long as the Tactical Firearms Commander believes no one is injured, the situation might not change for hours. Aaron has heard of situations like this lasting days before action is taken, something the relatives can never quite come to terms with.

'Fine,' his boss says eventually. 'But I want an update in two hours.'

'Will do, sir.' Aaron nods as he walks out the door, closing it behind him as he faces Kelly who is hovering the other side of it, waiting. 'I want a team briefing at 9,' he says. He'll be settled on the ferry by then and it means that in an hour he should hopefully have some updates he can then give the boss, particularly from the officers who are visiting the three home addresses, and hopefully also on the two other women Franklin saw entering the building, although this could prove trickier when they have nothing to go on so far.

'I want to come with you,' Kelly tells him. 'You need a scribe; I can do that.'

Aaron pauses, considering the fact she is seven and a half months pregnant. But she is right. He needs a DC to gather the info, and there's no one he'd rather have at his side than

Kelly. 'Let's go then,' he says, conveying more confidence than he feels in his decision to leave the station. Because the boss is right. In two hours anything can happen; it could all be over having culminated in nothing, or it could all be over with an innocent person or persons dead. All Aaron can do is hope he's making the right choice.

# Ede

Ede finishes the call to her neighbour as the kettle boils. She feels like she has betrayed her granddaughter, saying too much about Jennie. Ede has more or less admitted she doesn't think Jennie has made enough of her life, but only out of concern for her. The world is so much bigger than the Isle of Wight and full of endless opportunities, if only Jennie would take the chance to explore it.

She makes two cups of coffee in preparation for Majorie's visit and sits idling over her phone and the message she's just sent to her granddaughter, asking her what she wants for tea tonight. She assumes Jennie will see it as the olive branch it's intended to be. Theirs is a relationship where they don't have to spell things out. But, as yet, Jennie hasn't replied.

Often in the evening they'll sit side by side; Jennie on her phone checking websites like Pinterest and Facebook and Ede turning the dog-eared pages of a paperback she's picked up from a second-hand shop. They'll dip in and out of conversations seamlessly while being content in their temporary separate worlds, because they're comforted by the presence of the other beside them.

Occasionally, like in times like this, Ede will find herself imagining her granddaughter barely a matter of months ahead, sitting on her own, an empty space beside her and a dip in the cushiony recliner where Ede has indented it, and her eyes will well up with those damned tears she can't seem to get rid of. She has no idea how one of them will fare without the other. It's a thought she has never wanted to dwell on.

She pushes her phone aside and tells herself to stop being maudlin, reaching down to stroke her cat as she weaves around Ede's leg. 'What is it, Plum?' she says. The tabby turned up in Jennie's arms one day five years ago when she decided her grandmother needed something to care for other than her.

When Ede straightens up, she catches sight of the back of a figure moving towards her front door and, while it seems too tall to be Marjorie, Ede cannot think who else would be calling on her this early in the morning.

The doorbell rings and she gets up, moving to the window for a better view, peering through it to find a young man and woman standing on her doorstep. The man is leaning back and staring straight at her.

Ede frowns, trying to figure out who they are. The man is dressed in a black coat buttoned up to his neck and wears dark trousers, and Ede thinks he wouldn't look out of place at a funeral. He pulls out a badge that he holds up and Ede squints to look at it as she realises he must be a police officer. She glances at her watch as she pulls away from the window. 8.15 a.m., what could they possibly want with her at this hour?

Ede isn't a worrier by nature. She tries not to think ahead, despite her recent forays into Jennie's future without her, and so she doesn't panic at the sight of the police at her door. Besides, the only person she has to worry about is Jennie, and she knows exactly where her granddaughter is because she waved goodbye to her this morning as she left to go to The Boatyard.

She opens the front door and the police officer introduces himself and his colleague before asking if they can come in. Ede tells them that of course they can and opens the door wider. She directs them to the kitchen, where the three of them take a seat around the small round table that sits in its centre.

'Can I take your name?' he asks her.

Ede cocks her head, thinking it is the oddest question when it is he who has come to her home, but she tells him anyway.

'Mrs Hogan, we're looking into a vehicle that's parked at the Port Marina.' The policeman recites the make and model and the registration plate.

'Well, yes, that's my granddaughter's,' Ede says. 'She works at the café, she's there now.'

The officer nods, appearing to frown at the same time, pausing before he speaks again. 'And your granddaughter lives here, with you?' he asks.

'She does. Can you tell me what this is about?'

'Hopefully nothing at all, Mrs Hogan, but we do just have a couple of questions for you if you don't mind. Could you tell me what time she left for work this morning?'

'Yes. 6.40 or thereabouts,' Ede says. 'She was opening up for the early shift. Is there a problem?'

'And do you know if she was working with anyone else this morning?'

'No. I have no idea. I think at this time of day it would just be her.' Ede feels a fluttering in her chest, a sensation she doesn't like the feel of. 'There is clearly a problem, so will you please tell me what it is?'

'There's a situation at the marina,' the man replies, and in an instant Ede feels the blood drain from her body. He presses on. 'But as yet we don't have all the details. Mrs Hogan, is there anyone else in the house with you at the moment?'

'No.' She shakes her head, any thoughts of Marjorie popping by forgotten. 'But Jennie is okay, isn't she?' she says. And when he doesn't answer, 'What's actually happened?'

'As far as we know there is nothing to worry about,' he says and Ede nods eagerly, willing this to be true, yet he continues to beat around the bush. 'But we believe there to be some people inside The Boatyard and right now we are trying to ascertain who they are and what they are—'

'Please, just stop!' she says. 'I really don't know what you are talking about. Will you tell me straight what is going on, because while you are saying there isn't anything to worry about, I have a feeling that isn't the case at all.'

The officer nods gravely and finally the female constable next to him pipes up. 'We have reason to believe Jennie and some customers are being held inside the café against their will.'

'Oh my Lord,' Ede says, clutching a hand to her mouth.

'But my colleague is right in that, as far as we know, no one has been hurt. The police are doing everything they can to figure out what's going on so it can be resolved as quickly and safely as possible.'

'Jennie's being held hostage?' Ede cries, her eyes wide with fear. She realises that she cannot feel the tips of her fingers any longer, they have gone so numb, and her hands start to shake as she clamps them onto her knees to steady herself.

She doesn't have to wonder if Jennie is definitely there, she knows she is. Her granddaughter spoke to her this morning on her way out. 'Early one today, Gran,' she had said as she kissed Ede on the cheek. Besides, her Mini is parked outside the café.

Ede lifts her trembling fingers and touches the spot Jennie's lips had pressed. Her granddaughter's words had been sharper the previous evening, the second time this has happened in the last week, which is unheard of for them. But while it wasn't forgotten about this morning, because something that huge couldn't be, Jennie didn't act like she was holding a grudge. Theirs, after all, is a relationship built on a deep-rooted love.

'Mrs Hogan?' the officer is saying. 'Is it okay if I carry on asking you some questions?'

She looks at him, blankly. She is too busy trying to focus on breathing right now.

'Does Jennie open up every Monday morning?'

Ede frowns. It must come across like she is trying to recall, but that isn't it. She knows the answer, it's just that her head is spinning. 'No. Not every week. She was asked to, as a favour, I think.'

'Do you know who by?'

'No.' Ede shakes her head, though maybe this is important. It is hard to break through all the thoughts that are thrashing about when her world is tipping upside down. 'Who would be holding people hostage on the Isle of Wight?' she says, because she cannot fathom this. It sounds so absurd that she almost doesn't believe it to be true. 'Do they have a gun?'

'We don't know that,' the man says quickly, but Ede notices the look that passes between the two figures in front of her.

'You don't know that Jennie is okay either, do you?' Ede says, resting her hands on the table where they continue to shake, her cluster of rings rattling against the antique pine. The female officer pushes one of the coffee cups towards her and Ede stares at it before automatically taking hold of it. She glances at the other cup and for a moment she doesn't recall who she had made the drink for.

'We are currently trying to make contact with the people inside the café so we can ascertain what's happening.'

'You don't know if she's okay,' Ede says again.

'We believe no one has been harmed.'

'No one?' She looks up at him. 'Who exactly is in there?'

'Well, we believe there are two males by the names of Daniel Williams and Jacob Hamilton. Do either of those names mean anything to you?'

'No.' Ede shakes her head. She's never heard the names. 'Is it one of them who is holding Jennie hostage?'

'We don't know, Mrs Hogan,' he says patiently. 'They could well just be customers. A number of people were seen walking inside this morning.'

'But someone is keeping my granddaughter there?' Ede says. 'Against her will?'

The officer is staring at her, his thin lips flattening into an even thinner line. 'We are doing everything we can to find out right now what is happening.'

'I can't believe this,' Ede says, and releases a breath so deep that she feels all the air billowing out of her failing body. The idea that Jennie is in danger, inside her place of work. A place where she has always felt safe. What if something happens to her?

Ede is supposed to go first, not Jennie. This is not the natural order. But then, she knows better than anyone that death does not follow any rules.

'Has Jennie mentioned anything to you recently about working at the marina? Anything she thought seemed strange or wasn't happy about?' the male officer is asking her.

'Like what kind of thing?' Ede questions.

'Anything at all,' he replies, but when she doesn't answer he adds, 'Have there been any break-ins?'

'No, I don't think so.' She tries to sort through conversations, wading through the many things Jennie tells her at the end of the day. But while Ede's memory used to be spot on, more recently it hasn't been what it once was and nothing comes to mind. Her brain is empty.

Ede's concentration is broken and right now her focus is caught by the plants on her windowsill that need pruning. She pushes herself out of the chair and takes a pair of nail scissors from the drawer, carefully beginning to trim leaves. Ede has never been able to abide people who carelessly leave plants to die and rot.

As she concentrates on this task, something comes to her. 'Jennie said there was an argument outside the restaurant one afternoon.' She turns back to the officers who are watching her with curiosity. Now, the policewoman is nodding keenly in a gesture that makes Ede feel like a child who is doing well. 'But I don't know anything more about the detail.'

The woman makes a note of what Ede has said, though she looks more disappointed now.

'She's being held hostage,' Ede says, imagining her granddaughter tied up, a gun pointing at her face. She sees things like this on the news although she has never been good at looking at them. Both she and Jennie shy away from the atrocities happening around the world, because neither of them can bear to witness people's agony. Once, Ede had taken Jennie's phone away from her as she had watched silent tears falling down her granddaughter's cheeks, images of bodies lying on war-torn ground on its screen.

There are people who act when they see cruelty like this, but shamefully Ede is someone who buries her head in the sand. This is why she likes living on the Isle of Wight, because nothing bad happens here.

Until now.

Panic sweeps over her again as she wonders how Jennie will react. If she will keep quiet and do what she is told or feel some responsibility for her customers who are being held hostage with her. Ede prays it isn't the latter, but she knows Jennie too well. She will do anything for anyone whether she knows them or not.

'Yes, as far as we can ascertain they are being held inside,' the male officer is telling her again. 'Is there anything else you can think of?'

Ede shakes her head. There is nothing coming to her. Nothing at all.

'Anything?' the police officer questions. 'It doesn't have to be recent.'

'There've always been disagreements between boat owners and that kind of thing, but nothing that stands out.'

'What about Jennie personally?' he moves on. 'Is there anyone she's had any trouble with? Ex-partners, anyone who's caused a problem?'

'You think this is about her?' Ede cries.

'No, I don't think that,' he says quickly.

'So why did you ask—'

'We have to,' he says, gently, kindly. 'Jennie is working there and as far as we know the others are all customers. I assure you, Mrs Hogan,' he adds, 'there is nothing to suggest this is about Jennie, but right now we need to find out if there's anything at all you can think of, anyone who springs to mind who could have had an issue with either Jennie or anyone else on the marina?'

She shakes her head again, the slight movement sending a sharp stab through it and down her neck. She winces as she clasps her hand over the painful spot.

The female officer stands and fills a glass with water that she presses into Ede's other hand. 'Is there anything I can get you?' she asks. 'Do you need anything for your pain?'

'I just need my granddaughter to be safe,' Ede says, putting the glass down on the table. 'Your questions about the marina . . . You don't think this was random,' she points out.

'Right now we don't know why this is happening,' the female officer says. 'But I assure you, we are doing everything we can to resolve it. We have the best team working on it, led by a very experienced detective inspector.'

Ede desperately wants to believe this, but it is hard to when it is your own flesh and blood they are talking about.

'So, if there's anything else that comes to you, Mrs Hogan, please tell us. It may feel irrelevant, but whatever it is, we need to know.'

But Jennie doesn't have enemies, or nasty ex-boyfriends. There have only been a couple of men over the last twenty years, and no one she is still in contact with.

Ede's eyes fill with tears. 'Whatever is happening, it isn't anything to do with Jennie,' she says. 'It can't be. She's the loveliest girl you could ever meet. Everyone says so. Everyone tells me how wonderful she is. Maybe it's got something to do with the other person whose shift Jennie is covering. That has to be it,' she goes on. 'This is just like Jennie, to do someone a favour and then . . .' She breaks off, holding her hand up to her mouth. 'I don't remember if she told me who it was.'

'Don't worry about it,' the police officer assures her. 'We can find out.'

'Why did she have to go in this morning?' Ede cries before repeating, 'She didn't even need to. She shouldn't be there.'

# Rosa

Despite the fact Daniel isn't in bed like she thought he would be when she got home from her yoga class, Rosa still makes eggs Benedict for herself and sets about focusing on cooking, taking her time melting the butter and cracking egg yolks into a bowl.

She wonders where he has gone to write this morning, up so early after a late night pounding the keys of his computer, attempting to finish his latest book. She tries not to think about the creeping distance it's caused between them in recent weeks. Besides, she thinks, as she adds a little lemon juice to the eggs, there is nothing fundamentally wrong in their relationship. This is how it swings and dips when he is on the home straight, only weeks from a deadline, and she knows there isn't room in Daniel's heart for anything other than writing.

And isn't this what she loves about him? His passion for his books. Would she really have it any other way? she questions as she spoons out some Dijon mustard and adds it to the mixture.

Rosa tidies everything as she goes, making double the amount just in case her husband returns home soon. She strips off her sweatshirt as she stands in their too-hot kitchen, the underfloor heating warming her feet. He has turned the temperature up in the house again because he feels the cold, but it's ridiculous that she's standing in yoga pants and a cropped top in the middle of March. As soon as he is back, she'll need to ask him to turn it down again on the app he's installed on his phone. The one she really should get herself too, she thinks. She's always been so stubborn about conforming to new technology.

Plating up her breakfast, Rosa eats it one-handed with a fork as she leans against the kitchen doorframe and stares towards his office on the other side of the hallway. Through the glazed doors, she can see his laptop on the desk, closed, with a lead trailing out of it and into the plug socket. She sighs and wanders towards the doors, pushing them open. She has a thing about him charging it when he isn't here. She has visions of it overheating and catching fire and so she unplugs the lead and coils it up, placing it on his desk.

There's a woody smell in his room, a mustiness that isn't unpleasant. Maybe it's the oak of his desk, or the old books that sit on the shelves. His office is exactly what you might expect of a writer, dark brown wood and leather, spines of novels both old and modern, an array of colours adorning the shelves. These are the only things Daniel collects, this the only room that tells you anything about her husband. He has always been a private person. He is so unlike her.

'I like living in the present,' he told her once. 'I don't see the need to hang on to memories.'

Apart from books there is little else on his shelves, aside from a wedding photo of the two of them and a pair of interlinked wooden hearts she bought him three Christmases ago. Daniel isn't a keeper of the past and, in some ways, she admires the way he transitions through life without holding on to anything.

A small, latticed window looks out onto the hills, the view framed so that it looks like a picture. Whenever Daniel is in here writing, Rosa only sees the back of him from the hallway as he stares out onto the fields, deep in concentration. She wonders now if he's always wished they had bought somewhere by the sea again when they moved from Bembridge, and whether he only bought this house and moved to the countryside for her.

She glances at his laptop as she forks the last piece of egg into her mouth before placing her plate carefully on his desk and dropping down into his leather swivel chair, resting her fingers on its arms.

He would hate to think she is even contemplating looking inside his laptop, but Rosa is overcome with a sudden desire to glimpse the story that is taking him from her and leaving her with a shadow of a husband. She feels a nervous energy as she opens it and taps in the password. She knows it because they have no secrets, though this will be one because she won't be able to tell him she has gone behind his back.

Her breath catches at the thought of him suddenly appearing. If she hears his key in the lock, it will be too late to get out of his office. Rosa wonders whether she should leave it, but his manuscript has flashed onto the screen. Her eyes are drawn to the title *Death in the Quarry*. Underneath it the statement *working title* is bracketed.

Chapter One opens with a shocking scene, a young boy killed and a gruesome description of his body. Rosa reels.

She doesn't like violence, especially when it's so graphically described, and even more so about a child. Daniel has spared no detail. By instinct she pushes the chair away from the desk, as if to distance herself from the story.

She skims the next few paragraphs and then the subject takes a sharp turn, now dealing with an unassuming family beginning to question where their young child is. The writing is more poetic now, more like the Daniel she is used to, and Rosa wonders how much his work changes before she gets to see it. Does his editor take to it with a knife, slicing much of the gore away, knowing his readers won't like it as much as she doesn't? Or is this story a different tack for him?

The doorbell rings sharply, making Rosa jump. She closes the laptop with a snap and gets up quickly, pulling the office doors shut behind her as she found them before rushing to the front door. In the end she hadn't even been listening out for Daniel's car, she'd been so absorbed in the story. So surprised by her husband.

Standing on her doorstep are two men, one who looks much younger than Rosa, maybe in his late twenties, the other closer to her age of thirty-five. The older of the two has short dark hair that is almost black. He speaks first. 'I'm sorry to disturb you,' the man says. 'I wonder if we could have a moment of your time?'

'Yes?' Rosa asks.

He flashes a badge and introduces himself as a detective sergeant. Rosa opens the door wider for them to step inside. 'Is this about the burglary up the road?' she asks. 'Have you found out who did it?'

'No. It's not about a burglary,' he replies as they step

inside. The man pauses and looks at her. 'Would you mind if I took your name?'

'Yes. It's Rosa Williams,' she tells him. As the three of them hover in the hallway she has a sudden feeling of being underdressed, in a cropped top that could look like a sports bra and with the waistband of her trousers sitting low beneath her navel.

'And this is your home?'

'It is. Well, mine and my husband's.'

'Could we take his name as well, please?'

'Of course. Daniel Williams.' Rosa is intrigued but nothing more because already she thinks this is a story she can tell Daniel when he gets back. It's the kind of thing he'll be sorry to have missed.

'It's nothing to worry about, Mrs Williams,' the officer tells her, which immediately makes Rosa think it could be. 'We have your husband as the registered owner of an Audi TT,' he says, reeling off the registration plate.

'That's right.'

'Can you tell me if he was driving it this morning?'

'Yes. He's the only person who drives it.'

'And do you know where he is?'

'No.' Rosa screws up her eyes. 'Has there been an accident?'

'No, and the car is perfectly fine,' he tells her. 'It's parked at Port Marina. Do you believe that is where your husband could be this morning?'

'The marina? I don't know why he would be but if that's where he's parked ...' She trails off. She knows of the marina; they have a quaint coffee shop there called The

Boatyard that turns into a bar in the evenings. It's a lovely place to sit outside in the summer. Sometimes they have artists in who run classes outdoors. She's thought about asking whether she could do a yoga workshop there in the summer, to generate some new interest. But she knows little else about it, and it isn't particularly near. 'Why are you asking me these questions?' she asks.

'There's no need for concern, but we believe there is an incident currently taking place at the marina and we are trying to establish the ownership of all vehicles parked nearby.'

'An incident? What kind of incident?'

'We don't have any details we can share at the moment.'

'No, hold on,' Rosa says, confused. 'You're telling me there's an incident at the marina and implying my husband is there. And you're here now, on my doorstep, so I'm sorry, but there is clearly something wrong and I need you to tell me what.'

'Really there is very little else we know,' the older detective says, 'but we've had a report that the building has been locked down and yet there are a few people inside. Right now, we are trying to ascertain what this means. It really could be nothing, Mrs Williams, but that's why we are here. Because your husband's car appears to be there in the car park.'

Rosa reaches for the doorframe to steady herself. The officer's words spin around in her mind, making no sense, but she doesn't like the sound of them one bit.

'Do you know where your husband is supposed to be this morning?' he asks.

'No. He was gone when I got back from my yoga class. I assumed he was working somewhere but it could be anywhere. He's a writer,' Rosa explains. 'He must have gone there to write.'

Something is very wrong. There is no other reason the police would have come to her house.

'I'm going to call him,' she says, and runs into the kitchen, grabbing her phone from the table and pressing on his number. It goes straight to answerphone.

'I don't get it,' she says as she hangs up. Her heart is fluttering anxiously inside her chest. She taps a finger against her phone. 'I want to go down there,' she says. 'I can go, can't I?'

'We can't stop you going to the area,' he says.

'Then that's what I'm going to do.'

'But you may be better off staying here. You won't be able to get to The Boatyard itself because the road will be sealed off.'

'Oh my God.' Rosa clamps a hand over her mouth and bends double, clutching her other hand to her thigh. 'Is there a bomb?' She thinks she is about to be sick. All the recent yoga practice and breathwork go out of the window.

'No, we don't believe there to be a bomb. Mrs Williams, would you like to sit down?' The officer takes hold of her arm and leads her into their living room where he deposits her in the armchair that faces the window. It is the one that Daniel sits in sometimes, if it is sunny and he wants to read.

'Then what is it?' she cries.

'We don't know much at this stage—'

'So you keep saying! But what *do* you know?'

'We believe that someone may be holding them hostage,' he says eventually.

'No!' she yells. 'No. That can't be happening. The police must be going in there. They're getting him out?'

The man scrunches up his eyes. 'In situations like this we need to be very careful.'

'Careful? You're sending people to get him out, surely? If my husband is in there— Oh my God. What if he's already hurt?' The thought hits her like a truck. 'Do you even know if he's still alive?'

'We have officers at the marina and as far as we know no one's been hurt. Mrs Williams, I'm afraid at this stage there isn't much more I can tell you, but I would like to ask you—'

'I need to go down there right away,' Rosa says. 'I need to be there. You said I could, and I can't just sit here.'

'But first I do need to ask you some questions,' he persists. 'It's important we know who we might be dealing with.'

Rosa stares at them, the heavy beat of her heart thumping through her chest. Eventually she nods. Let them ask their questions. As soon as they're gone, she will go too.

She tells them again, Daniel has most likely gone there to write, though she doesn't know for sure because she'd already left the house this morning before he was even awake.

'You have a Ring doorbell,' the officer states. 'Could we look at that and see what time he left?'

'Yes. I have it on my phone,' she says as she pulls up

another app she never wanted in the first place but that Daniel installed on her mobile regardless. 'What difference does it make?' she says. 'If you know he's there?'

The officers don't answer as Rosa watches the video footage to confirm the time. The last image is of her returning to the house and the one prior to that is of Daniel leaving. It makes her catch her breath to see him, pulling the door to behind him, stopping for a moment to pat his pocket and check he has his keys or his phone before walking to his car. Her hand shakes as she holds the phone. She wishes she was able to stop him, tell him not to go.

Daniel left the house at 6.50 a.m. It is early for him, especially after such a late night working. The officer asks if she knows the names Jennie Hogan and Jacob Hamilton, but she's never heard of either of them. She tells them her husband works alone. 'He's a writer,' she says again. 'He would have just been wanting to write.'

She wants them gone from the house. She wants to get to the marina so she can be close to her husband. But their questions keep plaguing her and so she keeps answering that there is nothing more she can tell them. And she thinks of her husband who she loves to the root of her heart, writing, lost in thought, and caught up with the other early-morning customers when someone took them by surprise, locked them in and wouldn't let them go.

She tries to imagine how Daniel would have reacted; whether he was scared or if he kept calm. Whatever he felt, she knows the very first thing he would have wanted to do would be to message her because they have talked about it before, when they've seen programmes on TV interviewing people who've had texts from loved ones moments before disaster has struck.

But he clearly didn't have the time to do that. His phone has been switched off. And all these thoughts keep spiralling through her head until, finally, one settles. Because if Daniel *was* working there, why hadn't he taken his laptop with him?

# Liv

It should be comical that she is taking a pregnancy test sitting on the toilet seat in the bathroom of a restaurant, with her best friend Katy waiting for her to share the result instead of Jacob. And maybe it would be funny if Liv wasn't so bloody nervous.

She's often taken a test before her period is even due, hopeful, scared, ultimately crushed with disappointment. Telling herself to get it together, knowing they can start trying again in another two weeks. She pictures Jacob's face over the years and how disappointed he's always been when she has told him. This time she won't even bring it up if it's negative, especially as he hasn't said anything to her in the last week. By the time he gets home tonight, she'll have managed to convince herself she's already moved on.

This sense of detachment has become second nature to her and Liv senses herself shutting down now, in a bid to protect herself from the loss of something that never was. But then, she's practised at bottling her feelings, having done it throughout her life with two sisters who rile her constantly with their greed and materialism. 'The black sheep' is what her eldest sister calls her. Liv laughs in agreement because she'd rather be that than like them.

The test stick is balanced precariously on her bag at her

feet as she listens to strangers' footsteps outside the cubicle and the flushing of neighbouring toilets. Liv looks at the timer on her phone. Thirty-one seconds until she will allow herself to check. She watches it countdown, cancelling the alarm before it rings, and takes a deep breath.

'Shit,' she murmurs in disbelief as she stares at the one word on the test. She gathers it up along with her bag and leaves the toilets, walking back into the restaurant where Katy is waiting patiently. Her breakfast is long finished and her hands are wrapped around a near-empty mug.

'Well?' she asks.

'I'm pregnant,' Liv says. 'I'm pregnant. We're going to have a baby.' She laughs as her best friend jumps up and rushes around the table to hug her. Being with Katy is the second-best thing to having Jacob here, but she still wishes it was her husband she was sharing the news with right now. How she is going to get through the day without calling him she doesn't know, but she needs to wait for him to come home. She wants it to be perfect when she tells him. As perfect as he is, as perfect as the daddy he is going to be.

She laughs at how saccharine her emotions are. She can't quite get her head around what is happening because this news is too momentous, and Liv cannot stop beaming as tears stream down her cheeks, and for a moment she doesn't hear her phone trilling from her bag.

When she finally notices it, she rummages until she finds it, half-expecting it to be Jacob and wondering how she is going to hold back this news she is so desperate to share. But it isn't him, it's her elderly neighbour, who rarely calls Liv, which means there must be a problem with the house.

'Hello?' she answers.

'Liv?'

'Hi, is everything okay?'

'Well, it's just that there's a detective sergeant here wanting to speak to you, and I said you weren't in but that I would call and see where you are.'

'Oh?' She glances at Katy, her smile slipping. 'What does he want?'

'He won't tell me, dear. Do you want to talk to him?'

'I guess so,' Liv says as her best friend squeezes her hand in excitement.

'Is this Olivia Hamilton?' the detective says when he comes on the phone.

'It is. How can I help you?'

'My name's DS Raymond. Are you in the area?'

'I'm in Covent Garden, is there a problem?'

'Are you with your husband?' he asks.

'Jacob? No. He's working. I'm with a friend. Sorry, but what's this about?'

'Do you know where he is at the moment, Mrs Hamilton?'

'My husband? He's away on business, somewhere on the south coast. Please can you tell me if everything's alright?' she says. Katy is still holding tightly on to her hand and her anxious gaze unnerves Liv who looks away again.

'There's been an incident and we're currently trying to ascertain Mr Hamilton's whereabouts,' he says.

It's amazing how quickly her mind manages to scrabble together an image of the worst-case scenario. There's been an accident. A fire. Or a bomb maybe.

Threats like this are one more reason Liv wants to get out

of London. But then Jacob's not in London, she remembers. He is somewhere on the south coast.

The police officer is speaking again. 'We believe your husband is inside a café called The Boatyard. There have been reports of an armed robbery in progress,' the detective says. 'Although this hasn't been confirmed,' he adds, his tone suddenly wary, beginning to backtrack, like he has already said too much.

'An armed robbery?' Liv's heart begins to thump. She was right to panic. Jacob's meeting must have been in a restaurant, and someone's walked in with – what? – a gun? Now she imagines her husband crouching underneath a table, trying to send her a message, to tell her he loves her. Her heart contracts at the image, sucking the breath from her body.

'Like I say, the specifics aren't known. But we believe his car is at the location. Would you mind confirming the registration for me, please?'

Liv gives the details of the black BMW they had bought brand new last year. Jacob had always wanted a car straight off the showroom floor. Despite his earnings it wasn't something he could have afforded to have done on his own. Liv's money paid for it, or *their* money as she prefers to call it. *Liv's* as her father would correct, or, rather more accurately, *his*.

The detective confirms this is the car that is sitting in the car park of the marina in Newport.

'A marina?' she says now. She'd imagined her husband in the middle of a city like Southampton, near to whatever offices he was visiting. But what does it matter? He is there, and his life is in danger, and the new world that Liv, only moments ago, believed they were finally creating is beginning to break apart.

She begs the policeman to tell her what he knows, and he recounts what little he does: they believe there is a shooter in the café and that a handful of customers are being held hostage.

In return she answers his questions: she doesn't know the names Jennie Hogan or Daniel Williams, but maybe these are the people Jacob is meeting. Though she doesn't know for sure, she keeps saying, just like she can't tell if his meeting is with one or more of the two other females they believe to be in there too.

Liv thinks it's a small number of customers that they're talking about. She glances around the Covent Garden restaurant she is in and the steady flow of people filtering in and out.

'Where's Newport?' she asks. Though she knows the name, for some reason she isn't placing it.

'It's on the Isle of Wight.'

'No.' Liv draws back. It is like the detective has reached a fist through her phone and punched her. 'It can't be,' she adds, though of course it is. She *knows* it is, just that the Isle of Wight was never in her mind.

She lets go of Katy's hand by instinct. Her stomach has plummeted, a heavy weight dragging it to the pit of her gut.

'Mrs Hamilton?' he says as Liv's mouth drops open and Katy gapes at her.

Her other hand grips tighter on to the phone, her mind reeling with what this means. Her husband isn't just on the south coast, he is on the Isle of Wight. He has caught a ferry over to the island he grew up on; he possibly spent last night there if he was in a restaurant so early this morning. But Jacob hasn't told her about any of this.

'Mrs Hamilton?'

'Sorry?'

'I said, I wonder whether your husband has any interest in buying the marina?' he is asking her now.

'What? No,' she says, shaking her head. 'Why would he do that?'

'It is just a suggestion as it is up for sale.'

'Jacob's got no interest in boats.'

'What does your husband do for a job?'

'He's in insurance. He works in the City.' She can hear the mechanical sound of her own voice and imagines the police officer must be able to hear it too, but she cannot stop herself. Her heart is beating too fast. She can't pause the questions circling in her head, asking what Jacob is doing there.

'Does he have business on the Isle of Wight?'

'He might do,' she answers, though she is certain he doesn't because if he did, he would undoubtedly have told her. But, more significantly, he would have got someone else to go to the meeting instead of him.

No, whatever he's doing there, he decided it was important enough for him to go, and he has kept it a secret, which makes it implausible that it's anything to do with work.

'If it wasn't a work meeting, can you think of any reason why he might have gone to The Boatyard café at 7.15 on a Monday morning?'

Liv shakes her head again, utters a 'no', though unsettling

thoughts are swimming about. She comes off the phone after a request from the detective to meet him back at her house as soon as she can get there, and turns to Katy.

'They think Jacob's being held hostage,' she says, though her friend has heard every word of the conversation. Liv sinks down into her chair, one hand automatically reaching for her stomach, as if protecting the baby.

'God, Liv.' Katy is shaking her head. 'What do you want to do?'

'I need to go down there.' Her tone is lifeless, and she's already forgotten that she's mindlessly told the detective she'll go back to her house.

'Of course you do. Do you want me to come with you? I can drive.'

Liv nods numbly. 'He's gone back to the Isle of Wight,' she says. Every muscle in her body has tightened. 'He hates it there.'

'I know,' Katy says, because she does know this, she knows it as much as Liv does. As much as all of their friends do.

'He never wants to go there so why has he this time?' Liv says through gritted teeth. 'Why didn't he tell me?'

'I don't know, hon, I don't know.'

Liv nods her head numbly. Her thoughts drift; she is thinking of her unborn child, the life that is part her, part Jacob. The excitement of finally telling her husband they've got the one thing they have both so desperately wanted.

The love for this baby that she will now share with Jacob, a love that she cannot even imagine but is already beginning to make sense.

The fear that her husband's life is in danger, and that she might end up raising their child on her own. A single mother. Is that what she'll be?

'The bastard,' she hisses.

'Liv?' Katy responds.

'He must have been meeting her.' She ignores the look of astonishment on her friend's face.

Katy shakes her head in bewilderment. 'But Jacob—' she starts, frowning. 'No. Jacob would never. Who do you even mean?'

Liv doesn't respond. The idea that her husband has betrayed her comes to her with one sharp stab to her heart, a tiny part of her recognising the irony that this would have been the one thing he had hoped to get away with. And Liv knows that, one way or another, her life will truly never be the same again after today.

## Detective Inspector Aaron Field
### 09.00 hours

By 9 Aaron is on the ferry, watching it pull out of Lymington harbour. He'll be in Yarmouth by 9.40 and at the marina in an hour.

He has agreed a rendezvous point: they'll be using a van as their command centre, which will be parked at the top of the road leading down to the marina. This is where he'll meet the Tactical Firearms Commander and the FIOs and it is far away enough to be inconspicuous, because right now, the last thing he wants is to draw the attention of passersby. Once that happens it'll only be a matter of time before it reaches social media and the press.

Aaron settles himself at the front of the boat, in a wide booth with a 180-degree view of the Solent ahead of him and, in the distance, the Isle of Wight. He has commandeered a table by spreading his things across it, making it plain he doesn't want anyone else sitting near them, and waits for Kelly to join him with her steaming cup of milky tea. Thankfully, the ferry is relatively quiet: it's mid-March in the middle of a school term. There are no screaming kids running around, though there is a golden retriever who is interested in him, but Aaron doesn't mind that one bit.

Once Kelly returns, he makes the call to join the team briefing, allowing the various DCs to introduce themselves and then Sarah Connelly, his hostage negotiator.

'What have we got?' he starts when this is done. 'Any links between the three people we have names for?'

'Nothing that stands out, sir,' one of the team tells him. 'Next-of-kins are saying they don't recognise the other names.'

Jennie Hogan they know was working the early shift; Daniel Williams it appears was likely writing in the café; and Jacob Hamilton had made the same crossing to the island as Aaron is now, to attend a meeting. At this moment, all Aaron can do is work on the assumption the two men were customers, and it was nothing more than very bad luck on their part that they were in The Boatyard at the same time this morning.

'Have we checked phone records of the next-of-kins?' he asks. 'Any of them make any calls after they were spoken to?'

'Ede Hogan, no. And Rosa Williams and Liv Hamilton only made calls to their respective husband's mobiles, both of which went through to voicemail. Neither left a message.'

'Keep tracking their calls,' he says. The relatives could lead them to answers without even knowing it. 'Do we have names for the other two females?'

'Not yet.'

'Okay, let's start a wider search of vehicles parked in the area.' They need to know who else is in there, and right now all he has is that one woman has short cropped blonde hair, and the other is wearing brightly coloured leggings.

If this doesn't come to anything, and if the negotiator still can't make contact, Aaron's going to have to rely on members of the public coming forward with names of family members who haven't turned up for work, or who aren't where they're supposed to be. But they're not at that point yet.

'The landline keeps ringing out,' Sarah Connelly tells him. 'And the mobiles are still switched off, which isn't surprising.'

'Okay. It's been an hour and forty-five minutes since the gunshot was heard and we're as sure as we can be that no one has been badly injured or killed, but this is nothing more than an assumption. If it is the case, though, I doubt the shooter *wants* to harm the hostages, though again we can't rely on this.'

As far as Aaron is concerned the situation is as contained as it can be. He's done everything he should and could so far.

The briefing lasts no more than ten minutes, and they're drawing into Yarmouth when he receives a message from the FIO to report a possible three more cars in the area.

*I want registered owners of all three, and any that can't be contacted let me know,* Aaron responds.

So far, it's the only way of narrowing down who else might be inside: who the other two females are that Franklin Henderson has seen. And knowing that is the only step towards figuring out what this is all about, because he can't ignore that he's unsettled by the fact no one inside is talking.

# Gareth

Gareth Lombard's mind is a million miles away as he sits in the queue amid a tailback of cars waiting to board the 9.40 Wightlink ferry that will soon arrive in Yarmouth and take him to Lymington on the mainland.

The journey bores him. It's a waste of his time, but he has two choices: get a different job on the Isle of Wight or move his family away from the island. Only he doesn't know how to go about either. Eleanor won't leave, for reasons he doesn't truly understand, and getting another job is easier said than done.

He's kind of well paid, or well enough for a long-ago business graduate working in a car sales showroom in Portsmouth. It's a job that affords his family a nice semi-detached house and two cars. It's a job that means they don't have to worry, and this has always been enough for Gareth.

It wasn't his dream to be selling cars, but then what was? Gareth was the first of his family to go to university. His mum was so proud when he collected his 2:1. 'My own son with a degree in business management no less,' she had said, shaking her head with tears in her eyes. 'I can't quite believe it.'

'What comes next for you then, son?' his dad had quizzed

him over pizza that evening. 'The world's your oyster now, my boy.'

Gareth hadn't been sure what came next. He wasn't one to look ahead and make plans. He figured he would have the summer off and maybe contact some accountancy firms and look for jobs back in Hull where he came from, and where his parents still lived.

But five hours after they had finished their pizza and Gareth had said goodbye to his parents, he met Eleanor. And that was twenty years ago.

He is on the ferry an hour later than usual this morning because he had to run some errands first. As the only islander from the Audi showroom in Portsmouth, it always falls on him if a car needs dropping off or something must be picked up on the Isle of Wight.

With ten minutes to wait he gets out his phone and flicks onto the news sites, scanning the headlines before closing them down and opening Instagram.

It's not the usual choice for a forty-two-year-old man but Gareth has found himself in a routine of doing so every morning, because it's the only way he gets to keep up with what his wife is posting.

But this morning it isn't his wife's account that will tell him two things he doesn't know about her.

He is used to Eleanor calling herself an 'influencer'. She says it tongue-in-cheek but has managed to curate a mini-business of sorts out of it. She has created an account that shows a perfect family lifestyle. And while she doesn't get paid for running it, she seems to be gifted rather a lot of clothes and days out that keep their two boys happy. His wife is happy about it too, though it does mean they're reliant on Gareth's income.

She has 50,000 followers now. 'Oh my God, fifty thousand!' she had screamed down the phone to him recently, relaying it more nonchalantly to her mother later who, in turn, said she had no clue what Eleanor thought she was doing flaunting herself and the children online.

Gareth had watched his wife's face fall as he had done several times before when she'd been speaking to her mother. He'd expected this response, so he wasn't sure why Eleanor hadn't. His mother-in-law isn't one to lavish compliments or encouragement on either of them, or any interest at all come to that. 'Isn't it all so *fake*, Eleanor?' she had said.

'Don't listen to her,' Gareth told his wife that night. 'She doesn't even know what Instagram is.'

Eleanor had laughed in a kind of snort and shrugged it off like she didn't care. He doesn't know if his wife realises that she still seeks her mum's approval in everything she does. To him, it is blatantly obvious.

He also wonders if this is why she shows herself off to 50,000 strangers, and for that reason Gareth keeps supporting her. He would prefer if she could make a little money, and he doesn't particularly like that their life is bared for all to see, but sometimes it's just better for a husband to keep quiet and go along with things.

So he tells Eleanor how beautiful she looks and how gorgeous the boys are in their smart matching polo shirts. There will be a day when they refuse to wear them, but he'll worry about that when it happens. Eleanor is blinkered to the future: the idea of their boys growing up and, God forbid, ever leaving home. Whatever her mother lacked in maternal love his wife has in abundance. He's under no illusion that since she had the children he'll ever be enough for her again, and he made peace with it a long time ago.

Now, he looks at her latest post in which Eleanor is wearing a sweeping pale blue dress and arranging fake flowers that she was sent to promote from a new start-up business. The picture is all creams and muted colours, and she looks incredible. In another, the boys are sitting in the middle of the kitchen floor surrounded by fake pampas grass. At four and six years old they are adorably compliant.

Not so much in the mornings though. Gareth felt guilty leaving the house before 6.30 a.m. this morning and abandoning Eleanor to it. She was calling their oldest down so she could show him what she was making for his packed lunch, to check he was happy, though he wasn't responding. At her feet their four-year-old was crying for Eleanor to hold him, tugging on her new leggings as she grappled them out of his hands.

The leggings had also been gifted, and she was supposed to look like she was working out in them. He'd never seen any so bright, with their splashes of pink and orange over her legs. Gareth thought it looked like someone had tipped paint over her. Again, he didn't say as much.

This morning, he hurriedly kissed them all goodbye, leaving her to sort the school run as he always did. Not that she would have it any other way, he thinks as he closes his phone down and puts it in his pocket. Eleanor likes that her domain is taking charge of the children. She thrives on it.

At 9.30 Gareth is about to receive this morning's first

unexpected piece of news when the school calls him. 'Hello?' he answers tentatively, because the school never contacts him. It is always Eleanor they go to.

'Mr Lombard?' the school secretary begins. 'We have Ben in the office and I'm afraid he's just been sick all over the classroom floor.'

'Oh, I am sorry,' Gareth finds himself saying.

'Obviously we can't keep him here, so I was just wondering if someone could come and collect him.'

'Yes, of course. My wife should be around. I can call her if you haven't—'

'Oh, no, we have. We have tried her number twice, and also her mother's because she dropped Ben in this morning, but we can't get hold of either of them.'

'Her mother dropped Ben in?' he says, confused, thinking back to his wife and boys in their various states of dress and readiness when he left the house. Eleanor hadn't mentioned anything about her mother coming over, and certainly not about her taking the boys to school. It's unheard of that she would ask for her mother's help, and certainly not without telling Gareth she had to, because without a doubt she'd have asked him if he could do it first. His mother-in-law is strictly a last resort.

He thinks back to how he'd stolen a glance at his wife as he was closing the front door behind him, when she didn't notice him watching her. He'd thought she'd looked unusually distant as she hollered again for Ben to come down, though not once had she tried to stop her husband from leaving.

'Yes. She made a point of saying your wife had forgotten Ben's lunch box when she dropped the children at her house.'

'She dropped them *at my mother-in-law's*?' he says now, aware he is parroting back everything the school secretary tells him. He tries to think if he and Eleanor had a conversation he only half-listened to, but is certain they hadn't.

Gareth wonders what was on Eleanor's mind this morning when he was talking to her in the kitchen. What could possibly have happened in that short time for her to need to drive to her mother's? He gazes out of the car window and feels a ripple of concern, though he doesn't particularly know why.

His beautiful Eleanor – she's long been a mystery to him in so many ways. And yet she displays her life to strangers so freely. He could almost diarise her every day through the photos she posts. This unexplained change to her routine baffles him.

'Anyway,' the secretary is saying, 'can you pick Ben up?'

'Right, yes,' he says. 'Yes, of course I can. I'll be there in fifteen minutes.' Gareth ends the call and three-point-turns out of the queue, explaining to the man at the barriers why he needs to get out of the car park.

As soon as he is on the road and heading out of Yarmouth, he phones Eleanor, but as the secretary told him, her phone is switched off, which is highly unlike his wife at the best of times, let alone when the boys are at school. She's always on high alert in case there's a problem.

He leaves her a message and tells her he will collect Ben. He asks her where she is and says that she needs to call him because he really must get to work as soon as he can.

Next, he searches for his mother-in-law's number, hesitating for a moment before he presses call. He sucks in a breath as she answers, releasing it tightly from his chest. 'Oh, hi, Mary, I just had a call from the school.'

'I can't do any more favours this morning, Gareth,' she snaps at him.

He grits his teeth. 'That's not why I'm calling.'

'I'm in the middle of a hair appointment right now.'

'That's fine. I'm getting Ben anyway, he's been sick. I just wondered if you knew where Eleanor is.'

'I don't.'

'I thought she dropped the boys off with you this morning?'

'She did. But she didn't tell me where she was going.'

'She must have said something about why she needed you to take them to school? I can't reach her and I have to get to work.'

'She said she needed to go for a run to clear her head. Are you two having marriage troubles?'

'Troubles? No, of course we're not,' he snaps. He thinks Mary would like it if they were. A chance to put Eleanor down and tell her she always knew it was a mistake, marrying Gareth. 'Maybe she did just need to get out. Maybe the boys were playing up,' he suggests, though he knows this won't be true.

'She forgot to make Ben's lunch. I told the school when I took him in.'

'I know she made his lunch because I saw her doing it. He must have left it in the car,' Gareth says. Eleanor will be mortified to find out she's sent Ben off without it. She'll be more upset than their son. 'I don't understand,' he adds. 'Are you sure she didn't say anything else to you?'

'I'm certain, Gareth. I am not losing my mind.'

'I'm not suggesting you are, Mary,' he retorts. 'Anyway, don't worry, thanks for your time,' he tells her as he hangs up, shaking his head.

He's had to read between the lines of what Eleanor tells him about her childhood. Had to figure out for himself that neither of her parents had shown her much attention and he hates this on Eleanor's behalf.

His own beloved parents still live in Hull, and he doesn't get to see them anywhere near as much as he'd like. He still finds it odd that the grandparent they live nearer to is the one they can't stand.

But never mind all that now. He needs to find his wife so he can get to work, but mostly so he can find out why she took the boys to her mother's this morning when it's not something she would ever usually do.

He tries calling her again, twice more, before he arrives at the school. Both times he's diverted straight to her voicemail. As he parks on the road his mobile starts ringing again, and if Gareth wasn't already concerned, he is definitely about to be.

His phone blasts out Deacon Blue's 'Dignity' once more, the track he chose for his ringtone into the car, a withheld number popping up on the screen.

'Gareth Lombard,' he answers, assuming it to be a work-related call and realising he still hasn't told them he isn't going to be in any time soon.

'Oh, Mr Lombard,' a soft-spoken woman's voice says on the other end of the line.

'Speaking.'

'Yes, hello, my name's Violet,' she says. 'Your wife had an appointment with me this morning at 9.'

'Oh?' Gareth says, frowning because he hadn't considered any possible appointments his wife might be keeping from him, and now suddenly he has an image of her worrying over a lump or a mole that she hasn't wanted to talk about.

'Only she didn't show up,' the woman is saying, 'which is very unusual for her, and I was just wondering if you knew where she was.'

'She didn't show up?' he repeats. If this is the reason she left the children at her mother's so early, then why didn't she make it to the appointment? 'I'm sorry but I don't know where she is,' he says. 'I've tried getting hold of her myself.'

'Oh, I see. Oh, dear, in that case I'm glad I rang you. I have your number as an emergency contact,' she explains.

'Of course. I'm sorry I can't help. I don't know why she missed the appointment.' He tries to sort through what is going on here. Does his wife think she is ill, or do she and this Violet, who actually didn't introduce herself as a doctor, already know she is? Did Eleanor have an accident on the way to this appointment?

'Well, don't worry as far as I'm concerned,' Violet says gently. 'Usually, I like to take a payment for no-shows but, as I say, Eleanor has never let me down before. I thought to myself there must be a good reason why she hasn't shown up without letting me know.'

'Payment?' Gareth queries. 'What kind of payment?'

'Well, for the session,' Violet replies.

Gareth frowns. Surely his wife hasn't gone private.

That's not something they could afford to do, and if she was concerned enough to pay for a medical consultation, she would have spoken to him first. Perhaps it's not a doctor at all, he thinks. Especially when the woman's implied twice that Eleanor's been to see her more than once. 'Sorry, but what sessions are these?' he asks.

'Her counselling,' Violet says. 'She's been coming to me every Monday for the last six months. Mr Lombard, you did know this, didn't you? Eleanor told me you knew. We even talked about how you wanted to come with her for a session soon?'

Gareth shakes his head. 'Yes, yes, of course I know,' he lies. 'Don't worry. Her counselling, that's right.'

Violet is quiet on the other end of the line.

'Did she say why she thought it was a good idea for me to come?' he asks.

Violet hesitates. 'Maybe we should leave it until I've spoken with Eleanor again. I only wanted to check she was okay. When you get hold of her, please let her know I'll see her next week.'

'Right. Yes, I will,' Gareth says before finishing the second call this morning that has floored him. And now he is wondering not only what his wife could be needing to talk to a counsellor about, but how she might have got hold of the money to pay this Violet woman for the last six months without him knowing.

## Detective Inspector Aaron Field
### 09.40 hours

Aaron turns on the engine as he waits for the cars to start piling off the ferry. His boss's voice is shrilling through the car phone. 'How long until you get there?'

'About twenty minutes, sir.'

'And we still don't know what the situation is?'

'We're treating it as a hostage,' he tells the superintendent again.

Aaron hears the silence that follows. The pause that reinforces this is not a view that's shared by his superior. He's known his boss for the entirety of his twenty-six-year career in the force, from when Aaron started out. They couldn't be more different. Over the years Aaron has taken that to be a good thing, although he can't help but constantly feel the need to prove himself and his decisions.

'I have a hit and run and a dead body in a house in Eastleigh. I need resource that's currently being taken up by a hunch. I need certainty. Update me in another hour.'

'Will do, sir,' Aaron says as the call is cut. He ignores Kelly's raised eyebrows.

The traffic is slow as it crawls through Yarmouth until they're past the quaint town and on the A-road winding its way through the Isle of Wight countryside. One long snaking road that will take them all the way to Newport.

'I like it here,' Kelly muses as she looks out the window. 'It feels like you can leave everything behind, you know what I mean?'

'Not really,' Aaron mutters as he indicates to get past a particularly slow-moving Fiesta in front of him.

'I think if I lived here, it would mean a much slower pace of life. I wouldn't always be rushing to move on to the next thing.'

'I think I would get bored out of my brain,' he says as he presses on the number for Sarah Connelly.

'I still haven't made contact,' the negotiator tells him without preamble.

'Is that odd?' he asks. If they could reach someone inside, if there was some intel he could give his boss just to prove he is right, then that would at least be something.

'It's surprising. And it means we're working in the dark. We don't know what they want. But they've been in there nearly two and a half hours. People are going to start needing things: the toilet, drinking water. They can't all sit around for hours on end without moving. Whoever's doing this will need to talk sooner or later. They *want* something.'

'But what?' Aaron asks as another call flashes up on his car monitor, with the number of a detective sergeant from the Isle of Wight. 'What do they want with a waitress and the early-morning customers? And why here, at a café on the marina? Doesn't that seem significant to you?'

'I think probably, yes,' she tells him. 'But we need more to figure out why.'

'I'm sorry. I really need to take a call that's coming through, I'll ring you back,' he says before diverting into another conversation, because this is a line he really wants to pick up on. Why here, in some out-of-the-way café?

'Just to confirm, a block's been put up across the road into the marina,' the sergeant tells him, 'but we've had one of the relatives turn up. Rosa Williams, wife of that author bloke, Daniel Williams. Just wondering what you want me to do with her? I'm thinking sooner or later crowds are going to start gathering, probably more relatives.'

'We need to keep her somewhere out of the way. Is there any other building nearby that's safe?'

'There's the marine unit's base. We could use that.'

'Fine,' Aaron says. 'Just make sure she doesn't think she's going to get anywhere near her husband.' He thinks about what little he knows of the author. He has read a couple of his books. They're pretty good for crime that's written by someone with no background in the force.

The sergeant is right though. Given time, the rest of the relatives will start making their way there too. He can't expect them to stay away.

'No sign of any press yet then?'

'Not yet.'

'Good,' he says, though he doubts it will be long, and giving statements is not something he wants to be doing any time soon when they still have no idea what's going on.

'The owners of the marina have been reached as well, but neither of them are at home. One's at his second home in

Cornwall, the other on holiday in Tenerife. As far as they're both concerned, there's hardly been any interest in purchasing the marina and nothing that would cause this sort of trouble. The two of them agree they're on good terms with each other, neither has been able to shed any light on why someone has walked into The Boatyard armed with a gun. But they have given details of their CCTV cameras. Apparently, there are some hidden at the back that they installed five years ago when they suspected a member of staff of stealing. The cameras are still running, but no one else knows about them. Not even the staff.'

'And can we access them?'

'Seems like it can be done remotely. They're sending us details of the security company.'

'Good. Get hold of the footage,' Aaron tells him. 'Let's see if anyone might have got in through the back door. Or out,' he adds. 'Any news on the vehicles in the vicinity?'

'Two have been accounted for and driven away. There's still one remaining, a silver Nissan Juke, but we're unable to get hold of the owner. Messages have been left on her voicemail.'

'Okay, keep trying,' Aaron says, because they both know that if they don't manage to make contact, they'll have to assume this is a possible hostage. 'What's her name?'

'Hannah Parish.'

'Find out what you can about her. See if you can get a picture off social media that we can show to our witness. And I'll be there in about fifteen minutes,' he adds before ending the call.

'It is odd though, isn't it?' Kelly says as Aaron presses

his foot on the brake again. A tractor is ahead of them this time and there are too many blind spots to navigate getting around him. This is why he couldn't live in the country. He'd rather be sitting in rush-hour traffic jams in Southampton. At least there he knows what he's getting. 'That they're not answering?' Her head is buried in her phone as she taps away at the screen.

'I don't know.' Aaron shrugs. 'Could be a number of reasons.'

'But after all this time.' She looks up. 'Sooner or later, they'll want to be making demands or something, surely?'

He nods, trying to focus on the road. Their silence *is* unsettling. On the one hand it makes him wonder if he's got all this wrong, like the boss clearly thinks he has, and is pulling in a load of resource for something that doesn't need it. There could be another reason why a bunch of people have locked themselves in a coffee shop early on a Monday morning. It might not be legal but it wouldn't need the number of people he's brought in to deal with it, or the relatives to have been unduly worried. Then there's the gunshot, but he doesn't know for sure what Franklin Henderson actually heard.

He isn't going to dwell on that though. Not when his gut is telling him he's right.

But what *does* their silence mean? This is why he needs to talk to Sarah Connelly again. He wants to understand what the hell he might be dealing with here.

'I can't find anything on a Hannah Parish in the Isle of Wight,' Kelly says, waving her mobile in his direction. 'Doesn't appear to be on any social media.'

Aaron frowns. 'Nothing?'

'Not that I can see.'

Aaron pulls onto the road at the top of Port Marina just after 10 o'clock. He parks up in a side alley past the van that has become the command centre, where the detective he's just been speaking to is waiting for him.

'That's Rosa Williams,' he tells Aaron, pointing to a woman who is wandering up and down the road, looking in their direction as she stops by a bench. 'Said she didn't want to go into the marine's unit when we offered it. Said she'd rather be out here, so she knew what was going on.'

'Hope you didn't tell her none of us know what's going on,' Aaron mutters.

The DC laughs. 'And there's your witness – Henderson. He doesn't appear to want to leave.'

Aaron looks over at the man the detective is talking about. From where he stands, he'd put Franklin Henderson in his mid- to late fifties. He's well built, with a greying beard, wearing grey jogging trousers and a navy hoodie. 'Good,' he says. 'I want to speak to him again,' he adds as Henderson turns and catches Aaron's eye. He tries to work out what he sees in the man's expression but lands on nothing more than curiosity.

He ushers Kelly into the van where she can have a seat and pull up her laptop.

'We've had the security intel through,' the DC goes on. 'And managed to access the footage from the hidden cameras. From 17.30 last night when one of the staff locked up

The Boatyard, no one else has come in or out the back entrance since.'

'Who locked up?' Aaron says, and the DC gives him the name. 'Find out if she noticed anything suspicious yesterday,' he tells him.

'Already have. She says there was nothing. Plus, she makes a habit of checking there is no one left inside. She looked in the toilets and the rest of the space before she locked up and left for the night.'

'Right,' Aaron murmurs and the detective raises his eyebrows in response. They both know what this means. 'Just the five of them inside then.'

He goes through the list of people again in his head. Jennie Hogan, who was working the early-morning shift. Daniel Williams, supposedly writing his latest book. Jacob Hamilton, whose wife didn't even know he was on the island. And two more as yet unidentified females.

'Which means,' Aaron says, 'one of these five is our shooter.'

# Monday morning, 9.45 a.m.

*Why is no one coming in? This is what I keep asking myself. They know we are here. I have a view though a small window at the back of the road leading away from The Boatyard and a barricade has been put across, closing it off. It's being guarded by a man who keeps walking around. I assume they are stopping anyone from trying to get to the marina.*

*Do you know by now that I'm in here? I am sure you must. I wonder what they have told you, and what you think you need to do. Maybe you are down here, somewhere the other side of the barricade. That's what I would do if I thought your life was in danger. I would want to be as close to you as I could be.*

*You'll be telling them I don't deserve this to be happening to me and that they have to make sure I am safe because you could not bear it if I'm not. I can imagine you pleading with them to let you past the barrier. Desperate to get inside so you can haul me out safely. Not knowing that's the last thing I want.*

*Do they know it is me? They must have been questioning you, along with all the other relatives. What have you told them?*

*Or are they still trying to work out which one of the five of us it is? I can tell you from spending nearly three hours inside here there are some who are much more likely than the others to be holding a gun.*

*'What are you going to do?' one of them is asking me.*

*I tear my eyes away from the window and turn back to them.*

*'What are you going to do with us? We can't stay here for ever.'*

*My hand aches from how tightly it is still gripped around the gun.*

*They are right, we can't stay here for ever. I know that. The police know that.*

*I imagine you saying to me,* Had you even thought this through? How it's all going to end? *I had* thought it through. *I went through the possibilities. Maybe not as much as I should have done, I see that now. Only my mind isn't quite as straight as it should be. I suppose if it were, I wouldn't have walked in here and taken four people hostage.*

*'Please?' they say to me. They are shaking their heads, their eyes betraying how desperate they are.*

*They are afraid, as you can imagine.*

*But I am afraid too. Only no one will care about that, will they? My fear won't mean anything when all everyone will see is a potential killer, a psychopath.*

*If I walk out of here alive, they will lock me up and we'll be separated.*

*I feel like I might be losing my mind.* Haven't you already lost it? *I can hear you say. If the situation weren't so awful, we would laugh at that.*

*Yes. I probably have. After all, no one in their right mind does something like this, do they?*

*I'm afraid I might not see you again. Whatever happens from now on, life has changed.*

*I'm sorry for that. I am so sorry, and I really hope you will understand that. I love you. You do remember that, don't you?*

## Detective Inspector Aaron Field
### 10.10 hours

Working on the assumption that the gunman is one of the five people their witness saw walking into the café this morning hasn't helped him figure out who's behind this, let alone what it is they want. It doesn't help that Aaron still doesn't know who two of the people inside The Boatyard are.

The relatives of the ones they have identified have shed little light. They'll have to be questioned again. Aaron needs to *know* what their loved ones were really doing at the marina so early on a Monday morning.

What he also needs to understand is why *here*. Even more so now he's at the marina himself, because he can see it's an unusual choice for holding a bunch of people hostage.

He returns the call to Sarah Connelly that he'd cut short. He knows his negotiator will ring him the moment she makes contact, but first he wants to ask her opinion on the situation. As he waits for her to pick up, Aaron walks away from the van and towards the top end of the road where the lane veers off onto a couple of side roads. It isn't until you go much further that you reach a residential area. Thankfully, this means the immediate area is quiet, and that they can go unnoticed for now. He stands for a moment, looking down at the road that weaves towards the marina, the blockade further down stopping anyone from getting there.

'Still no luck,' Sarah tells him when she answers. Obviously, this is making her job harder. A hostage negotiator works on the basis that this is a transaction. Each party has something the other one wants, but until they know what that is, there is little they can do.

'I figured as much,' Aaron says. 'But talk me through what kind of person we're looking at here. Who's going to walk into a pretty little coffee shop in a marina on the Isle of Wight and hold up what appears to be four innocent customers. Or three and a waitress,' he adds.

The ones they know of so far are family people with normal lives, holding down jobs, no criminal records, and they have people who love them. At first sight nothing points the finger at any one of them in particular, but Aaron knows there is always more beneath the surface.

'Good question,' she replies. 'Typically, someone takes hostages for one of three reasons.' She begins listing them. 'Psychological, criminal or political. I think we can work on the assumption this isn't political,' she continues. 'They are your social protesters, your ideologists, terrorists. Whoever is inside that café doesn't want to talk to us, or at least not yet. If they have a cause, they'd want us to know.

'It could be a crime gone wrong,' Sarah goes on. 'They've been cornered, most likely trying to rob the place, but that seems unlikely in this case given a number of factors like the time, location and taking a risk with unsuspecting members of the public.'

'Which leaves psychological,' he fills in.

'The most likely,' she agrees. 'But we don't know the cause. Mental health is of course a big consideration. They're suicidal, disturbed, something in their life has gone very, very wrong and they don't see a way out. They're seeking vengeance or else they're just full of rage.'

Aaron nods. These are things he knows, but it's good to hear them again.

He needs to understand who these people inside *really* are, what they have been doing lately, what their family members have noticed, even the smallest of things that don't mean much to them but nonetheless could mean *something*.

Kelly will be profiling the people they know of, checking GP records for histories of depression, suicidal tendencies, substance abuse, anything that could be of interest. They will need to talk to everyone who knows the people inside that building. And, of course, there are still the two females who haven't been identified.

'Shooters,' Sarah is saying, 'are driven by mental illness. This is an impulse, it's emotional. Obviously, our man or woman in there today hasn't walked in, shot everyone and walked back out again, which means this situation isn't your typical shooting. So, we need to consider other aspects: romantic motivations, loss, grudges, disputes.

'It's the location though,' she adds. 'This is what's stumping me. It's such an odd choice. 7.26 on a Monday morning. An otherwise quiet boatyard. Why here? What are they hoping for? They aren't getting the immediate reaction they would in the middle of a city. Do they even want to be noticed?'

'You're right,' he agrees. 'It's what I keep coming back to. Why the hell here? It feels remote,' he says. Much more so now he is standing at the top of the road looking down rather than seeing the images on his screen. The marina is out of the way. You can see nothing more than the roof of The Boatyard from here. 'Like they don't want any attention.'

'I think it feels personal.'

'It does.' It's exactly what Aaron's been thinking. Someone knows The Boatyard opens early for breakfast, but were they expecting Jennie Hogan to be working today or someone else? Was the place supposed to be empty?

'Jennie Hogan wasn't meant to be doing this shift originally,' he tells the negotiator. He needs the investigative teams to find out whose shift she was covering this morning.

'That could be something,' Sarah agrees. 'Or one of the others might have been targeted. Perhaps followed here and then whoever it was took their chances.'

'And the rest are collateral damage?'

'Probably. After all, if we're looking at the probability this has something to do with the marina or one of the café staff, then a number of customers have got caught up by accident. Either way, it means there're unwanted people inside, and that could go some way to explaining why they aren't making contact.'

'How do you mean?' he asks.

'This isn't what they hoped for. They don't know how to move forward with whatever they had planned,' she suggests.

Aaron sighs, not liking the idea of that one bit, but he knows there's a lot in what she says. Almost three hours is a long time not to be making any contact, and they need to start figuring out why.

He thanks her and finishes the call, mulling over the options of the marina being a target or the idea that one of the people inside that building has a stalker. Someone likely to act without thinking through the possibilities of how this is going to end.

Across the road he can see Rosa Williams, her body facing down towards the marina, but her head twisted round so she can watch him. Her arms are wrapped around her body. She's wearing an oversized hoodie, but it looks like she's shivering. She seems haunted as she stares straight at him.

Daniel Williams is a local celebrity, a semi-famous author who made an appearance on TV only a week ago. He must have a fan following – maybe people who like him a little too much, as well as those who don't. Does that make him the most likely target?

It feels unlikely that someone tracked Jacob Hamilton all the way down here from London. Plenty of people could have known Jennie Hogan might be here this morning, or was their suspect expecting to encounter someone else – someone whose shift Jennie ended up covering?

Aaron makes his way back to the van where he opens the door and pokes his head inside. 'I need names for everyone on the staff directory at the marina and every boat owner too,' he tells Kelly. 'And I need intel on Daniel Williams,' he adds. 'See if anyone has a grudge against him, comments on fan sites, that kind of thing.'

He looks back towards Rosa Williams. There's an officer already at Liv Hamilton's house and he needs another back at Ede Hogan's, but he can talk to Rosa himself. The family members need to know what the police are currently thinking. They need to be considering at least the possibility that *their* relative could be responsible for this.

'Any luck getting hold of the owner of the Nissan Juke parked in the vicinity? Hannah Parish's?' he asks the FIO who is sitting in the back of the van.

'No, sir. No answer on Parish's mobile and we've tried her address too. No one at home, although there is a car on the driveway, a light blue VW Golf belonging to a Connie Parish. Sisters,' he adds.

'Tried calling her?'

'I have but can't get hold of her either.'

'I think we need to add Hannah to the list,' Aaron says. 'Car unaccounted for nearby and she's another one we can't reach. See what we can find out about her, without losing too much focus on the ones we know for certain are inside.'

He rubs his chin as his mind goes back to the last call he had with his negotiator, and the fact they aren't making contact, and whether she's right when she says this isn't turning out as the hostage-taker was expecting.

If that's the case, no one knows how they're going to act. Firearms are prepared and ready to go when needed but that's down to him. Aaron is the one who calls them in and, though he knows the time isn't yet, he can't ignore the feeling that someone is going to get hurt. And that when they are, it'll be his fault.

# Liv

Liv allows the tears to roll silently down her cheeks as she sits in the passenger seat of Katy's car, driving down the A3 from London towards Portsmouth. She cannot catch her breath. It sticks in her throat each time she inhales a gulp of air. She doesn't know what part of this horrendous mess she is crying for. Whether it's that she can't share the news of the baby that's already growing inside her with her husband, or if it's that she doesn't know if he's going to walk out of that building alive. Or perhaps it's the part of her that fears why he is there in the first place.

She turns and looks out of the window as Katy speeds past other cars, going too fast, hitting 85 m.p.h., but the journey is set to take them two hours and forty minutes in total, and they both know it's unlikely they'll make it before *something* happens.

One way or another this will surely be over by the time they arrive. *One way or another,* she mouths out of the window. The stretch of the journey ahead feels like it's pulling away from her, like she might never get there, or at least not in time.

She quells the need to scream from the frustration rising inside her, burning through her veins. Everything is beyond her control.

'You know, I don't buy it,' Katy says. 'I really don't think Jacob would be having an affair. He adores you, Liv.'

She closes her eyes as she leans back against the head-rest.

'I know it doesn't make any sense why he's over there without telling you,' her friend goes on, 'but there'll be another explanation. To jump to that—'

'There was someone,' Liv says. 'Jacob and I bumped into her once on the Isle of Wight.'

Katy peers at her but doesn't say anything.

Liv can remember it so clearly: the little pedestrianised street and the quaint coffee shops and independent gift stores selling handmade fudge and ornaments with seagulls perched on top of them. She just can't remember the name of the town. 'Jacob was holding my hand, and we were laughing about something or other, and then suddenly he just froze. I asked him what the matter was because he looked like he'd seen a ghost. His face had visibly gone paler.

'And then I realised he'd recognised someone,' Liv goes on. 'This woman ahead, walking straight towards us. They both looked at each other and said hello, but she had the same look of horror on her face as he did.'

'Who was she?'

'I asked him, but he just shrugged it off and said she was an old girlfriend he hadn't seen in years. He told me it was a bit embarrassing. But he'd let go of my hand by then and he changed the subject fast, telling me he wanted to go and look for something in the sports shop.'

'Maybe that was all it was though?'

Liv shakes her head. 'No.' She has bumped into a couple of her exes when she's been with Jacob and knows it can be cringey, but the way he'd reacted – like he'd seen someone he definitely shouldn't have, like he'd been *caught*. 'I don't know what it was, but when I looked back, she had stopped walking and turned around to watch him. And there was something about it that made me think she was more than just an ex.'

'When was this?' Katy asks.

Liv shrugs. 'A year ago.'

'You can't seriously think he's been having an affair for the last year,' Katy replies in disbelief.

Liv doesn't know what she thinks. The police officer had told her they knew of three female hostages. A Jennie Hogan, but also two others they hadn't yet named. The woman she'd seen could be one of them.

'Jacob hates going back to the Isle of Wight,' her friend points out. 'He never does. How's he supposed to see this woman? And *when?*' she asks.

'I don't know,' Liv says. It's true that he couldn't find the time to keep hopping over there without her knowing, but then he does have the occasional work trip. And maybe he has been lying to her about them.

She sighs. It's so hard for her to cut through the facts when half of them are missing.

They fall silent again and Liv sinks back into her thoughts about Jacob, and his mother too this time, the woman Liv adores but whom she needs to coax her husband into visiting.

Joyce lives on the south of the island in the pretty coastal town of Ventnor. Here holidays are the bucket-and-spade type, with picnics on the beach and ice creams falling out of cones. Liv has stood on its promenade many times watching families with their tiny children, always wondering about the possibility of them one day moving there.

'Never,' Jacob has told her with grave determination. She knows it isn't an option in his opinion, but his mother has no one else and one day, in a future that isn't far off, Liv knows, she will need them.

Joyce is the antithesis of her own parents, whom she also loves though in a very different way. Joyce epitomises everything Liv would like to be as a mother herself: a giver of love that is all-encompassing, a solid presence who is always there even when she knows her son makes no effort to see her.

Theirs is certainly not a relationship that has broken down, or at least not in the way that they've fallen out. It is deeper-rooted than that. She is part of a life he was desperate to escape from as soon as he could.

Jacob craves the childhood Liv had. Holidays in five-star hotels where the ice cream wasn't stuffed between wafers and tasting of sand but instead piled into a tall glass with a long silver spoon and whatever selection of sweets you dreamed of sprinkled on top. He sees the glossy magazine-cover version, not the mechanics behind it – like the dad who worked round the clock, and the mum who shouted if Liv or her sisters got dirt on the pristine white bedding.

It's like Jacob has forgotten the luxury of his own memories of biking down to the beach when he was ten, hanging out with friends until it grew dark. The kind of freedom rarely given to a child in London.

Still, his mum would have been waiting for him to return, with a home-cooked meal ready and wanting to hear about his day. Nowadays she is desperate to see more of him. She's always asking Liv if they might be popping over any time soon, with a hasty, 'No pressure, love, I know what busy lives you both lead,' resigned to her sadness, knowing it won't happen, though through no fault of her daughter-in-law's.

'There's nothing there for me, Liv,' Jacob has said to her in the past. 'What do you think I would have done for a job?' She remembers how his eyebrows had peaked as he looked at her, a smile hanging off the corner of his lips as he said, 'We don't all have the luxury of being born well off.'

Getting a job in the city, earning big bucks, holidaying in Thailand and the Maldives swathed in luxury rather than in a caravan in Bournemouth . . . These are the aspirations that drive her husband and keep him well away from the Isle of Wight.

Liv wonders if Joyce ever revisits the way her son couldn't wait to get away at the age of eighteen and if she's come up with the reason why. Perhaps she has. Perhaps it is only Liv who is in the dark.

There *has* to be more to it than she realises, Liv thinks. To hate this place as much as Jacob does. Or is it just an excuse so that she doesn't collide with his past?

'Jacob adores you,' Katy is saying now. 'Please hold on to that.'

Liv nods solemnly as her gaze drops down to her belly. She's dreamed that things will change when they have a family of their own, but right now she doesn't even know if her husband will still be alive by the end of this journey.

'Only . . .' Liv starts in response, but her words dry up. She can feel the questioning burn of Katy's gaze. 'I mean, he works so late these days,' she goes on eventually. 'And then he doesn't always come straight home. He goes to the gym or the pub on a Friday night instead of coming back like he always used to.'

She can sense Katy frowning, but doesn't want to look at her friend. Doesn't want to tell her that he hadn't even asked when her period was due this month.

But she shouldn't even be entertaining these thoughts right now. 'Forget what I said,' Liv tells her. If her husband is having an affair, she will find out soon enough now. 'Innocent until proven guilty and all that,' she murmurs.

'Exactly,' Katy says, nodding emphatically, her gaze flicking between Liv and the road ahead. 'Do you want to stop and get something to eat or drink? You didn't touch your breakfast.'

Liv shakes her head. 'I'm not really hungry.'

'You need to look after yourself now,' Katy says. 'You and the baby. You have someone else to think of.'

'Is this how it will be from now on? One way or another, will it just be me and the baby?'

'Liv—'

'I know,' she says. 'I know.' She wasn't going to go there, and yet she can't help herself. Her husband has lied to her, and she will find out why and then she is going to have to confront it. She cannot ignore it.

'Jacob loves you,' Katy reminds her, but her eyes are focused straight ahead this time and there is a catch in her voice like she might be beginning to query that herself. 'Let's just take one thing at a time. All that's important right now is his safety.'

Katy is right, of course she is. Liv shouldn't be worrying about whether her husband is having an affair or not, or even whether he still loves her, when he might end up dead.

'Oh God,' she groans, as she wraps her fingers over the slight curve of her otherwise flat stomach that until this morning she had thought was caused by bloating. She is an awful person. A horrible, horrible wife not to be directing all her energy into praying for his life. What must Katy think of her? Only every time Liv imagines the horror of her husband being held hostage, the image of another woman springs into her head, sitting alongside him in a shared tragedy that will for ever bind them in ways Liv won't ever be able to understand.

'Jacob's life is in danger and yet right now I'm angry with him. I'm so bloody angry.' She sobs at the admission. 'I love him so much and I don't want him to die, and I don't want to lose him, but he's lied to me. He's kept something from me, and we don't have secrets. And I know I should trust him, but I don't.' The truth of this burns into her heart, making it ache deeply.

'This might have nothing to do with another woman, or an affair, or any of the things that you think it does. And even if he was meeting that woman you saw, it could be as friends. Maybe he just wants to talk to her, or she needs him to, and he didn't want to tell you. Liv,' her friend begs, 'please. We just need to get there, and you need to speak to him.'

Liv nods, numbly, through the tears streaming down her face. She is glad Katy is here and no one else. She can't bring herself to talk to her parents yet. It's a sad admission that they wouldn't bring her the comfort she needs and so she'll speak to them later, when she knows more.

Her head feels like a snow globe. Like someone has shaken her up and all the tiny snowflakes are her thoughts, floating around, refusing to settle. She tries to catch hold of one, a memory of a happier time for her and Jacob.

His birthday last year. Hakkasan in Mayfair because Jacob's favourite food is Chinese. Just the two of them at his request. His eyes had been drawn to the tight-fitting red dress she was wearing. 'God, you look so good, Liv,' he'd murmured in her ear in the doorway to the restaurant. She'd kissed him, then playfully pushed him away.

She tries to smile at the memory, but it was over a year ago. On his latest birthday three weeks ago, he didn't want to go out. She wanted to book a restaurant, but he told her he was too tired and Liv said she understood because he was working so much.

She feels a tightness in her chest at the memory and tries to let go of it. She is being ridiculous. Her husband still loves her. She loves him, like she always has.

But then she wonders what he would have said tonight if someone hadn't walked into the marina with a gun, and she hadn't found out he was on the Isle of Wight. Liv would have given him the pregnancy test wrapped up as a gift and Jacob would have opened it and laughed and hugged her, telling her how excited he was.

Now she has no idea if that would have been true. Only she would have believed him because she wouldn't have had any reason not to.

# Rosa

Rosa feels like she will be sick. There is a hysteria brewing inside her, and she cannot stop crying. As soon as the police officers left her house, she grabbed her sweatshirt and got in the car, calling her parents who are visiting her sister in Scotland to tell them. Her dad told her they would get a flight as soon as possible.

'Hang in there, darling, everything's going to be alright,' he had said to her calmly, though they both knew her parents wouldn't make it back for hours. Rosa had hung up, tears trickling down her cheeks, feeling even more desperate as she got in her car and hurried to the marina.

She wishes they were here with her. It would be so much easier if her dad was by her side. He wouldn't need to say anything, just his presence would be enough. He adores Daniel, almost as much as he does her. 'I think you're marrying your dad,' her mum had laughed once before their wedding. 'Look at them out there in the garden, trying to fix that old shed up. Two peas in a pod.' Rosa had felt a warmth spread through her. They both knew she had found The One.

Now, the police aren't letting anyone past the barrier that closes off the only route to The Boatyard and so she is wandering back and forth, no idea what to do, but desperate to be close to the man she loves. She cannot bear the idea of being cooped up inside the building they have tried to usher her into.

'Do I have go in there?' Rosa had asked them.

'No, you don't have to be anywhere,' she was told.

'Then I need to be outside.'

Since then, she has been watching a detective who arrived ten minutes ago. He too is pacing up and down the road on a call. He has glanced in her direction more than once.

Rosa feels her life suspended in a moment of time, invisible strings tugging at it that she has no control over. She wants to run past the barriers so she can be with Daniel but, at the same time, she wishes she was back in the sanctuary of her home.

She looks up to the sky, tears still stinging her eyes as she tightens her arms over her chest. Rosa had thought she would have held it together better in a crisis. Daniel is always telling her how strong she is, but then she has never been tested like this before. Up until today, she has largely escaped drama and heartache.

The detective emerges again, walking up the road, heading in her direction. Rosa wipes a hand across her face and straightens up, trying to pull herself together. When he reaches her, he introduces himself as DI Field.

'What's happening?' she asks.

'Shall we go inside?' He nods towards the building they had said she could sit in.

'I don't want to.' She prefers being here where she can see the barrier and the police officers scuttling around. If anything happens, she will be able to tell. Locked away in a building with no view, she would only be imagining the worst.

'Okay, that's fine. We can talk here,' he says.

'Why isn't anyone going in and getting them out?' she asks. 'Anything could have happened inside there, and no one can even tell me if my husband is hurt. For all we know he could be *dead*.'

The tears stream down her face again as she shouts the last word and her hands shake against her body.

'As far as we know, everyone inside is unharmed,' the detective tells her gently, though his face is blank in that poised way she supposes he has learnt to perfect, because of course they can't know this.

'*How* do you know?' she asks him.

'Mrs Williams, is there anyone you can call, someone who can be here with you perhaps?'

'I *want* to be with my husband,' she says. 'And how do you know he isn't hurt?' Rosa repeats the question.

'Because we have a team who are experts in these kinds of situations, and everything about this one leads us to believe that is the case.'

She studies his face, searching for the truth in his words. They cannot *know* this, of course, but she desperately wants to believe him. 'Then why isn't anyone going in and getting him out?' she asks again.

DI Field turns back to the marina. 'Right now the best route is to continue trying to make contact and, in the meantime, find out what we can about the hostage-taker and figure out what it is they want.' He turns back to her. 'Experience shows that sooner or later whoever is in charge will want to talk, and when they do, we'll be ready.' He adds a smile, like he truly believes it is this simple. 'The most helpful thing you can do for your husband is to talk to us.'

'I've already told one of your officers everything I know and that's *nothing*. I didn't know my husband was coming here this morning. The chances are *he* didn't even know until he left the house.' Rosa pauses as she thinks again of his laptop sitting on his desk and briefly wonders what he was doing here when he can't have been writing. 'So, what else is there to say?'

'There may be no more to it than that,' the detective agrees. 'And your husband may just have been unfortunate this morning, but we can't be certain that's true. There could be something you don't realise you know, something that could help us.'

'Of course he's been unfortunate,' she says. 'What else could it be?'

'Maybe you could talk me through his movements this morning,' DI Field suggests calmly.

'No.' She shakes her head. 'You implied something else. Like there is more to it than Daniel just coming down here to write. Do you think he's involved in something?' she asks, a different kind of fear now crawling over her skin.

The detective hangs his head ever so slightly to one side, which makes Rosa shiver and clench her arms tighter around herself.

They know something they aren't telling her. Something about her husband.

The pause he leaves is interminable but she doesn't know what to say and so she doesn't say anything.

'We don't know anything for certain,' he says eventually, though this does nothing to calm her. 'But I need you to help me. Tell me about his writing. He writes crime novels, doesn't he? I see he was talking about it on TV last weekend.'

'You think this is because of that?' she gasps. 'Because he was on TV? That doesn't make any sense.'

'I'm just trying to pull a picture together and I *need* you to help me, Rosa,' he says again. 'The more you can tell me, the more we can work out what is happening and get everyone out safely. Perhaps there's someone Daniel's mentioned lately who's taken a dislike to his work or there are some bad reviews that have upset him.'

She shakes her head. 'He gets bad reviews occasionally, but no more than any other author. Daniel knows it comes with the territory but he chooses to ignore them now.' He didn't in the early days as he trawled Amazon and sites like Goodreads, ignoring the good ones and focusing on the bad as if he was trying to punish himself. 'Is this what you're thinking, that someone was after him? You think that's what this is all about?'

'It's one possible avenue of inquiry,' the detective admits.

'No, that can't be true. He would have told me if there was anything I needed to know. He hasn't mentioned anyone being angry with him for anything he's written. And anyway, why would they be?' she says. 'He's just an author. It's all fiction.'

Daniel doesn't have crazy fans. People like his books. But now Rosa wonders whether he would tell her if there was anyone worrying him because it would be just like him to want to protect her from it, knowing she would panic.

What if he's been getting threats that he's kept hidden from her? Has he been looking out of his office window when she doesn't realise, watching shadows scurry through their garden? And all the while she's been in the dark. Until now, when they've taken it too far. The detective is asking if he can see the Ring doorbell footage for himself. Rosa frowns but reaches into her pocket for her phone and pulls up the app again.

'What are you looking for?' she asks when she finds the video and passes it to him for him to play. 'How's watching Daniel leaving the house going to help?'

The detective doesn't answer her, but says, 'Has your husband worked from The Boatyard before today?'

'I don't know. I have no idea where he writes most of the time. You think someone knew he was going to be there?'

The DI is too busy studying the video on Rosa's phone to answer her. 'Does he have a working routine?' he says instead.

'No.' She shakes her head adamantly, because routine is one thing Daniel doesn't have.

'Does he ever work with anyone when he writes in coffee shops?'

'No. The only people he meets are his agent and editor, but they're both in London. He always goes there to meet them, and he would have told me if they'd come to the Isle of Wight.'

'He's a good author,' DI Field says now, passing Rosa her phone back. 'I've read a couple of his books. I enjoyed them.'

She has no idea what to say to this.

'He must enjoy what he does?'

'He loves it.'

'When was the last time you spoke to your husband?'

'Last night. I went to bed about 9 o'clock and he was still working.'

'Did he seem okay?'

'Yes.' Rosa frowns. 'He was fine. It's not as if he could have known this was going to happen or he wouldn't have gone to that café.' She stares at the detective, trying to fathom what he is actually asking her. Does he really think Daniel would have knowingly walked into danger this morning if he has been receiving some kind of threat? That isn't him. He'd go to the police, just like she would. Daniel's not the kind of person to think he could sort it out himself.

'Have you noticed anything different in his behaviour or actions in the past week?'

'No.' She shakes her head.

'Anything out of character?'

'You really think someone is after him?' she says.

But DI Field doesn't answer. He stares at her intently instead, as if trying to find the words to confirm that actually this is the only line of inquiry they're following. It means Rosa isn't expecting the next words that come out of his mouth.

'I'm sorry for all these questions, but it's important we know all that we can about your husband and everyone else inside that building. Mrs Williams, has Daniel ever suffered from depression or had any kind of mental health issues?'

'What?' She shakes her head in confusion. 'What are you talking about?'

'I'm going to be frank,' he says, plainly. 'There are five people inside The Boatyard.' The detective pauses, gesturing in the direction of the marina but never taking his eyes off her. 'And one of them is responsible for holding the others hostage. And right now, we don't know which of them it is.' He pulls back as he waits for her reaction.

Rosa feels it coming in slow motion – the pieces of what he is saying, clicking into place like a jigsaw. 'You can't be thinking . . .' she says. 'No. You can't seriously be suggesting this might be Daniel?' He doesn't speak and so she goes on. 'No way.' She laughs, incredulous. 'It is not my husband. You can rule him out.'

'I'm afraid we can't rule any of them out until we know more.'

'That's why you're asking me all these questions? Why you want to see footage of him leaving the house? You're not worried someone might be stalking him, you think he is the one doing this? No!' she cries. 'This can't be happening.' Every minute that passes it is getting worse. Isn't it bad enough that her husband is in there at all? But for them to suggest he is the cause . . . 'One minute you're implying someone wants to hurt him, and the next that he wants to hurt other people?'

'Mrs Williams,' he says again, trying to calm her, 'we don't know *who* is behind this. I'm sorry to upset you but it *is* one of them.'

'Daniel's my husband. There's no way.' She shakes her head. 'It's one of the others. Ask them what their relatives are doing in there.' She gestures around her, even though there is no one else nearby. She is the only one who has come down here. Is she the only one who *knows*? Is Daniel the only one they suspect?

'We are. Of course we are,' he says.

'It's not Daniel,' she says, firmly.

He tells her that if there is anything she thinks of, or remembers, to let him know and apologises again before he walks away, over to the van that is parked a little way down the road. She watches him disappear into it then turns back to the phone that is still in her hand and opens the Ring doorbell app again, her hands still shaking.

Replaying the video of Daniel leaving the house this morning, she zooms in on her husband. His head is bent as he hurries to the car and pats his pockets to check he has his keys or his phone. The car beeps, its lights flash to show it is unlocked. Daniel glances back at the house, up at the bedroom window.

She looks at him more closely, pausing the video and expanding the pixelated image of his face to try and read his expression. Is there something in his eyes or is she just looking for it? Has he been hiding something crazy from her like threats?

But no, he can't have known what he was walking into this morning. He couldn't have unless the detective's implication is right, and this is somehow something to do with him. *One of five of them*, as he'd said to her.

She calls her dad again. 'The police are questioning me,' she says.

'What about, darling?'

'They said it might have something to do with Daniel.'

'Oh Lord.'

'He might have someone stalking him or something like that,' she says at first.

'They actually said that?' he asks.

'They implied it. Oh God, Dad. I don't know what to do.'

'I know, my darling. We've found a flight and we're on our way to the airport now.'

Rosa nods, but what is the point of that anyway? Even once they have boarded a plane, it will take an hour to reach Southampton, and then another two to get to the Isle of Wight. 'They said something else,' she goes on, words sticking in her throat like hard lumps. She hesitates, not wanting to say them aloud. But this is her dad. And she tells her dad everything. 'They suggested it could be him. That Daniel could be the one who has taken the others hostage.'

He laughs, incredulous. 'Well, that's the most ridiculous thing I have ever heard,' he says.

'I know. I know,' she says, with mild relief.

'They're just looking for a reaction from you, you know that, don't you?' he says. 'They cannot believe that.'

'Yes. I'm sure you're right,' she says, nodding. 'It's just . . .' She pauses.

'Just what, darling?'

'Just he's been so engrossed in his book lately. You know how he gets. And he was so worried about the interview last weekend. I've barely seen him lately.'

'But this happens every time he's nearly finished one.'

Rosa nods. 'I know, Dad. I'm sorry. He's been so worried

about this book, that's all. But he kept telling me he just needs to get it right.'

'Doesn't he always?'

'I told him that, but he said this one's different.' She remembers how she'd been rubbing Daniel's back as he stood at the kitchen sink filling himself a glass of water a few days ago. She'd leant in to hug him, but he'd tensed under her touch. Somehow it had got to him. 'But you're right. Of course you're right.' Rosa pauses. 'Dad—' she begins.

'Yes, love?'

She is about to tell him the one other question DI Field had asked. If Daniel had ever suffered from depression. But how can she when she'd lied in response? In the end she says, 'I'll call you as soon as I have news.'

Now she focuses back on the image of her husband's face again as it fills the screen on their doorbell app. The opening words of his book have stuck in her mind, sharply unwanted in their raw, gruesome horror.

Eventually Rosa closes the app and puts her phone in her pocket. She wonders if DI Field is questioning anyone else like he did her.

And if they in turn will question if this is the work of the person they love.

She holds a hand over her mouth, gasping at her own realisation that this is what she is doing. Daniel isn't capable of causing such horror, not her sweet loving husband who neatly folds her pyjamas and leaves them on her pillow for her when she has got up earlier than him, as she does most mornings. At weekends he leaves a chocolate mint on top as if she's staying in a hotel. One day she found the box of them in his bedside drawer and the sweetness of the gesture nearly broke her heart.

When she closes her eyes, she can feel the trail of his fingers lazily running up and down her arm as they cuddle up on the sofa and binge Netflix series like *Grey's Anatomy*. Her choice, and he's happy to oblige. He doesn't crave gore and crime and violence. He only started writing it because he said he wasn't funny, and he wouldn't know where to start with romance.

This is who Daniel is, not the awful person the detective has made her imagine. But she can't take it back now – that fraction of time when she thought he could be capable of this.

# Ede

Jennie's place of work is supposed to be a safe space. Somewhere she isn't going to come to any harm. Ede's granddaughter would have walked through its doors this morning and thought of nothing more than the chores that needed to be done and how long it would be before she could have a break. Whether it would be busier than it has been lately. Which customers she might meet.

Jennie has always loved talking to people. She does it with ease, whatever their age and their background, she finds the right things to say to them. Ede has often sat at the bar in The Boatyard with a coffee and been mesmerised by her granddaughter's ability to get strangers to share their life story. 'It's easy,' Jennie says. 'Everyone wants to talk about themselves.' She has too much time to give everyone.

But then, this morning, someone walked in with a very different kind of backstory. One that, whatever it was, brought them to a point in their life where they thought the only option was to lock the doors of the café and refuse to let Jennie or any of the other customers out.

A nutter, *a psychopath*. Who else would do something like this? Someone who knows they have nothing to lose, and this is what Ede fears the most.

*

'I should be there,' she says to her neighbour who has just boiled the kettle for the second time without making either of them a drink. 'I shouldn't be sitting here idly doing nothing.'

Marjorie turned up just as the police were leaving, bellowing, 'Who are *they*?' as she strode up the path to where Ede still stood in the doorway of her cottage. Marjorie's face was awash with undisguised interest while, meanwhile, Ede's aging heart was thumping erratically.

'Someone's locked down The Boatyard,' Ede told her. 'Jennie's being held hostage.'

Marjorie stared like she didn't believe her, and still, an hour later, they are both milling around the kitchen suspended in the same disbelief.

'I'm not sure we should go down there,' her neighbour tells her now as she finally refills the coffee mugs with freshly boiled water.

'Then I don't know what to do,' Ede murmurs and finds herself beginning to cry once more.

All the things she has done for her granddaughter and all the things she has wanted to, and now Jennie needs her more than ever and there's not one damned thing Ede can do about it.

She's had to be tough all her life. Tough when her daughter was drinking herself sick and not looking after Jennie as she should have been. Then again when Shona died and left Ede at the age of fifty-eight to take care of her granddaughter and pick up the pieces. And once more when her husband passed away ten years ago.

She will not lose Jennie. She knows this with fierce

determination. Ede won't have one more person taken from her.

'There must be a reason why they've chosen The Boatyard. That's certainly what the police seemed to think,' Ede says. 'They kept asking me questions about the place,' she goes on. Although she is sure she has already uttered these words, for once Marjorie doesn't pick up on it. 'They think Jennie is the only hostage who works there. They think it could have something to do with her,' she says, wondering now if this is what they said or suggested, because Ede is struggling to remember everything they told her.

'I cannot see how it could have anything to do with Jennie.'

'It can't,' Ede agrees, shaking her head adamantly in denial. 'Only she wasn't supposed to be working there this morning. And so, what if it has something to do with the marina, and Jennie's got caught up in it by accident?'

She breathes out as another wave of panic courses through her. *Think*, she tells herself. Maybe there is something she knows that can help. Something Jennie has told her. Ede could hold the key to the reason her granddaughter's life is in danger, and meanwhile her addled brain is letting Jennie down. If anything happens to her, it will be Ede's fault.

What has Jennie told her lately? So much and usually it is also so little. Often it will be trivial things, like what someone was reading or how much milk they get through with all the fancy coffees she makes. Jennie tells her grandmother all about her days, every day, reliving them patiently because she knows how interested Ede is in the detail.

But there is nothing that comes to her, at least not in the

last few weeks. So maybe she needs to think further back than that? In the last months, perhaps. There has to be something, one thing, a little fragment that neither of them thought important at the time.

It comes to her then. 'Oh,' she says, 'there was a man.'

'A man?'

'Jennie told me about a man. A while back, last November maybe. She said he was pestering her, and I told her she needed to report him to the owners, but she brushed it off and said he was harmless.'

'You think he wasn't?' Marjorie asks, clasping her hands together, like she is in *The Thursday Murder Club*.

'I had a feeling at the time she wasn't telling me the whole story,' Ede goes on. 'But she didn't want to say any more.'

'That's very Jennie,' her neighbour says. 'She never wants to worry you.'

She is right. Jennie is always trying to protect Ede, like she doesn't realise what her grandmother has already had to go through. Nothing can shock Ede after the terrible things she heard come from Shona's lips: the cursing; the drunken threats; and then, the very worst of them all, when she told Ede how she wished she had never had a child.

Ede tightens her hands into fists at the memory of Shona's words. She hadn't meant them, or this is what Ede tells herself, though some part of her probably had when she didn't have the capacity to care for herself, let alone anyone else.

The day Jennie was born, Ede made a promise to the little girl: she would make up for any absence of love from a mother who couldn't give it, and a nameless father who didn't even know she existed. And Ede has honoured that promise a hundred times over.

But right now, she needs to focus on the man Jennie had mentioned. The last time, before Christmas, she had checked in with her about him, Jennie told her he hadn't been around for a while. 'It's not boating season. I probably won't see him for a bit.'

That had been the end of it then, and Ede was pleased. She had forgotten all about him until now.

'Can you remember anything about him?' her neighbour asks.

Ede nods. 'I need to talk to the police,' she says. 'Come on, we're going down to the marina. You'll come with me.'

'Do you remember his name?' her neighbour asks as she collects her handbag from where she had dropped it in the hallway.

'I do,' Ede says. She remembers it because it was so unusual. 'He was called Franklin Henderson.'

## Detective Inspector Aaron Field
### 10.30 hours

Aaron has called for another team briefing at 10.30. It starts with the news that the negotiator still hasn't been able to make contact. The hostage-taker still doesn't want to list their demands or create a reaction. Sarah Connelly repeats what she told Aaron earlier: given the circumstances, she wonders if they don't want to make a point at all, and likely didn't want anyone to know they were here.

'It's an otherwise quiet marina early in the morning,' she says. 'Franklin Henderson's presence was probably unexpected.'

'What does that mean then?' another detective asks her. 'What do you think could be happening in there?'

'We don't know for certain, but my feeling is that they don't know how to react, which is why they aren't answering. Right now, they could be feeling trapped, and that raises the stakes. Something's gone wrong, which will make them desperate. And that means finding another resolution to what they planned. But without talking to them, I can't make any progress. I really want to be reassuring them right now, and I can't do that.'

Aaron sucks in a breath. 'And not being able to identify which one of them *is* our hostage-taker makes the job even harder. We can't even start trying to release hostages even if we could get through to them, when we don't know who is involved and who's an innocent party.

'We're also having to profile five different people, when as yet we don't know the identity of two of them.' He sighs before pressing on. 'Okay, let's start with what we've got on them so far. Jennie Hogan: our only link to The Boatyard. According to her grandmother, Jennie doesn't usually start her shift until 11 a.m. on a Monday, so who was supposed to be opening up today? What was their reason for not coming into work, and did they ask Jennie to cover their shift? Have we got a full list of staff yet?'

'We have,' Kelly says. 'We're working our way through, making contact with everyone on it, but so far we haven't been able to get hold of the manager. It seems she's the one who holds the rota and no one we've spoken to so far was supposed to be doing that shift.'

'Keep trying to get hold of her. Get someone to her home address,' he says. 'See if anyone has an idea who should have been working and if there's any connection between them and any of the people inside.

'Ede Hogan – who's at her house?' he goes on.

'An officer has just been again, sir, but there's no one there.'

'Great,' he mutters. 'And Liv Hamilton?'

'Officer at the house says she never came home, but he's

spoken to her again and apparently she's on her way down here. Seems she didn't know her husband was at the marina either, but odder still, she didn't know he was on the Isle of Wight at all. He told her he had a meeting on the south coast, which feels like a strange way to word it. That's not an expression I'd have used if I was getting a ferry over to an island. And particularly so if I used to live here like Jacob did.'

'You're right,' Aaron says. 'Find out if Hamilton caught a ferry this morning or last night. And someone should speak to his wife again. We need to keep talking to family, and not just the next-of-kins. We want others too – friends, work colleagues, the ones who know things that spouses don't.

'I've spoken with Rosa Williams,' Aaron goes on. 'She's adamant she didn't know her husband was here, and doesn't believe he had anyone stalking him, but what have you dug up on him, Kelly?'

'Daniel writes under the name D. L. Martin,' she starts. 'I've been through his recent television interview but there's nothing contentious, although he does talk about setting his latest novel on the Isle of Wight, which he's never done before. But he didn't want to talk about it on TV. He shut the interviewer down pretty quick when she tried to probe him for more information.

'Other than that, he's written five crime books, all of them set in cities,' she goes on. 'He's always lived on the Isle of Wight, but his online bio doesn't say much. This was his first appearance on TV and, so far, it doesn't look like he's generating more than the usual number of nasty comments. In fact, I can't find anything really negative online, apart from a few one- and two-star reviews on Amazon by readers who didn't like the books, but nothing personal.'

'Okay,' Aaron says. 'Keep digging. See if there are any fans who comment more than others, and double-check to see if any of them are names we already have.'

'Do we think it's odd that neither of the wives knew their other halves were here today?' a sergeant on the call asks.

'Tell me what you mean,' Aaron prompts.

'Well, people usually know where their husband or wife is or have a vague idea of what they're up to if they're going out or meeting someone.'

Aaron nods though he couldn't tell anyone where his wife is right now. But he knows, in part, that's his fault for not listening properly. Then again, he's sure he'd remember if she were meeting a friend or doing something outside her usual routine.

He doesn't know if there is anything in what the sergeant says or not. Possibly each situation can be written off with a simple reason why they haven't told anyone where they were going this morning, but it's a thought that's worth keeping hold of. After all, right now, they have little else.

'Medical records?' he asks Kelly.

She shakes her head. 'Not yet. It's going to take some time.'

He chews his lip in thought as he looks up the road to where Franklin Henderson was hovering earlier, but the man has disappeared.

'Do we hold a press conference?' someone is asking. 'It could be a way of finding out if someone isn't where they should be. Not turned up at work, that kind of thing.'

Aaron lets out a deep breath. 'Not yet,' he says.

'I don't know how we find out about the other two women then,' the team member goes on.

Aaron agrees, but he doesn't want to involve the press yet. Doing that will only attract public attention and raise questions they can't answer.

'We have one name: Hannah Parish,' he says. 'Who we still haven't been able to contact. Do we have anything on her?'

'We've done a bit of digging,' the DS tells him. 'Nothing out of the ordinary again. She's a student counsellor, specialising in teenagers. Thirty-nine years old, single, currently lives with her sister and brother-in-law.'

'See if she turned up for work this morning,' Aaron tells him. 'The car's still there and we've been trying her phone for over an hour . . .' He doesn't bother finishing the sentence. The inference is obvious.

The more hours that pass, the more agitated Aaron is becoming, and he can't help but think that the people inside The Boatyard will be doing the same. He ends the team briefing and turns to Kelly. 'Someone knows something,' he mutters.

He doesn't know how long they will hold out inside, and he doesn't just mean the person carrying the gun. There are four others locked inside that building, and it won't take long for one of them to try and be a hero. And as soon as that happens the outcome is never good.

# Hannah

Hannah Parish opens the door of the small classroom that's been renovated into a counselling space for her, and lets fourteen-year-old *Lacey* in. She isn't actually called Lacey, but for the purposes of confidentiality Hannah calls all her young clients by a different name.

'I saw you at the weekend,' Lacey says.

'Did you?' Hannah cocks her head. She won't ask where because she doesn't want to get into a conversation with one of her students about her life outside of these four walls. However, she's surprised Lacey's jumped right into conversation when there have been sessions when she's barely uttered a word. Lacey has been coming for therapy at the school for nine months now and it took two of them for her to start talking at all.

'You were with another woman,' the girl says. 'Is it your girlfriend?'

Hannah stifles a laugh at her directness. 'No. It was my sister,' she relents.

'Really? You don't look anything like her.'

Hannah shrugs.

'She looks a lot older than you.'

Connie is eight years older than her, but Hannah isn't going to encourage this discussion.

'And her hair's a lot shorter than yours,' Lacey points out. 'I think that makes her look older.'

Again Hannah doesn't reply, though she thinks short hair suits Connie. Her sister had it chopped off a couple of years ago, but now the maintenance feels relentless with it being so cropped.

'She could even be your mum.'

'No.' Hannah evades eye contact as she catches Lacey looking at her. 'Not my mum.'

'What?' the girl asks.

'What do you mean, *what?*'

'You looked funny when you said that.'

'I'm glad you're talking today,' Hannah says. 'But why don't we talk about you instead?'

'I don't want to.'

'Did you have a good weekend?'

'Why did you look funny when I said she could be your mum?'

'I don't think I did,' Hannah insists while thinking, *God, this girl is good*. Lacey could become a detective or even a counsellor herself if she ever finally sifts through her own issues. Of which there are many, Hannah realises, and they haven't even touched the surface of them yet.

Were this not one of her students, Hannah would tell them the truth about why she felt the tic twitching in her left cheek when Lacey asked the question, a tell-tale but involuntary reaction she can't avoid. But she won't divulge anything about her own life, least of all the fact her parents are both dead.

'What did you do this weekend?' Hannah tries.

'Saw some mates, nothing much.'

'That's good,' she says. 'You went out with friends?'

'Mates, not friends.' Lacey speaks abruptly as she looks away and out of the window, chewing on her lip the way she does when she's agitated. It's an emotion that derives from hurt.

Hannah realises that she shouldn't have said what she did. She'd used a trigger word. Two months in, one of the first things Lacey had told her was that she didn't have any friends, and as far as she's concerned there's a distinct difference between that and mates.

Lacey screws up her eyes and Hannah knows she has monumentally cocked up. She shouldn't make mistakes like this when she's been working with troubled teenagers since she graduated. She's glad she's already had her job interview this morning, because otherwise she'd be going into it with a complete lack of confidence.

She wants this permanent role. She *needs it*. It's security and comes with a pay increase and more hours. Right now, she's trying not to think too much about the fact the interview only lasted half an hour.

Hannah doesn't say anything to Lacey, hoping the girl will fill the silence. She knew early on in their sessions that the root cause of Lacey's problems was her inability to form friendships. She remembers nearly asking the girl once, *Do you want them?*

She knew it was a ridiculous question when it's what every teenager craves, and yet Hannah could tell Lacey from her own experience that sometimes they are more trouble than they are worth. You can't rely on friends, only family. That's how it is for her anyway.

She wonders, briefly, what Connie is doing right now. Hannah only managed to send a quick thumbs-up emoji when she was out of the interview, but Connie will want to know more.

It is also her sister's birthday today, Hannah's job interview being the key reason she's said she can't take the day off to be with her. She'd overheard Connie in her bedroom on the phone to her husband when Hannah left for work. He must have called extra early to wish her a happy birthday, apologising again for not being on this side of the world for it. Connie professed not to mind. 'I'm forty-seven,' she'd told him two weeks ago. 'It's hardly a milestone.'

She was still on the phone when Hannah needed to leave to walk the five miles to school so she could wear in her hiking boots. Her other love, as Connie would say, rolling her eyes. 'Hiking and your students. You're obsessed with both.' And so it meant Hannah didn't get the chance to chat and make her own apologies for not being with her sister today.

Connie had wanted her to take the day off once she'd heard her husband wasn't in the country, a swift U-turn on having no desire to celebrate.

'I have my interview,' Hannah had pleaded. 'I'm sorry, but you know I can't.' The timing was bad but there was nothing she could do about it.

'You could try being less committed,' Connie had muttered, pretending to sulk as she'd sat on her sister's bed and picked up the book that was on Hannah's bedside table, waving it in the air as if to prove a point. '*Understanding the Child's Brain*. This is what you read for fun?'

Hannah had taken the book off her sister and put it back on the table. Her sister's table in her sister's spare room to be more precise, though Connie called it Hannah's now as she'd been living with them for so long.

'Don't ever make out you are anything other than a part of this family. This is *us*,' Connie had said when Hannah had settled into their home. 'The three of us. There is no one else. And you know . . .' she had gone on as she had stared straight into Hannah's eyes. 'Well . . . anyway, you just know.' Connie shrugged before turning away.

Yes, Hannah did know what Connie was saying but would never utter aloud. Hannah came first and she always would. Connie loved her younger sister more than she did her own husband.

Hannah feels guilty about it. But then, she feels guilty about many things. She wonders what her students would think if they realised how much of a mess she is. She couldn't expect them to listen to her if they did. But doesn't it make her a better counsellor?

*I am good at my job,* she tells herself now, turning her focus back to Lacey. Who else does she know who would give their all to help the ones in trouble, or in pain, or the lost ones crying out for attention? Hannah is there for every one of them, and in the times when she hasn't been enough, she's been wrung out with regrets like she was their mother herself.

She does it for a reason. *Guilt.* That nasty word again.

Connie knows all about it, because they have always shared everything since their parents were killed. Hannah and Connie know everything about each other. Except what Connie is doing right now on her birthday, Hannah thinks wryly. Her sister never did tell Hannah her plans.

But anyway, she will get the lowdown over dinner tonight, when she'll also be able to fill Connie in on her own rather short interview.

In the end Hannah doesn't apologise to Lacey for using the word *friends* and when the girl doesn't fill the silence, says instead, 'What did you do with your mates?'

Lacey shrugs, then tells her, 'You were sat in a coffee shop by the way, not that you're interested.'

'I'm interested in *you*,' she says. 'But for some reason you want to talk about me today?' Hannah smiles. 'I'm not very interesting.'

'What's it like to have a sister?'

'You have a sister,' Hannah points out. 'You have three.'

'Yeah, but they're younger than me, and they're a pain in my arse.'

'Yes, well, I'm sure all younger siblings are,' she jokes.

'I mean, what's it like to have one you get on with like you do with your sister?'

*You don't know that I do,* Hannah wants to say. Or rather, *How do you know I do?* Because they do get on, better than anyone else she could imagine getting on with.

Hannah knows they were in Ryde when Lacey must have spotted them, the town they like to go back to every now and then because it reminds them both of their childhood. Happier times in the years before Connie reached her teenage summers and didn't want to hang out with Hannah any longer, and back when their parents were still alive. Good wholesome memories of a time when it was still the four of them.

'All you need is one person in your life to count on,' Lacey is saying, spouting something Hannah would have told her once, only she knows the girl means it. This is all she wants. 'How often do you speak to her?' Lacey is asking. 'I bet it's every day.'

Hannah smiles but doesn't reply. She needs to get Lacey off the topic that she is becoming obsessed with. She will hyperfocus on this relationship if they aren't careful.

'How many times will you message her today?'

'Please can we move on,' Hannah urges.

'Answer me that first.'

'I won't message her,' Hannah says. She has sent the one emoji but that will be it.

'Not at all?'

'Not at all. I don't turn my phone on when I'm working. Now, please. Let's talk about something else.'

# Gareth

Gareth sits in his car outside his son's school for a moment before going in, his head spinning from the conversation he's just had with a woman called Violet and the news that his wife has been seeing a counsellor for the last six months. And there was the one before that, when his mother-in-law told him Eleanor had left the boys at her house this morning, without telling him any of her plans.

When he eventually climbs out of the car and gets to the school office, he finds Ben waiting for him with a sick bowl on his lap and a face that's as white as a sheet.

'Mr Lombard?'

He glances at the school secretary, shaking his head to reset his focus. 'Sorry, yes. How are you doing, Ben?' He hadn't been conscious of the fact he was lingering there, silent, lost in thought.

His son looks up at him with wide eyes and begins to cry.

'He hasn't been sick again, but he needs to stay at home for forty-eight hours, I'm afraid.'

'Right, of course. Come on then, let's get you home.' Gareth holds out a hand for Ben to take and picks up his son's school bag with the other.

'Where's Mummy?' Ben sobs as Gareth leads him through the playground and out onto the street to the car.

'Mummy's a bit busy at the moment so I'm going to take you home while we wait for her to come back,' he says, strapping his son into the car seat, stopping to give him a smile and run a hand through his soft hair. Busy doing what he has no idea, not when her phone keeps taking him straight to voicemail.

'I want Mummy.'

'I know,' he says softly. 'She'll be back soon, I promise. Come on, let's get home and into some PJs. Then you can snuggle up on the sofa and watch TV. Does that sound good?'

Ben doesn't respond and so Gareth closes the car door and walks round to the front, sliding onto the driver's seat while glancing at his boy through his rear-view mirror. It doesn't surprise him that Eleanor's the one Ben wants: she's the one both their sons always want. Gareth is second best, but he's alright with that because he kind of figures it's the way it should be.

He tries calling his wife again on his way home, but her phone is still switched off. Eleanor's mobile is never off. It is her work, her lifeline. She's forever updating her posts and checking her Instagram account. And she won't switch it off for fear the school will call her to say one of the boys is sick. Not having that access would be like 'losing my arm, Gareth', she'd once told him.

Gareth could laugh at the absurdity of it now. The one day Ben needs her, and she's nowhere to be found.

'Where are you, Eleanor?' he mutters quietly to himself. Either his wife's gone AWOL or something bad has happened to her. As far as he can see, there are no other options.

He makes a call to work and explains the situation to his unsympathetic boss who grunts in response and tells him to get into the office as soon as he can. Gareth hangs up and drives home because he has no other choice. Which is a good thing; he has never been good at making decisions. It's one of many things that irks Eleanor about him.

'Just choose one, Gareth,' she'll often mumble when he's deliberating over two dishes in a restaurant. 'It isn't that hard.' The boys will already be colouring in their books, waiting for burgers that haven't yet been ordered, and Eleanor's fingers will be tightly gripping the stem of her wine glass.

'Okay, I'll go with this one,' he'll say, smiling at the waitress as Eleanor will then smile at her too, with a slight roll of her eyes, and one of the boys will ask if their burger is ready yet. His wife has the patience of a saint when it comes to their children.

The last time they went out for dinner, Gareth had booked the restaurant, a table for two. 'I thought it would be nice to have a date night,' he'd said, excited at the prospect of an evening alone with Eleanor.

'Without the boys?' She had frowned. 'I don't know, I don't really want to pay a babysitter.'

'No, no, that's fine,' Gareth said. 'Just an idea.'

He changed the booking to four people, not wanting to unravel her response, or dwell on the way his wife's eyes had narrowed when he'd suggested going on their own.

Now, Gareth lets out a deep sigh as he lets himself and Ben into the empty house. He feels a fluttering in his stomach as his breath catches.

He takes Ben upstairs and finds the Spiderman pyjamas that Eleanor has neatly folded and left on his pillow with his blue ted on top. Gareth helps his son into them and then leads him down to the sofa where he tucks him under a fluffy grey blanket.

In the kitchen he tries calling Eleanor again but there's still no reply. Her phone takes him straight to the sing-songy message on her voicemail. He hangs up and thinks about calling the police, but he can't decide if that seems too ridiculous. 'Where did she say she was going?' they'd ask.

'Out for a run,' he'd tell them.

'Well then, that's probably what she's doing, Mr Lombard.' He imagines them sighing at his overreaction.

Gareth is prone to over-reaction. Another thing Eleanor has pointed out. He worries about the boys and how they are at school, whether they have friends and if everyone is kind to them. 'For God's sake, Gareth, are you trying to make an issue?' she has said.

'Of course not.'

'Then stop questioning everything.'

Maybe if he had done more than skim over the details of his own school life with her, she might have understood him better, but then people like Eleanor could never really understand what it's like to suffer at the hands of bullies. And so, Gareth has never given her the chance to prove him wrong. Perhaps she might have pleasantly surprised him.

'When's Mummy coming?' He turns to find Ben standing in the doorway.

'Soon.' He smiles. 'What are you doing walking about? Do you fancy some toast maybe?'

Ben nods solemnly as Gareth sends him back to the sofa. He pulls out some bread and pops it in the toaster then taps *Violet counsellor Isle of Wight* into the search bar on his phone.

It agitates him how quick his mother-in-law was to suggest they're having marriage troubles. He doubts she has any idea Eleanor is going to counselling. She would have said as much outright if she did, taking some warped pleasure in it too. No, her observations weren't based on that. So is there something else he is missing?

Not much more than a dozen results come up on the screen, so he works his way through them, visiting their websites, starting with the ones closest to where they live in the centre of the island. He is four down when he finds the name – Violet Richards. She is based in Newport, only three miles from here.

Gareth tries to think if there's been anything different in the last six months, but nothing comes to mind. People can hide things; he knows his wife certainly can. When he first met Eleanor there was an air of mystery about her that both reeled Gareth in and scared him rigid at the same time. Two people could not have been more different.

He scrolls through Violet's website, but nothing signals what help she might have been giving his wife. Only Eleanor will be able to tell him that. Violet would be silenced by client confidentiality if he called her back, he thinks, as a WhatsApp message pings up on his screen.

Gareth opens it. It is from one of the guys on the football team group, a prolific texter who likes to share minute details about his life that no one wants to hear about.

*What's going on at Newport marina?* the message says. *Road blocked off and police up there.*

Gareth frowns. The marina is no more than ten minutes from his mother-in-law's house. He opens up WhatsApp as a couple more replies to the group pop up.

*No idea, mate.*

*You been arrested again, Tucker?*

*Nah mate. I heard about it too. Seems serious,* Ian Tuck has written. *Heard someone walked into The Boatyard with a gun.*

Gareth's heart skips a beat. He flicks onto the news website and searches for incidents at Newport marina, but nothing comes up. He has an uneasy feeling even though there's no reason to believe Eleanor is there.

But then it's just *so* close to Mary's house.

He calls Ian Tuck's number. 'Do you know what this is about?' Gareth asks him.

'My brother's been doing some work down there lately. Says some guy's walked in with a gun and has a bunch of hostages. Customers who just went in for their breakfast by the sound of it,' he says. 'Why do you want to know?'

'Hostages? Do they know who?'

'No idea, mate. Why? You know someone who might be down there?'

'No. I don't know.' Gareth pauses. 'I mean, maybe Eleanor.'

'Shit, really?'

'She's probably not,' Gareth hastily says. It sounds ridiculous; he's getting carried away with himself. 'Never mind,' he says instead. 'Just wondered what it was all about.' He hangs up, staring at the toast that has just popped up.

But Gareth is now thinking about his wife being held hostage, a situation far more likely if she did actually need some time to herself before her counselling session. She would have left the boys with her mother, gone for a run in her new exercise gear, snapped a few selfies, and then stopped at the marina for coffee, with plenty of time to get to her appointment for 9 o'clock.

He dwells on the idea until it becomes a reality in his head. Stealing a glance at his son, who is smiling at the TV, Gareth shuts his eyes in disbelief that this is even remotely possible. When he opens them, he pulls up a number for the local police station in Newport, dials it, and tells the man who answers that he's concerned his wife may be caught up in the incident on the marina. Eleanor would be proud of him for making so many decisions.

'Do you know that your wife was there this morning?' the man asks him.

'She might have been,' Gareth says. 'I can't get hold of her.' He gives Eleanor's name and details. 'I'm sure everything's fine,' he adds, because he desperately hopes it is.

The man on the other end of the line puts him on hold. Gareth waits, chewing on a thumbnail. When the man returns, he asks more questions.

*What was she wearing?* Gareth describes the colourful leggings and the orange top she had on when he last saw her in the kitchen. He only remembers the outfit because it was so bright.

*What time did she go to The Boatyard?* He tells them it could have been any time after 7 a.m.

Gareth is told a detective will call him back immediately,

the urgency causing an instant surge of panic to course through him as Ben's laughter rings out from the living room. It is a sound that, in any other circumstance, would bring him joy, but right now it tugs at him.

He spreads butter and Marmite on the toast and takes it through to Ben, his heart beating erratically. He doesn't have to wait five minutes before his phone rings. When he answers, a man introduces himself as DI Aaron Field from Hampshire Police, who tells Gareth he is overseeing the investigation. 'I understand you think your wife may have been at The Boatyard this morning?' he says.

'Yes,' Gareth replies, because she might have been. He has no idea. He just wants an answer.

DI Field goes over the details Gareth's just told the man on the phone: the clothing his wife was wearing; the timing.

'I can't confirm your wife is definitely involved.' The detective pauses before adding, 'But there's a high possibility she is.'

'Oh God.' Gareth's heart sinks. He knew it, despite not wanting to believe it. 'Oh God, no.' But maybe, he thinks, maybe there's a chance it isn't her . . . Only the detective is asking him more questions now and deep down he knows it is.

'Why was your wife at the marina this morning?' the DI says.

'I don't know,' Gareth replies. 'For coffee?' Does it really take a team of detectives to work that out? Why else would she be in a café?

'Is it somewhere she goes often?'

'I don't know,' he says again, shaking his head as he tries

to remember if she's ever mentioned it. 'She might do,' he adds. He could probably find out by trawling her Instagram photos.

'Do you know if she could have been meeting anyone there this morning?'

Gareth should have just told the truth from the start. His lie is already beginning to take hold. 'I don't know,' he answers, because this, at least, is the truth.

'So, what do you know?' the DI persists.

*I know she's been lying to me for the last six months,* he thinks. *I know she has a reason to talk to a counsellor about things I have no clue about.*

Gareth has never been good at lying; a pool of red will appear on each cheek if ever he tries, like when they are playing cards and he can't help but laugh. His wife is different though. Eleanor has a frightening ability to keep a poker face. She must have been optimising this over the last six months as she waved goodbye to him every Monday morning when he left for work.

The truth is, Gareth would have been supportive if she had spoken to him about the counselling. Eleanor must know this – he does whatever he can to make anything she wants happen. When she conjures up holiday ideas on a whim, he moves some money around so they can do an albeit watered-down version of what she's fallen in love with on social media. Eleanor works hard to be gifted all the luxuries he can't afford, but he does work hard too.

'I don't really know much,' he admits in the end. It seems to sum things up perfectly.

Perhaps the DI can detect the resignation in his voice,

but Gareth is still surprised when the next thing he says is, 'Mr Lombard, how are things between you and your wife?'

'I'm sorry? Why would you ask me that?' The question brings a lump to Gareth's throat, which makes him suck in a tight breath. It's the second time he's been asked as much this morning.

He suddenly wonders whether there is something they already know about Eleanor. Does DI Field know why she is in The Boatyard this morning? Do they know about the counselling? Are they better informed about his wife than he is?

He falters over the question because he'd thought things were perfectly fine until about an hour ago. But he cannot bring himself to tell the inspector what he now knows. And besides, what difference does it make to them? 'My marriage is good,' he says. 'We are happy.'

'Is there anyone your wife has mentioned meeting recently, maybe in passing?' the DI asks now.

Gareth stares out of the kitchen window and onto their back garden where a bright red slide and various balls and ride-on toys are scattered across the lawn. He no longer knows what he paid for and what has been gifted to them.

'She meets some of the school mums,' he mumbles. That's about all he can offer, and he hardly thinks the primary school's PTA are involved in taking people hostage at a café.

But other than that Eleanor doesn't see anyone. There are no school or university friends she keeps up with. As a family, they don't see anyone as much as Gareth would like to. Their small social lives circle around whoever is in favour at the moment, and right now that's the parents of kids from the school who he doesn't think either of them have much in common with.

'Do you know if she's friends with Jennie Hogan?' DI Field asks.

'No,' Gareth says adamantly. That isn't a name he's heard.

'Daniel Williams or Jacob Hamilton?'

'Daniel Williams the author?' Gareth says.

'You know him by that name?'

'Well, yes, because he's local, I suppose. Or rather he comes from the Isle of Wight. But also, he bought a car from me not that long ago.' It was a vague claim to fame at the time and one he'd told Eleanor all about. For once she was interested in what she otherwise laughed off as his boring work stories. It wasn't every day you had an almost famous person come into the showroom.

'I've read all his books,' Gareth goes on. Eleanor has read them too, though she didn't think they were any good.

The DI isn't interested in the books. 'So, you know Daniel Williams?'

'No. I don't know him. He just bought a car from me. Why are you asking? Is this who else is being held hostage?'

'We believe there are five people inside the building,' DI Field tells him. 'And right now we're working on the assumption that one of them is the hostage-taker.' He pauses. 'We need to ascertain who.'

'Oh,' Gareth says, the names spinning round in his head with the only one he has heard before settling at the front. Surely it isn't Daniel Williams. Unless it's research for his next book. But what kind of sick person would go to those lengths to research a book? Is that what crime authors do? They'd end up in prison, surely.

'Mr Lombard?'

'Yes?'

'Is there anything more you can tell me about Eleanor?'

'Like what?'

'I've just told you, we're looking at five people inside a building and one of them has taken the other four hostage.'

'I know but—' It dawns on him then. 'Hold on, you're asking if— No!' Gareth exclaims. 'Oh my God, no. This isn't my wife. Eleanor's just a normal person. She's got a family. She's a mum.' Of course she hasn't got hold of a gun and held a bunch of people hostage.

'Every one of the people in there has a family. They're all normal everyday people just like your wife.'

'I don't . . .' Gareth falters.

'Are there any issues at all that you can think of? Any worries that may have been concerning her, changes in her behaviour?'

How quickly things have taken a dark turn as the situation spirals even further out of Gareth's control. He's finding it harder and harder to grasp on to the Eleanor he is married to as images of her flash through his mind. He sees her as he always does when she's not in front him: in a series of picture-perfect portraits. Stills from a movie that capture her frozen in a moment of time. Much like her Instagram account.

'No,' Gareth says as he feels the burn of two red splotches sear his cheeks. He hasn't *seen* any changes in her behaviour at all but wouldn't the fact she has been seeing a counsellor count?

But whatever is happening at the marina today, it has nothing to do with Eleanor. He knows this without a shadow of a doubt. He only needs to look at their boy, giggling at the TV, to know his wife wouldn't do anything so stupid.

# Ede

Ede drives to the marina, Marjorie sitting in the passenger seat beside her, fiddling with the seat belt as she complains she can't get comfy. As they reach the top of the road, Ede sees that they can't get all the way down it to The Boatyard. A barrier is closing off access, meaning she has to turn around and park up on a gravelled area to one side.

'I do want to be here for you, Ede,' Marjorie is saying as they get out of the car. 'But I don't know how long I should leave my Ray all by himself.'

Ede sighs. 'Then go. I'll call you if there's any news.' She starts walking ahead, as fast as her legs will take her. There is a man speaking on his phone, standing outside a van, who turns and watches them coming and she's conscious of what they must look like: Ede with her walking stick clacking on the tarmac; her gangly neighbour in that ridiculous multicoloured patchwork coat she insists on wearing, scurrying behind.

'No, you need me to look after you too,' she is protesting.

Maybe Ede shouldn't have brought her. Ede would be better on her own, without someone fretting over her as if she can't do anything for herself. Up until six months ago no one made her feel that way because Ede Hogan was a strong and independent woman in her seventies. 'A force to be reckoned with,' Marjorie would say. But then, up until six months ago, Ede hadn't sat in a doctor's room to be told she was dying.

She has tried to come to terms with her prognosis. It is the circle of life after all, even if seventy-eight doesn't feel like a good age these days, but her own parents had passed away in their sixties so she supposes she should at least be grateful she has made it this far. She isn't though. Last summer, Ede had thought she had many more years left in her. Though she supposes she could cope with dying if it wasn't for the thought of leaving Jennie behind.

When they reach the man who has been watching them, Ede says, 'I'd like to talk to whoever is in charge.'

'I'm Detective Inspector Aaron Field,' he says. 'Can I help you?'

'My name is Ede Hogan, and my granddaughter is in that building.' She gestures towards the marina. 'Please can you tell me what is happening? Why isn't Jennie out of there by now?'

'We're doing everything we can,' he says. 'The situation is contained.'

'You mean Jennie is contained, and no one is doing a damned thing to get her out?'

'I can assure you our priority is getting everyone inside the building out safely,' he says. He cocks his head and chews down on his lip. She wonders if he expects her to believe him. 'Actually, I do need to ask you some questions, Mrs Hogan. Maybe we could go and find somewhere to sit? There's a building at the top of the road—'

Ede turns and looks up the way they have just come. She shakes her head solemnly. It was enough of an effort getting here and that was downhill.

'Then maybe we could just go and sit down on that bench?' he suggests.

'Fine,' she mutters, as if she really doesn't need to sit, when they must both know she does. Marjorie follows as they cross the road.

'Jennie is the only person inside the building, as far as we know for sure, who has any link with The Boatyard,' he tells her as they slowly walk over to the side of the road.

'So you do think it has something to do with this place,' Ede says, just like the officer who came to her house suggested.

'We can't rule it out. It could have something to do with the marina, and your granddaughter might somehow have got caught up in it.'

'There was a man who was bothering Jennie last year,' Ede tells him. 'I remembered his name. It was Franklin Henderson.'

'Franklin Henderson?' the detective repeats as he straightens his back. His eyes veer away from hers and Ede looks about her, but there is no one else around apart from a young woman in a top that's far too big for her. 'Can you tell me what happened?'

'She didn't tell me much, but he was pestering her. I told her to report it, though I doubt she did. The thing with Jennie is that she gives time to everybody, even the odd ones.'

Jennie had said once that you never know what people

are going through. They get some lonely people at The Boatyard who like to talk because they have no one else to chat to, and Jennie would never turn any of them away.

'It means she never knows who she's talking to,' Ede goes on.

The detective is nodding slowly, a curious expression on his face as he says, 'Franklin Henderson is the man who made the call to the emergency services this morning. He was the one who witnessed Jennie and four others entering the building.'

'Oh,' Ede says, frowning. 'Well, I guess that means it isn't him then.' She thinks about the coincidence of it though, whether it means anything still, even if the man isn't inside the building. 'Who *do* you think it is?' she asks.

'We're looking at every possibility,' DI Field says to her, which suggests they don't have a clue.

'But he saw four people go in there this morning. So, do you think it's one of them who is holding my granddaughter hostage?'

This time the detective hesitates before saying, 'At the moment we're working on the assumption there aren't any other people inside the building.'

'So you do,' she deduces as she turns around and looks about her, wondering whether the lone woman hovering in her oversized top is another relative. She looks to be freezing in her thin baggy pants that do little to hide the fact there's nothing of her. Ede watches her for a moment, wondering what her connection is to whoever is inside, before the woman turns and walks away.

'You were given two names earlier,' the detective says. 'Daniel Williams and Jacob Hamilton. You say you don't know either of them?'

'I don't,' she replies, shaking her head.

'We now believe there's a woman called Eleanor Lombard in there too.'

'I haven't heard of her either.'

'How about Hannah Parish?'

'Parish?' Ede repeats as she thinks about the name. There were Parishes on the Isle of Wight. 'I remember a Lisa Parish.' She was about Shona's age. 'I think she had daughters but I don't remember their names. Is she in there too then?'

The detective turns towards the marina. 'No. We don't know that she is. It's just a possibility we're investigating.'

'It was years back anyway,' Ede continues. 'They lived nearby but it's a small island, Detective. Everyone has a link to someone, somehow. I knew them when my daughter was still around. She died. Twenty years ago now.'

'I'm sorry to hear that.'

'Jennie's mother,' she tells him, though she doesn't know why she's sharing this. 'She was an alcoholic. Eventually her liver couldn't take any more.' Ede's eyes well up. It shouldn't keep surprising her when they're persistently doing so these days, but Ede thought she had got past the stage of tearing up when she talked about her daughter. She feels the need to look away from the detective now; it might be pride, or something else she can't quite put her finger on.

'Lisa Parish and her husband died too,' Marjorie chips in. 'Do you remember, Ede? They died in a car accident.'

Ede nods, pulling herself together. 'It was a couple of years after Shona. Tragic way to go.'

'You kept in touch with them?' the DI asks.

'No.' Ede shakes her head. 'But you hear things,' she says. 'You can't do much around here without everyone else finding out.'

'That's true,' Marjorie agrees, with a *humph*ing sound that suggests she doesn't like it, when she's always the first in line for gossip.

'Did Jennie know the daughters?' DI Field asks.

'Not that I know,' Ede tells him, thinking back. 'But then she didn't bring many friends back to the house.' In fact, Ede can't remember her bringing a single person home once she'd started secondary school. Ede had asked her a number of times if there were any girls she wanted to invite for tea, but at some point, she gave up.

She knew *why* Jennie didn't want anyone around. You tended not to when you had a mother who was either sleeping off a hangover or just tucking into another vodka when you got home from school.

The detective is asking, 'And now?'

Ede shakes her head. 'She's never mentioned a Hannah.' She pauses then adds, 'I told the other officer earlier Jennie doesn't usually do this shift.'

'Yes,' he says. 'And you don't know whose shift she was covering?'

'No. *Someone* must have asked her though because she doesn't normally start until 11 on a Monday. Shouldn't you know who it is by now? I would have thought it was important.'

'We don't have that information yet,' he tells her.

She stares at him. 'Whoever it is –' she waves her hand about '– don't you think, if they were supposed to be there this morning, they are the intended target?'

'It's something we're looking at.'

'No one would want to hurt Jennie,' Marjorie tells him as Ede closes her eyes, willing the tears to stop but they keep coming regardless. There is an eddy of emotion swirling inside of her. The idea of Jennie's life being in danger, the short future of her own, and the loss of her daughter, all whipping up like a tornado.

'Everyone loves Jennie,' Ede adds, biting her lip as the tears cascade down her cheeks. 'We had a fight last night. It was the second one in a week. We never fight.' She opens her eyes again and looks at the detective. She can feel Marjorie shifting next to her, no doubt wanting to know what it was about. 'I need to tell her I'm sorry.'

'What did you have a fight about?' the detective asks.

Ede shakes her head. She regrets saying anything. 'It was nothing,' she says, because she cannot tell him the truth.

# Detective Inspector Aaron Field
## 10.45 hours

'Where's Henderson?' Aaron pulls the door of the van shut behind him as he climbs inside. 'I need to speak to him.'

'Don't know, sir. I thought he was still hanging around,' Kelly replies.

'Well, he isn't.'

'Everything okay?'

'Ede Hogan's just mentioned that he was bothering Jennie Hogan last November. She doesn't know how exactly, but she knows there was some unwanted interest from him.'

'You think it might mean something?'

'I don't know,' he says. 'I don't see how, when he called this in. He's clearly not the one holding the gun, but . . .' Aaron trails off. But what? But it's too much of a coincidence that the one name that's been handed to them is that of a person they've already linked to The Boatyard?

He hits redial on Franklin Henderson's number and waits for it to connect. As it rings, he says, 'And please can someone get Ede Hogan and her neighbour up to the marine unit? Get them a cup of tea. She doesn't look well.'

The phone rings and rings until Franklin eventually picks up.

'Would you mind meeting me back here?' Aaron asks.

Silence. Eventually Henderson clears his throat. 'Yes. Of course. It'll take me at least ten minutes to get back though.'

'Ten minutes is fine. I'll see you then.' He ends the call and turns to Kelly. 'Someone has a potentially unhealthy interest in Jennie Hogan. Isn't this what we've been looking for? And yet the guy's on the outside of the building.' He rolls his eyes and sighs. 'We need to know who was supposed to be working that shift today. Chase up whoever's trying to make contact with the manager. Someone must know who it was.'

Franklin Henderson arrives at the marina exactly ten minutes later, by which time Ede Hogan and her neighbour are ensconced in the marine unit.

In the absence of any privacy, Aaron leads his witness to a spot along the roadside, away from the barrier. 'Thank you for coming back,' he says.

'Has something happened? Down there?' Henderson nods down the road.

'No. The situation is still contained.'

Henderson doesn't respond and Aaron tries to figure out what he makes of him. Close up, the man looks much older than his fifty-eight years. The skin around his blue eyes is hooded, his face weathered. No wedding ring, Aaron notices, or mark where one might have been. He has the look of someone who's spent the entire night on his boat.

'We don't believe Jennie Hogan should have been working this morning,' Aaron starts.

'Is that so?'

'Do you know who was supposed to be opening up the café?'

'No,' he says. 'I wouldn't have any idea about anything like that.'

'Someone may have asked her to do their shift. Information like this could be important.'

Henderson nods but doesn't reply.

'How well do you know Jennie?'

'As well as I know any of the staff here. Like I told you, she's been here seven years, so . . .' He stops, shrugs.

'But you said you and she were friends.'

Henderson squints as he appears to look off into the distance. 'Well, maybe not so much friends . . .'

'Did you see her outside of The Boatyard at all?' Aaron asks, with the distinct sense that the man's demeanour has changed since they last spoke two and a half hours earlier.

'No,' Franklin answers, chewing on one corner of his lip.

'Never?' he persists.

'What's this about?'

'Her grandmother tells me that you've been bothering Jennie. Maybe you were more interested in her than she was in you?'

'That's ridiculous,' he says. 'This is all ridiculous. Why are you asking me these questions? How's it going to help you get those people out of there alive?'

There is something off about Franklin Henderson's behaviour. His vague answers are lacking in substance compared to the detailed descriptions he was happy to offer at the start of the day. 'Your name came up,' Aaron says. 'And right now we need to follow every line of inquiry so that we *can* ensure Jennie and the others are safe.'

'Well, clearly this has nothing to do with me,' he says, waving a hand in front of himself as if to add, *because here I am*. 'Do you really think I'd have phoned this in if I was in any way involved?'

*People do all kinds of strange things*, Aaron thinks, but what he says is, 'Jennie Hogan is the only person associated with this place and so we're working on the assumption she might have been targeted. If you *are* friends with her then anything more you can tell us would be extremely helpful.'

Henderson regards Aaron as he takes this in. 'Jennie's a nice girl. We've chatted. She takes the time to talk to me when some of the others don't bother,' he adds flatly. 'If she ever thought I'd taken too much interest in her, then I'm sorry about that. It wasn't my intention. Now if there's nothing more, I would like to be on my way,' he adds. 'If that's okay?'

'That's okay,' Aaron says, watching him curiously. 'But keep your phone on, please. There may be some more things we need to run by you.'

Henderson pats his pocket, which Aaron supposes is to confirm he will, and then turns and walks back up the road.

'There's something he's not telling me,' Aaron says to Kelly when he gets back inside the van. 'He seems different from earlier when he couldn't wait to share everything he'd seen. Now it seems like he's holding something back. I don't know. Maybe he is, but it's not relevant. Perhaps he did come on to Jennie, but that doesn't mean he's involved in holding her hostage. How can he be?' he muses. 'Speak to the staff again,' he tells her. 'See if anyone has *anything* to say about him. I want to know what his relationship with Jennie Hogan really was.'

'Will do, sir, only . . .'

'Only what?'

'I just wondered if this is where we need to be focusing resources when the guy's here, outside the building. I really don't see how he can have anything to do with the hostage situation.'

'The image isn't always that clear though, is it?' Aaron says. 'And while we're at it, see if there's any connection between Henderson and any of the others.' He doesn't know how, but he's certain the man has more to say than he's letting on.

# Hannah

Mondays bring one student after another. It's the most popular day for appointments after difficult weekends at home for the children.

Lacey's session has finished, and now Hannah has a different student in front of her. *Abbie* sits on the sofa opposite. She turns sixteen tomorrow and doesn't want to be at school any longer. Just like Hannah at her age. She couldn't wait to get out, though for her it was futile to fight her parents on it. Not when they were so set on her and her sister taking A-levels and going to university. She wonders what they would think if they could see her now, working in the same school she was so desperate to leave.

They would be proud, and they'd see that Hannah doesn't do it for the money. If she did, she'd go private rather than work through the council. But then, she wouldn't reach the kids who need her most: the ones whose parents can't afford counselling, or who don't care enough to invest in anything that will actually help.

Abbie reminds Hannah of herself. It's just one of the reasons she's grown more attached to this young girl than she has to the others.

Hannah watches her chewing a nail then picking at the dry skin around it when she takes it out of her mouth.

Beneath the long sleeves of her sweatshirt there are thin lines of scars on her wrists.

'How are things at home?' Hannah asks gently.

Abbie shakes her head. Her eyes that are too large and wide for her elfin face stare at Hannah hauntingly. 'He did it again last night,' she says eventually. 'He came into my room when Mum went out.'

'Oh, Abbie.' Hannah can't imagine how unsafe Abbie must feel in her own home. Every family should be like Hannah's was, a perfect haven, until that was taken away from her. A family of four sliced in two, leaving her with Connie who has since become her everything.

She had left Connie's birthday card on the kitchen table this morning. Along with the others that have come through the post over the last couple of days. Hannah wonders if she had been too abrupt when she told her sister she couldn't take the day off. Maybe Connie was more pissed off with her than she'd made out. And she would have done it if it was Hannah's birthday. She has a don't-care attitude that Hannah doesn't. She doesn't care about her job as a dental assistant. Connie wouldn't have agreed to an interview on her sister's birthday, she'd have told them straight it would have to be another day.

It's amazing that two sisters could turn out so different. Connie's laid-back attitude makes Hannah feel even more uptight in comparison.

'Can we go outside?' Abbie is asking, gesturing past the window. Hannah nods and grabs her coat from the back of the door. They walk around the school, talking a route that avoids the classrooms with large windows where kids would see them. Instead, they go through the doors that lead onto the staff car park. Abbie stops outside and takes a deep breath, wrapping her arms around herself. Hannah pauses too and waits until the girl is ready to talk.

There is a nip in the cold March air. Hannah shudders as she looks up at the darkening sky. There is something foreboding about the clouds that are collecting overhead. She shouldn't be here, she suddenly thinks. She should be with her sister. Connie had wanted her today, and Hannah isn't there for her. Sometimes she just needs to let go and do the things that are most important. But it's too late to do anything about that now.

It is a thought that passes when Abbie tells her, 'I want to do something. You know, about him.'

'Okay.' Hannah refocuses, but Abbie has started walking again, lost in her own train of thought.

It is too late for regret, Hannah thinks, and she will make it up to Connie tonight. Her sister has already bought two pieces of sirloin, a bottle of Chablis and announced that Hannah will be cooking for her. If she was annoyed, then it won't last long.

'I can't let him get away with it any longer, can I?' Abbie says.

*No*, Hannah thinks. 'Not if this is what you want to do,' she says.

'Will you come with me?'

'Of course I will.' She has been longing for this day for thirteen months, desperate for Abbie to find the courage to speak out about her stepfather.

'I don't know how my mum will react.'

'No,' Hannah says. 'But you can't control that. You can only control what you do.'

'She won't believe me,' the girl says softly.

Abbie comes to her in her dreams. Her *nightmares*, rather. The child is slipping over the edge, the place itself not specific, its background a dark cavern. It's not something she wants to talk about with anyone or try to pull apart to decipher the meaning. She already knows what it means.

In her dreams Hannah sometimes hangs a hand over the edge, but she doesn't ever reach her. Other times she just stands there. Never is she able to save her.

Hannah does something else she shouldn't do and wraps her arms around Abbie, feeling the girl fold into her. She wants to say that maybe her mother will believe her, but Hannah doesn't think it's the truth.

# Liv

By the time she and Katy reach Southampton, Liv has replayed the last time she saw her husband in her head so many times that she has lost count. She has been trying to recall if anything seemed off with him last night, but nothing springs to mind.

He'd asked if there was any part of her looking forward to a night at her parents' house as he took a jacket out of the closet and sat on the bottom stair to pull on his trainers. She laughed and said, 'Not really.' Then shrugged and told him it would be okay, she just wished he was coming with her.

Jacob stood up and kissed her on the cheek. He looked into her eyes as he said he wished he could too. 'I won't bother calling tonight as you're out; I'll ring you in the morning,' he'd said.

'Remember I'm meeting Katy for breakfast.'

He nodded, whether he had remembered or not. 'I'll call you in the office when I'm out of my meeting.' He had kissed her again and told her he loved her and then left the house as she'd gone upstairs to finish getting ready.

She'd pictured him spending the evening sitting in his hotel room, maybe eating in the restaurant. Not catching a ferry to the Isle of Wight.

His whole evening and morning have been filled with lies and yet still she cannot see them in his words and actions. And there would have been more before that too in the plans he made to get there and the tickets he purchased, or maybe his PA purchased for him. Conversations with whoever he is meeting, because he *will* be meeting someone. Liv's thoughts dwell upon an affair because what other explanation is there?

She knows Jacob's PA, the woman who would have booked his hotels and diarised his meetings. They work in the same building, albeit a floor apart, but Liv can't bring herself to ask her what she knows about Jacob that Liv doesn't. As soon as she airs her dirty laundry in public there is no going back. Liv saw it happen with her own parents.

Katy pulls off the road into a petrol station, telling Liv she won't get far the other side if she doesn't fill up now. Inside the service station, Liv uses the bathroom, remembering only a couple of hours ago sitting inside a very different one in a Covent Garden restaurant, seeing the word *Pregnant* on the test stick.

Her joy then was like nothing she's ever experienced, knowing her life was about to change, but it was supposed to be for the better. Now Liv doesn't see any future for herself that will bring her anything but pain.

Katy is still on the forecourt filling her car when Liv comes out of the toilet and so she wanders up the aisles of the small store, stopping by the chocolate bars.

Jacob would always want one on a journey like this. 'Choose it for me,' he would say. He didn't mind what, he's obsessed with chocolate. Every Christmas she buys him a chocolate advent calendar *and* one of those netted stockings filled with bars.

Liv hovers now, her heart contracting at the memories as her eyes trail the selection. Her fingers reach for a Yorkie and she grasps it in her hand, moving on, her attention caught by the discounted rolls of wrapping paper at the till. She takes a tube of paper covered in multi-coloured stripes and hands them both over to be scanned.

'What have you got there?' Katy asks, appearing behind her.

Liv looks down at the two items as if, for a split second, she has no idea how they got there. 'I always planned to wrap up the test to give to Jacob. It seems stupid now.'

'No, it doesn't.' Katy takes hold of Liv's hand. 'You'll get the chance to give it to him.'

'Will I?' She looks at her friend. 'I don't even know why I bought these,' she mutters as she picks them up anyway and they make their way back to the car. She dumps them both on the back seat and climbs into the front.

Silence envelops them again as they crawl through the city. They need to get to the other side of it to reach the ferry terminal. Liv leans her head against the headrest and watches the people outside of the window going about their lives; teenagers scurrying by with their heads in their phones, couples holding hands, mothers pushing prams. She feels an emptiness at seeing them. It isn't just the fear of what she's heading into, it is more than that. Liv feels a sense of loss already, for what she thought she had, and what she hoped her and Jacob's future would look like.

She turns and opens her mouth to voice this to Katy but

what would she tell her friend? That she isn't even sure she's been happy lately?

Instead, she says nothing and picks up her phone that she'd left in the car when they went to the garage. 'Oh God, I've had a missed call.' It's an unknown number and so Liv calls it back.

'DS Bantham,' a voice answers.

'It's Liv Hamilton, I think you called me.'

'Mrs Hamilton, we'd like to ask you a few more questions. Is it safe for you to talk? Are you driving?' It's the detective she had kept waiting at her house, who has already called her once on the journey and knows she isn't driving.

'I'm not,' Liv tells him again. 'Is there any news?'

'The situation's still the same.'

'So, Jacob's okay?' *He's still alive?*

'As far as we know, no one has been hurt.'

'But you told me it was an armed robbery, so what are they still doing in there? Why hasn't anyone given them the money so they can get out?'

*Why* is someone robbing a café on the Isle of Wight? Katy had asked earlier. Of course, neither of them has the answer.

'We don't know why your husband and the other hostages are being held inside,' the detective tells her before asking if she recognises the names Eleanor Lombard or Hannah Parish. She tells him she doesn't. She's never heard Jacob mention an Eleanor or a Hannah, but then she doubts she would know any name from his past. She is certain he never told her who the woman was they had bumped into a few years back.

'How did your husband seem last night?' DS Bantham is asking her now.

'Seem?' Liv repeats. She's already deduced that he seemed normal as he lied to her about his plans, and yet she isn't sure what difference it makes to the police. Unless they know something? 'What does it matter how he seemed?' she asks uneasily.

The detective hesitates for a moment before he tells her, 'We believe there are only five people inside that building including your husband and the others whose names I have told you.' Another pause before he goes on, 'What we don't know is who is responsible for this situation.'

Liv frowns. 'Okay,' she says, still not understanding what he is getting at.

'That's why I need to ask how your husband has seemed to you lately. Maybe he's done something out of character or there's been behaviour that's caused you concern?'

'Hold on,' she says. 'What exactly are you getting at?' She catches Katy glancing at her. 'You're not trying to suggest Jacob is doing this? Are you joking?' Liv says. 'What the hell would my husband take a gun into a café for? Where is he even supposed to get one from?'

'We don't know who is responsible for this situation and that's why it's important we know if there is anything—'

'Of course there isn't,' she cries, her heart racing. 'He's not the one holding people hostage. So don't waste your time thinking he is.'

'We need to ask the questions, Mrs Hamilton,' he tells her calmly. 'Until we know who, and what, we're dealing with, we can't get your husband and the others out of there safely.'

'Well, it isn't him!'

'We need access to Jacob's medical records,' he tells her.

'We're getting them for everyone. But it would speed things up if you could tell me anything important.'

'Like what?'

'If there's anything we need to know. History of depression, mental health problems, that kind of thing.'

'No,' she says adamantly. 'There is nothing. You can look at his records and see that for yourself.' Jacob never even goes to the doctor; he barely ever takes a paracetamol if he has a headache. 'You're barking up the wrong tree,' she tells him.

'Is he for real?' Katy snaps when Liv puts the phone down. 'Why on God's earth would this be Jacob?'

'It isn't,' Liv says. 'Of course it bloody isn't.' There is not one scrap of doubt in her mind. She might not know everything about her husband, but she knows *this*.

'Liv, do you think you should call your dad?'

'What for?' She turns to her friend.

Katy hesitates before replying. 'Do you think maybe you should get some legal advice?'

Liv stares at her. She has no clue what she should be doing anymore. Every time she thinks it can't get any worse, something else hits her. 'I don't know,' she says eventually. 'I don't know how much more I can take.' She shakes her head in disbelief as she stares at the blank screen on her phone. 'I'm calling Jacob's PA,' she says eventually. 'I need to know what he was supposed to be doing this morning.'

Liv finds her number and dials it. 'It's Liv,' she says when his PA answers, the next words ready on her tongue, but she doesn't get a chance to say them.

'Ohmygod, Liv. Are you okay? What's happened? I heard about Jacob, and we're all obviously going out of our minds here. Is he okay? Have you heard anything?'

'How do you know?' Liv says, taken aback that they already do.

'I had the police on the phone, asking loads of questions.' The PA pauses, hesitating. 'It took me totally by surprise. I didn't even know he had left London; I didn't book anything for him. I can't believe it.'

Liv bites her lip, closing her eyes. The police have already spoken to people at the office, but the detective didn't see fit to tell her that.

'Did he have a meeting?' Liv asks.

'He has one today. Not till 2 p.m. though.'

'Where?'

'Reading.'

'But that's—' She stops herself. That isn't *down south*. That's an hour and a half's journey from home at the most. He wouldn't have needed to leave the house until after midday.

'Oh, I better cancel it, hadn't I? God, I'm so sorry, Liv. You must be so worried. Is there anything I can do?'

'There definitely isn't anything else in his diary?' she asks.

'No. He just blanked it out.' The PA pauses again. 'It says he's working from home this morning. Oh, did he mean his mum's?'

A ball of nausea surges into Liv's throat. Her hands shake as she mutters that he probably did and hangs up the call, tossing her phone in the direction of her bag. Does she know *anything* about her husband? Has she been so naive as not to realise she is married to a man who can lie so easily?

Right now, the only reason she wants him to walk out of that building alive today is so that she can look him in the eye and get some answers, she thinks. But as quick as the thought comes it is washed away by guilt, leaving her hollowed out with fear that she may never again see the man she loves.

# Gareth

Gareth paces back and forth, pounding the downstairs carpet of their three-bed semi.

He wants to drive to the marina, but he can't take Ben with him. He wants to call Violet Richards, but he knows any counsellor worth their salt won't tell him anything. He wants to scream but his six-year-old son is one room away, oblivious to the fact his mummy's life is in danger. And that's the way Gareth needs to keep it.

He is trapped inside his own house. It doesn't escape him that his wife is the one who is *actually* imprisoned, but this is his home and he usually loves it here.

Eleanor has made everything about it comfortable and cosy. Whenever he gets home from work candles are lit and there's a soft glow emanating from the many lamps. The walls are adorned with photos of the boys in white IKEA frames, up and down the stairs and hallway. The boys' toys are usually spread out over the floor but, every night, they are tidied away into one of the many wicker boxes that fit snugly into the cube storage shelves. His wife has created a sanctuary for them but now he just wants to get out of it.

He's so desperate for more news of Eleanor. He may as well be a million miles away for all the good his persistent pacing is doing her. Gareth feels like a prisoner in his own body too, unable to show any emotion when his son is looking at him like he is now.

'Is Mummy coming home soon?' Ben asks again, his wide eyes peering out over the top of the blanket he's cuddled under in the living room. His plate has been discarded at his side; at least he seems to be holding the toast down.

'Yes. Soon,' Gareth murmurs. He is not enough for his boys; it is Eleanor they want. He might have accepted this previously but today he wishes he could be all the comfort his son needs.

He has to keep it together even though he feels like he is falling apart.

Now he's thinking of the wine he and Eleanor shared last night. He's thinking of the sound of her laughter, and how she'd wanted to open another bottle, even though he had to be up early for work. She already knew the next morning she'd be waiting for him to leave the house so she could pack the boys off before unburdening herself to her counsellor.

Gareth opens the door to the back garden and steps outside. He has a missed call from work, no doubt checking if he's actually coming in, but he cannot bring himself to call them again and so he ignores it instead.

*What* would his wife have been unburdening herself of this morning? Would it have been about him? The life they have created together for their boys?

He strides to the end of the garden until he gets to his shed and then stands there for a moment, staring at it, before doing something he has never ever done before. He balls his hands into fists and pummels the wood, which splinters and crumbles beneath them, cursing under his breath with words he would never usually use.

Blood trickles down his knuckles. His sudden outburst has surprised him, but just for those few seconds the pain felt good. Only as he looks up and turns back to the house, he can see Ben in the garden by the kitchen doorway watching him again, his eyes as wide as saucers. 'Son, what are you doing out here? It's too cold to be outside,' Gareth calls as he walks back to the house.

Ben's eyes drop to Gareth's hands. 'You're hurt.' His little boy looks horrified and takes a step away.

'Oh, no, silly Daddy was just trying to fix the shed. It doesn't hurt. It looks worse than it is,' he says, stepping past Ben to run his hands under the cold tap in the sink. As the water runs red, pooling in the plughole, Gareth knows he cannot start losing it like this. He never loses it.

Their home phone trills out and makes him jump. He leaps to grab it, but it's his mum's voice on the other end, and it surprises him to hear her, as much as it does her that he has answered.

'Oh, darling,' she says, 'is everything alright? What are you doing at home?'

His heart sinks into his hollowed body and he feels everything draining out of him. 'I'm looking after Ben,' he says. 'He was sent home from school.' He smiles at his son who is standing by his side.

'Oh? Poor lamb. Where's Eleanor then?'

'She's—' He stops himself. 'Actually, Mum, I can't really chat.'

'Oh, not to worry, I was just wanting to check something

with her that I've bought for your birthday. I don't want to get you the wrong thing.' She laughs, trying to make light of the fact she probably runs everything she buys for any of them past Eleanor first.

'That's kind, Mum. I'll get her to call you back later.'

'Oh, well, don't bother her,' she says. 'I know how busy she always is. I didn't know if this was a good time to call her or not, but I know she can easily ignore the home phone if she wants to—'

'Mum,' he interrupts her, hating the way she sounds so desperate to please. He reads between the lines of what his parents think, because neither of them would ever tell him straight. He remembers how they were from the start, the first time he took Eleanor back home to Hull to meet them.

'She's very bubbly, isn't she?' his dad had said.

'Oh, yes, and incredibly beautiful, darling,' his mum had added. 'Well, she's very lucky to have *you* anyway,' she'd gone on to say, smiling.

Gareth had smiled back in much the way he keeps smiling today. They all knew Eleanor was out of his league. But his two closest friends, to whom Gareth had shown Eleanor off at the pub that same weekend, hadn't said as much either. They'd nodded, looking impressed, and slapped him on the back when she wasn't looking. And later into the evening he'd laughed along nervously, ignoring the simmering unease that was developing. It felt like he was trying to combine two different worlds, and that it might all go terribly wrong. He was already out of his depth.

His mum had caught him the following morning as they

were leaving to go and pulled him to one side so Eleanor couldn't hear what she had to say to him.

'Just don't be grateful, Gareth,' she had said as she kissed him on the cheek. He didn't understand what she meant, or rather he did but he didn't want to.

He was just as surprised as his parents and friends that Eleanor had chosen to be with him. Maybe none of them thought it would last, and they were all on edge as they waited for the inevitability of her finishing with him.

But she didn't. And by the time they were in their late twenties they were married. And by thirty they'd moved back to the Isle of Wight, for reasons that weren't wholly apparent to Gareth, and within a couple of years they had two amazing boys together. And some days Gareth looks at her Instagram posts and wonders what the hell she sees in him with his greying hair and balding spot, and a wardrobe she's forever changing. But he doesn't dare ask. All he knows is that if she were ever to leave him now, he wouldn't want anyone else. He would rather live on his own with the boys reluctantly visiting him every other weekend than give his all to someone else. The thought of doing that again drains him.

He ends the call to his mum with the promise Eleanor will phone her later. A promise he knows it might not be possible for her to keep. Speaking to his mum will be the last thing his wife wants to do, if, God willing, she is back at home with them all tonight.

Gareth knows what their marriage looks like to the people around them. He isn't blind or naive, but he fell in love with Eleanor soon after they met, and he hasn't stopped loving her since. The wives of his two close friends don't have much time for her and as a consequence, they rarely spend much time together anymore. If you broke it down, you might think that Gareth has chosen his wife over his old friends, and maybe he has. But it doesn't matter. His family unit is what he cares about, and now it is up to him to make sure he can pull it back together again.

And preferably by 3.15 when Jack, his youngest, comes out of nursery.

'I need to take you to Grandma's,' he says to Ben, ignoring the look of horror on his son's face.

Gareth's call to his mother-in-law is short.

'I need to bring Ben over to you.' He talks in a hushed voice as he sits on the edge of their bed, trying not to listen to his son wailing downstairs that he doesn't want to go. 'It's an emergency.'

'The police were waiting for me at the house, Gareth,' she screams. 'When were you thinking of telling me my daughter is being held hostage?'

'As soon as I knew for sure.'

'Well, they seem pretty certain to me,' she cries. 'They have literally just this minute left my house. I was about to call you.'

He tries to see past her anger and put it down to fear for her only daughter. 'I need you to look after Ben for me so I can go to the marina,' he says.

'And what exactly do you think *you're* going to do, Gareth?'

He grits his teeth. 'I'll be there in ten minutes,' he tells her as he hangs up and goes downstairs, ushering Ben into the car outside.

His son's face is smeared with tears as they make the short trip to his grandmother's house. 'Why isn't Mummy looking after me instead of her?' he sobs.

'Daddy's going to get her,' Gareth says, smiling into the rear-view mirror, the lie cracking his heart in two. If anything happens to Eleanor, he can't imagine how his boys will cope. Surely this is what his wife is thinking herself. Now Gareth can't stop picturing her, knowing this will be what is going through her head. How desperate she will be to survive for the sake of their boys, how scared she must be that there's a chance she might never see her sons again.

He cannot rid himself of this image as he pulls up at Mary's house and tugs a sobbing Ben up the path to the front door. Mary's face is expressionless as she opens it, staring at Gareth and then dropping her eyes to her grandson. 'Come on in then,' she says to Ben eventually, a crack in her voice that Gareth doesn't miss. 'Shall we bake some cookies?'

'Thank you,' Gareth says as he urges his son inside. 'I'll call you as soon as . . .' He doesn't know how to finish.

Mary frowns as she ushers Ben into the house and tells him to look for the cats. 'The police were asking questions about Eleanor.'

'What kind of questions?'

'When I last saw her, what her state of mind was. I had to tell them the truth,' she goes on. 'Eleanor was in a weird mood this morning. Something was bothering her.'

Gareth wonders how he hadn't noticed it himself. His wife had been distracted before he left for work, but she can be distant at times, not quite in the room with him.

Last night he had watched her from the kitchen as she

lay on the living-room floor with their boys, immersed in a tangle of limbs and a love so deep. Not for the first time he wondered how it would feel to be a part of that instead of standing on the sidelines of his family.

'I didn't notice anything,' he says to Mary eventually. 'I don't think she's been any different.'

Has he not been looking closely enough? Or is he just so hardened that he has closed himself off? *Self-protection*, he calls it. The reason why he would never try to join their huddle on the floor. He's scared none of them will want him.

'Do you think she was meeting someone at the marina?' Mary asks.

'I really don't know.' Gareth's whole body sags with defeat. He feels sickened by what has happened today. 'Did you know that she's been having counselling?'

The look on his mother-in-law's face tells him she didn't.

'I don't know why.' He shrugs. It all feels so hopeless. He isn't going to get any answers standing on Mary's doorstep.

He turns to walk back to his car, but as he reaches the gate his mother-in-law calls out to him. 'Gareth!' He turns. 'Just bring her back safe,' she says.

He closes his eyes, inhaling a deep breath as he nods at this small and simple but momentously huge request from her. A rare show of emotion, an even rarer belief in his capability, that makes Gareth determined he will do just that, whatever the cost. But first, he thinks, he is going to pay a visit to Violet Richards and see if the counsellor will tell him anything.

## Monday morning, 11.10 a.m.

*The phone keeps ringing, and I have tried to ignore it. I figure that for as long as they think they can reach us they won't try by any other means.*

*But I can't keep listening to it ringing and so I go over and rip the cord out of the socket. There's a moment of blissful silence and peace, knowing they can't contact us. Not until they send in the firearms unit anyway.*

*One of them starts up again. They have been relentlessly talking to me in the last hour. Trying to reason with me. 'If we go now, we can talk about this,' they say, tears streaming down their face as they have been all morning. 'We can tell them you never meant to harm us. It isn't too late.'*

*'Of course it's too late,' I reply. My own eyes briefly fill with tears, but I turn away before they can see that. They are looking for a sign of weakness, waiting for me to break.*

*'No! No, it's not,' they carry on. 'This is just a situation that's got out of hand and we can tell them that, and they'll understand—'*

*'Just stop,' I shout. I am looking out through the window again, at the people by the barricade, trying to pick you out, but I do not see you. I don't know if I want to or not. A part of me wants to feel you near me, but there is another that fears I will fall apart if I get a glimpse of you.*

*Maybe I should stop looking. I pull myself away and turn back to the room, catching sight of the one who keeps watching my every move, trying to figure me out. They won't say anything, they haven't all morning. They just keep following me with their gaze, waiting for me to trip up, perhaps ready to make their own move when they think I least expect it.*

*I drop the phone cord that is still in my other hand and kick it to one side, staring back at them.*

*'I don't see what you think is going to happen,' another pipes up. I turn slowly towards them. 'What I suggest is that we all walk out of here calmly now, one by one, with our hands up.' They have watched too many dramas on TV and think they know how it's done. They've been trying to talk me into letting them walk out of those doors for the last hour.*

*Shut up, shut up, shut up! They won't stop with their questions, like they are the ones in control. Do they forget, I am the one with the gun? I take a step closer to them until eventually they fall silent. 'Enough,' I say quietly, staring them in the eye.*

*They are bugging me the most. More than the one who keeps crying and pleading with me, and the one who is watching me and the other one who keeps muttering over and over that they shouldn't be here.*

*'Please. You don't need me here. This isn't anything to do with me. Can't you just let me go? I shouldn't be here,' they cry.*

I KNOW YOU SHOULDN'T BE, *I silently scream.* BUT THAT'S YOUR FAULT. *Any sympathy I had for her has long since dissipated. She, after all, is the one who has screwed this all up for me.*

\*

*Is this how it feels to lose your mind? To lose control of yourself? I don't know how to stop it. I wish you were here to tell me. You would find the right words where I can't.*

You haven't lost your mind, *you'd calmly say*. You just couldn't see another way out. *You wouldn't believe that, but it's what you would tell me.*

*I know, deep down, you will never understand how the thought of coming in here today kept scratching and clawing its way into my head until I began to think there was no other option.*

*But I am not a monster. I do want to let them go. I want us all to go. I am as trapped as they are, and they know this.*

*The longer I keep us all here, the more chance there is of one of them reacting, coming for me, trying to end this hell. My bet is on him, the one who thinks he's in control, but then you never know for sure. You never know what someone is capable of.*

## Detective Inspector Aaron Field
### 11.15 hours

Gathering intel on the names they have so far is slow when there is only so much resource Aaron can haul in. It's been confirmed that Hannah Parish showed up for her job at 7.30 a.m. and has been there ever since. Aaron's fifth and final person is still unknown, an unidentified female they can't even try to profile.

'It all points to it being the only one we know nothing about, doesn't it?' Kelly muses as she looks over her shoulder to where Aaron is sitting in the back of the van.

He tends to agree. But then he also knows too well that things aren't always obvious.

The van door opens and the FIO pokes his head in. 'Some journalist from a local website wants to know what we're saying.'

'We're not saying anything,' Aaron replies. 'It's got out then?' He turns to Kelly.

'Must have,' she answers as she taps at the screen of her iPhone. She nods as she says, 'Yep, someone's got hold of it and posted on social media. I take it you don't want to do a press conference?' she asks him. 'Or release a statement?'

'No.' He hesitates. 'If asked, we'll release one. But for now, we call editors and ask them to back off. It's a fluid investigation and I don't want any repercussions making matters worse. The legal press will do as we ask at the very least,' he mutters.

The FIO ducks out again, leaving just him and Kelly in the van. 'Let's go through each of them again,' he says. He will go over and over the details of the people inside that café until he finds a crack.

'Okay. Jacob Hamilton,' Kelly starts. 'Travelled on the 19.20 Wightlink ferry last night from Portsmouth to Fishbourne. Got to the Isle of Wight at 20.05. Bought a return ticket for 10.20 this morning. That would have left him plenty of time to get to his 2 p.m. meeting in Reading.'

'And he lied to his wife about this little trip.'

'And his PA didn't know about it either. Supposed to be working from home this morning. I guess the most obvious explanation would be an affair?' Kelly shrugs.

'If that's the case then he was possibly with someone else last night and came here for breakfast on his own, or he was meeting them here. Get someone over to his mother's house,' Aaron tells his sergeant. 'Find out if she knows anything. She could recognise one of the names. Be sensitive though, she might not have heard the news about him yet.'

'It doesn't make much sense that he'd travel here from London to walk into an out-of-the-way café with a gun,' Kelly says.

'Agreed. Likely Hamilton's not our guy, though we're

not ruling any of them out as yet.' He gestures for her to continue.

'Jennie Hogan. Still no contact with the café manager, which means we still don't know whose shift she was covering this morning. And re: Franklin Henderson, the general consensus from the other staff is that he keeps to himself, goes into The Boatyard a fair amount but doesn't really talk to any of them. Except for Jennie.' She pauses, deliberately. 'Apparently Jennie Hogan has been seen with him outside the café. On his boat,' she adds.

'Really? He told me he hadn't seen her outside of The Boatyard. I suppose he thinks his boat doesn't count?'

'Though I still don't get what he could have to do with anything. Not when he's the guy who called it in and we know exactly where he is.'

'Do we though?' Aaron says. 'The man keeps disappearing. I want to get on his boat, take a look around,' he murmurs, more to himself than Kelly. The FIO will be able to show him which one it is. 'Get him on the phone,' Aaron continues. 'Tell him to meet me there.' He'll tell Henderson it's because he wants to check his field of sight to The Boatyard for himself. Then he'll ask if he can take a look onboard. He won't be able to if Henderson refuses, but the man's response will most likely tell him something.

'By the way, Liv Hamilton and a friend have arrived from London,' Kelly tells him. 'One of the sergeants has taken them to a side room in the marine unit, but I didn't know if you want to have a word with her?'

So that's three of the relatives gathered here. Ede Hogan and her neighbour are also in the unit, and Rosa Williams is still striding back and forth at the top of the road. Aaron wouldn't be surprised if Gareth Lombard turned up any minute. All of them are denying having any knowledge as to why their loved ones are here and dismissing any suggestion that they could be the one holding the gun.

But he is sure one of them knows something. There is a story behind one of those people in the café. Something that hasn't been shared.

Aaron wonders if it's not such a bad idea for all the relatives to meet. Get them inside the marine unit, introduce them to each other. He could have someone sat quietly in a corner, pottering about mindlessly. It's amazing what can come out when people forget they're being watched.

He tells Kelly he's going to head up there and start making some introductions himself. As he opens the van door she says, 'If only we could make contact. At least strike a deal to get the ones out who shouldn't even be a part of this.'

'None of them *should* be a part of this,' he reminds her, though he knows what she means. If they could free at least some of the hostages, they'd feel like they were making progress.

# Ede

Ede feels drained and the pain of every throbbing muscle in her body is getting unbearable. She lifts one of her trouser legs and rubs her calf. If she were at home, she would take herself to bed with a dose of morphine. She didn't bring any in her rush to leave the house.

She tries not to give into it too much during the day, but the nurses are forever telling her how important rest is. 'Listen to your body,' one of them has said. 'Don't put too much pressure on yourself. And *don't* work yourself up over anything. Stress doesn't help anyone.'

Ede has never been one to do what she is told, but these days she doesn't have much choice. Still, she should be able to cope with a bit of pain. But it is more than that today, she acknowledges. There's a pressure in her that feels like it is pressing from the inside out, and while she keeps trying to ignore it, the wretched feeling won't let her.

She wishes she could get her thoughts straight and try and remember who asked Jennie to cover their shift this morning, but this important piece of information still eludes her.

Jennie should never have been here. Both their days could have looked so different if only her granddaughter hadn't done what she always does and said yes to anyone asking a favour. People take advantage of her kindness and usually it doesn't matter, but today it's changed the course of everything. Today it might be the difference between life and death.

'Would you like a cup of water?' Marjorie asks.

Ede shakes her head. 'I think I need to stretch my legs,' she says. 'Who do you think it was that they took into the side room? Another of the relatives?'

'I guess so,' Marjorie tells her. 'Do you want me to find out?'

'They won't tell you anything,' she says, pushing down on her stick and groaning when a sharp pain rises through her leg. 'I'm okay,' she adds, brushing away Marjorie's hand as she straightens her back. 'One of them could be related to the gunman,' she murmurs. 'That's likely, isn't it? Her or that other woman outside? They say there are two men in there. Surely one of these women may be married to them.'

A feeling brews inside of Ede that she doesn't like. It resembles something like hatred, only she doesn't know who she should be aiming it at.

*Is it you?* she thinks as she catches sight of the woman prowling the street outside of the window. She's a skinny, pretty little thing with long hair tied back in a ponytail and is chewing on a thumbnail. She looks like she is about to break down at any moment, refusing to come inside this building that Ede has been ushered into, choosing instead to pace back and forth on the pavement. Her pale face is streaked with tears and she has a deeply haunted expression.

Or maybe not her. Possibly it is the other two who have

just been taken into a room out of the way. Ede catches the attention of the woman outside who is now staring through the window at her. Ede lifts one of her hands in something resembling a wave, but the other woman doesn't respond, instead she stares blankly back.

Ede shrugs as she unsteadily heads towards the door that is suddenly thrust open with surprising force, letting in a burst of bracing fresh air. DI Field is standing the other side of it, asking the woman with the ponytail to come inside.

'Ah, Ede,' he says, when he sees her. 'This is Rosa Williams. Come in and let's get you a cup of tea,' he says to the other woman.

Reluctantly, Rosa steps inside and the DI follows, closing the door behind him. He turns into one of the rooms at the back, out of sight.

'Hello, I'm Ede,' she says to Rosa. 'My granddaughter Jennie was working at the marina café today.'

Rosa gives her a pained look. 'Rosa. My husband Daniel is in there too.'

'Daniel Williams,' Ede says, recalling the name she was given as DI Field reappears with a police officer who says she is going to make everyone a cup of tea.

The detective slips back out again. From behind Ede, Marjorie is saying that she would like a cup, before forcing a conversation with the officer about Ray and his lunch, and how she really doesn't know how long she'll be able to stay here.

Ede wants to ask if Marjorie thinks she can't hear her. She'd like to tell her to go home if that's what she wants, but she knows her neighbour won't leave her. Besides, right now Ede is more interested in talking to the young woman whose husband is inside the building with Jennie.

'It's hard to know what to do, isn't it?' she starts.

'I can't bear it,' Rosa says.' They won't tell me anything. They have so many questions but no answers.'

'That's true.'

'They—' The young woman pauses, darting a glance towards the police officer before lowering her voice. 'Have they asked you if it could be your granddaughter?'

'They have. But Jennie has never hurt anyone in her life. This isn't her doing.'

'Nor Daniel's,' Rosa adds quickly. She lets out a breath and rolls her eyes, seeming a little relieved by Ede's answer. 'Why would someone do this? Whoever it is has to be crazy. Someone's got to know who they are. People don't just get hold of a gun and take a load of hostages without their wife or husband knowing they're capable of it.' Rosa pauses. 'Don't you think?' she adds.

'You're right. They must be crazy. There's certainly no sanity in an act like this,' Ede says. But she doesn't entirely agree with Rosa. People can hide all manner of things when they really want to.

She has seen this first hand with her daughter, her husband too. And Ede knows because it is all she's been doing herself lately.

She looks down at her hands as the thought of her own mortality hits home yet again, scrunches her fingers, flexing them as she tries to rid herself of the numbness that is creeping over them. Her skin has turned papery and her thin wedding band hangs loosely on her ring finger.

This will become Jennie's when she is gone. Everything will be Jennie's, though Ede doesn't have much.

'Tell me what's going to happen,' she had demanded of the nurse who talked to her of breathing exercises and meditation. 'I want to know it all. I want to know how this is going to end.'

She remembers how the nurse had frowned at her, but Ede made a gesture as if to say, 'Go on then.'

She listened intently, nodding in all the right places, keeping her face a blank canvas to prove that she could take what she was hearing. But halfway through she had already made up her mind. This wasn't the way she was going to leave. Jennie wouldn't be suffering through these final weeks, days, hours and minutes caring for her. Ede would die on her own terms.

She brought the subject up with Jennie a week ago, and again last night after her granddaughter refused to listen to her the first time.

'If you get on a plane to Switzerland, you're going on your own,' Jennie had screamed at her. Ede had never seen her so riled and unmoving in her opposition.

'I need you to listen to me,' Ede had told her calmly, because she had thought this through. It wasn't some stray notion that had come out of the blue. She'd been sitting on her decision for weeks before she spoke to Jennie, only she couldn't leave it much longer now. 'What lies ahead isn't going to be pretty. I want us to say goodbye on our own terms. I don't want you to have to care for me or sit by my bed wondering when it's going to end.'

In truth, she'd thought Jennie would understand. She'd

expected the two of them to go abroad together. Despite her granddaughter's palpable pain, Ede was by now so committed to the decision that she found she couldn't, and wouldn't, back down.

Besides, she knew it was right. She had nursed her own daughter to her death. Sparing Jennie from that was her prime concern, and given time, which she did not have, she was certain Jennie would see that.

But it seemed she didn't. 'Gran!' Jennie had cried. 'You aren't even trying to live.'

Ede had nodded, letting Jennie have her say. She had been trying to live, but the consultant had made it clear any course of treatment was unlikely to have a high chance of success at this stage. They'd talked about quality of life at the end, and she had made the decision she wasn't going to put her body through any more.

Whether she liked it or not, Ede's time was up. She would stop feeding her body the chemicals that were making her feel worse, and as far as she was concerned if she sped up the inevitable with a trip to Switzerland, that would be the best outcome for Jennie.

Her granddaughter, however, did not agree. And after today, Ede is wondering if she was too hasty in talking about trips overseas. Last night she didn't want to listen to Jennie. Ede wasn't being selfish; she was being anything but. Ede was thinking of what Jennie wanted, because Jennie would *not* want to live through what Ede had when Shona died.

And yet, of course, Jennie doesn't know about any of that. She doesn't remember how bad it got because Ede had carefully hidden it from her.

As a young girl Jennie had seen too much already. Her mother turning up at the school gates drunk and swaying, laughing raucously and holding a finger to her lips with a mocking 'Oops!' if Jennie ever said anything. She would have been an embarrassment to anyone, but for a teenage daughter the cuts would always run the deepest.

Ede knows now she won't go to Switzerland. Today has taught her that. She has been looking at it entirely the wrong way, her decision based on what she thought was right for Jennie, but not what Jennie wants.

Her granddaughter's words reverberate in Ede's mind. 'How can you consider leaving me even one day too soon?'

Ede smiles to herself now, knowing that as soon as Jennie walks out of that café, she will tell her she has changed her mind. She will apologise for ever considering it. Say she didn't mean it. It was a stupid idea. Of course, she will not leave Jennie even one second before she has to. Theirs is not a goodbye that will come too soon.

Ede gulps back a sob before it lodges in her throat and turns to Marjorie, who is calling over that there is a nice cup of tea on the table for her.

She should probably go back to her chair and drink it, but she finds herself turning to Rosa, carrying on their conversation. 'Actually, I believe plenty of husbands and wives don't know a lot of what their other half is up to. People hide things from the ones they love the most.'

She finds herself staring into Rosa's big brown eyes. 'It happens, doesn't it? You see it on the news. Someone is suffering, and their family don't realise how much, and then they suddenly flip out and go around shooting people.'

Rosa stares at her in horror, shaking her head as if she cannot quite believe the words that have just come out of Ede's mouth. She has surprised herself with them really, but stands by their veracity.

Eventually Rosa clears her throat and says, 'If that's the case, how can you say there's no way your granddaughter is responsible?' Her words are loud enough for Marjorie to hear.

'What did you say?' she barks from her chair.

But Ede ignores her neighbour as she muses, 'I don't suppose I can. But then, I have known Jennie since she was a baby. I am the one who brought her up. She lives with me; I have always been the closest person to her. I know that girl as well as anyone could know another person. I know what makes her tick,' she says, 'and I know what her demons are.'

Ede pauses and inhales deeply. 'I don't know that I could have said the same for my late husband, if I'm being honest with you. I don't know anyone who could say the same for someone they've known for less than half of that person's life.'

Rosa looks horrified as she seems to consider what Ede has said and starts shuffling nervously. Ede recognises that it might have come across as a pointed comment, but that wasn't her intention. She was only saying how she felt.

'I just wish the police would do the one thing they keep saying they aren't going to and would get in there. Do *something* at least,' Ede mutters, 'instead of prowling the road, questioning the wrong people about things that are irrelevant.'

She can't imagine what scars this will leave on Jennie.

You don't walk away from life-threatening situations and remain unchanged. Life is going to be different for every one of them after this.

But Rosa is still visibly shaken. 'You're pointing your finger at my husband,' she says.

'I'm not,' Ede tells her. 'Though I do believe what I said is true.'

'I know my husband inside out.'

'I'm sure you do, dear,' Ede sighs. 'All I'm saying is that these things can happen, can't they? As much as all of us protest it's not our partner or our sister or our child . . . well, it must be someone's.'

# Rosa

Rosa takes a step back from the older woman. She doesn't want to listen to her anymore. This is why she didn't want to come inside this building, to be cooped up with strangers hurling accusations that Rosa has been trying to ignore. It is like Ede Hogan has been able to see Rosa's deepest fears, festering in her mind, and is plucking them out to the surface.

The life of the man she loves beyond anything is in danger, and yet it hasn't taken much for a seed of doubt to be planted and take root in her.

*He left his laptop behind this morning.* That is all, it is nothing more than that.

Or is it that Daniel seemed a little more detached from her this last week? When she felt like she was trying to reach out for him, but he wasn't quite there.

Or that the detective inspector had wanted to know if her husband had ever suffered from depression.

Ede Hogan has returned to her seat and is talking to the woman next to her. Rosa turns away, starting to gnaw at her thumbnail once more. She has held three things back from the police on purpose. Daniel would surely ask her why.

*I took my notebook and pen with me,* he would tell her, a look of surprise on his face that she is even questioning this small act.

*I haven't been detached, Rosa, it's always like this in the lead up to the end.* You *know that.* She does know that, of course she does. He would be upset that she didn't speak to him if she'd felt neglected in any way. She doesn't think she did until today.

*And the last thing? Well, that was years ago.* He would look at her in horror. *When we first met I was suffering, but I haven't felt like that since.*

She believes this is true, but at the same time she never really knew the root of his depression. They hadn't spoken openly about its cause, only about how they could make it better. 'Who are you, Daniel Williams?' she remembers asking him the first time he visited her flat.

'Who are you?' she had asked again when he only smiled in return. All he had told her was that he thought he would be happy now, and she had readily accepted his answer, because she believed they both would be. But who was he before her?

# Gareth

Gareth stands on the path in the counsellor's front garden. Violet Richards lives in a one-room-wide semi-detached property on a street filled with houses that look identical. There is a gate to one side with a small bronze plaque on which her name followed by a handful of letters are engraved. He presumes this is the entrance her clients use.

Now he is here, he doesn't know why he has come. There is a reason his wife has chosen to pay a stranger to talk to instead of him, and maybe he should respect Eleanor's privacy. But on the other hand, Gareth thinks if he could just tell Violet what has happened today, she might open a window into Eleanor's life for him, just a crack, so he can peep inside.

He has always thought of his wife as an enigma. Eleanor is beautiful, with her long blonde hair and flawless skin. No one would contradict him for saying as much. The world opens up for beautiful people like her. He has seen it with his own eyes, the way people bend over backwards to help and always want to hear what she has to say.

He'd seen her around the university campus plenty of times before they first spoke. She was like a ghost drifting around the periphery of his life. Gareth would never have plucked up the courage to speak to her first. Most men like him don't approach girls who are glaringly out of their league.

But Eleanor came up to him, at the end of the night of their graduation ball. She asked him to buy her a drink, her eyes sparkling, her cheeks flushed from the Mojitos she'd already drunk. Gareth willingly obliged. It was a story to tell his friends if nothing more. Why, two hours later, she asked him if he wanted to meet for coffee in the week he had no idea, but no way was he going to decline.

Eleanor was going places. He believed that from the start. Women like her always are. She had dreams of a career in fashion and thought she might try living in Paris. These were the things she told him when they met three days after the ball.

*What happened, Eleanor?* Were they all just words? He didn't want to ask the question when they started dating, and the weeks turned into months, and then years, and Eleanor said she wanted to move back to the Isle of Wight rather than Paris. Gareth was as in the dark as his friends and family undoubtedly were. He didn't heed his mum's advice; he was a little grateful. Or maybe it was more than a little.

The fact remains, his wife has always been a mystery to him. And he rather hopes Violet might shed some light on her.

Gareth presses his finger on the doorbell and takes a step back, holding his breath as he waits. A woman who is no more than five foot tall answers the door and looks curious to find him looming over her.

'Hello, are you Violet?' he asks.

'I am.'

'My name is Gareth Lombard, we spoke earlier.'

'Oh, yes, of course.' She frowns. 'What are you doing here? Is everything okay?'

'No,' he says. 'Actually, everything's very much not okay. I don't know whether you've heard but there's a man holding people hostage in the café on the marina and Eleanor is inside and that's why she didn't make your appointment this morning.' The words tumble out before he can draw another breath.

Violet is staring at him in shock. 'My goodness,' she says eventually. 'That's just – that's awful.'

'And the police have been asking me questions about her and what she's doing there, and I haven't told them yet about her sessions with you, but I think I probably should. Don't you?' he says.

'I don't know,' she replies, her mouth still hanging open.

'Why is she coming to see you?' he asks now. He is so desperate for an answer that he knows deep down he won't get.

'I can't tell you what we talk about, you must know that.'

'Is it about me?' he says. 'About us? Our marriage?' As he asks her, he realises just how much he doesn't want it to be. How he wants it to be about anything but, because anything else he could deal with.

'I'm sorry . . .' she says, with a shake of her head and a darkening of her eyes.

Gareth feels his whole body slump. It is, he knows this. Violet Richards doesn't need to say anything.

'We're happy,' he tells her as he stands on her doorstep. 'Our marriage is solid. I mean, I know it doesn't have the energy it did in the beginning, but what marriage does after near enough twenty years?' He laughs at the absurdity of the idea. 'We don't argue,' he insists. 'We don't even bicker. And we spend every weekend together as a family. We're always taking the boys to the farm or the beach, back over to the mainland. And I never complain about going there, even though, God knows, I could do without making that ferry run again when I already do it five times a week. But it doesn't matter when it makes the children happy, does it?'

'Mr Lombard—'

'I mean, sometimes I would just like to chill out at home, but I do it because it's what she wants. What they all want,' he goes on.

'Gareth, please,' the counsellor says gently, holding up a hand to stop him. 'I'm sorry, but I really can't talk to you about Eleanor or your marriage.'

Gareth feels himself deflate. 'I know,' he tells her. 'I'm sorry. I didn't mean to . . .' He waves his own hand about. 'I'm going to the marina now. I'm going to get her out,' he says with a defiance he hopes will stop this woman looking at him with pity.

He doesn't want pity. He wants his wife. And he is going to show Eleanor, and her mother, and this woman he has only just met but who knows Eleanor better than he does, that he will do whatever it takes to save her.

## Detective Inspector Aaron Field
### 11.30 hours

Aaron surveys The Boatyard from a distance as he walks onto the marina, to the bridge, where Franklin Henderson's boat is moored on the other side. He has Sarah Connelly on the phone again.

'We can't even connect the calls any longer,' she tells him. 'My guess is they've disconnected the landline. To be honest I'm surprised it took them this long if they didn't want to talk, but it was the one thing keeping me hopeful that they didn't want to lose a connection with the outside world.'

'And now?'

'It's been over four hours and we have nothing. We still don't know who we're dealing with.'

Aaron doesn't need any reminders of that. 'What are we missing?' he mutters as he crosses the bridge. The water is as flat as a sheet of glass, long dark shadows from the boats stretching across it. He's always had a slight fear of pools of water where he can't see what's lurking beneath the surface, and today the light makes it feel more menacing.

He reaches the boat he is looking for and climbs onboard, staring back at The Boatyard. This is where Henderson would have had a reasonably good view of the hostages walking in one by one earlier this morning.

'Someone knows something,' Sarah says. 'They always do.'

Aaron watches the FIO walking Franklin Henderson along the route he himself has just taken.

'Mr Henderson, thank you for coming back,' he says when they reach him.

Henderson stares back, giving the distinct impression he isn't happy about the fact Aaron is standing on his boat.

'I needed to see it for myself,' the DI tells him, gesturing towards The Boatyard.

He doesn't reply as he joins the inspector on board. Aaron has scouted around as far as he can. He already knows the door to the cabin is locked.

'Do you mind if I have a look inside?' he asks.

'I don't see what for.' Henderson's gaze is flicking between Aaron and the locked cabin door. He seems twitchy, Aaron thinks.

There's little he can do without the man's consent. They certainly don't have grounds for arrest of their one and only witness. 'Just while we're here?' he says.

Henderson sighs. 'I don't know if I have the key,' he replies, one hand in his pocket, as if searching for something Aaron already knows won't come to fruition. He's surprised when Franklin eventually produces it, muttering that he does as he sticks it into the padlock and opens the door.

Aaron raises his eyebrows at the FIO, to convey he really wasn't expecting this, and waits for Henderson to enter the cabin first. He's taking his time, his broad build blocking the doorway and any view of the inside. It takes him a moment to step in and allow Aaron to follow.

Aaron's eyes sweep around the small kitchen area as Henderson stands to one side. He is watching the detective intently but doesn't say anything or move as Aaron gestures to another door and opens it to find a double bed filling the small space, a toilet cubicle to the left.

Nothing glaring stands out, which isn't a surprise when Aaron isn't looking for anything in particular. It's a standard boat, everything tidied neatly away in cupboards, the way he supposes it needs to be when the cabin is so compact. Aaron opens one that is filled with crockery – a couple of everything. It isn't until he makes his way back to the door that Henderson finally says, 'What is it you think you're looking for?'

Aaron doesn't answer the question as he steps outside on deck and eventually off onto the sanctuary of dry land. 'Thank you. Nice boat you have here. I'd be doing the same as you if I had one: sitting on deck with my coffee, watching the world go by.'

'I like it,' Henderson replies as he locks the door and steps off too. He is watching Aaron tentatively, waiting for him to make the first move and lead the way back over the bridge.

'Has Jennie ever been onboard?' Aaron asks as they start walking, the FIO trailing behind.

'No,' Henderson tells him.

'Oh? One of the bar staff says they saw her on your boat once?'

'Well, they were mistaken,' he says abruptly. 'I never have anyone on my boat.'

'Perhaps they were wrong,' Aaron says, glancing at the man, who is now staring straight ahead of them. When they eventually reach the barrier at the top of the road, he watches the witness walk back to his car.

'Why did he just lie?' he says to the FIO, who shrugs in return. 'Does he seem nervous to you?' Aaron asks. Because he sure as hell seemed it to Aaron.

# Ede

Ede is sitting inside the marine unit building, with a blanket wrapped around her shoulders that Marjorie has given her. Her neighbour keeps watching her, fretting that she is getting too cold and saying she really doesn't look right.

'Of course I'm not right,' Ede has said to her. 'I'm not going to be right until they let Jennie out of there.'

Marjorie keeps frowning and huffing beside her, fiddling with the blanket until Ede swipes her hand away. 'Maybe you should get home to Ray and give him his lunch?' she says, though she doesn't really want Marjorie to leave her.

'He doesn't eat till midday,' Marjorie responds, making no move to go anywhere. 'Besides . . .' she says, but doesn't finish her sentence. *Besides, Ede needs her more*. She is grateful to Marjorie for being here. As much as she fusses, Ede wouldn't want to be on her own today.

Her body feels like it is beginning to shut down. She heard what the nurse said about how harmful stress can be, but Ede is trying to look past that. After all, there is nothing she can do about it right now.

So she continues to sit here, wrapped up like an old lady, breathing as slowly as her mind allows her to, trying to ignore the glances Marjorie is giving her and not think about how awful she must look to make her neighbour so concerned.

She accepts another cup of tea, though she hadn't finished the last, and watches Rosa Williams who is hovering by the door, ready to scurry out any moment.

The two women, who have been inside one of the back rooms, suddenly appear and Ede looks up. 'This is Ede Hogan,' the police officer tells them, awkwardly, 'and Rosa Williams. Ede's granddaughter and Rosa's husband are also inside the building. This is Liv Hamilton and her friend, Katy Richards. Liv's husband is in there too.' She looks sheepish as she makes the introductions, as if she really doesn't think it's a good idea to be doing so. They all turn to look as the door opens and DI Field brings someone else in. A man this time, who is nervously running a hand through his hair. A man called Gareth Lombard, the detective explains, whose wife, Eleanor, is inside The Boatyard.

The DI glances at each of them in turn, waiting for a reaction they all avoid giving. He nods at the police officer and walks over to her, leading her to a corner of the room where they talk together in hushed voices.

Ede feels herself bristle at the idea that they have all been brought in here for a reason. One by one, she looks at the strangers she has just been introduced to.

Liv Hamilton is a petite woman with mid-length highlighted blonde hair that hangs down her back in perfectly styled waves. She looks stunning in a long camel coat and dark jeans and a button-down green silk shirt. She seems out of place here, this smartly dressed lady who is potentially married to a killer.

She skims past the friend to the only man in the room apart from the detective: Gareth Lombard, who looks uncomfortable in his grey suit, white shirt and bright pink tie. Ede feels a sudden affinity to him, though she isn't sure why. Perhaps it's because it is his wife inside the building, and Ede believes this must be the work of a man.

Either way, do the police still believe one of them is related to the person holding her granddaughter hostage? The idea that they might sends a shiver down her spine. She clutches the edge of her seat to steady herself, the thought of it making her dizzy.

DI Field starts bustling about in the back and the female officer comes over to Ede and crouches down in front of her. 'Mrs Hogan, are you feeling alright?' There's a look of concern in her eyes.

'Of course I'm not alright,' Ede says, forcing strength into her voice. 'I am only going to be alright when my granddaughter walks out of there unharmed.'

The woman nods slowly. 'We are doing everything—'

'So you say,' Ede interrupts. 'And yet nothing is changing. She is still inside, and you still have no idea who is holding her there. Do you?' She isn't talking loudly, but it's loud enough for the others to hear because she senses them listening.

'We're looking at a lot of information right now,' the officer starts.

'So, no, you don't. Tell me, what is your theory?' She lowers her voice this time. 'Which one of us is related to a shooter?' She waves her hand around her with a tug that causes her pain and makes her drop it back down to her side.

'That's not something I can share,' the officer says quietly. 'Mrs Hogan, are you sure you're okay?'

'Of course, you can't share it because you don't know, do you?' she replies, coldly. 'Or do you know? Are you just not telling us?'

The officer grimaces but doesn't answer.

'Was there something else you wanted?' Ede asks. She is being rude, and she hates being rude, but she cannot help it. Pain is coursing through her, reaching her head. The situation is beginning to drown her in anxiety. Her focus keeps flitting between Jennie and how much worse she herself will feel if she doesn't get back and take her morphine soon.

'I just wanted to check you're alright.'

'I'm fine,' Ede tells her. 'Thank you,' she adds. It angers her that the police won't give her answers. Surely they can't be this much in the dark? They must have an inkling.

She is certain they know more than they are letting on. She is also certain they have dragged her and the other relatives together here for a reason.

The police officer gets up and moves away and Ede turns to Marjorie. 'What do you make of all this?' Her neighbour is eyeing each of the people in the room in turn.

'They all look as frightened as each other,' Marjorie replies.

'But what if one of them is related to the shooter?' Ede hisses. 'Are the police expecting us to fight it out between us?'

Marjorie looks over her shoulder to where the police officer is seemingly distracted by her phone. 'I think they have nowhere else to put everybody,' she says.

Ede *humph*s as she looks about her. She wonders which of them knows more than they are letting on. She is certain that one of them at least suspects their husband or wife could be capable of getting hold of a gun and taking it into the café.

She doesn't regret one bit what she said to Rosa earlier, even though she obviously upset the author's wife by voicing her opinion. She believes she is right in saying that no one knows everything there is to know about their spouse.

Ede came down to the marina to do something helpful for Jennie. Sitting here, draped in a blanket and sipping milky tea, isn't getting them anywhere. 'I'm sorry,' she announces, before she thinks about what she is about to do, 'but someone here is likely related to a shooter.'

Gareth Lombard's face pales. Rosa wraps her arms more tightly around herself.

'Which could be you, of course,' Liv Hamilton says. It doesn't surprise Ede that she is the one who has spoken out.

Ede feels the room crowding in on her. It's not a small space but suddenly it feels like they are all looming on top of her. She forces herself to stand, feeling Marjorie's hand on her arm as she does so, glad when her neighbour gets up with her.

Pressing down on her stick for support, Ede loses her balance as she leans too heavily on her left leg, which buckles under her weight. 'Oh!' she cries out. She hadn't meant to, and she ignores Gareth Lombard's hand that stretches out to her as she rights herself, straightening her back slowly and then arching it, waiting for the blood to flow and the tightness in her muscles to ease like it normally does.

'We may as well discuss the elephant in the room,' she addresses the small group. They are all staring at her with varying degrees of horror; Rosa looks like she is going to be sick any moment, and Liv Hamilton studies Ede with open interest. She sees what could even be a flash of respect in the younger woman's expression.

'I'll go first,' Ede says. 'My granddaughter Jennie opened up the café this morning. And, one by one, four other people came in. But one of them brought a gun with them. And if we believe what the police are telling us, one of us –' she pauses '– most likely knows who that person is.'

She looks at everyone in turn. It feels like they are creeping forward, forming a jagged circle around her, though no one has moved.

Liv Hamilton's friend has taken hold of Liv's hand in a show of solidarity. Ede watches, frowning, as her other hand slips automatically to her stomach. Is she pregnant? Either way, it's too late to stop now.

'I think it's time everyone starts asking themselves if their loved one is capable of doing something like this,' Ede presses on, searching their faces one by one.

Gareth Lombard looks around at the women, as if expecting one of them to say something. It doesn't surprise her that he's ruling his wife out.

Rosa Williams has silent tears trickling down her cheeks. Ede squints at her. She is certain this is the woman who is holding something back. Everything about her demeanour seems off to Ede, and she is about to question her when Liv speaks.

'I know my husband,' she says, but there is something in her voice that makes Ede thinks she doesn't quite believe this. 'This isn't him. How can you be so sure it isn't your granddaughter?'

'Because I have known that girl her entire life,' Ede says simply, as she has already told Rosa. 'I was witness to the moments that shaped her. When you meet someone as an adult you only see them from that point on. They've already painted a portrait of the person they want you to see.'

'That's ridiculous,' Liv says, but her wide eyes make Ede think she is striking a chord.

'Is it? You only have to consider criminals who offended when they were young and then served their time and were given a fresh identity when they walked out of prison. The whole world might know what they did when they were a child, but the person who marries them today has no idea it's the same person.'

She can feel shock at her words reverberating around the room in palpable waves. Ede wonders if she has gone too far. There is a buzzing in her head, and she looks up to see what is making the noise but there is nothing there. She shouldn't have done that because now the room is beginning to spin.

'Everyone needs to ask themselves if they're married to someone who is capable of this,' she goes on as the buzzing swarms louder and closer, and her vision begins to blur.

Still, she clocks Rosa step backwards, closer to the doorway, trying to extricate herself from a situation she cannot handle, and Ede believes she is right about this woman. There is something she isn't telling them, and Ede wants to ask her what that is. 'Because one of them is,' she goes on, before clutching a hand to her chest as she falls to the floor with a heavy thump.

# Rosa

The old woman kept speaking and Rosa knew she couldn't be in this suffocating room any longer, surrounded by the faces of people who were either in this with her or else related to the person threatening her husband's life.

She was trying to back her way out and had reached the door when Ede Hogan fell to the floor.

Now the elderly woman who was standing with her is shrieking as the police officer races over. A flurry of activity and concern, no one knowing what they should be doing to help, but everyone trying to do something. The police officer crouching on the floor beside Ede is taking control. DI Field has appeared and an ambulance is radioed for. Rosa and the others are told to step back. It all happens so quickly.

Ede Hogan looks too pale to be okay, or even to be moved from where she has been rolled into the recovery position. Another officer has raced through the doors now, making them bang into Rosa as she rushes past. There is talk of making sure nothing is broken.

Rosa takes her chance to step outside, leaning against the wall for support as she gulps down a deep breath of cold air. She can hear Gareth Lombard shouting. 'Where's this going to end?' he is saying. 'How many more people are going to get hurt today?'

Rosa wipes a hand across her face, mopping the tears that keep streaming down it. She wraps her arms around her shaking body, disappointingly aware of how little use she is to Daniel when she is such a mess.

'Could you all step out, please?' she can hear DI Field saying to the group still inside.

Gareth is undeterred. 'I want you to get my wife out of there. I need to be able to tell my boy his mum's okay. He knows there's something wrong – he keeps asking for her.'

'Please, Mr Lombard, you need to let us do our job.'

'She was right though, wasn't she?' Liv Hamilton and her friend appear in the doorway. Liv tugs at her coat to wrap it tighter around her. 'Someone here *is* related to a potential killer.' She stops short when she sees Rosa.

'This is unbearable,' Gareth says as he joins them too. 'The police know more than they're telling us,' he adds angrily. 'They have to.'

'You think they know who it is?' Liv asks him. 'Because I don't think they do. That's why they're asking us so many questions, waiting for us to turn on each other.'

He stares at her but doesn't answer as the sound of sirens in the distance pierces the air. An ambulance is coming. DI Field is leaving the building, making his way up the road, his pace quickening as he goes.

'Ede said someone must know deep down that the person they are married to could be capable of this.' Rosa turns back to the others, willing one of them to give something away. *Anything.* Just one little gesture, some sort of reaction. But if they do, she doesn't see it.

'Is your husband?' Gareth asks her.

'No!' she cries.

'Or yours?' he says, turning to Liv.

'No.' She shakes her head adamantly, glaring back at him defiantly. 'There is no way—'

'Well, we're all going to say that, aren't we?' Gareth goes on.

Rosa wonders if there is a shred of doubt in any of them, or whether it is just her. She might as well have turned Daniel in for the thoughts that have been scuttering through her head this morning.

But Daniel has never shown her anything but kindness and love. He has never given her any reason to think there is a side to him she doesn't know about. Though her boyfriend before Daniel had turned out not to be the person she thought he was.

She hadn't seen it coming. Neither had her parents. Her mum found him charming, her dad liked him too. But everything changed the moment Rosa received a blow to the side of her face in the heat of an argument. There was a look of pure anger in her ex's eyes that vanished the moment he hit her. The apologies came quickly, along with the promises it wouldn't happen again, but she didn't stick around to find out. Her parents' love-filled marriage had taught her she was worth more than that.

But Daniel isn't like that. Daniel is the sweetest, most sincere man she has ever met. She is no longer the naive young girl she had been. Only when you have been burnt once, the scars never heal completely.

Rosa struggles to breathe as she holds a hand to her throat. The others are staring at her now as if this means she knows something. *I don't,* she wants to yell at them, but she's incapable of uttering another word.

She takes a step backwards, turns and walks away from them. She doesn't have to stand here, listening to their accusations when the voices in her own head are already doing enough.

'I know you, Daniel,' she murmurs.

'What do you know?' Liv is calling behind her. 'There's something, isn't there?'

Rosa's heart sinks. She didn't mean to say that aloud. She spins around. 'No,' she cries. 'And can you honestly say you know absolutely everything about your husband?'

Liv doesn't reply, but Rosa notices the way her friend tightens her grip on her arm. Only she doesn't have the strength to question the others anymore. She just wants to get away from the marina, to stop dissecting evidence and questioning her husband, playing the footage from her Ring doorbell camera, over and over, until the images of him no longer mean anything.

Rosa keeps walking back towards her car, the voices behind her blurring.

The sun has gone behind a bank of cloud that brings a chill to the air. She craves the sanctuary of her home. She needs to feel close to Daniel in their space, not have the memory of him tainted by police questions and the oppressiveness of the darkening marina.

At home she parks at the front of the house, aware of the Ring doorbell camera following and recording her as she lets herself into their home. Slipping off her shoes, Rosa kicks them into a corner of the hallway and lingers for a moment looking into Daniel's office.

Opening the doors, she steps inside his room again, soaking in the scent of his musky aftershave. She has such a deep longing for her husband.

She'd been in the middle of reading his manuscript earlier, the thing that has torn him from her lately. Now she thinks that if he was being stalked or receiving harassing emails, the evidence will surely still be on his laptop. Rosa sits down at his desk again and opens his computer, heading to his email folder.

How surprisingly easy it is to access is a stark reminder of just how trusting her husband is. Rosa tries to console herself with the knowledge that if he had anything to hide, he would surely change his passwords.

She scans the most recent email, working her way down the list and through the usual spam from companies he uses: Amazon, Vodafone, HSBC. Scattered among them are messages from his agent and editor, his publicist, and others from readers that have come via his author website.

But there is nothing unusual, or worrying, here. And certainly no message from any of the names she's heard today. Besides, she thinks now, calmer, why would anyone have a grudge against Daniel? His books are entirely fiction, they aren't based on people he knows or situations he's ever been in.

Her mind strays to the opening she read only hours earlier, the brutality of it still making her stomach coil, and thanks God that story isn't real.

There cannot be another reason anyone would want to hurt Daniel, other than the fact he's a writer. Daniel would say himself that without this status, he is no one.

'You're my husband,' she's said on more than one occasion.

'You know what I mean, my love,' he's told her. 'I mean writing is everything I do. I'm not sporty or even that social. I write. That's who I am.'

She told him this can't always have been true. Before he started writing, who was he then? She wanted him to realise there is more to Daniel Williams than his job. Or maybe Rosa wanted to comfort herself that this is the truth, when she can sometimes be jealous of this passion that consumes him.

'I was nothing before that,' he said, teasing her as he kissed her. 'Nothing before *you*,' he added at the last minute.

Rosa opens the latest email from his agent which was sent six days ago, last Tuesday. It was three days after Daniel appeared on TV and so she expects it to be about this.

```
Hi Daniel,

After our call this morning I have spoken
with the editorial team, and needless to
say they're disappointed. But ultimately,
they understand this is your decision. If
this is what you really want to do, then
I am behind you.
Let's chat soon,

N.
```

Rosa frowns at the contents, with no idea what he's decided that has disappointed everyone so much. She scrolls down to older threads. But these are about book-signing events and latest sales figures, the good news that he has secured a deal with an Italian publisher for his latest title. All are details he's shared with her. Everything but his disappointing decision.

She goes into his sent folder and finds Daniel's reply to his agent.

> Decision made. I definitely don't want to write it anymore. But thanks for your understanding.
> Daniel.

She opens others he has sent his agent but there is nothing more and it strikes her how Daniel's tone was much more formal, more abrupt, in his last response. Every other message begins with a friendly hello, he always asks how his agent is, and mostly he signs off with an informal 'D'.

Rosa flicks quickly through the rest of his emails but nothing else stands out.

She sits back, a desire to call his agent creeping over her.

Rosa finds her number at the bottom of the email and taps the digits into her phone. 'Hi, it's Rosa Williams here,' she says when the agent answers. 'Daniel's wife.'

'Rosa?' she gasps. 'I'm so sorry, is there any news? I had the police on the phone half an hour ago, they told me Daniel's being held hostage.'

'You've heard?' she says, surprised, but then surely she shouldn't be after her conversation with the police. Only their call to his agent makes her even more certain they think this has something to do with her husband. 'No, there isn't any news.'

'I'm glad you called me . . . I didn't have your number. Is there anything I can do?'

'I don't know,' Rosa says. 'I don't know what *I* should be doing.'

'Of course you don't. I can't imagine. It's unbelievable.'

Rosa nods, but doesn't answer for a moment before saying, 'What did the police want?'

'They just had questions about Daniel. Was I aware of any negativity towards him, had he mentioned anyone to me who had been in contact with him or given him any bad press, that kind of thing. To be honest they were really digging into it, as if they wanted me to come up with something, but I told them there was nothing at all I could think of. Daniel doesn't get anything like that. He isn't that kind of person.'

'That's all?' Rosa says. 'They wanted to know if anyone was targeting him?'

'Yeah, I guess. They asked a whole load of stuff: about him and whether I've noticed anything unusual lately. They really think he's been targeted?'

'I don't know,' Rosa admits. 'I don't know what they're thinking. They made me feel as if that might be the case.' She hesitates before adding, 'Are you sure there's nothing you've noticed?'

'About Daniel? No,' she says. 'There really isn't.'

'It's just . . . I saw an email from you. You said you were disappointed with a decision he'd made?'

'Oh, about the book, you mean? Well, yes, but obviously that's not anything the police will be interested in, I didn't even mention it to them.'

'What was it about?'

'You don't know?' she says, clearly surprised. 'Daniel told me last Tuesday he wasn't going to carry on writing his latest book. The one he's been working on for the last nine months. The one he was due to send the first draft of to me and the publishers in four weeks' time,' she adds in an exasperated tone. 'He said he wanted to write something else instead. I assumed you knew he'd had a change of heart?'

'No,' Rosa says. 'I didn't. You mean the one about the boy whose body is found at the start, dead in a quarry?'

'That's the one. He'd previously sent me the first twenty thousand words and I told him it was his best yet. I truly thought it was. I tried to talk him out of this decision obviously, but he was adamant. There was nothing I could do. I take it you can't shed any light on his decision? I couldn't get a proper answer out of him as to why he doesn't want to finish it, let alone publish it.'

'I can't tell you anything,' Rosa says. 'I didn't know.' She'd thought he was still working on it. He has been shutting himself away in his office every evening, working into the early hours of the morning on what Rosa now supposes is a new idea. Only he hasn't mentioned any of this to her. Even when she's asked him how his latest manuscript is going, he's told her it's fine and not uttered one word about abandoning the original idea. Why wouldn't he tell her if he's scrapped a book he is a month away from delivering?

She enters his Word folder, searching for the start of another novel. But there is nothing there. 'What did he want to write instead?' Rosa asks.

'I've no idea,' the agent tells her. 'He was so vague about it. I asked him for an outline of what he was thinking so I could send it to his editor, and he said he'd do it, but that was last Tuesday and he hasn't sent anything. To be honest, Rosa, I don't think he has another idea. At least not one he's happy to share. And certainly nothing that would warrant throwing away such great work for.'

'I don't get it,' Rosa says. 'This is all so unlike him.'

'It is,' the agent agrees. 'But listen, none of this matters right now, does it? Not with what's happening today.'

'No,' Rosa murmurs, catching herself. 'No, of course it doesn't.' She thanks the agent for talking to her and promises to let her know if there is any news.

Rosa ends the call and stares at the screen. Only two weeks earlier they'd had a conversation about this book. They'd been for a Sunday afternoon walk and found a local pub where they could have a roast. They had sat in front of a log fire and shared a bottle of Malbec, talking about anything and everything, his books just a part of their long conversation.

But she could see his excitement bubbling on the surface when he spoke about what he was writing. It was clear in the way he'd pressed towards her, his fingers curling around the stem of his wine glass and his other hand gesturing animatedly as he too told her he thought this was his best book yet.

So what happened to him since then? One week and an appearance on TV and as far as she knows there is nothing else.

Rosa might have just told his agent it doesn't matter right now, but she isn't so certain that this is the case.

# Hannah

Hannah knows Abbie won't leave her head for the rest of the day. The girl always manages to get inside it, prodding at places Hannah doesn't want to go to. But today Hannah won't be able to focus on anything much when she knows what lies ahead for the girl, telling the truth about her stepfather. She prays Abbie's mother believes her, though she doesn't hold out much hope for that. And even less that she will stand by her daughter.

Hannah has half an hour to eat an early lunch and write up her notes on her morning sessions before her midday appointment with *Harvey*. She takes the tuna sandwich she made early this morning out of her bag, unwraps the foil and takes a bite, wiping mayonnaise from where it drips on her fingers.

Her thoughts drift to her sister and how Connie is spending her birthday. Maybe she should break her rules today and give her sister a call. Just to check in on her. Connie was distant with her last night, their conversation trivial. Hannah can't imagine her sister being upset with her over today, and yet she can't think what else her mood could have been dictated by.

Whatever was on her mind, she wasn't sharing it with Hannah. There is nothing about Hannah that Connie doesn't know, and she imagines it's the same the other way around. But then Connie hadn't mentioned Hannah's interview when they'd gone to bed. Hadn't wished her good luck. Something was bothering her.

She takes another bite of her sandwich and finds her phone in her bag now, switching it on, surprised to see Connie hasn't replied to the short text she sent after her interview. In fact, she hasn't even been online on Whatsapp since 7.01 a.m. and there are several missed calls from an unknown number.

She's about to listen to her voicemail when a sharp knock on the door makes her look up. It's only 11.40, but Harvey is pushing the door open and striding in. 'I'm early,' he says, with no hint of apology. He's wearing a black beanie, his blond hair poking out under the front of it.

Hannah gestures to a chair, still chewing on the last bite of her sandwich. She holds a hand over her mouth as she speaks, 'That's fine, but what have you done to your face?' His right eye is bruised and above it is a line of stitches cutting into his hairline.

Harvey shrugs. 'Got into a fight.'

Hannah purses her lips. 'Who with?'

'I don't know. Some guy.'

'Come on. What happened?'

'He thought I was coming on to his girlfriend.'

'And were you?'

'Maybe.' He gives her a lopsided grin that makes him wince with pain then laugh in response.

'Harvey,' she sighs. He reminds her of someone she once knew, but she tries to put it to one side because she likes

Harvey and doesn't want her view of him to be tainted by memories. Especially not bad ones.

'Sorry, Miss,' he says with one eyebrow raised. He has his phone in front of him and keeps swiping on it.

'Can I have that?' She holds out her hand. 'You shouldn't have your phone on in school.'

He shrugs and clicks off the screen, turning it over in his palm, but he doesn't hand it over. 'I was just reading the news.'

'I doubt that,' she replies as her own phone flashes with a message and she automatically looks down but it isn't from Connie. 'Sorry,' she mutters and turns it off, tucking it back into her bag quickly, aware of Harvey's amusement and judgement that she isn't living by the same rules. Hannah won't look at it again till she leaves now.

'There's some gunman down the marina,' he tells her, waving his phone at her. 'I was just reading about it.'

'On the Isle of Wight?' she asks as he nods in response. 'Which marina?'

'Newport.'

'What do you mean, a gunman? Has he shot anyone?' Hannah immediately feels sick. The marina is only five miles away from Connie's house and that makes it too close for Hannah's liking. She shuffles awkwardly in her chair, already looking forward to today being over. Now all she wants to do is call her sister and check she is alright, just to put her mind at rest even though she knows that sounds silly. But she will have to wait until Harvey is gone.

# Detective Inspector Aaron Field
## 11.45 hours

Aaron is craving a cigarette. A bad habit he gave up almost two years ago. But smoking was his thinking time and, right now, he needs to think. He takes out the packet his wife gave him, with the stupid white fake sticks she makes him carry. He didn't want to start vaping and so she made him these replica cigarettes.

He sticks one in his mouth now and pretends to light it, then holds it between his fingers, flicking imaginary ash onto the ground and hoping no one is watching. He's got to admit it feels kind of realistic, but he must look ridiculous.

The ambulance has left and taken Ede Hogan to hospital. He hopes to God she'll be okay, because even though it's not his fault she collapsed, he can't help but feel in some way responsible. Though he has to hand it to the woman. Aaron can see what a strong character she is despite her ailing health.

He taps his finger on his little white stick again as he heads back to the van. With Ede taken away, and Rosa Williams having left, the only relatives still here are Liv

Hamilton and Gareth Lombard. He assumes Liv and her friend are back inside the marine unit, but he can see Gareth pacing up and down the road, demanding news from officers that they can't give him.

There are others here too by now. A small crowd has gathered behind the barrier and will start swelling soon enough with onlookers wanting to share things they can't even see, but who have their iPhone cameras ready to video any action they can upload to their social media accounts. Magpies with a desire to be in the midst of the trauma among the expectant journalists with their own cameras.

'These lot will be jostling between themselves to get the news out first about whatever they believe is happening,' he mutters to Kelly as he climbs into the van. 'Not that anything is.' The Boatyard itself is as quiet as it was after the gunshot was fired. You'd think it was nothing more than closed for the day.

He looks out the window as he closes the van door. 'They want answers we don't have. What the hell are we missing?'

He's been trying to wrap his head around what's important and what isn't: Franklin Henderson's potential friendship with Jennie Hogan; Jacob Hamilton neglecting to tell his wife that he was on the Isle of Wight; Eleanor Lombard's mother who has now told them Eleanor had dropped the kids off at hers this morning and her husband, Gareth, hadn't had any idea. Are any of these things relevant?

Henderson was nervous with Aaron on his boat, that much is true, but Aaron won't be getting a search warrant any time soon when the guy can't be viewed as a suspect.

Sarah Connelly has to be right. The lack of communication with the outside world must surely mean that this isn't what the hostage-taker had planned. And now whoever it is doesn't know what to do. Their choice of timing and location points to this being personal. *But why? Why are they doing this?*

All he has linking any of them is one small connection that feels totally irrelevant: Daniel Williams bought a car from Eleanor Lombard's husband. But the link is too tenuous surely, especially when, like Ede has said, the island is such a small place.

'Has anyone got hold of the café manager yet?'

'Yes. Sorry to say but that's something else that isn't going to help,' Kelly tells him.

'Jesus, what?'

'Finally got hold of her. Says she's been sick all night and hasn't been answering her phone or front door. And she says that no one was scheduled for the early shift this morning. Jennie offered to fill it.'

'Great,' he mutters. 'Another dead end.'

Wider searches aren't picking up any other vehicles that can't be accounted for. Hannah Parish's car is the only one still parked in the area, but they know she's at work. The only way Aaron is going to find his unidentified female is by putting out a public appeal.

'I'm sorry.'

'Yeah. Me too,' Aaron mutters. 'There has to be a connection between two of them, though. If everything points to this being personal, then two of them at least must know each other.'

'None of the relatives have heard any of the other names,' she points out.

'So they say.'

'You think one of them is lying?'

'Either that or they don't know.'

'Because it's been kept a secret?'

Aaron doesn't respond. 'Ede Hogan knew the surname Parish,' he recalls.

'But Hannah—'

'I know. Isn't here. But Ede also said this was a small island and everyone on it has a link to someone else, somehow.' He pauses, thinking. 'How many schools are there on the Isle of Wight?'

Kelly starts tapping on her keyboard. 'Forty-seven primary schools, six secondary and one that goes all the way through. A couple of them are centred around the Newport area.' She points to her screen. 'It won't be easy finding out where they all went though.'

'Except when there aren't that many secondaries, we can access school records. I want someone on it. Start with the nearest schools and report back if there's even one connection,' he tells her.

It only takes fifteen minutes. Aaron is outside of the van, on his phone to the Tactical Firearms Commander, when Kelly calls out with the news they have been waiting for. 'Sir, we've got a link.'

He ends the call and heads back into the van. 'Go ahead,' he urges.

'Jacob Hamilton and Daniel Williams were at school

together. Same year, same class, from the ages of eleven to sixteen. After GCSEs Jacob stayed on to do his A-levels and Daniel left to go to college.'

'Damn,' he says, nodding, with a stir of something akin to excitement. 'They know each other?'

'I think so,' Kelly replies.

'Which school was it?'

'St Joseph's.'

'And the others?'

'Jennie Hogan and Eleanor both went there, but they were different years, and in different classes. A hundred and twenty kids in every year, so it was a big school.'

'But does it mean anything?' Aaron murmurs, testing the connection. 'I mean two of the guys were in the same class, but they could have just bumped into each other again by chance this morning?'

'I guess.'

He shakes his head. 'But it happens on the day someone walks in and takes them hostage. Isn't that too much of a coincidence?'

Aaron senses something brewing inside him, a feeling that he will try not to get too excited about. But he's due a break. And what if this is the one they're after?

# Liv

Liv doesn't know anyone called Daniel Williams like DI Field is asking her. She hasn't heard of the author D. L. Martin. She doesn't read crime novels, and she's told them Jacob doesn't either. Her husband doesn't read *any* novels, she hasn't once seen him pick up a book.

The detective keeps pressing her, overly interested in a connection between Jacob and the author. 'They were at school together,' he tells her. 'In the same year. I'm surprised your husband has never mentioned the fact an old school mate is now a famous author.'

'I don't know that they were mates,' Liv says. 'It's not a name I've ever heard.'

DI Field seems frustrated with her when he finally gives up. Either that or he thinks she is lying. His expression suggests he might, but Liv doesn't care. The last half-hour, after Ede Hogan collapsed and was rushed to hospital, has drained what smidgen of energy she had left.

As soon as he is out of earshot, she turns to Katy. '*Is* this Daniel guy famous? Have you heard of him?'

Katy shakes her head as she googles D. L. Martin, fingers working overtime on her iPhone. She pulls up images and shows Liv a picture. Liv takes her friend's phone and stares at it.

Daniel Williams is tall and slender, kind of good-looking in a studious way, though the images are author shots, smiling but sensible. He has a goatee beard and light brown wavy hair. 'Chances are Jacob barely even remembers him,' she says.

'Maybe he's a local celebrity,' Katy suggests.

Liv hands back the phone. 'What's it going to be next?'

'What do you mean?'

'It's one thing after another.' Liv pauses. 'Do you think Ede is going to be okay? She didn't look it.'

'I know, I hope she is.'

'She reminded me of Jacob's mum, the way she looked so frail. She must have been scared for her granddaughter. I wonder why the girl's parents aren't here,' Liv says.

'Who knows?'

'I think I need to tell Joyce what's happening.' She thinks of her mother-in-law, blissfully oblivious in her home in Ventnor. 'Before she hears it from someone else.'

'I agree,' Katy says. 'Why don't you call her?'

Liv nods but doesn't make any move to do so. She wonders what everyone here is really thinking, and whether she's the only one who has no idea what their husband is doing at The Boatyard.

She still hasn't told her own parents. It's a sad thought that they wouldn't make any of this any easier for her. 'Do you think Jacob's caught up in something?' Liv says.

'Caught up in what?'

'I don't know,' she admits. 'I mean, maybe he was supposed to be meeting someone here today. He could have got himself involved in some dodgy business. What if he's got on the wrong side of somebody?'

Liv is clutching at straws because she doesn't have any answers. If this was happening anywhere other than the Isle of Wight, she would pass it off.

'There has to be a reason he's come over here. He wasn't just popping out for a coffee. So, if it wasn't another woman . . .' Liv trails off. 'Either way he lied to me; whatever he's doing, he didn't want me finding out.' She gives a hollow laugh. 'That didn't work out well for him, did it?'

She lets out a long breath before continuing. 'Actually, I don't think I should call his mum. She's going to be beside herself. I need to do it face to face.'

'Come on then, let's go,' Katy says. 'The police will call you if there's anything you need to know.'

It's a twenty-minute journey to Ventnor on the south of the island. Halfway there they eventually join the winding country lanes that Liv is familiar with by now. She directs Katy onto her mother-in-law's road, and down to the end where a police car is parked outside her house.

'Shit,' Liv mutters as Katy pulls over and she jumps out of the car. 'They've already told her.'

'Probably only just,' Katy says, leaping out too and following her up the path to the front door. The garden is more overgrown than Liv remembers it being last time, weeds sprawling onto the path that they need to step over, and the curtains in the living room are still pulled closed. The house and garden are falling apart, Liv realises. It's become too much for Joyce to look after on her own, and they didn't even know, let alone step in to help.

'It wasn't like this last time we were here,' Liv says as she presses her finger on the doorbell. It's no excuse. She is cross with herself for letting it get to this point, but more so with Jacob who refuses to help his own mother. What kind of son allows his mum to struggle in her own home like this?

Katy doesn't answer her as the shadow of a figure appears behind the frosted glass of the door. A police officer opens it, and Liv needs to tell him who she is. Satisfied with her explanation, he lets them in, saying, 'Your mother-in-law's in the kitchen. She isn't in a good way. I was just on my way out actually so I'm glad you're here, I didn't really want to leave her.'

'I wanted to be the one to tell her,' Liv says, aware this is also her fault. She was trying to avoid hurting her. She'd *thought* it would all be over by now.

Liv hurries down the short hallway and finds Joyce sitting at a small round table, eyes wet with tears, hands shaking as she grips on to a cup that rattles against its saucer.

'Liv,' she gasps as she sees her daughter-in-law appear. 'Oh, thank goodness.'

'I'm here,' Liv says as she bends down and wraps the small woman in her arms. She can feel that her mother-in-law has lost weight in the last three months and doesn't know if it's something else she should be worried about. At eighty-one, Jacob's mother is much older than Liv's. She had Jacob when she was forty-two. By the time he left school she was already sixty.

Liv pulls away and sits at the table and Katy kisses Joyce on the cheek. They have met a few times, once at Liv's wedding but also over the years when she has come to stay with them in London.

The police officer, who has been lingering in the hallway, tells Liv that someone will be in touch before retreating to let himself out the front door. When they hear the door close Liv reaches over the table to take hold of Joyce's hands.

'He says Jakey is being held hostage,' Joyce says.

'Yes. We've been down at the marina,' Liv tells her. 'But they aren't letting anyone near The Boatyard.'

'What's happening? Are they getting him out?'

'They will,' Liv tells her. 'But right now they say the best thing for them to do is keep trying to contact the hostage-taker.' She imagines that as soon as they go in things could take a turn for the worse. 'They don't believe anyone is hurt,' she adds.

'I didn't know Jakey was coming over,' Joyce says. 'He didn't tell me.'

Liv bites her lip. 'I didn't either.'

Joyce glances up. 'You didn't?'

Liv shakes her head. 'I don't know why he's here. There's nothing more I can tell you than you likely know yourself.'

'I see.' Her mother-in-law frowns. 'It doesn't really make any sense then, does it? I mean we both know Jakey hates coming over here. He hardly keeps it a secret.'

Liv smiles sadly. 'I was told there's someone in The Boatyard who Jacob went to school with. Daniel Williams?'

'Yes, I remember Daniel. The police officer was just asking me about him.'

'Was he?' Liv says, turning to the front door, as if expecting he might still be standing there, listening to them. 'What did he want to know?'

'Just about their friendship. Daniel's a writer now, you know? Not that I've read any of his books. They're all about murder and things like that, though he has done very well for himself, I believe.'

'They were friends then?' Liv questions.

'They were for a time; actually, they were very close in the first couple of years at secondary school. Not so much later on when they were older. Like I said to the police, as far as I know they never kept in touch after school,' Joyce says. 'I told Jakey about Daniel when he first had a book out. I saw it in Tesco and sent him a photograph, but he wasn't interested. You know what he can be like.'

'He'd definitely know Daniel again then,' Liv says. 'When he went into the café this morning, he would have recognised his old friend?'

'Oh, yes, I would have thought so for sure.'

'Do you think he might have been meeting Daniel there?' She doesn't know if this gives her any hope or not. Liv isn't even sure what she *is* hoping for any longer. That she does know her husband after all? Right now, all she wants is the truth. Then she can deal with whatever that brings her.

'I don't know why he would have done that,' Joyce says. 'Not if they didn't keep in touch. But then, who knows with Jakey? He can be very secretive, can't he? He always is with me, anyway. Hopefully not with you though.' She stops abruptly and glances at Liv.

Liv smiles, refusing to comment; she won't bad-mouth Jacob to his mum. The only thing they should be focusing on now is him getting out of that place safely.

Katy suggests making everyone a cup of tea and Liv nods in agreement, watching her friend pick up a cloth and wipe it over the counter first. Liv hadn't noticed it when she first sat down, but the surfaces are dirty and there is a sheen of grease lining the top of the small standalone fridge.

She can't face that today. Next time she will broach the subject of getting a cleaner for Joyce. Instead, as Katy finds her way around the kitchen, Liv decides she needs to ask her mother-in-law something they have never discussed. 'Why *did* he want to leave the Isle of Wight so much?'

She has always shied away from this topic, not wanting to hurt Joyce's feelings, and maybe this still isn't the right time. But they both know how desperate Jacob was to go and, right now, Liv needs some answers about her husband.

'Oh, my dear, he couldn't wait to get away the moment he left school. As soon as he was eighteen he told me he was going, and there was nothing I could do to stop him. I knew it was coming, he was such a difficult teenager,' she goes on. 'Always angry and shouting at me, so different from the way he used to be when he was a little boy, when he'd cuddle up to me on the sofa and tell me he loved me.

'I didn't want him to go,' she says. 'I love him, you know I do, but at the same time the house was a lot calmer after he left. I didn't realise how on edge I was all the time until he wasn't living here anymore. That's a horrible thing to say, isn't it?'

'No. And I can't believe we haven't spoken about it before.'

'I was so pleased when he met you.' Joyce smiles. 'I finally knew he'd found someone who was going to make him happy. I just hoped he would make you as happy.' She reaches over and takes hold of Liv's hands, squeezing them gently.

'Why do you say that?'

'Oh, you know.' She dips her eyes and then turns to look out of the kitchen window. 'He didn't really treat some of his old girlfriends very well.'

Joyce pulls her hands away and curls them into a ball on top of the table. Liv tenses. She knew Jacob could be a bit of a lad, but it's another thing to have his mum say he was outright unpleasant to women. 'What do you mean by that?' she asks, tentatively.

'He was just very – dismissive of them, I suppose. They used to call at the house and I'd hear the way he spoke to them. I mean he wasn't nasty or violent or anything like that,' Joyce says. 'Just . . .' She shakes her head. 'Not very thoughtful.'

Liv glances at Katy who is watching them both, one hand resting on the counter beside the kettle. *Isn't that just the action of a typical teenage boy?* she thinks as Katy rejoins them at the table. 'Mrs Hamilton, do you recognise either of these other names?' Liv doesn't know if her friend has stepped in to change the subject on purpose, but Katy has her phone out and is reeling off the names she has kept in her notes. 'Jennie Hogan or Eleanor Lombard?'

'No. The policeman asked me about them too, and I told him I didn't. But here,' she says as she pushes a pad and pen across the table. 'Maybe you could write them down and I'll see if I can find his old yearbook. Some of the photographs might jog my memory.'

'That's a good idea,' Katy says. 'For all we know, these are the women's married names anyway.'

'Can I get you girls something to eat?' she asks suddenly as Katy goes back to finishing the tea. 'I haven't even offered you anything and you must be hungry. Shall I make you a sandwich?'

Katy smiles. 'Actually, I'd love that, thank you. But let me do it.'

'Nonsense. I need something to keep me busy.'

'You should have something too.' Katy glances at Liv.

'I don't feel hungry,' she mumbles.

'You need to look after yourself,' her friend says.

Liv throws her a look.

'She's right,' Joyce says. 'Worry can ruin your appetite. I'll make you both something, I only have cheese though, so I hope that's okay?'

They tell her it is and as she starts fumbling in her kitchen to prepare sandwiches Liv doesn't want, Joyce starts talking again.

'Jakey and I were so close when he was little. It was just the two of us and I think we relied on each other because of it. But then, almost the day he hit thirteen, he pulled away from me. He started putting gel in his hair and wanting to wear trendy clothes. I think he was embarrassed that I was much older than all his friends' mums. It's not unusual nowadays, is it? But it was back then, and he didn't think I was very cool to be around, and he certainly didn't want them all hanging out at our house any longer. I lost him then; he was always out.'

'I'm so sorry,' Liv says, imagining how hard this must have been on her when she had no one else.

'He took everything out on me. I know they say that's what all teenagers do but what he was doing felt different, more targeted somehow,' she goes on.

'What was he like with his friends?' Katy asks. 'With Daniel, for instance?'

'Daniel was always coming round to the house when they were eleven, twelve. They used to spend a lot of time together for a couple of years, mostly skateboarding at the local park. Daniel was never into football, that was always Jakey's thing, but Jakey would make him stand in the garden in front of the goalposts while he kicked footballs at him. And Daniel just seemed to take it.

'I liked him though. He was such a nice boy, gentle and kind, and always so polite with me.' She smiles. 'I used to tell Daniel he needed to stand up to Jakey more. If he didn't want to spend his evenings standing in the goal then he needed to say so, but he never did.

'Here you go.' Joyce places two plates of cheese sandwiches on the table. 'You eat these, and I'll go and see if I can find that old yearbook, shall I?'

The sight of the white bread filled with slabs of Cheddar turns Liv's stomach.

'Who is he?' she says as she looks up at Katy. 'I don't know the man I married.'

'That's not who Jacob is anymore.'

'Don't.' Liv stops her. 'Don't keep defending him.' She stares at the plates of sandwiches, watching as Katy prises one apart to look inside before she takes a bite. Liv wonders if everything they have discovered is even a shock to her, or whether she has been burying questions she's always had about her husband, deep down inside where she doesn't have to confront them.

## Detective Inspector Aaron Field
### 12.00 hours

At midday Aaron holds another team briefing. He begins with the news that Daniel and Jacob were at school together, and that Jacob's mother has since confirmed the boys were close friends in their early teens. 'But what does it mean?' he questions the team. 'Apparently they haven't kept in touch. So was this morning a coincidental meeting? Or, even if they did arrange to meet, does that have anything to do with the situation at hand?'

'I want old classmates spoken to,' he goes on. 'See if there's any history between them as boys. Something that happened in the past. Meanwhile, will someone please tell me we've got something on our fifth person?'

'Nothing, sir,' one of the sergeants reports. 'No one else has come forward with a misper, or anyone not where they should be. Still the only vehicle in the vicinity unaccounted for is the Nissan Juke. But we know Hannah Parish is at work.'

Aaron doesn't like this. Something about it doesn't sit right. He pulls up a map that shows St Joseph's, where Hannah is working. 'It doesn't make sense,' he says, tapping his finger on the screen. 'The school is ten miles away from where she's parked her car. And her home address is midway between the school and the marina. Do we have any idea how long the vehicle has been there?'

'A resident in the street confirmed it was there before they left the house this morning at 7.15,' another of the team tells him. 'But that it wasn't there last night. No one else can say when it arrived or confirm that they've ever seen it before.'

'So, what reason would Hannah Parish have for driving east of her home, and five miles in the opposite direction from where she works to park her car this morning?' Aaron asks. 'And then how did she get to the school?'

'She could have met someone she knew to share a lift?' Kelly suggests.

'Would you drive in the opposite direction to do that? If you're en route they'd come to you,' Aaron says. 'And if she wanted to walk into work she wouldn't head off in another direction.' He shakes his head. 'Someone else was driving her car. Isn't that a more reasonable explanation? Our unidentified female,' he says. 'Has anyone tried her sister again?'

A muttering of 'no's confirms they haven't. 'Right. Priority is locating her. And I want two officers sent to the school where Hannah is working. Is it the same one Jacob and Daniel attended? Has anyone checked to see if Hannah Parish or her sister attended too? If not, get on it. As soon as she comes out of whatever meeting she's in, I want her spoken to about the possibility of Connie Parish or anyone else driving her car today. If she isn't out in the next half-hour have her interrupted.'

# Rosa

Long after her call to Daniel's agent, Rosa is still sitting in her husband's office, staring at the manuscript that he has almost finished and had excitedly confided in her was his best book yet. But then made the decision not to finish for reasons not even his agent understands.

He has poured his soul into this piece of work for the last nine months. Eighty thousand words to date, the story itself fully formed. At the end he has written an outline of the few remaining chapters. Everything has been worked through.

Rosa knows the impact his decision to stop writing this book will have: he won't hit the publication scheduled for next July. Starting again means not completing a first draft for another ten months, which will result in pushing the release of that book back a year. Most importantly, they'll have to go a whole twelve months without the income they'd anticipated.

And Daniel hasn't shared any of this with her.

She makes the cursor take her back to the start of the novel again and her eyes trail the opening paragraphs once more, the graphic details still making her wince.

She leans back in his office chair a little further and carries on reading. Soon, she is eight pages in, one chapter read and another started. For a while Rosa has almost forgotten where her husband is and what is happening to him. She's too absorbed in his story.

She steels herself with a breath that catches in her throat before she closes the abandoned document. Sitting here in his office isn't going to help him. She needs to get back to the marina so she can be close to him. Though, in some ways, she'll never feel closer than she does here, surrounded by everything he loves.

She gets out of his chair and walks over to his bookcase, letting her fingers trail the spines of the novels he's collected over the years.

She stops at one of the shelves where there is a photo of them on their wedding day; Rosa in a slim-fitting, floor-length ivory gown with her hair styled in a low bun. Daniel is beside her in a deep grey suit and a red tie that matches the colour of the bridesmaid's dress. He is cupping Rosa's face between his hands as he leans forward to talk to her. Neither of them knew the photo was being taken but it's by far her favourite one of that day.

She remembers the moment so clearly. All he had said to her was, 'I love you.' Three words that you would expect to hear between a bride and groom on their wedding day and yet he'd said them with such passion and desire that Rosa knew, without one shred of doubt, he meant them with every fibre of his being.

Now she touches his face in the picture with one finger. 'I love you too,' she whispers to her husband. Her heart aches that he isn't with her, and that the man she loves more than anything in the world is in danger. What she hates the most is that she could even have considered for a second he was part of something he hasn't told her about.

*And yet there* are *things you haven't told me,* she thinks as there is a ping from his laptop, an alert that an email has come through.

Rosa goes back to the desk and pulls up the inbox, but the email is a generic one from his bank asking for feedback. She stares at the folder and the list of names and subject headings in front of her, when she realises she hasn't checked his deleted folder.

It would kill him to know she is invading his privacy, but would he expect her not to snoop at a time like this? She tells herself it's for his safety, because of course there could be correspondence from someone: a stalker he hasn't told her about; someone crazy enough to walk into the marina with a gun.

Rosa scans the messages over the last few days. Most of them are spam, all of them from businesses and nothing related to his work.

Then suddenly she pauses, her fingers stilling the mouse beneath her hand as she recognises a name she has only learnt today: Jacob Hamilton.

It is an email that was sent exactly one week ago, last Monday, which was only two days after Daniel's television appearance. It is one that Daniel had moved straight to his bin.

She opens it up, her fingers twitching nervously at the prospect of what the message contains. Her heart starts to hammer in her chest, the blood rushing through her ears, pounding and making her light-headed.

*You will be there? Next Monday?*

She reads the one line over and over. Goosebumps prick at her skin. So Daniel knew he was going to The Boatyard this morning after all. He got up and left the house with an arrangement that he hadn't told her about.

She needs to call DI Field. Now.

Only Rosa can't pull herself away from Daniel's computer. There is something chillingly vague about the message, the tone so impersonal from someone who is supposedly an old friend, brusque and demanding.

And then there is the fact it was delivered and received on the same day Daniel told his agent he was no longer going to write the story he had been working on for ten months. Two hours earlier, in fact, she realises when she notes the time stamp on the mail. She *has* to assume the two are linked.

She blows out an unsteady breath, pushing her hands against his desk to wheel herself away from it.

This isn't a coincidence.

She needs to tell the police.

Why hadn't he mentioned to her he was meeting an old friend? What reason could he have had for keeping it a secret from her?

She must call DI Field, now, she thinks for the third time. She reaches for her phone in her pocket and pulls it out, her fingers trembling as they clutch on to it. Her mind plays out what this might mean.

'Oh, Daniel,' she says aloud. She drops the phone on the desk, stands up. She knows she has to make the call but how can she?

She has no idea why Daniel had sent an email to Jacob

saying, *You will be there? Next Monday?* And why he then moved the message to his bin. But what she does know is that it doesn't look good. And if she tells the police Daniel sent a demand to Jacob that brought him to the marina this morning, she knows what they will think. They will *think* that Daniel is the one to blame.

There is so much she's already kept from them, she realises, as she turns to their wedding photo. Her heart thumps as she reaches for his mouse and hovers the cursor over the delete button.

# Liv

Liv feels dizzy. And maybe it is the fact she is pregnant, and she hasn't eaten much today, but she thinks it's more likely down to her mother-in-law's words that keep swimming around in her head. Listening to Joyce talk about a younger version of her son. A man who was frequently angry and who took it out on his mum, the sweetest woman Liv knows.

She's always thought Jacob was probably an arrogant teenager, just by looking at old photos of him. He was sporty and good-looking, often wearing a smirk, with one eyebrow raised in that cocky way she used to fall for in boys herself at that age. With hair that hung down in curtains either side of his face, Jacob had the boy-band image Liv wanted to date. Girls would have loved him; she would have too if she'd known him back then. But it would have been a short-lived relationship. Girls like Liv knew boys like Jacob didn't hang around for long at that age.

She got him when he had matured, when he had been out in the world a bit and survived on his own without his mum doing everything for him.

Or that was what she thought. And maybe this is still the case, she tells herself as her hand rests on her stomach, protecting what she already loves fiercely. Whatever happens, this is her priority now.

And maybe her husband isn't having an affair. And when she shares the news of their pregnancy with him, he will wrap her in his arms and tell her how much he loves her as he explains his innocent reason for being here.

Liv feels a shudder rippling through her body and closes her eyes tightly. She isn't even sure if this is what she wants.

Regardless, none of this means her husband is going to walk out of that building alive, Liv thinks, with a crashing realisation that it doesn't matter what Jacob used to be like if he ends up dead. And she knows that *isn't* what she wants. God, no. More than anything, she prays Jacob is okay. Whatever he has done, he is the father of her unborn child.

'I want to leave,' she says to Katy. 'I want to go back to the marina.' Upstairs, her mother-in-law is rummaging about, searching for the old school yearbook she's so keen to find. Katy had told her it was a good idea, but Liv couldn't care less about it.

She needs fresh air more than anything, she can't breathe inside this house any longer. Everything is made worse by the thought of trawling through old images of Jacob, his classmates and girlfriends. Her husband's past is smothering her in a blanket of dread.

'What if something has happened?' she goes on. 'What if all the time I'm just sitting here in my mother-in-law's kitchen, the gunman has started shooting everyone? I'm not going to know. They're not going to call me.'

'Liv, that's not happening,' Katy says, but they both know it could be. None of them know how this is going to end. 'Though I get that you want to go back to the marina, we just need to wait for Joyce to come back first.'

'Do we?' Liv mutters. 'No, of course we do. I just don't know that I want to see whatever it is she's looking for.' Liv almost wishes they had never come in the first place.

Finally, they hear Joyce's footsteps as she slowly descends the stairs. Liv gets up to meet her; she worries about her mother-in-law falling, so unsteady on her feet that Liv holds out a hand to help her.

Joyce is clutching a small hardback book, but she doesn't mention it for a moment as she looks into Liv's eyes and gives her hand a squeeze.

Liv cocks her head, trying to work out what she's attempting to communicate but isn't saying. Is there more about her son she's remembering?

'What is it?' Liv questions.

'Oh, I don't know,' Joyce says. 'Maybe I shouldn't have spoken about Jakey like that. Not with him—'

'He's going to be fine,' Liv says, determinedly. 'You know Jacob, he's strong. He won't let anything happen.'

Joyce smiles, wanly. Her eyes are filled with fresh tears. Liv has the urge to tell her she is pregnant so that she can give her something to be happy about. Knowing she is going to have a grandchild will do that. But before she has the chance to say anything, Joyce says, 'I found the yearbook.' She waves it in the air like a prize.

Liv allows her to lead them back into the kitchen where she opens it up on the table and begins to flick through the pages.

Images of girls with high ponytails and hair slicked down either side of their smiling faces bounce off the paper. Pretty boys with floppy hairstyles. All of them are in the last year of their GCSEs, which means they must be sixteen, or just about to be.

She turns another page, and Liv sees a photo of her husband. He is young, fresh-faced and holding a football in front of him as he grins at the camera. *Jake*, it says he prefers to be called, a name he has never answered to as long as she has known him, insistent everyone uses his full name, pulling a face at the idea she could call him Jakey.

Liv scans the short bio on him. He loves football and rugby and being with his mates. He is going to be rich when he grows up.

Her fingers twitch as she turns the page and his picture disappears. She wonders if Katy had clocked that last sentence too. If she has recognised that he got his wish when he met and married Liv.

They turn a few more and a handful of photographs fall out from the back. His mum picks one up. It's an image of a group of kids, Jacob in the middle, his arm slung over the shoulder of a girl with a 'Rachel Green' hairstyle. 'Elle,' Joyce says, tapping the photo. 'That was one of them. I'd forgotten all about Elle until now. But Jakey went out with her for quite a while.'

Liv takes a closer look at the picture. The girl is pretty with flawless skin and bright blue almond-shaped eyes that are staring into the camera. 'Elle,' she murmurs as she turns to Katy. It's the woman she and Jacob had bumped into in town a couple of years back, Liv is sure of it.

'Do you think it's Eleanor?' Katy is saying as she starts tapping on her phone. Liv stares at the screen as the search for *Eleanor Lombard, Isle of Wight*, brings up a link to her Instagram account.

Katy clicks on it, scrolling through the many, many posts and photos till she comes to one that shows Eleanor, standing next to a man and two young boys.

'My God,' Liv says as Katy enlarges the picture. 'It's him! That's her husband, the one from the marina. That's Gareth Lombard.'

## Monday afternoon, 12.05 p.m.

*Of course, they all know why they are here. They knew as soon as I took out the gun and told them to walk around the back. The moment they finally recognised me. They just hadn't been expecting to see me after twenty-five years.*

*I wondered if they thought I had changed. I have been thinking the same about them, trying to reach a conclusion over the hours as to whether they are the same people they all were back then.*

*One of them had said my name aloud and one by one I watched as their faces fell, putting two and two together, slotting the pieces into place, their gazes drifting from my face to the gun in my hand in horror. I could see their fear was genuine, but still I wondered if it was anything like the fear I had once felt at their hands.*

*'Do you still think about that day?' I turn to the one who has been silent all morning. 'Do you feel any guilt?'*

*They clear their throat, their eyes darting towards the others and then back to me. 'Of course I do,' they say eventually.*

*Good. It should be seeping through their pores. It should be the first thing they see when they open their eyes and the last when they go to bed.*

*'Tell me what happened,' I demand.*

*'Nothing happened,' another of them says. It's all I ever*

*expected from him. I don't think people change that much. We all stay the same at our core.*

'You were bullies,' I hiss.

He doesn't deny this.

'You were killers.'

'No, we weren't.'

I see the others looking at him. I want the truth. I want them to tell me everything that happened that day. I want them finally to admit what they did.

I bet the people who love them now don't know. They won't be able to imagine being married or related to someone who made another person's life so awful that they didn't want to live any longer.

Neither is it likely that they know the people they love once killed someone, lied and got away with it.

They have never been punished. It was covered up and made out to be an accident that had nothing to do with them.

'We didn't kill anyone,' he is saying to me, the same denial they made all those years ago.

I knew it wasn't true then and I know it isn't now. I was never able to prove it but all I want is for them finally to tell me the truth.

# Hannah

At 12.15 Harvey walks out of Hannah's room. As soon as he is gone, there is a rap on the classroom door. It swings open and the nicer of the two ladies from the school office pokes her head around it, smiling at her.

'They tell me it's nothing to worry about,' she starts, 'but the police have been on the phone asking about you this morning.'

'Asking about me?'

The lady nods as she pushes the door open wider and comes into the room. 'And now they've turned up to see you. There's two of them arrived and they said I didn't need to disturb you when you were in with someone.' She looks about her as if she has never been inside the little room before which makes Hannah feel inadequate in her tiny space. 'So, I don't *think* it's anything serious.'

'Do you know what they want?'

'When they called, they just wanted to know if you'd turned up at work today and I told them you had and so they said that was fine and it was all they needed to know. But then they showed up here five minutes ago and said they needed to speak to you as soon as you're free. They're waiting at the office for you, but shall I send them down here?'

Hannah frowns. 'Yes, yes, do that,' she says. 'But it seems odd, doesn't it? Why did they want to know I'm here?'

The lady smiles and shrugs and Hannah assures herself it must have something to do with one of her students because it wouldn't be the first time the police have wanted to talk to her. She tells herself it has nothing to do with what Harvey has told her about the marina.

'I'll wait for them here,' Hannah says.

The lady nods and begins to back out of the room. 'They did say something about your car,' she adds.

'My car?' Hannah questions. It's parked on Connie's driveway. She left it at home this morning as she walked into work. If this does involve one of her students, have they found out where she lives?

As she waits for the two police officers to arrive, Hannah plucks her phone out of her bag and switches it on again. She waits for it to flash into action, but there's still nothing other than three missed calls from an unknown number, which she now assumes must have been the police.

Hannah opens the doorbell camera app to see what the last movements on Connie's driveaway were. She sees that no one has been on it since 7.04 a.m. when her sister left the house and went straight to Hannah's car, getting in it and driving off until she is out of sight.

Hannah's stomach plummets. She was blocking Connie's car in this morning. She realised as she was leaving for work that her sister's car was parked behind hers, and she had no way of getting out. But Hannah had left her keys in the usual place on the rack in case Connie needed them. The two of them are forever moving cars out the way – or if they are in a rush, they take whichever is easiest.

'Ms Parish?'

Hannah looks up to find two policemen standing in the doorway. She is still preoccupied with thoughts of where her sister would have been heading at that time, in too much of a hurry to move the cars around.

'Yes, come in,' she says.

'Thank you,' the taller of the two says as he steps inside. The other follows and closes the door behind him. It feels too intimate with the three of them huddled in the small space. She regrets not meeting them at reception. But they are here now, and they begin to tell Hannah why. Her car, it appears, is parked in the vicinity of an ongoing incident and they need to rule it out of their investigations.

'My sister was driving it this morning,' she tells them as ice-cold dread crawls over her skin.

'Connie Parish?' the policeman asks her, and Hannah says yes, aware they already know her name.

'What is this incident?' Her heart beats wildly; she's desperate for them to tell her it is something other than what Harvey was talking about.

'Hopefully nothing for you to worry about,' he says, and Hannah tries to focus on the word *hopefully*. 'But we do need to locate your sister. Do you know where she's supposed to be today?'

'No. It's her birthday and she has the day off and . . . she didn't tell me what she was doing.' Hannah holds up her phone. 'I watched her leave the house just after 7, but I've no idea where she went.'

*She is at the marina.* She knows this and yet she cannot bring herself to ask him because there is still a part of her that is hoping Connie isn't, and that this is about something else.

What she also doesn't say is that her sister never leaves the house this early, not even for work, and especially not when she has a day off.

'There's a hostage incident at the marina,' the policeman says, confirming her worst fear. 'At The Boatyard café. Is this somewhere your sister might have gone?'

'I don't know. She's never mentioned it.' Hannah slides one hand over the back of her neck. Her hairline feels damp with sweat. The café is not somewhere they have been together, and if Connie has been before, Hannah thinks it's the kind of place her sister would have told her about. They share things like that with each other, tell each other every minute detail of their everyday lives.

'Would you mind trying to contact your sister?' he asks. 'Is there any other way you can get hold of her other than her mobile?'

'No.' Hannah screws her eyes up. 'Not if she isn't at home.' She presses for her sister's number, number one in her favourites list as she is in Connie's. Her husband is second.

'I speak to Hannah more,' Connie had laughed once when he'd asked her about it, not that he minded. He knows their close bond is something he couldn't expect to change, and neither has he tried.

Hannah waits for the call to connect as bile rises in her

throat. Her jaw is tense, a dull ache begins to seep through her muscles.

When it switches to answerphone, she tells Connie to call her immediately, begging her sister to ring her back and say where she is.

'I'm worried,' she tells the officers. 'I don't know why she has her phone off. Connie never has her phone off.' Her sister is forever complaining that she can't get hold of Hannah in the days when she is working. It's one of the reasons Hannah switches hers off, because she knows she would otherwise be bombarded by messages.

'Would you mind describing your sister to us?' he asks her.

Hannah does so, noticing the look that passes between them and the moment of silence that follows.

'What is it?' she says.

'I think there's a chance your sister was seen walking into The Boatyard just after 7 a.m. this morning and—'

'No!' Hannah cries, a scream so primal it shocks her. The taller policeman reaches out to grab her as if she is going to fall but Hannah clutches her head in her hands, fingers clawing into her scalp. 'She can't be there.'

'We need to ask you some questions,' he is saying to her. 'Can you think of any reason at all why your sister would have gone to the marina this morning?'

'No, I don't know why she would go there.'

'And has everything with your sister seemed okay to you recently? Has she done anything that is out of character? Have you had any reason to be concerned about her lately?' he is asking with a renewed sense of urgency.

'What?' she says, confused as to why they are asking her these loaded questions. 'No, of course there's been no reason for me to worry. What do you mean?'

'Maybe you know some of these names,' he is saying to her now. The speed of the turn in his questioning disorientates her. 'Have you heard the name Daniel Williams?'

Hannah feels the blood drain from her body as she clutches on to the edge of her desk.

'Ms Parish?' the officer is asking. 'Do you know that name?'

Yes. Yes, she knows the name, but she can't bring herself to tell the police officers as much.

'I don't understand,' she says in a whisper as he asks her again if she knows Daniel Williams' name. 'I don't understand,' Hannah repeats, as her mind trails back to the conversation she had with Connie once, not long after their parents had died, a night when the darkest of stories were shared.

# Gareth

Gareth feels numb as he hovers on the outer edges of the crowd at the marina, by the barrier. The number of people who have arrived, driven by a sickening curiosity, has grown.

The police are scurrying off in different directions, gathering intel on what's happening. They aren't sharing anything with him, though they know more than they are letting on. He is convinced of this now.

Ede Hogan's words keep going round in his head. She was right: one of the five of them inside that café is responsible. He thinks it must be one of the two men; it makes sense that this is something a man would do. Women don't do things like this.

His thoughts stray to Daniel Williams whom he met on two occasions last summer when the author came into the Audi garage where Gareth works, first to look at new cars and then to purchase one. He'd been so chatty and friendly.

Gareth mentioned he'd read his books, and the author had thanked him, shaking his hand. He seemed so nice when they spoke, so unpretentious. Gareth remembers how he'd said as much to Eleanor that evening. She was playing with the boys in the garden when he got home.

He'd called out: 'Guess who came into the showroom today?'

'I don't know,' she'd said with disinterest, her mind on the boys and not on him.

'The author, D. L. Martin. His real name's Daniel Williams. He came in to buy a brand-new Audi.' That caught her attention. Eleanor stopped what she was doing and stared at him. Gareth was pleased he finally had a story to share.

'Did you speak to him?' she asked.

'Yes!' he told her. 'I'm the one who sold him a car.'

She shook her head – a strange reaction, he'd thought at the time – as if she didn't believe he could sell a car to someone famous.

'What did he say?'

'Oh, nothing much, we were just chatting,' Gareth told her. 'I said I'd read one of his books and told him it was really good. He thanked me,' he added while Eleanor just kept staring at him.

She had started frowning and he'd felt wrong-footed. 'And he didn't – didn't ask anything about you or anything like that?'

'About me?'

'Oh, it doesn't matter,' she said.

'Why would he ask anything about me?' Gareth had questioned her, but she'd moved on, asking the kids what they wanted for tea, and the subject was dropped.

He'd forgotten the strange turn their conversation had taken, but he recalls it now. And the way Eleanor had brushed him off when he remarked on it, saying she didn't mean anything by it, but later had peppered him with questions.

Did Gareth miss something back then? Was there a hint of something in that conversation that he hadn't seen at the time, because he wouldn't have been looking for it?

But that's all changed. Now his wife is being held hostage in the same building as Daniel Williams. Now it no longer feels like a coincidence.

And just because the man was friendly and talented doesn't mean he's not a nutter. In fact, isn't it more possible that someone who writes about criminals for a living and delves into their deepest, darkest thoughts might possibly be a little unhinged?

Gareth couldn't conjure up anything so morbid. He doesn't have the ability to dive into the psyche of a murderer or describe a rape in all its disturbing detail. He's not creative, as Eleanor has pointed out several times. The last time she did so was when he helped the boys make a birthday card for her.

His eyes stray beyond the barrier towards The Boatyard, and Gareth feels a sharp kick of adrenaline. He grabs the arm of a police officer who is guarding the roadblock. 'I think it's the author, Daniel Williams,' he tells her. 'I remember something.'

'What is it that you remember?' she asks him urgently and Gareth tells her the story. She frowns at him then and looks like she is waiting for more.

'I think they might have known each other,' he says at the end. 'My wife has been in that building for five hours now!' he cries. 'How is this going to end well?' He can't stop imagining Daniel Williams now with a gun in his hand, pointing it at Eleanor's pretty head.

Does he plan to shoot everyone and then himself too? Or does he think he can somehow walk out of this unscathed?

*Is it even him?*

Gareth eyes the barrier and the officers who are keeping guard as he takes a step closer. Eleanor would tell him he doesn't have it in him. But he does. He could make a run for the marina if he wanted to.

# Detective Inspector Aaron Field
## 12.30 hours

There is a buzz of activity on the road leading down to the marina now that the public and press are aware there's an incident unfolding there live. Stories of varying degrees of accuracy are popping up on social media. Amateur video footage of Aaron and his team.

He watches the officers out of the van window, the ones who are keeping the onlookers from creeping too near to the barrier. But there are some encroaching nonetheless. Like they can't get close enough to the danger.

Mobile phones are held in the air, trying to catch a moment they can share, just to say they heard the news first, that they were there.

'They make you sick, don't they?' Kelly murmurs.

Aaron raises his eyes in agreement. 'Any news on Ede Hogan?' he asks. 'Can we find out how she's doing?'

'Sure.'

The poor woman had clearly pushed herself too far. 'Okay, I want another update at 13.30.' Another hour, he thinks. How long is this going to last?

The last five minutes have brought them another piece of news: that Jacob Hamilton used to date Eleanor Lombard. Three out of the five people inside The Boatyard knew each other when they were teenagers. *This* he cannot ignore. This means something. What he doesn't know is if they knew the others in there too.

'They knew each other between the years 1997 and 2003,' he says. 'What if something happened in that time frame?'

'But whatever it might have been, surely none of the victims believed there'd be any risk in meeting up today,' Kelly points out. 'Or they wouldn't have come.'

'Possibly,' he agrees, his gaze searching out the one remaining relative who is still at the marina. Gareth Lombard is hovering on the periphery of the crowd, among those closest to the barrier. The rest of them have all gone. Ede Hogan in an ambulance accompanied by her neighbour. Liv Hamilton to her mother-in-law's driven by her friend. Rosa Williams had disappeared a while back now. In fact, he hasn't seen her since Ede collapsed, and he doesn't know where she went. 'What access do we have to Daniel Williams' computer?' he asks.

'Nothing. His wife assumes he has his laptop on him.'

'Get someone to their house to check if she's there. The woman couldn't get down here fast enough earlier, so why has she suddenly left again? Get them to check she isn't mistaken about his computer.'

'On it.'

Aaron's mobile starts ringing. He turns away from the van's window. He's been having to field questions from local journalists: *Why are they doing this? How do you know all the hostages are still unharmed? How do you know one of them isn't dead?* Truth is, he doesn't.

'DI Field,' he says, picking up the call. It is the officer who's gone to St Joseph's School.

'Sir?' he says. 'I think you're going to want to speak to Hannah Parish.'

'Her sister's in there?' Aaron guesses, turning back towards the marina.

'It appears she is. But it's more than that. I think Hannah might know what's going on,' he says. 'She knows the names of everyone inside that building. All of them. I have a feeling she knows who's responsible for the hostage-taking. And why they're doing it.'

# Hannah

Every inch of Hannah feels numb, like it's no longer a part of her. She's been this way ever since the policemen arrived in her room, confirming they believe her sister is caught up in a hostage situation, reeling off a list of names: *Daniel Williams; Jennie Hogan; Jacob Hamilton.* Eleanor too, though Lombard, Hannah assumes, is her married name.

She knows of every one of them. And the fear that rippled through her with each name he read out, meant she knew that, somehow, they're the reason her sister is at The Boatyard too.

She inhales a tight breath as she silently climbs into the back of the marked police car they tell her will take her to the marina where someone will interview her.

Hannah needs to get her head straight on the ten-mile journey to where her sister is, before she talks and tells them everything she knows.

Flashes of her and Connie's conversation keep darting through her mind. The wine they had shared that night, too much of it, and the truths that had come out in consequence. They were both grieving their parents and so desperately in need of comfort that it was no wonder they sought solace in one another.

She has to tell the truth. She has no choice, she understands that. She must tell it for the sake of her sister's safety, and before it is too late.

Could Connie really do something so stupid?

Hannah has no idea anymore, not when it's clear she already has.

She needs to cancel her afternoon appointments, she thinks. Ironically Hannah's had to take time off work today after all. It was what Connie had wanted her to do in the first place.

If she had, things could have been so different.

The police car weaves through the narrow lanes. News this shocking reminds her of the night she was told their parents had died. Connie was the one to get the call from the police then, as their dad must have put the eldest daughter's number into their phones as an emergency contact.

Half an hour earlier, Hannah had called their parents from work and asked them to pick her up. It was dark and raining heavily and she didn't want to hang around at the bus stop getting wet. 'It's not safe,' she moaned, which she knew would do the trick. She thought nothing of her father's safety, driving in those conditions, and they were the last words she ever said to her parents.

Hannah had hung up the phone with no *I love you*, or *drive safely*, because these aren't the words a twenty-four year old thinks to use even when she is far too old still to be calling her parents for a lift home.

But Hannah knew they wouldn't mind. They did everything for her and her sister. They still would now if luck had let them live.

Now she is thinking back to her conversation with her sister last night, which hadn't been any better. Hannah didn't tell Connie she loved her. She hadn't poked her head around her sister's door this morning to wish her happy birthday because Connie was on the phone to her husband.

Instead, she had snapped at Connie last night that she was being snippy. 'What's wrong with you?' she'd bit. Was her sister seriously pissed off that Hannah hadn't taken the day off, even though it would have meant missing her job interview? The last words she'd spoken to Connie were a brusque, 'I'm going to bed.'

What if she doesn't get the chance to tell her anything else? Situations like this – they often don't end well.

Hannah stares out of the car window, clutching her bag tightly in her lap with hands that are trembling and fingernails digging into the leather.

*Why, Connie?* she thinks, leaning her head against the glass. *Why have you done this?*

Hannah should have tried harder last night, when she *knew* Connie was upset by something. But the way she seemed to be discounting the importance of the job interview had annoyed her too much.

They should have talked. If Connie had opened up and told Hannah what the matter really was, none of this would be happening.

There is nothing she can do to turn back time. Connie was never going to admit to whatever was going through her head. Turns out they do have secrets after all.

Hannah's phone starts ringing from where it sits in her

lap. In an instant she thinks of her brother-in-law who has no idea what is happening either. But he is the other side of the world in Japan. Nine hours ahead. He probably hasn't tried calling Connie again since this morning and remains blissfully unaware of what his wife has done.

Hannah picks up her phone and looks at the screen to see Abbie's number flashing.

She hesitates a moment before picking it up. She doesn't have the capacity to think of anyone other than Connie right now. But Hannah can't ignore a student in need. 'Hi?'

'I just wanted to speak to you again.'

Hannah can see that they are only around the corner from the marina. She knows that Abbie needs her more than ever; the girl's face when she left counselling earlier was pale and haunted, desperate even. She has no one else to turn to but Hannah.

But Connie needs her more. And Connie will always come first.

'I'm sorry,' Hannah says. 'Something's come up. I can't talk to you right now.'

'Oh,' Abbie says. 'Erm, but—'

'I'm so sorry, really I am. I'll call you later,' she says, though she fears she has already let the young girl down.

## Monday afternoon, 12.33 p.m.

*'It was you who started it,' I say. The tears continue to drip down her face, but I know she is crying for herself rather than anything she did to me in the past. 'But you know that, don't you? You were the one who began bullying me.'*

*Girls can be such bitches, can't they?*

*They manage to find the weakest point before sticking the knife in and giving it a twist, finding the one thing that will hurt their victim the most. I guess it wasn't hard. I was an obvious target for someone like her.*

*It started simply. 'You called me Fatty. "Hey, Fatty, what have you got for lunch today? A few pieces of cake?" It wasn't very original,' I add. That's probably why they didn't recognise me straight away when they came in today. It took a while but eventually the pounds had dropped off. 'Make sure you don't get too skinny,' Mum had said to me, like my weight was always going to be the focus of attention.*

*Girls like her don't stop to think about how, after insults like that, your life will for ever be shaped and controlled by even the smallest of sniggers.*

*She was the ringleader. The one who delivered most of the jabs. Soon she was joined by her mate, and though her words weren't as cutting, it was her silence that hurt more. She could have spoken* out. *She had plenty of opportunity but chose not to say anything. She could have put a stop to it at any time she wanted. She had the chance to change everything, and it was worse that she'd once been my friend too. A true friend for a time.*

'I was young,' she says now, shaking her head. 'I was just a child myself; I didn't know what I was doing.'

'You knew,' I tell her. 'Of course you knew. It didn't stop. For months I had to listen to you as I walked back from school. It was like you had nothing better to do than sit on the wall and wait for me. Me and Raff,' I add.

At the mention of his name I glance around the room, seeing which of them flinches.

Rafferty Jones became my best friend when I was thirteen. We weren't in the same classes, but he lived around the corner, and we found solace in our friendship and a mutual love of American sitcoms, spouting lines that only each other would recognise.

Raff started waiting on the corner to walk me to school, and would then hang about at the playground gates at the end of the day for me. He made out it was because we lived so close to each other, but I knew he thought he could somehow protect me.

Each time we saw the two girls waiting, he started engaging me in some conversation about what was on TV that night, his expression serious, as if he really was so engrossed in whatever he was telling me he didn't even hear what was being shouted at me.

'Come on,' he'd mutter occasionally, pulling me along. 'Sticks and stones . . .'

'Yeah, yeah,' I'd say. 'Words will never break me.'

I say to her now, 'You used to call him my boyfriend. Like that was the worst thing you could say to me. "Got yourself a boyfriend, have you?"' I sneer in an imitation of her voice. Then they *would laugh as our cheeks reddened and our steps quickened while we scurried on past.*

It started off so trivially, and yet the damage was already inflicted. The cracks in my confidence; the anxiety of simply walking to and from school.

We began going back to Raff's house at the end of the day, which was closer than ours, and we'd sit inside his dad's shed in their back garden. His parents had put an old sofa in it and set up a small TV. Raff was their only child, and they loved him more than anything. His mum would bring us lemonade and a plate laden with strawberries, Jammie Dodgers and Mini Rolls, because we'd once agreed they were our favourites. I didn't tell Mum how much I had already eaten before I came home for tea because I didn't want her commenting. I knew full well that stuffing my face with chocolate was the worst thing I could do when I was already overweight.

I felt safer in Raff's old shed than I did anywhere else. No one could get to us there. I was comforted by The Fresh Prince and Saved by the Bell. *Those times were slices of heaven.*

Then we'd discuss how we shouldn't hide from the bullies but stand up for ourselves by learning self-defence. Raff showed me some moves in his garden. He'd bounce on the spot with his hands in front of his face like he thought he was a professional boxer, telling me how he'd learnt to jab and upper-cut. I'd dive out the way of his flailing arms and hope I never had to leave it to Raff to settle a physical fight. But he didn't give up.

Or not until their little twosome doubled in size. Then it was clear there could be no fair fight. And though the newcomers weren't around as much as the other two, it was worse when they were. The ringleader would get more vocal, showing off, doing anything for a laugh at my expense with two boys to witness her.

*You knew Raff, you went to his funeral, but at the time you had no idea just how much of a friend he was to me.*

'Which one of you put the note through my door?' I say to them now.

I can remember that day as if it were yesterday. I have played it through in my head so many times over the years, keeping the memories crystal clear. I can even remember the book I was reading when I heard the sound of gravel thrown against my windowpane: Ender's Game, Raff had lent it to me.

'Because I knew it was never Raff,' I go on.

Though at the time I didn't know this for sure. I had looked out of my window and caught a glimpse of his bright red bike cycling off into the distance. I'd assumed it was him and so went downstairs to go out the front door and call him back, but there was a note on the doormat.

**Meet me in the woods. I've got a surprise!**

What I did know was that something didn't feel right. Raff had never done anything like this before, and yet it looked like his handwriting, even though it had clearly been written in a rush. But he'd know I wouldn't want to go in the woods on my own, and I couldn't work out why he hadn't waited for me.

I became certain the note wasn't from him yet I didn't know what to do. In truth, I didn't want to go anywhere. A tingle of fear was beginning to creep through me. But Raff might be in trouble, and if he was, I'd never forgive myself if I went back up to my room and carried on reading.

'Do you really think I didn't know it was you?' I say now.

Of course I had to go into the woods. I wouldn't leave Raff there. They knew this too.

*So I dragged my own bike out of the garage and cycled the ten-minute journey to the woods, leaving the bike on the edge as I crept in and out of the trees, searching for him. At first, I didn't call out his name because I didn't want to draw attention to myself, but after half an hour of looking in vain I began calling for him in earnest.*

*I scoured the length of the woods, back and forth, but there was no sign of him. Eventually I left, clueless as to why they'd led me there in the first place.*

'Do you ever imagine how his parents were told that their only son was dead?' I go on. 'Do you picture his mum's face when she came home that evening to find a policeman waiting at her door, telling her they've found a body? That they believe her only child is dead? Because I do,' I say. 'I will never get it out of my head.'

That sweet woman with the bouncy permed hair, with her denim dungarees that always had one shoulder strap falling down and green wellies she'd wear to dig the flower beds in her garden.

A year later, and she would be dead too. I was surprised she managed to survive as long as twelve months without her son.

Raff was lying at the bottom of the quarry. His mum and dad were told it was a tragic accident and that no one else had been seen at the scene.

Of course, they never got over it. All they had left was each other and it turned out that wasn't enough. They separated within six months and then after his mum died, his dad moved away from the Isle of Wight, keeping in touch with no one from his past.

I didn't get over it either. I suffered through school assemblies on the dangers of the local quarry and how we must not think of going there alone. I listened to muttered condolences and sat through the funeral service.

They all went too, the four of them, standing with their parents and pretending to care and look sad, daring to look like it had nothing to do with them.

But I saw it in their eyes: the way they looked at me, startled and afraid. The way the bullying stopped in an instant. And the way their little group started to fracture until it shattered.

I search their eyes now. Their varying degrees of guilt and fear. I will get the truth out of them one way or another before any of us walks out of here today. I will do what I came to do.

# Hannah

The police car parks up on the side of a road and Hannah looks out of the window. Further along she can see a crowd of people. 'Is that the marina down there?' she asks as the car door opens on the far side and a man leans in.

He is tall and has glasses perched on top of his head. His eyes are wide with anticipation but at the same time he looks frazzled. 'Hannah? I'm Detective Inspector Aaron Field.' He tries for a smile but it's more of a grimace; she imagines his whole day must be hanging on what she can tell them.

Hannah nods and climbs out of the open door that he shuts behind her as he gestures towards a building. 'We can go inside. There's a room we can talk in.' She stares up at its white-rendered walls and double doors.

Outside it is a woman who looks to be in her mid-thirties, immaculately dressed in a long camel coat and dark jeans. She is flanked by another woman the same age and an older lady whose gaze is trained on the pavement. The woman in the expensive coat pauses to stare at Hannah as she follows DI Field into the building. Frowning, she opens her mouth to speak, but the detective is pushing the doors open and hustling her inside before any words can be spoken.

'Who was that?' Hannah asks him. 'The woman outside.'

He doesn't look back. He doesn't need to. 'She's one of the relatives,' he tells her. 'Jacob Hamilton's wife.'

Hannah's mouth makes an O. She blows out a breath. She is glad the doors have shut behind them and DI Field is leading her into a side room. He closes them inside and they are on their own.

'Would you like anything to drink?' he asks as he indicates a seat.

'No. I'm fine, thank you.'

She sits and he pulls up another chair for himself. There is a TV in the corner of the room, a trestle table and a small back window that looks out onto the side road beyond. There are two extra chairs that aren't occupied and the whole room feels bare and lacking in comfort.

'Is it correct you told my officers that you've heard the names of all the individuals we believe are inside The Boatyard?' DI Field leans towards her, urgently. 'Eleanor Lombard?' he starts as she nods, and then he reels the other names off to her.

'I have,' Hannah says. The sheen of sweat that was pooling around her hairline is trickling into the creases of her neck. It sticks to her skin, cold and clammy.

'How do you know them?' he asks.

'We used to live near them,' Hannah tells him, trying her best to keep breathing through the hard lump that has lodged in her chest. 'When we were younger. They were all local.'

It surprises her he doesn't already know this, especially if other relatives are here like he says. But then, she imagines, the others inside the building haven't spoken to anyone else about each other. After that one and only time when patches of the story were shared, Connie and Hannah don't speak of them either.

'Do you know *why* they are all in The Boatyard?' he prompts. He needs the answers quickly, and she needs to give them to him. The sooner she does, the quicker they can help her sister and the others. Only he cannot understand just how hard it is for her to tell him what she knows.

'I do,' she says.

'I need you to tell me, Hannah. Once we know we can work on getting your sister and all the others out safely.'

Hannah nods, but she doesn't really know where she should start. Eventually she decides that maybe the best place is the beginning.

'There was a boy,' she begins. 'A boy called Raff, short for Rafferty but everyone called him Raff.'

The DI screws his eyes up, frowning in concentration.

'If you search for him online, you'll find him. Rafferty Jones. It'll say he died in an accident at Bluestone Quarry.' Hannah pauses. 'Only that isn't the truth,' she adds. 'He was killed.'

The detective's mouth opens in surprise. He clearly wasn't expecting this.

'But those who killed him got away with it,' Hannah goes on. The skin on her arms is covered in tiny goose-bumps and, despite the jumper she is wearing, she's visibly shivering.

She watches how the detective's gaze travels in the direction of the marina even though they cannot see it from inside this room, and how his eyes narrow as he starts to piece it together. 'All of them?' he questions, making a sweeping motion with his hand. 'All of the people inside were responsible?'

'No. Not all of them,' she tells him. 'One of them was his best friend.'

He turns back to her, realisation dawning. 'His best friend?' he repeats.

She nods. Neither of them say it. That this is the one who's responsible for what's happening today.

## Monday afternoon, 12.37 p.m.

*I turn my attention back to her: the ringleader. I tell her to stop her tears. 'They're too late,' I hiss.*

*They each played their part. Besides her there was her sidekick, my old friend who didn't speak out when she could have. Then there was the one who carried the plan through, and finally the one who made sure they could cover it up. At least, this is how I have always imagined it.*

*What I do know is that they were probably protected by their families but more importantly the police weren't looking for a killer. Everything worked out just rosy for them.*

*I wonder if they know I spoke to the police about them once. It was six months after Raff died and I plucked up the courage to talk to the officer who not only lived nearby, but was the one who'd had the awful job of telling Raff's parents their son was dead.*

*'I don't think it was an accident,' I told him.*

*He looked at me with a frown that conveyed he thought I was mad. 'What are you talking about, kid?'*

*'I think someone killed him.' I pulled out a notebook where I had been recording the evidence I had been gathering, and handed it over to him, open on the page where I'd begun making notes.*

*He took it from me and stared at the pages, his eyebrows beginning to rise. 'This is your evidence?' he said to me. 'Against the* kids you have listed here?' He prodded a fat finger against the list of names and chuckled as he passed me back my notebook, and I felt my face flush in splotches of red that crawled down my throat. 'Stay out of trouble,' he said to me, pointedly.

Like I was the one doing something awful. Like I was the one who had killed someone.

I was right to think no one would ever believe me.

I tore the pages out of my notebook, one by one, as tears streaked my face. I ripped each of them into tiny shreds and flung them out of the open window of my bedroom, letting the wind carry them away. There was nothing I could do, and it became a cruel lesson that life isn't fair. But then again, we know that, don't we? I don't need to tell you that.

'We've told you: what happened to Raff had nothing to do with us,' Jacob says. I turn to him. It doesn't surprise me he's the one remaining adamant. He has been like this all morning; defiant, trying to maintain control.

His lip is curled into what comes across as a snarl, and whether he means it to or not, in a flash I see the way he used to laugh at me, leering, with that lopsided grin I used to hate but all the other girls seemed to love.

The sight of Jacob Hamilton makes me sick. Or Jake as we knew him then. Did he use his full name when he started work? Or when he met his rich wife?

Twenty-five years ago, just like we buried Raff and his mum, I'd decided I had no option but to bury the truth of what happened. My best friend was dead and there was nothing I could do to bring him back. Maybe there was no alternative but to get on with my life.

*I thought that if I didn't see Jake and the others any longer, I could gradually begin to forget. After all, there were only a couple more years left of school until everyone went their own way, scampering off in different directions to live their lives. If they were out of sight and out of mind, then I wouldn't have to think about them anymore. They couldn't cause me any further pain.*

*Only it wasn't that easy. I didn't forget. And I certainly never forgave. In fact, I couldn't help myself listening in to snippets of gossip if I heard one of their names mentioned, as I wondered what they were doing and how life had turned out for them, comparing it to my own.*

*Over the years it became even easier to keep track of what they were up to with sites like Facebook meaning I could dip into their lives whenever I wanted. I knew when one of them met someone, got married, where they went on holiday. It wasn't an obsession, but I also couldn't help myself.*

*Jacob was the first one whose picture I saw again. Ten years ago, on Facebook. I'd like to say he just popped up but that isn't how it happened. I was falling down a dark rabbit hole, searching out their names, looking for ways to torment myself, for reasons none of us can ever understand, but we do it nonetheless, don't we?*

*Really it would have been nice never to have seen his face again, but there it was smirking on the screen of my phone.*

*His smattering of posts and photos told me everything I needed to know about him. Though he isn't much of a social media user himself, he makes up for his few posts with a number of 'friends' and plentiful details highlighting his university and career successes like it is a CV.*

*I studied Jacob's progress with disgust over the years, scurrying up the corporate ladder like a rat, only ever interested in* himself. He works in the City, clearly making enough money to afford his fancy lifestyle in London, and he married a woman called Liv, who is naturally beautiful. I wonder how she ended up with a self-centred arsehole like Jake Hamilton and whether she could imagine how her husband used to snatch my rucksack off my back and rummage through it, making out he was looking for something to eat, because surely someone my size would have plenty in there.

'Yes, but I don't believe you had nothing to do with it,' I say to him now, taking a step closer to him. His eyes flash with defiance.

'Have you ever told Liv about what happened?' I ask him.

He swallows at the sound of her name. 'Don't bring my wife into this,' he says after a beat.

Ah, I have hit a nerve. Is it possible he actually loves someone other than himself? 'I don't expect you have,' I go on. 'Does she know about the way you asked me if I had ever been kissed?'

He probably doesn't even remember it. Not like I do.

'You came right up to my face,' I say, taking a step closer. 'Asking if I had been, just to try and amuse your friends, and then you said, "Would you like to be kissed?"'

Jacob frowns but to my surprise doesn't say anything.

'And then you ran your finger down my cheek.' I can still feel it now. How such a small gesture could feel so intimate. I had closed my eyes, so I didn't have to see him grinning at me, pushing down the vomit that was rising into my mouth. 'And then you said, "Oh, it looks like you're enjoying this," and you laughed. And they all laughed at me too.'

I remember the way he leant closer, the heat of his breath searing my skin. I wanted to pull away, but I couldn't move.

*'And then you said, "Nah, you're alright. I'd rather not." Do you remember any of that, Jake?'* I say.

*I had never been more repulsed by anyone, and yet when I had opened my eyes, he was still smirking at me, one eyebrow raised like he truly believed every girl in the school must love the idea of being kissed by him.*

*Mum once called him cheeky. 'He's got a naughty side to him,' she'd laughed, like that was a good thing.*

*Yes, he had a naughty side to him. He was a murderer. Jake Hamilton was a murderer, just like all the others.*

I thought Jacob would be the hardest to get to the Isle of Wight within a week. But it turns out people jump through hoops when they're scared of their past being revealed.

All it took was a message on LinkedIn, from a fabricated username, suggesting it might be from one of the others. One of them is going to speak, *it said.* We need to talk.

The date and time were given: Monday at 7 a.m. at The Boatyard café on the marina.

I'd set the wheels in motion with that first message. I remember how my hands were shaking as I hit send, throwing my phone down on the table in front of me, clutching a hand to my mouth as I considered what I was doing.

No. It was the right thing. I needed it. I wanted the truth, an admission of what had happened that day. I wanted them to feel just a fraction of what I felt and to understand true fear like Raff would have done at the quarry. Let them stare their own death in the face, begging for their lives like he would have done.

I imagined them then as characters in a puppet show, with me holding their strings. Finally, I would have control.

*Do you think you might have understood if I told you what I was thinking? There's a chance you would. I could imagine you saying, 'I'll go in there with a gun myself.' But you wouldn't have meant it. You'd have thought I was joking, really, and when you realised I wasn't, you'd have talked me out of it.*

'I'm telling you the truth,' Jacob says. 'We weren't anywhere near the quarry when Raff died. We had nothing to do with it. We told you that then, and I'm telling you again now. Whatever you think happened, it didn't. So this – this has to stop. You have to stop.'

I lift the gun and point it in his face, watching his boldness waver as I brush my finger against the trigger. 'Just try me,' I mutter. Right now, I want him dead.

# Liv

Liv watches as the main doors to the marine's unit building close behind DI Field and the woman he was escorting into a side room.

'She knows something,' Liv says to Katy. 'What does she know?' *Who is she?* Liv wonders. Someone new, someone they haven't seen down here before.

'I don't know,' her friend says, shaking her head. She peers at Liv, frowning. 'She could be a police officer?'

Liv doesn't think so. There was such a sense of urgency in the detective's face as he ushered her in, like she had something he wanted.

'There's so many people here,' Joyce is saying as she holds on to Liv's arm.

Liv isn't sure it was the right choice bringing her mother-in-law here, but she had to get out of her house. The pictures of happy smiling sixteen-year-olds in the yearbook were starting to swim in and out of focus. Jacob's, Daniel's, and then Eleanor's too. Even now their faces are imprinted on the back of Liv's eyelids, and she doesn't know how she will ever erase them.

There is more to this than her husband having an affair. She knows it must be the case that this goes further back, which makes it feel more sinister. It is bigger than his having another woman, a situation that she now thinks she could cope with. Whatever this is, it means that someone lured her husband to the marina this morning to hold him hostage – potentially to kill him because of it.

Liv shudders as she lets out a low cry. Who is she married to?

She cannot begin to imagine what Jacob has done to warrant this. She doesn't know where to start, but what she is acutely aware of is how easy it has been to believe him guilty of something.

And now she is thinking that she is having his baby and so, no matter what happens, if he walks out of this alive, he will always be in her life. Despite his past, she cannot walk away from him. She is trapped; tethered to her husband by an unborn child.

It is a crushing realisation that not only is she married to a man she does not know, but she has already given up on the person she once believed she loved.

## Monday afternoon, 12.44 p.m.

*While Jacob keeps protesting that they weren't at the quarry when Raff died, I notice the way Eleanor's eyes flick towards him nervously, her lips slightly parted like she wants to say something but doesn't dare. It is like it always was with Jacob in charge. Not even a gun being waved in his face is breaking them. It is not how I imagined today going for a number of reasons.*

*Eleanor wasn't always so nervous. She was the ringleader at the start and was just as outspoken as Jacob. Has she changed so much? Does being a mother do that to you?*

*'You have children of your own now, Eleanor,' I say to her. 'You must see that what you did was wrong.'*

*She nods her head, almost imperceptibly as if she doesn't want to admit it out loud.*

*Her eyes don't leave me as I wave the gun in Jacob's face. Her hands are trembling as they have been all morning.*

*'I know it was,' she says in a whisper. 'I know how awful I was, and I'm sorry.'*

*'Are you?' I ask. 'Would you be sorry if you weren't here, right now?'*

*'Yes,' she says, adamantly. 'I've always regretted it.' Her eyes are pleading with me, but I cannot work out if it's true or if she's*

*just scared for her life. Maybe motherhood hasn't changed her and she's just the same self-centred person she always was.*

*Pretty, skinny Elle Malone. Jacob wasn't really interested in me or Raff, he just got his kicks from making his girlfriend laugh. When it comes down to it, everything happened because of her. I have wondered over the years who I hated most. Jacob or Eleanor? It is a fine line.*

*'Why did you do it?' I ask her. 'Why did you think it was okay to be so cruel?'*

*'I don't know,' she whimpers, shaking her head. 'I don't know.'*

*'You need to try harder than that, Eleanor,' I cry as I swing the hand that is holding the gun so it points at her.*

*'Because I was unhappy,' she sobs, her eyes staring at the barrel of the gun. 'Because I thought that if I could make someone else unhappy then I would feel better about myself. I don't know,' she begs, looking up at me now. 'I was a teenager. I don't know why I did or said the things I did. I was a stupid child myself.'*

*'You made my life miserable. You made me feel like I was worthless,' I tell her. 'You had the power to make everyone around you do whatever you pleased,' I add, waving my arm to indicate the others. 'Because of how you looked. And you knew exactly what you were doing.'*

*The tears continue to flow down her face as her teeth bite into her bottom lip.*

*'You still do it now,' I say. 'I've seen your Instagram posts. All you want is for everyone to see what a perfect life you have.'*

*'My life isn't perfect,' she says. 'It's anything but.'*

*I cock my head, intrigued by her sudden burst of honesty.*

*'Why do you think I do that? Why do you think anyone posts*

*their life on social media? I only show everyone the parts I want them to see.'*

*My hand curls around the gun, gripping it tighter.*

*'I've spent the last six months in therapy,' she cries. 'I'm scared every time my boys are out of my sight that something bad is going to happen to them. I have a mother who puts me down at every possible opportunity and a husband—' She stops abruptly.*

*'And a husband . . . ?'*

*Eleanor shakes her head. 'This isn't why we're here,' she says, quietly.*

In a way it is, *I think. 'Humour me,' I tell her. 'A husband who – what?'*

*She blinks, lets out a breath. 'A husband who I don't believe I've ever been in love with.' She wipes away the tears that are pooling on her cheeks. 'I have no one I can call a close friend and as my counsellor has helped me realise, I never have had. I imagine anyone reaching adulthood looks back at girls like me and realises that I was only ever* perceived *as popular. No one* actually *liked me.'*

*Whatever I expected from Eleanor today, it was not this. 'You had* my *friend,' I tell her, my gaze flicking to the woman beside her. Our eyes lock, briefly, before I turn back to Eleanor. But even as I've uttered those words, I know she is right.*

*'Please, let me go. My boys are my world. They'll be coming out of school soon and they won't know where I am.' The pain in her face is real – the idea that she won't be at the school gates to meet them is palpably too much for her to bear.*

*Tears stream down her cheeks. She can't look away from me, even for a second, as if she's scared that if she turns away for too long, I might pull the trigger.*

*There were plenty of occasions inside Raff's dad's shed when we had talked over the idea of killing them and laughed about it in the full knowledge we would never do anything so abhorrent. There were many times I would have liked to, but that isn't what today is about.*

*I don't want to kill her. I don't want to kill anyone. But they don't need to know that.*

*'What would you do if they were being bullied?' I ask her.*

*'I would do anything,' she says. 'Anything to make it stop.'*

*My hand falters on the grip. A momentary lapse and I want to drop the gun to my side in defeat. I am so tired. We have been here so long. And Eleanor's honesty has shocked me. She seems so genuine. Maybe I could let her go, so she can make it to the school gates on time.*

*But then inside my head I hear her laughter again and her words come back to me. The sight of her long legs swinging casually over the wall as I rounded the corner; the feeling that I might wet myself. Every day I'd prayed she'd leave me alone. She never did.*

*'If it wasn't for you none of this would have happened,' I say. 'Raff wouldn't be dead.'*

*'I didn't kill him,' she cries as Jacob calls out her name to stop her speaking.*

*'Elle!' She stops and his tone is calm as he says, far too pleasantly, 'No one killed Raff. He had an accident.' His eyes flash a warning to her. He is scared after all, I realise now. He thinks if they admit the truth, I am going to kill them.*

# Gareth

The police are scuttling around, faster-paced, more urgency in their actions. Something has changed. Or this is how it seems to Gareth. Though what, he does not know.

He keeps among the crowd gravitating to the barrier, as if by moving closer they may get a sense of what's going on. He couldn't bear it stuck up at the top of the road. One by one all the other relatives had dispersed anyway until he was the last one remaining at the marina.

He has been standing here a while now, contemplating what he can do. Deliberating over whether to make a run for it, knowing he doesn't actually have it in him. It wouldn't be a wise move.

But still, he is better off down here, close enough to hear the rumours that circulate.

'They're going in,' someone near to him says.

'In?' Gareth replies. 'Into The Boatyard?'

The man who said this is a head shorter than Gareth. He nods in response. "Course they are. What do you think all this sudden commotion is about?'

Gareth frowns, nodding himself too now, urging the man to carry on, because he obviously knows more than Gareth does. He might be a journalist who has seen this kind of thing before. He could shed some light on what course of action the police are plotting.

'Then what?' Gareth asks. 'I mean what will they actually do?'

'Well, they'll send the firearms unit in, won't they? I mean those guys will be hovering round here anyway, you know that, right?'

Gareth looks about him, but he cannot see anyone noticeably carrying a firearm.

'They'll be down there, watching the place. They'll have their guns trained on the building, ready to open fire.' The man acts it out, using his hands to mimic holding a rifle.

Gareth frowns and the other man makes out he is firing, the recoil startling him.

He leans closer. 'And then – shit!' He whistles through his teeth, pressing his hands together and then flailing them out like an explosion. Then he stands back and grins at Gareth with a display of crooked teeth.

'Why are you laughing?' Gareth asks him. He no longer thinks this is a journalist with any important insight.

'Well, who knows what happens then, mate,' he says, still smiling. 'You just need to watch this space.'

Gareth stares down at the man. 'My wife is in that building.' His hands are clenched into fists that he's never come close to using before he hit the garden shed earlier today. A surge of anger rises within him. 'We've got two boys who love her more than anything in the world and I don't know that she's going to come out of there alive. So why are you laughing?'

'Okay, mate, steady on,' he says, chuckling again but more nervously this time.

'Don't laugh,' Gareth tells him as he jabs a finger at the man, who's now regarding him with curiosity. 'And don't you dare whistle like this is just some source of entertainment for you.'

People around them are stopping conversations and turning to look in their direction as they creep a little closer.

Someone holds their phone up to Gareth's face, their expression blank; unmoved by anything other than getting some good footage to share on social media.

'What are you doing?' Gareth shouts as he lurches forward and grabs for the phone, stumbling as the man behind it jumps out of his way. 'Stop filming me!'

A burst of mocking laughter rises, and he looks about to find the culprit among the sea of faces surrounding him.

Gareth is back in the playground again, a ten-year-old boy being taunted by the others for having curly hair and needing to wear bulky prescription glasses.

In his head he hears the chants: *Four-eyed freak, Gareth!* He remembers the day a boy in Year 6 grabbed them and tore them off his head, throwing them onto the ground so kids could take it in turns to jump on them.

Long before he met Eleanor, Gareth had cut his hair short and started wearing contact lenses.

'Your lovely curls,' his mum had said to him, as she touched a tuft of what remained on his head. She looked so sad, but it was easier to give in to the bullies than to stand out.

But today Gareth isn't in the mood to let anyone laugh at

him, or film him, or make out that this is nothing more than entertainment in their otherwise dull existences.

'Who laughed at me?' he says. 'Which one of you thinks it's funny that my wife is being held hostage by some mentalist?'

'Looks like *you* might be the mentalist,' someone shouts out.

Gareth is shaking. His hands are trembling and his legs feel like jelly, but he is ready to punch one of them and it doesn't matter who.

Imagine if they caught that on camera and uploaded it to YouTube. He doesn't know if his wife and boys would be proud of him or not, but he wouldn't be proud of himself.

'How do you know it isn't your wife who's holding everyone hostage?' another man asks him in a serious tone of voice.

That does it. It's the moment Gareth curls his fist into a ball and punches the man squarely in the face.

'Oh my God!' someone cries as the commotion is quickly broken up by one of the police officers readily on hand. The man's nose is bleeding. Blood pouring out of it.

The policeman grips on to Gareth's arm and steers him out of the crowd. 'Aren't you Mr Lombard?' he questions.

Gareth feels like he has been punctured, breath emptying out of him in one sharp puff. He feels like he wants to cry. 'I didn't mean to do it.'

'You can't go around hitting people,' the officer mutters.

'Will he press charges?' Gareth asks. 'I need to pick my boys up from school if . . .' He tails off. If Eleanor can't do it, is what he is imagining.

Gareth doesn't know what he would do without the only woman he has ever loved. He can't envisage a life without her. He has been with her since he was twenty-two years old.

It doesn't matter that she's been having therapy, all that matters is that she's getting the help she needs. He will stand by her whatever happens next. He'll be there, like he's always been there. All he wants is to have her back with him and the boys.

But now look at him. He has let all of them down. He is being led away by a police officer for punching someone. What if he goes and gets himself arrested? Who will look after their boys now?

## Detective Inspector Aaron Field
### 12.50 hours

Aaron steps outside the room and calls Kelly on his mobile. 'Rafferty Jones,' he says. 'Died in June 2000. Find out what you can about his death.' He fills her in on what Hannah has told him so far, and even though there will be little information if it was ruled an accident, he wants to know everything he can.

'Do we think she's telling the truth?' Kelly asks.

Aaron thinks of Hannah and how haunted she looked as she told the story. 'I don't see why she would lie,' he says before being momentarily distracted by the crowd. 'What the hell's going on at the barricade?'

'Gareth Lombard punched a journalist.'

'Great,' he mutters.

'Good for him, I say. So, this is all about revenge?' Kelly reverts back to the topic in hand. 'What do you think's going on inside there? It feels like the stakes have been raised somehow.'

'I don't know,' Aaron sighs, rubbing his chin. 'I need you

to speak to Sarah Connelly urgently. One way or another we need to make contact with them.'

It's been five and a half hours since five individuals entered the building. He dreads to imagine what might be unfurling and still hopes they can get them out safely. But right now, Aaron isn't confident it's going to end well.

'My God,' Kelly murmurs. 'They got away with murder then?'

'Until now,' he says and, though he won't admit it, soon he will consider where his sympathies lie. And whether the only person he actually feels sorry for inside that building is Connie Parish.

## Monday afternoon, 12.50 p.m.

'No one killed Raff. He had an accident,' Jacob has warned Eleanor. *On the other side of her, Daniel places a hand on her arm. I'm not sure if his gesture is for reassurance or to get her to stop talking.*

*Daniel Williams the writer, who has been watching me all day like a hawk, like he is trying to second-guess my next move when it must be clear to him I have no idea what it will be myself.*

*He doesn't say much but when he does his words are thoughtful.* 'We all need to work out where we go from here,' *he says, calmly.* 'How we get ourselves out of this situation.'

*He'll be wishing it's one he hadn't got into in the first place. A message was sent to Daniel through his author page, saying the four of them needed to talk urgently.* They're reopening the inquiry into his death, *the message had read, and we need to* make sure our stories are straight.

*This is one story he definitely won't want published.*

*Daniel is looking at me earnestly.* 'I don't think you want to hurt anyone,' *he goes on.* 'So let's focus on what we have to do to get us all out of this situation safely.'

'Not until I hear the truth,' I tell him. 'Until then, we're not going anywhere. Though I don't imagine you want it coming out, do you, Daniel? Not when you've got so much to lose.'

*He parts his lips, ready to speak, and yet it feels like he's weighing up what I just said.*

'How important is your career to you?' I say. 'More than your wife?'

'No. There's no contest,' he replies, earnestly. 'I love my wife more than anything in the world.'

'Then why not come clean and tell me what happened? So we can all get out of here?'

*I know it isn't that simple. I am sure Daniel does too as he weighs up whether admitting his part in Rafferty's death will secure his escape.*

'I saw you at Bluestone Quarry six months ago,' I say.

*Daniel pulls back, dropping his hand from Eleanor's arm.*

'You were sitting on a rock and you had a notebook with you. At first it looked like you were sketching. But then I realised you wouldn't be drawing. Art isn't your thing, writing is. You were making notes.' *It's a guess, but the way he flinches tells me I'm right.*

*He looks down at his feet only briefly before he meets my eyes again, because he hasn't taken his gaze off me the whole morning. I've been thinking it most likely that Jacob would be the one to lunge for me. I have kept just enough distance from him in case he does. But now I wonder if it's more likely Daniel would.*

*He is the cleverest by far of their little group. He was the one I thought I might be able to get through to. The last time I saw him this close in the flesh was the day of Raff's funeral when I'd escaped out of the back of the church just before the end of the service. I made the excuse that I needed the toilet, but the reality was I couldn't breathe. I'd wanted to die myself.*

*I was standing with my back to the cold stone of the wall, waiting for you and Mum to come out, when suddenly Daniel appeared.*

*He had walked out too for whatever his own reasons were, but I liked to think they were the same as mine to some degree. Maybe he couldn't breathe either.*

*When he spotted me, he looked like he'd seen a ghost. He just stood there, staring, wide-eyed and fearful, and I did the same in return. I was plain terrified whenever I saw any of them, and in that moment I saw my terror reflected back in his gaze; he was afraid I knew what they had done.*

*Other than my one-time friend, I felt like I knew Daniel better than I did the others in that group. Maybe because of the poems he'd been writing since the age of eight that were published in the local magazines I'd find scattered on our coffee table. I thought someone who expressed themselves with such heartfelt emotion must be a good person.*

I tell him this now. 'I always thought you'd be the one to come clean. I didn't think you would be able to live with what you'd done,' I say.

He recoils at this, visibly shuddering. I cock my head. 'You can't, can you?' I guess. 'Has it always been there? Is that why you were down at the quarry?'

'No. That isn't why,' he says.

'You're lying. Why are you lying to me? Why can't you just tell me the truth?'

Because as soon as he does his career will be over. He's got so much more to lose than he did back then. I'd tried and failed to get him to admit it outside the church; the only hope I have now is that maybe he'll come clean if he believes his life is at risk.

*Back then, my breath had caught in my throat with all the things I wanted to say to him as we stood there staring at each other, but all that came out was, 'I know what you did.'*

*He didn't collapse in a heap on the ground, admitting it was all their fault and begging for my forgiveness. Daniel didn't say a word. In the end, he walked off, looking back over his shoulder just once.*

*But he didn't need to say anything. He hadn't denied it, and I'd seen the sheer panic in his eyes. I knew outside that church that I was right in believing one or all of them had murdered my friend.*

*All I could do was watch him walk away until eventually he disappeared. I was still shaking when you and Mum came out. She said to me, 'I think we should go home now.' I didn't want to; I wanted to go back to Raff's house where I thought his mum would have made sandwiches for everybody. I wanted to sit in his dad's shed and watch reruns of* Saved by the Bell. *But instead I had started sobbing loudly.*

*'We should never have come, it's too much for her,' Mum said. And so I never went to their house or sat in his dad's shed ever again.*

*Maybe Daniel isn't the one who is going to admit what they did after all. Perhaps I've been giving him too much credit and he isn't as good a person as I used to think. How can he be when he's happily lived with a secret like this for more than half his life?*

'Your fans are going to find out what you did,' I say to him now. 'And your wife. So, one way or another, you must know it's all over for you anyway.'

# Rosa

'What have you done?' Rosa whispers to the screen of the laptop, the email from her husband to Jacob Hamilton glaring back at her, her finger still poised over the delete button. Does she erase the evidence? Is that the person she is?

She holds a hand over her mouth, her fingers trembling against her lips.

*You will be there? Next Monday?*

The police were right; this is all because of her husband.

Theirs was supposed to be a marriage based on trust. A love story that has flourished from the moment they first spoke on that bench in the park, to where they are now. For twelve years Daniel has been by her side. As she grew up through her twenties and into her thirties, he has been her rock, and she has never once imagined life without him.

Is it him? Is Daniel the one holding the gun? She no longer sees an alternative option.

A text message comes through from her dad telling her their flight from Scotland has landed in Southampton airport and asking her what has happened in the hour they have been out of contact.

She doesn't know how to respond. It'll break their hearts to think of their son-in-law as anyone other than the Daniel they know and love.

Rosa looks at her watch and realises with a sickening sense of dread she's been away from the marina for too long. She doesn't know what's going on down there and needs to get back. Anything could have happened there while she's been at home.

She springs out of the seat, closing the laptop with a snap, leaving the email untouched. Then she grabs a coat from the hook on her way out and gets in the car, making the journey back as her mind flicks through memories of her husband, searching for anything over the years that might have warned her Daniel was someone she didn't really know.

But there is nothing. Not one thing that comes to her.

She pulls over in the same space she had parked in earlier and jumps out of the car. A bigger crowd has gathered around the barricade further down the road since she's been gone, and there's a palpable sense of urgency in the air. It is a buzz that wasn't there when she left.

Something has happened, she is certain of it. She picks up her pace, running towards the gathering and searches for DI Field. She finds another police officer in his absence.

'My husband, Daniel, is in there,' she says to him. 'What's happening?'

'Mrs Williams?' He looks over his shoulder and steers her away from the crowd. 'Why don't we go back up the road and get you settled. I can get someone to come and talk to you.'

'I just want to know what's happened,' she cries as he takes her by the elbow and manoeuvres her away. 'Is he hurt? Is he *dead*?' she screams. Or is it that they know it is him?

Rosa stops in her tracks.

'As far as we know, nothing has happened inside The Boatyard. There's every reason to believe your husband is okay,' he tells her. 'But someone will come and speak to you.'

Rosa glances around as they walk back up the road, spotting Gareth Lombard standing on a grassy verge, a police officer by his side. He looks as crazy as she feels right now.

'I'm fine,' she says, shaking the policeman's hand off her. 'I can make my own way.' She doesn't want to be led away. She *wants* to know what the hell is going on.

'Okay,' he says eventually. 'But you'll need to make your way to that building.'

'I will,' she tells him as she waits for him to finally to leave her and make his way back. She watches him talk into his radio as he looks over his shoulder at her, making her feel like she's the criminal.

'Hey,' she shouts out to a man with a camera. 'What's happening?'

'Don't you know?' he says, his eyes almost dancing. 'There's a gunman in The Boatyard. He's holding four people hostage.'

'Of course I know that,' she says. 'You said "he". Do they know it's a man?'

He shrugs and frowns at her. 'No clue. I guess it could be a woman. But the police seem to know what's going on. They've been interviewing someone up there who arrived in a police car.' He points to the marine unit where Ede Hogan had collapsed earlier. 'We think she must know something. DI Field, the one who's in charge, he's been with her for the last half-hour.'

The detective must know what has happened. Maybe, somehow, they have found Daniel's email by now. What does it matter if she deletes it from his computer, when someone else has already received it?

She bends over and throws up on the grass as the man jumps out of the way. She doesn't want to believe this is her husband. Daniel wouldn't do anything like this. Not the man she loves, the man she has shared a bed with every night for the last twelve years.

'You alright, love?' the man says, still backing away from her as her phone starts ringing from her coat pocket. She pulls it out to see *Dad* on the screen.

Rosa presses to accept the call and puts the phone to her ear.

'Rosa? Honey, what's happening? We've landed in Southampton and we're in a taxi to the port. Did you get my message?'

'I think it might be him, Dad,' she says. 'Daniel.'

'Oh dear Lord, Rosa, of course it isn't!' She hears her mum in the background, asking what's going on.

'Dad, I found an email he wrote to someone,' she goes on. 'And I don't know what to do.'

'Darling, we're on our way. We're getting there as quickly as we can, don't jump to any conclusions. For what it's worth, your mother and I – we don't believe this is down to Daniel,' he tells her. 'We don't believe there's a bad bone in his body.'

Rosa nods in response and tries to take some comfort from what he's saying, only she can't stop flashes of Daniel's latest book from slicing through her mind like a thousand knives.

'Only *I* do,' she tells her father with a disquieting realisation. 'I do believe it.'

# Ede

Ede can hear a buzz of activity around her though she can't distinguish any of the voices. Stark white lights find their way through the crack between her eyelids, but it hurts too much to keep them open.

Her body is sore, like she has run a marathon, though why anyone would want to do that Ede has never been able to fathom. Memories come back to her in scraps. Marjorie's early-morning phone call while she was dusting. The police officers on her doorstep. The marina. Jennie.

*Jennie.*

Ede struggles to open her eyes against the glare, blinded by panic and the flickering fluorescent tubes above her. Her body feels like it has been strapped to the bed she is lying on, but she is in too much pain to move. The wires that snake out of her aren't holding her down, just dripping what she supposes is much-needed morphine into her bloodstream.

*Jennie?* She tries to call out. If anything happens to her—

Tears spill from Ede's eyes, trickling down her papery cheeks. If only their last conversation hadn't been what it was. What if the last thing Ede had the chance to say to her granddaughter was that she wanted to end her life in Switzerland?

What a stupid thing to say when there is so much more

she could have voiced. Age is supposed to bring wisdom, and Ede thought she had this in abundance when she was writing a letter to Jennie, one her granddaughter would only receive once she was gone.

Ede had wanted to articulate all the things she has tried to say over the years but has never quite got right. How she had such big dreams for Jennie. She had choices and talent; she could do so much with her life.

Ede refuses to believe it is too late for Jennie. The girl isn't even forty years old yet. She is half her grandmother's age and time is still on her side.

The letter that Ede has left alongside her will at the solicitor's was one of the hardest things she has ever written, knowing she would not get to see Jennie's face when she reads it.

In it she's asked her granddaughter to look at her life and ask herself if she is happy. *Don't be afraid of the answers,* Ede has written. *Because you are bound not to like them all.*

She wrote that she only finally became content with her own life when she reached her early sixties.

*By then I had experienced enough to know what I wanted. I'd lived through grief and come out the other side. As you will again,* she assured her.

*But please, Jennie, all I ask is that you find out what it is you truly want. And maybe it won't be the dreams of travel I had for you. And that is fine. It may be that, once you have searched your soul, you conclude that you don't want to be anywhere other than the place you are in right now. And that is also fine.*

*All I ask is that you are honest with yourself. If the answer is that you would rather be somewhere else, then I beg of you, go.*

*Start living!!* She had finished with a couple of exclamation marks in an attempt to make it light-hearted.

Ede had thought the letter rather poetic when she had finished and laid her pen down. She wished someone had done the same for her when she was younger. The wisdom that only comes from old age hadn't been imparted to her; her parents had died when she was in her late thirties.

With the final chapter of her life ahead, Ede has also been questioning what she's done right and wrong over the years, and every one of those questions centres around Jennie, because there is nothing more important to her.

Did she tell her she loved her enough? *Yes. She is certain of this.*

Did she always put her first? *As much as she could.* Though there were times when her own daughter absorbed Ede's focus.

Did she ever take her eye off the ball? *Yes. When Jennie was a teenager, she certainly did.* Because for a long while Shona desperately needed Ede, and her heart was consumed with fear for her daughter.

There is a memory that sticks in Ede's mind, and it is one she has never been able to let go of. One evening Jennie had walked in the door from school with a prize in her hand.

'What's that for?' Ede had asked her, taking it from the girl and reading the engraving.

'Most improved in English.' Jennie had shrugged. 'It's no big deal.'

'It is a big deal!' Ede had told her. 'Oh, I am so proud of you. I wish I could have been there to have seen you collect it.'

Jennie didn't reply but Ede caught the way her granddaughter's cheeks flushed red.

'Your mum would have too,' Ede went on, watching her carefully, knowing she was missing something.

'Where is Mum?' Jennie asked, a faux-lightness to her voice.

Shona was in bed, Ede remembers. Sleeping off another hangover.

The next day Ede was waiting in the post office queue when someone she vaguely recognised leant forward and said to her, 'Congratulations to your Jennie. I saw her collecting her prize yesterday.'

It turned out there had been a ceremony that parents were invited to, and yet Jennie hadn't mentioned it to either of them. When asked why, she told Ede that she didn't think it was important.

Ede understood this wasn't the truth, but she didn't press it. She knew exactly why Jennie hadn't invited either of them. She didn't want her mother there for fear she would embarrass her, but she wouldn't invite Ede without her. She would rather have no one than make her mum upset.

Even now this particular memory breaks Ede's heart. It is the goodness in her granddaughter that always shines through.

There was a period when Ede found it harder and harder to get Jennie to open up about anything. But then, that wasn't surprising when, at the age of twelve, she nearly lost her mum, and Ede was back and forth to the hospital to see her daughter rigged up to machines that kept her breathing. All while holding as much of the horrendous truth back from Jennie as she possibly could.

Maybe Ede did let some things slip then, because she had to. There was no choice but to get a key cut and give Jennie instructions for making herself snacks and how much TV she could watch. Dinner became later than Ede would have liked, bedtimes no longer a routine. Some nights Ede wondered how long it had been since Jennie had last had a bath.

These were the years when she might have been able to persuade Jennie to carry on her studies, go to university, travel the world.

But then look at her now – you would never guess the childhood she'd endured if you met her; the damage that having an alcoholic for a mother and an absent father could have done. Jennie will do anything for anyone.

When Marjorie was sick, it was Jennie who ran all her errands and queued for prescriptions, with no regard for catching anything herself when she dropped them off. When someone else up the road broke her leg, Jennie cooked their meals for a fortnight.

Yes, her granddaughter is the kindest person Ede knows.

A coursing pain sears through her head, bypassing the morphine trickling into her veins. Ede looks to one side, searching for a button to press to call for help. She cannot find one. She opens her mouth to yell, but no sound comes out. She is trapped in a nightmare that she no longer has the energy to fight, and she fears she might die on this bed without knowing what happens to Jennie.

And this, she realises, is the worst possible thing to bear.

# Detective Inspector Aaron Field
## 13.00 hours

There's a knock on the door to the room where Aaron is interviewing Hannah Parish. It opens and one of his sergeants pokes his head round. 'Sir? Franklin Henderson's here and he wants to speak to you.'

'What does he want?'

'He won't tell me. Says it's you he must speak to.' The sergeant shrugs.

Aaron frowns. 'Okay, find somewhere for him to wait and I'll get to him as soon as I can.'

'He says it's urgent. Says you'll want to hear this. He seems quite agitated to be fair, sir.'

Aaron glances at Hannah. This *is urgent*, he thinks. 'Two minutes,' he says to her as he gets up and leaves the room, closing the door behind him.

'Make sure she doesn't go anywhere,' he tells the sergeant. 'Where is he?'

'Waiting outside.'

Aaron goes out to where Franklin Henderson is hovering. His eyes are narrowed, as though he is trying to work something out. As though he isn't entirely sure he knows what he wants to say.

'I'm in the middle of an interview,' Aaron says as he approaches.

Henderson nods and looks down at his feet. His hands are shoved inside the deep pockets of his coat.

'You have something urgent to tell me?' Aaron prompts.

'You mentioned some names to me earlier,' he says, finally looking back up at Aaron. 'The people who are inside. The ones I saw going into the building this morning.'

'Yes?'

'I said I didn't recognise any of them, but that's not completely true. Jennie did mention them to me once. The author guy, D. L. Martin . . . She used his real name.'

'Okay?' Aaron questions, wondering where this is going.

'There was an article in the paper about him. Someone had left it on the counter and Jennie was reading it. She said she knew him.' Franklin pauses. 'I don't know why, but she didn't seem herself so when she finished her shift, I asked her if she wanted to come back to my boat. She said she did. She clearly wanted to talk. And that's when . . .' He falters. 'That's when she mentioned the other names to me too.'

'What did she say?' Aaron asks.

Henderson shakes his head. 'Nothing specifically. Nothing that made much sense. But I could see how worked up she was and then suddenly she said she didn't want to talk about them anymore. Said they weren't worth it, but . . .'

'But what?'

'But I had a sense she really didn't like them.' He stops, shrugs. 'Not one bit, though I didn't find out why.'

'And this is what you needed to tell me now?' Aaron says. 'When you could have said as much this morning?'

'I didn't want her to get into trouble. That's why I didn't say anything. She's a good girl, Jennie. I know she is.'

'Mr Henderson—'

'I know I should have said earlier,' Henderson replies. He squints, looks away.

'That isn't what you dragged me out here for, is it?' Aaron says.

A shake of his head. 'Not all of it. I own a gun. It's legal,' he insists. 'I keep it on my boat. Jennie asked me about it when she saw it that time.' He pauses, turns to Aaron. 'When I met you back on my boat, I noticed it was missing.'

'Oh God,' Aaron groans.

'But I know Jennie.' Franklin Henderson is pleading with him now. 'And I know she would never hurt anyone. She's not that kind of person.'

'And yet she's taken your gun,' Aaron says, his voice rising with frustration. 'Which means Jennie Hogan has been holding four people hostage inside that building for almost six hours, and *you* could have stopped that so much sooner,' he spits, shaking his head in despair.

He only just manages to stop himself from adding that if anything happens, this is all on Henderson.

# Monday afternoon, 1.00 p.m.

*I know you must still have so many questions, Gran. Like why didn't I tell you I was being bullied at the time?*

*I assume you can guess the reason: you had enough going on with Mum. But I know you will hate that I didn't. Regardless, you will blame yourself.*

*You knew I was friendly with Raff, but you didn't know how much. You, Mum and I went to his funeral, but neither of you understood how much I was hurting. Mum managed to stay sober until after the service, but she had been in hospital only the week before. I could see the pain in your face: you never let on, but you thought we were going to lose her too.*

*I didn't bring friends back to the house, and you likely understood that was because of her, but you never questioned it. Mum was slowly dying, and that took precedence over the silly, childish things happening to me and so I chose not to burden you with them.*

*Yes, maybe they weren't silly or childish. And if I'd confided in you, you would have helped me at the time. I might have got the support I needed, and, in turn, moved on with my life. We might even have brought them to justice for what they did.*

*And perhaps if I had told you what they were doing from the start, Raff would still be alive. I often think of that too, though I try not to dwell on it.*

*I know it's too late now, but I can tell you the day it started was when Mum turned up at my school for a parents' evening when I was thirteen.*

*I half-thought, half-hoped, she might have forgotten about it. I'd written the times on the calendar for her that morning and told her which entrance she needed to go to. I said to enter the school through the staff car park at the back, and definitely not to go in the front entrance where the other kids and I would be. I wrote those instructions on the calendar too.*

*I'm sure you knew I would much rather you'd attend than Mum, but I still couldn't do that to her, not when she told me she wanted to come. So instead, I bit my lip as always, and convinced myself it would be okay.*

*I saw her as soon as I left the school building, making my way over the playground to the front entrance. She had ignored my instruction to enter via the back, but that was to be the least of my problems. Mum was snaking towards me, kids hopping out of her way as she zig-zagged over the tarmac.*

*Her top was falling down on one shoulder, and I could see the blue lace on the cup of her bra. Mum didn't care about things like that. Topped up with vodka, she didn't realise all the other kids were standing and staring at her, mouths wide open in excitement.*

*I couldn't decide whether to ignore her and hide, or to walk up to her and steer her out of their sight as quickly as I could, when suddenly she toppled forward like her feet were hinged to the ground and fell flat on her face. I don't think she even thought to put her hands down to stop herself.*

*Horrified, I rushed over. 'Mum, are you okay?' I was pleading, despite being aware of the crowd gathering around us, too concerned she'd seriously hurt herself because she wasn't answering.*

*I expected to see a pool of blood start seeping out from underneath her. She was immobile. I thought she was dead.*

*Then she just started laughing, her whole body convulsing with how funny she thought it all was. I rolled her over and she lay on the ground in the middle of the playground, holding up her arms to the sky as she slurred, 'Isn't it all so beautiful, my darling?'*

*Two days later, Eleanor was obsessed.*

*'Your mum had her vodka yet this morning?' she'd shouted at me on the way to school. My face flushed red with embarrassment. 'Is she too drunk to realise you need new shoes?' She looked down at my black patent leather shoes that we'd picked out that summer, scuffed on one toe already. I'd tried to cover it up with black marker because I knew we couldn't fork out for another pair so soon.*

*I was too mortified to say anything to you about Eleanor, and so I didn't breathe a word. Mum didn't make it any better for me, leaving the house in a nightie that barely covered her arse, walking to the corner shop barefoot and coming out with a paper bag-wrapped bottle as I was walking home one day.*

*She could have been beautiful, couldn't she? With her sun-kissed olive skin and her long dark hair. She was only in her thirties then, and I always thought I could have been proud of her in a different life.*

*I don't blame you for not noticing what they were doing to me, Gran. I can't bear the idea that you will blame yourself. I made the choice not to tell you. It is all on me.*

*Besides, when we had buried Raff, the bullying stopped. They weren't bothering me any longer. They avoided me then.*

*And so, I survived the last eighteen months of school, leaving as soon as my GCSEs were done, knowing I didn't have to see them anymore.*

*You kept asking me what I wanted to do with my life, if I wanted to go travelling, not understanding that the idea of that made me feel sick.*

*I couldn't imagine doing any of the exciting things you hoped I might. I was too scared to try anything new for fear something awful would happen. I carefully chose the people to surround myself with, the ones I knew wouldn't hurt me: neighbours we had known for years; friends of yours that you trusted. It was easier to find jobs I could walk away from if the people I worked with turned on me. And so I found comfort in the mundanity of routine and lack of pressure, and I believed that comfort was all I wanted.*

*They had ground me down to a much smaller version of the person I could have been, and while you saw the path I had chosen as a waste, to me it was simply survival.*

*Life carried on like this for a number of years. Maybe ten, fifteen of them passed with me trying to pretend I'd let go of what they did to me and Raff. I didn't confide in you; I didn't go to therapy. I kept pushing down the memories, burying them deeper and deeper where the truth couldn't hurt me.*

*But each time I overheard one of their names mentioned in passing, it chipped away at me. Then, as you know by now, I started searching for them myself: online on Facebook, Instagram, wherever I could.*

*And instead of continuing to lie buried, my resentment started to resurface. All four of them were achieving great things in their careers, getting married, having children, while I was stagnating, never having moved on.*

*I did a double take when I was walking down the high street in Newport five years ago and Daniel's face loomed out of a Waterstones window at me. A cardboard cut-out of him, dressed in a navy V-neck jumper with a white open-collar shirt poking out, his expression so serious as he looked off to one side.*

*Daniel had written their crime thriller of the month. He had made the* Sunday Times *Bestsellers List. Daniel had found success in doing something that he loved, and the idea of it brought a bitter taste to my mouth.*

*I went on to read every one of his novels. Always on my Kindle so you never saw. I hated how good he was: the crime writer who had once committed a crime himself. I remembered how I had once dreamt of being a fashion designer, picturing myself on the living-room floor aged twelve drawing costumes, feeling a bubbling excitement that the world was my oyster. Back then, I thought I could be whatever I wanted to be. We were told that often enough.*

*And as I stood on the pavement outside Waterstones, staring at Daniel, I hated him for following his dreams when I hadn't. I hated every single one of them, all over again. It felt like the day I was told Raff was dead.*

*Still, I tried to move on, but now with more bitterness and regret. And then, two years ago, you told me you were sick. You went through treatment but eighteen months on, we were told it hadn't worked. The doctors advised if you did nothing more, you had months, not years, ahead of you.*

*You told me you couldn't do it any longer. You wanted quality of life, not quantity when the last year and a half had made you feel so awful.*

*I begged you to try again. It was selfish of me, but I couldn't bear to lose you a day too soon.*

*You remained adamant. It was better this way, you said. It was the way it was meant to be.*

*I have never felt fury like it. Just embers at first, a flicker that burnt inside me but would soon start to ignite and take hold. I wasn't angry with you, though it might have seemed that way at times. I was angry about everything that had gone wrong before. And I was angry at the thought of facing a future without the only person in the world I loved in it. How the hell was I supposed to carry on without you?*

*Three weeks ago, you sat down at the kitchen table, picked up a fork that you speared into a lamb chop and told me, 'I want to go to Switzerland. I want to do this on my own terms, before I get too sick.' You tried to explain your reasons, that it was better for me to remember you like this, rather than months down the line when you'd become too poorly, but I refused to listen. You knew how hurt I was, but you had no idea how much my brain was spiralling.*

*I couldn't think straight. I didn't know where else to direct my rage than at the four of them. How dare they get away with taking Raff's life? With taking mine too in a different way. I wanted them to pay. I wasn't going to hurt them, but I wanted the truth to come out, and I wanted to see their lives spectacularly unravel because of it.*

*This was my plan.*

*The Boatyard was supposed to be empty this morning. No one was coming in until midday; my own shift wasn't even supposed to be starting until 11, and though I'd mentioned briefly that I was happy to open beforehand, I hadn't said it would be as early as 7. A cold morning in mid-March: the marina is always dead.*

*I didn't mean to fire the gun first thing; I didn't want anyone knowing we were here. As soon as I had their confessions, I was going to let them go and then watch the fallout.*

*Clearly it hasn't panned out as I hoped.*

*We are all getting desperate, for various reasons. They're desperate to walk out of here alive, I'm desperate for one of them to tell me what happened at the quarry. But without any assurance I will let them go once they do, they aren't prepared to take that risk.*

*I veer between thinking the most likely person to break will be Eleanor or Daniel. Daniel's eyes keep tracking me and I wonder what's more important to him: if it's that his career will landslide now, or that his pretty wife will leave him when she finds out what he has done.*

What about your ex-friend? *you're probably thinking. Why isn't she telling you the truth? She's the only one I haven't told you about yet, Gran, because she broke my heart the most.*

*Like Raff, I never brought her back to the house when we were friends. We met the first week of secondary school, when we sat next to each other in class, and I liked her immediately.*

*Over time I told her things I had never admitted to anyone before. Things like the fact Mum embarrassed me. It felt like someone had punched me in the stomach when I first told her how much I dreaded Mum turning up at school, and how sometimes I hid if I saw her on the way home, so she didn't do anything mortifying in front of the other kids. She said she understood how I could feel that way but still love her.*

*In turn, she said she felt like an only child too, the gap between her and her sister was so big. And that their parents put pressure on them to work hard at school and she already knew they were expecting both their girls to go to university. She made out like these were bad things, to make me feel better, but I thought her life sounded idyllic.*

*I looked forward to going into school to see her every day but at ten-past three, when the final bell rang out, our friendship ended for the night. She didn't come back to mine, and she never invited me to hers either. Maybe because she knew I would see how perfect her family really was.*

*I wasn't surprised that by Year 9 she wanted to make other friends. During the summer her social group expanded while mine suddenly halved in size. We'd clearly drifted apart, and I couldn't really blame her. But then she became best friends with Elle Malone, sitting on the wall outside of school alongside her, mute, pretending what Elle said was funny and too scared to speak out for fear of being ostracised by the so-called popular girls. She never once stood up for me.*

*I think she was the one I wanted to see most today. It was her I wanted to confront, to look into her eyes and ask why she stood by and did nothing.*

*Only she never came.*

*Her sister must have picked up the note I had to post through their door because Hannah is the only one not on social media. And now Connie is sitting here, telling me she shouldn't be.*

*And so, I can't ask, 'Why did you do it, Hannah? Do you think your job absolves you from what you did all those years ago? Do you think working with troubled teenagers makes up for the two lives you helped destroy?'*

*I squeeze my hand tighter around the gun. It is the only thing that helps me regain any control. The walls are closing in tighter. The room feels like it is getting smaller. I cannot look at these people for much longer.*

'If one of you doesn't speak out now, I will pull the trigger again,' I cry.

# Hannah

Hannah waits in the room on her own. DI Field told her he would be two minutes, but it's been longer than that.

Something must have happened. She shuffles to the edge of her seat, wondering whether to stay put or leave and find out, but he wanted her to stay here for him, and Hannah has always followed the rules. Well, almost always.

She feels like she is going to be sick. Waves of nausea have been rolling over her. Sweat beads her forehead. He can't expect her to sit here when lives are in danger, and she is to blame.

Eventually the door opens, and he walks back in and sits down again in the chair opposite.

'My sister shouldn't be there,' she tells him once more. She can't imagine what Connie is doing trapped inside The Boatyard. Her sister will always think she can take care of everything for Hannah. The one and only time she has ever confided her story before now was the night she told Connie, not long after their parents' death.

They had shared secrets, although Connie's were insignificant in comparison. But for Hannah the relief of unburdening herself was immense. She believed she was to blame for them dying. It wasn't just the fact they were coming to pick her up, it was that she deserved it too. Karma.

But Connie could never have anticipated what she was walking into today. She will crack at some point, Hannah fears.

'None of them should be there,' the detective says, grimly.

Tears spill from Hannah's eyes. She nods, agreeing. Her job does not make up for any of this. How conceited of her ever to think she could compensate for what they did by helping others, when the one person she should have helped was Jennie.

But right now, Jennie is holding a gun, and Connie's life is in danger.

Suddenly a loud bang undulates through the air and makes the detective leap out of his seat and rush out of the door.

'What was that?' Hannah cries, close at his heels.

'Stay here,' he tells her, but she follows him outside regardless.

A flock of birds rises rapidly to the skies.

'What was that?' she calls out again, panicked, but he is already running down the hill. He doesn't answer. He doesn't have to. She knows what she heard.

## Monday afternoon, 1.10 p.m.

'Fine!' Daniel says, holding up his hands. 'I'll tell you the truth, Jennie. Just, please, lower the gun.'

I clench my hand around it but lower it slightly.

'It was a prank that went wrong,' he starts. His eyes are glassy as he shakes his head. 'It wasn't supposed to happen. Nothing bad was supposed to happen to him.'

I let go of a breath that feels like it has been lodged in my throat. I'd imagined feeling an instant release when one of them told me. I wait for it to come.

'Daniel . . .' Jacob interrupts, but his tone is resigned.

'Tell me,' I say. 'From the start.'

'I don't even remember whose idea it was in the first place,' Daniel goes on.

'It was mine,' Eleanor chips in. Her hands are shaking as she clutches the bright fabric of her top and twists it. 'I thought it would be a laugh.' She releases one hand and wipes it across her face.

Daniel glances at her then turns back to me. 'Elle wrote a note and gave it to Jake to put through your door. He threw some gravel up at your window and cycled off because he was the quickest and – well, no one else would do it,' he says. 'The idea was that they—' He pauses, clearing his throat. 'That we were just going to tie him up to a tree,' he corrects. 'You were supposed to find him.'

*Daniel visibly shudders and I look at Eleanor who is gaping back at me. She cannot dry her tears quickly enough.*

*'Why?' I say. 'Why were you doing that?'*

*'I don't know.' He shrugs. 'I think everyone was bored. It was something to do, something that was supposed to be a joke.'*

*I feel a swell of disgust rise in my throat. 'You were bored!' I choke. 'He died because you were* bored*?' When Daniel doesn't reply I wave my hand, gesturing for him to go on.*

*'I didn't want to do it,' he says, his words nothing more than a whisper.*

*'Don't you dare put this all on me!' Jacob shouts out.*

*'I'm not. I'm to blame as much as you were. I didn't do anything to stop it. Hannah didn't either,' he says to me. 'We went along with it. We could have said something at any time.'*

*'What happened?' I ask. 'If you went to the woods, how did you end up at the quarry?'*

*'Raff kept running away from us. I don't think anyone had realised how quick on his feet he was.' He looks over at Jacob and waves his arm towards him. 'We,' he says, emphasising the word while trying to convey it was mostly Jacob, 'were chasing him.'*

*'You were too,' Jacob spits.*

*'You were whooping like you were in some rodeo!' Eleanor cries out, turning to Jacob, but taking a step away from him at the same time. 'It was nothing more than a game to you.'*

*'Shit!' he laughs, shaking his head, looking up at the ceiling. 'You think you can all turn the tables on me now? Jennie knows every one of you was there. You've told her as much.'*

*'Anyway,' Daniel goes on, like he's desperate not to lose momentum. He must be thinking that as soon as he gets the story told he is out of here. 'Suddenly we were out the other side, at the*

end of the woods where you reach the quarry. And Raff came to a sudden stop. Probably because we all knew that if you went over the edge of a fifty-foot drop, you'd break a bone at the very least.'

I had always hated it there. The water had run dry back then. It was disused and eerie, and I knew the moment they said Raff's body was found at the bottom that he would never have gone there on his own.

Daniel closes his eyes. 'I still see his face,' he says. 'He knew he had nowhere to go.' He lets out a breath and I feel the tears trickling down my face, the ball of grief and loathing twisting itself into knots inside me.

'He shouted "Boo!"' Daniel says, gesturing towards Jacob. 'It made Raff stumble backwards.'

'You're making shit up now,' Jacob shouts.

'No, he's not,' Eleanor says in a whisper.

'And then he said, "Fine, we'll tie you up here instead,"' Daniel continues, as if Jacob hasn't even spoken. 'And he kept walking towards Raff, and I knew – I just knew that if he wasn't careful, Raff was going to step right off.'

'He must have been so frightened,' I say. My hand trembles upon the butt of the gun. Daniel is sobbing too now, turning away from me, his expression agonised.

'We called out to him to stop. I told him we'd had our fun and we should leave.' He turns to Jacob. 'But you were having none of it!' he cries. 'Every time Raff stepped one way, you mirrored him like you were doing some kind of tango, and you –' he points a shaking finger at Eleanor '– you just stood there laughing.'

Her tears keep coming. There is no denial.

'But we did nothing to stop it happening,' Daniel says. 'And Raff kept getting closer and closer to the edge and Elle had stopped laughing by then,' he recalls. 'And I remember that so clearly. Because we all knew something bad was going to happen, but it was too late to stop it.' He clears his throat, making a horrible whining sound as he does so. 'Raff took a step too far and he went — he disappeared over the edge. He screamed, but then there was this awful silence and none of us could move. We all just stood there, like we were frozen until Elle said, "You need to look." Or something like that, but I couldn't bring myself to look at her, because I didn't know if she was talking to me or not.

'In the end, I went to the edge — I had to crouch down because I was shaking so much — and I looked over and saw him. And I am so sorry,' he cries. 'I am so sorry for what we did.'

I can't listen anymore, Gran. I can't bear to imagine Raff lying at the bottom of the quarry, knowing they did nothing to help.

'You just left him there,' I yell. 'You left him, and you made out you weren't anywhere near.'

'I was only fourteen,' Eleanor pleads. 'And we were so scared. We thought we would end up in jail and we made a stupid decision to say nothing, because he was gone. It was too late, and we didn't know what to do, and — oh God!' she cries. 'Please, it was wrong, but we didn't know what to do.'

'You got away with killing him. You all just moved on and lived your lives as if nothing happened—'

'No. Hannah didn't,' Connie says, finally. 'My sister still pays for her part in this. She's never forgiven herself for what happened. Why else do you think she does the job she does now?'

I laugh out loud at this. 'Are you kidding me?' I spit. 'You think being a counsellor to teenagers is paying for the fact someone is dead because of what she did?'

'Jennie, you have the truth,' Daniel cuts in. 'And you'll do with that whatever you need to, but please, you have to let us go. We can walk out of here and we can admit what happened, but you don't want to do this any longer. You don't want to hurt anyone.'

'No!' Jacob shouts then. 'No, she doesn't get to do whatever she wants. She's held us in here all day. And it was an accident. You heard that, right? It was an accident. But this isn't! Holding us all hostage, locked up, waving a gun in our faces for hours on end . . .'

'Shut up!' I cry. 'All of you.' Their noise is deafening, and I can't think straight, Gran. I'm already pushed to my limits. And what does it matter if they walk out of here and tell the truth? I am going to be the one who is handcuffed and led away. I will be the person arrested and sent to prison. Not one of them. They'll get away with it all over again.

So God, please, tell me, Gran, what do I do?

It all happens in a split second. I don't see anybody lunging at me from the side. I don't feel Connie Parish coming for me until she slams into me, trying to wrench the gun out of my grip.

'Do something!' she is yelling at the others.

It's one split second, but I see how they all react: Eleanor taking a step back; Daniel freezing on the spot he has been standing in; Jacob coming for me.

Connie twists my wrist, and I pull my thumb back. One flick of the trigger and it goes off.

Bang.

This time the scream that follows is nothing like the first. When that bullet had fired into the ceiling, no one thought they were in its line. This time it is a blood-curdling gargle of a scream, followed by the thud of a body as it hits the floor.

# Detective Inspector Aaron Field
## 13.13 hours

Aaron is running down the road, heading towards the crowd, his heart thumping with the exertion and the shock of the noise he heard: a second gunshot from within The Boatyard. The one thing he has been dreading all day.

To his right, he sees Kelly climbing out of the van as he passes it. 'Stay where you are,' he calls to her. He doesn't want her down there, seven and a half months pregnant. She's been vital today, but he only agreed to her coming knowing she could be safely ensconced in the van.

Her face says she knows what she's heard, but then everyone in the crowd knows. Shrieks of fear are blended with anticipation. All of them forgetting the relatives whose only concern is the safety of their loved ones inside the building. Hannah is still at his heels.

Aaron pulls out his phone and calls the Tactical Firearms Commander. 'What's your situation?' he asks.

'We're ready to go.'

It is up to Aaron to make the call. One shot could mean

anything: potentially even that Jennie Hogan has shot herself. He can't wait around for someone else to get hurt.

'Go!' he commands, before turning to where Kelly is still standing. 'Get the paramedics down there,' he yells.

Aaron has had a bad feeling something was going to go wrong. He knew it was only a matter of time until everything imploded. No contact in six hours. And now he knows the motive is revenge, a desire that is often impossible to control.

'What's happening?' Hannah shouts from behind as he picks up his pace again. He turns to find Liv Hamilton has followed them too.

'You need to stay back,' he says to the women.

'No way. My sister's in there.'

'And my husband,' Liv adds.

He no longer believes any of the relatives has been lying to him. They have all most likely been kept in the dark: Liv, Ede, Rosa and Gareth, who is still being restrained by an officer to Aaron's left. 'Fine. You can all come with me,' Aaron says. 'But we stay well back. We won't be going anywhere near the building, you got that? We'll be keeping at a safe distance.' As long as he can keep them away from The Boatyard, they don't need to be caught up among the journalists and the rubberneckers.

They stare back at him and Aaron takes his chances, beginning to lead them past the barrier and away from the crowd of onlookers. He is followed by Hannah, Gareth and the officer who was with him, then Liv, whose friend stays behind with Jacob's mother.

A voice calls out, 'Wait!' Aaron turns to see Rosa Williams running after them. 'I heard a gunshot.' She scans the small group, eyes settling momentarily on Hannah who she hasn't seen before, turning back to Aaron as she asks, 'I'm right, aren't I?'

*Really?* he thinks. Every one of them is here apart from poor Ede who still has no idea this is her granddaughter's doing, or how much Jennie has been suffering.

'Come on,' he says by way of answer as he leads them to a spot some distance from the building still, but where there is a clear line of sight to the front doors. His heart thumps as he watches these, telling the officer to keep them back. Under no circumstances must any of them think they can go any nearer.

He is in the middle of warning them again when the doors open and two firearms officers walk out, flanking a woman in handcuffs.

'That's Jennie,' Hannah says.

Aaron detects a note of anguish in her voice and can't help but feel his heart sink at the sight of her.

He blocks out the questions that are being fired at him, his thoughts all on Jennie Hogan and how she must have thought she had nothing to lose any longer. How's she going to tolerate the fact she's the one who will come out of this the worst off yet again? The others won't pay for what happened all those years ago. Rafferty Jones's death was an accident, but she won't see it that way.

Jennie has blurred the lines between right and wrong today. Some people will undoubtedly agree that the others deserve to pay for their past actions and that maybe she was right to exact revenge.

But fair or not, it isn't Jennie's right to decide. The victim has become the predator, and at the end of the day what she did was wrong. No matter that anyone might have done the same in her position.

Besides, Aaron is certain they will all pay in some way. They may not be charged with Rafferty's death, but the fallout of what they did will affect marriages, families, careers, in ways they might not comprehend today, but they will.

Jennie's face is taut with fear as she looks about her, perhaps searching for her grandmother. Aaron holds out his hand in a gesture for the group behind him to stay where they are. He needs to tell Jennie himself.

He walks over to her. 'Jennie Hogan?' he says. 'DI Field.'

Her eyes are hollowed out from what he guesses is exhaustion. 'Is my gran here? I can't see her.'

'She was,' Aaron says. 'I'm afraid she's been taken to hospital.'

'Oh God.' Her already pale face goes a shade whiter. 'What's happened to her?'

'She collapsed. We'll get an update for you on her condition.' He kicks himself that he doesn't already have one. He hasn't had the chance to talk properly to Kelly since he asked her to get one.

'She collapsed because of me,' Jennie cries, her legs buckling beneath her. She would fall to the ground if she wasn't handcuffed to one of the firearms officers.

'We'll make sure you know how she is as soon as we can,' he says. There is nothing more he can tell her.

He watches as she's ushered into a police car, and waits for the engine to start and the car to roll away.

'Sir?' An officer appears in the doorway to The Boatyard. 'One fatality,' he says as the hostages begin to be led out.

'Shit,' Aaron mutters as he hears someone shrieking from behind him.

'Daniel!' Rosa races forward. 'Oh my God, Daniel.' She is crying as she races into the arms of her husband. 'I thought you were going to die,' she sobs, her relief palpable. 'I thought I was going to lose you.'

Aaron can't take his eyes off Daniel Williams who wraps his arms around his wife's tiny frame, resting his head on top of hers as he closes his eyes and appears to sink into her. Even from here, Aaron can see how the strength has been drained from him. He looks defeated as he clings to her, and she to him. Aaron wonders, briefly, how someone who is as relatively well known as Daniel is will move on from today.

Eleanor is led out now. Everything happening so quickly. Sirens blaring urgently in the distance, getting closer. Aaron notices her clock her husband, holding her hand up in a wave as he runs towards her. She breaks down as he reaches her, gripping on to his jacket with both hands as she rests her head against his chest.

There is a tenderness in the way Gareth Lombard holds his wife's head in his hands, tears streaming down his face as he looks into her eyes. He is murmuring something Aaron can't decipher.

The reunions bring a lump to his throat. He can only imagine what each of them has gone through today: the fear of not knowing if the person they love is going to live or die. He has seen it too many times in his job.

His *job* today was preservation of life. But one of them

is lying dead in the building, He will have to answer for his actions, be judged on whether or not he made the right decisions.

'Who's the victim?' he says to the officer. Connie Parish or Jacob Hamilton. He glances back to where the depleted group of relatives stands, to Hannah and Liv who are both in the grip of fear as they gape at The Boatyard.

As he's given the name and is told what happened, his eyes seek out the woman to whom he needs to break the news. This never gets easier. They teach you to distance yourself, but it never gets easier.

Aaron walks back towards Liv and Hannah, and the officer who is still with them, his heart thudding.

'Connie!' Hannah cries as he watches her gaze flick from him to the building behind him. 'Connie!' she shrieks, louder this time as she sees her sister emerging from The Boatyard. He glances over his shoulder as the sisters run towards each other then quickly turns back to Liv who is shivering, her arms clutched to her chest.

'Where is he?' she says, her voice catching on the words. 'Where's Jacob—' She breaks off, as if she has seen what she needs to know in his face.

'Mrs Hamilton, I'm sorry,' Aaron tells her. 'There was a struggle. Someone grabbed for the gun, and I'm so sorry,' he says again as she begins shaking her head in denial and telling him no. She doesn't want to hear it, but he has to go on. 'Jacob died straight away.'

'No,' she says. 'No, that can't have happened,' she begs as the words wash over her. 'He can't be dead.'

'I'm so sorry,' he says again.

'No,' she wails, and he can hear the pain in her voice, see it in her eyes. He wishes there was anything he could do to take it away from her. But there is nothing. Absolutely nothing. 'I'll find your friend and mother-in-law,' he tells her. 'And I'm going to get an officer to stay with you. We'll answer any questions you have with whatever information we know as soon as we have it.'

That doesn't mean anything to her. The woman has lost her husband today. Her life has shattered irretrievably. 'I'm so sorry,' he tells her again.

# One month later

Daniel Williams is too close to the edge. His legs could give way any moment, and it wouldn't take much for him to step forward and jump. There is a compulsion, it's even been named something like 'the call of the void', or 'high-place phenomenon'. He briefly researched it once for one of his books about a woman who couldn't help herself from taking flight off a tall building. Daniel didn't understand it then but in this moment, he does. To be so dangerously close and hold the power of that decision.

'Daniel, get back,' Rosa calls, but there's no real worry in her voice. She is more concerned that the edge of the precipice might crumble beneath his feet and give way. He feels her hand on his arm as she gently tugs at him, and he steps back like she wants him to do.

'I only came here that once, a few months ago,' he says, 'when I was writing the book. I didn't want to; I'd avoided it for years.'

'So why did you?' she asks.

'Because I thought if I was going to write a story about it, I needed to see it. My memories were—' He cuts off. 'I didn't think they were all that clear, but when I came back, I realised I remembered everything about that day. Everything,' he adds, shaking his head to try and rid it of the thoughts. 'Nothing's really changed about this place.'

'How are you feeling now?' she asks him.

'Glad you're with me.' He looks at her and smiles, eyes glistening with tears as he shrugs and holds out his hand to her. She clenches it in her own. 'Rewriting the story was supposed to be therapy for me,' he tells her, gazing back at the void of the quarry. 'That day never left me, of course it didn't. How could it? I always felt this need to talk to someone about it, tell someone what we did.'

'You could have told me.'

'No,' he answers, quickly. Then, 'If I did that, I would have burdened you with a terrible truth you'd have had to hold on to. It wasn't that I didn't trust you,' he says. 'I just didn't want it eating away at you. For you to be left wondering whether you should tell anyone or not. I don't think you would ever have betrayed me?' he says. There is a question in his voice.

'No,' Rosa says. 'I don't think I would.' She has asked herself this a lot in the last month. If her husband had confided in her what had happened, would she have gone to the police? Or would she have decided there was no point in bringing up the past – a tragic accident that happened all those years ago? They'd have assumed everyone had moved on with their lives, that it would do no good. They would have told each other this, whether they believed it or not.

But she wouldn't have been able to tell her parents. And there would have been nights when he was working on his latest book, and she was alone, curled up in bed, when unwelcome thoughts would have broken in. Sharp knives twisting in her gut, asking how she could live with this dark secret.

Daniel is right, it would have eaten away at her.

'I didn't want to tell anyone, not a counsellor or anything like that. I wouldn't have trusted anyone other than you,' he says. 'So, the next best thing was for me to write the story, changing it in places so it didn't come back at any of us. And I guess I found the whole process cathartic even though I don't know I'd ever have got as far as allowing it to be published. I still believe there'd always have been a moment when I told my agent I didn't want to write it any longer. I don't know.' He shrugs. 'I don't know if that's really the case, but it's what I thought when I started.

'I think this is it now,' he says. 'I think this is the end.'

'The end?' she says. 'What are you talking about?'

'Of my writing. I don't see how I can carry on after everything that's been said about me.'

'No. You can't stop,' Rosa urges him. She can't imagine her husband not doing the one thing that makes him happy. She can't envisage what their life would be like if Daniel didn't write. Yes, he has come off the worst, in some respects, by virtue of the fact he is a well-known author, and his name alone creates headlines.

The press were like vultures once they'd caught on to this aspect of the story, after the excitement of the release of the hostages had passed and they'd had their fill of the death of Jacob Hamilton at the hands of a local waitress. Then they'd wanted the nitty-gritty of why it had happened and how each of the old school friends had been summoned there to pay for their part in a death that happened twenty-five years before. Then it was Daniel's name that had stirred the most interest.

'You'll be yesterday's news soon enough,' she tells him.

'I don't know.' He sounds resigned already, like he's made his decision. 'I don't know it's even important.'

'Oh, Daniel,' Rosa says as she turns him to face her, looks into the eyes of the man she loves. 'It *is* important,' she says. She doesn't know how to take this hurt away from him.

'Don't worry. This isn't going to send me off down another spiral. It's nothing like it was back then.'

She understands this, at least. His depression when they met was caused by a hanging cloud of dread. He couldn't shake off the memory of his part in what they had done, and he couldn't talk about it with anyone. Now at least he can discuss it with whoever he wants. They have the opposite problem when everyone on the Isle of Wight knows what happened.

'Thank you.' He leans forward and presses his lips against her head, holding them there as she asks what for. 'For being there, for coming with me today. For not once judging me or making me feel like you were going to leave me.' He pulls away then and she looks at him curiously.

'What is it?' she asks, because she fears there is something else. Something he isn't telling her.

'Nothing.' He shakes his head, sharply. 'There's nothing,' he says again. 'And thank you for not questioning if it might have been me holding that gun,' he adds, with a small laugh.

Rosa smiles back at him, burying her head back against his chest. 'Of course,' she murmurs as he wraps his arms around her and holds her. She won't tell him there was a fleeting moment when she didn't believe in him. Or that she had told her dad as much. No good would come of that. Despite everything that has happened, some secrets are better kept to yourself. 'I love you more than anything,' she tells him.

On Wednesday afternoon Gareth is waiting in the school playground, Jack's small hand clutching on to his as he waits for Ben to appear at his classroom door. 'Can you see your brother yet?' he asks, forcing cheer into his voice while his heart thumps a little too fast for his liking. It's silly that it does but it's such a new arrangement, him picking the boys up from school, and he is prepared for some backlash from one of them.

He sees Ben then, peering around the teacher as he searches the playground. Most likely it is Eleanor he is looking for, but he sees his father and then his brother and holds up a small hand in a wave. Ben nudges the teacher and must tell her he can see his dad because she looks in Gareth's direction, smiles and ushers the child out of the queue forming behind her.

'Hey, how was your day?' Gareth beams when Ben gets closer.

''S'okay. Someone brought reptiles in. I held a snake.'

'Did you? That was very brave. I don't think I could have done that.'

Ben shrugs. 'Are we going home?'

'No, we're going for pizza and soft play, aren't we? Remember?' Gareth asks, still grinning like an idiot.

'Yes. I remember,' Ben says.

'It's that one with the really high bumpy slide that Mummy says you both love.' The one Eleanor hates because there are too many blind spots where she can't see the boys. 'Make sure you keep an eye on them at all times, won't you, Gareth?' she has told him, more than once.

'Of course I will. I'll look after them like they're my own,' he had joked. She had stared back at him with horror and so he added, 'Eleanor, I'll look after them.'

She knows he will, but it doesn't stop her worrying. He feels for her really. He might think she over-reacts, but he also acknowledges her anxiety is sky-high when it comes to their boys. This new arrangement will test her. Having to relinquish control every Wednesday, and then next weekend he's having them for two nights.

'What are you going to do with them?' she has asked him. 'Will you please come and stay at the house, and I'll go somewhere else for the weekend?'

'Where would you go?'

'I don't know. My mother's?'

'Eleanor,' he sighed. They both know how much she would hate that.

'But it means the boys can stay in their own rooms, and it will be better for them. They'll be less confused—' She broke down then. She's been breaking down a lot over the last month. She was in tears every night for three weeks and then, since he moved out into the guest house three roads away from their home, she has cried on the phone to him too.

Maybe the best thing for the boys is for Gareth to spend every other weekend in their home. Whatever they decide must be in their sons' best interests. But next weekend his parents have booked an Airbnb in Lymington and so he's taking the boys there. 'For a mini holiday,' he has said to them. They don't want to go without Eleanor and so he's still unsure it will happen, warning his mum it might only be him who turns up.

Gareth braves a smile as he straps them both into the back of his car.

'What do you think the future's going to look like, Gareth?' Eleanor has asked him. 'Are you going to keep working in Portsmouth? Are you still going to live on the Isle of Wight? Are you going to want to take the boys over to the mainland every other weekend?' There is always such panic in her voice.

'I don't know any of that,' he's told her. 'We're just going to have to work it through in time.'

'It wasn't supposed to be like this!' she cried when he stood in their kitchen three days ago on Sunday. The boys were playing in the garden. 'When we got married, it was supposed to be for ever.'

'I know,' he said. 'And it breaks my heart too.'

'Then why are you doing it, Gareth?' she had shrieked.

'Eleanor,' he pleaded, and she carried on crying as she stared out at the garden, to where Ben was pushing his brother down the red plastic slide. 'You know why this has happened. We've been through it. Right now, it's for the best.'

She turned to him. 'Right now? You think you can walk out on us, and then come back home whenever you want?'

'That's not what I'm saying.'

'I can't believe you're doing this to us. To the boys.' She gestured out of the window.

'You don't love me, Eleanor,' he said.

She had stopped arguing then, gulping back sobs.

'And it's good that it all came out, because it had to. You've been seeing a counsellor for six months and I knew nothing about it. You'd been putting money aside to pay for it without telling me. And frankly, that isn't a good basis for any marriage.'

'Because I didn't know where else to turn.'

'Because you weren't happy,' he pointed out. 'Honestly, I don't think you've ever been happy with me.'

It breaks him to admit this, but he knew it and his parents knew it too. Turned out his best friends did as well, though none of that surprised Gareth. Eleanor didn't exactly hide her disdain over the latter years, but even in the beginning she never showed him love. He was just there: comfortable and reliable Gareth. Someone she never had to worry about in a world where Eleanor worried about everything. Not just the boys, but never being good enough too, all the things that were starting to come out in therapy, and that he's pretty sure they're only cutting through the surface of.

'But this isn't making me happy either,' she had pleaded.

'I know. But I don't know what else to do about that,' he told her. 'I just know that right now we both need space to work out what the future's going to look like.'

He arrives at the soft play car park where he lets the boys out and they run to the doors, not looking back for him as they push them open and let themselves in. They're already at the counter when he makes it inside, suddenly caught up in their excitement.

Gareth finds a table as close to the inflatable hell as he can, orders a coffee and sits down as his phone rings.

'Is everything okay?' Eleanor asks him.

'Of course it is.'

'Okay. Just call me if you need anything.'

'I will,' he tells her, patiently. He imagines her sitting in their beautiful home, alone, no idea what to do with herself when she doesn't have the boys' tea to make, or games to play, or questions to ask about their day. He feels a pang of guilt that he knows he shouldn't, but it is there nonetheless. He doesn't want Eleanor to be hurt. He still loves her. He always will when she is the mother of his boys.

In truth, he would love for none of this to have happened. He would like nothing more than for his wife to turn around a month from now and tell him how much she wants him home, but he has a strong feeling that won't happen.

Plus, something has broken in him this last month. It's not just that his wife's been confiding in a stranger that she isn't happy in her marriage, or even that she's been keeping a secret from him about a young boy who died when she was a teenager. Or that Eleanor was a bully when she was at school, and she could never comprehend what being bullied does to anyone; did to him. It's the combination of all these things that gave him the courage to suggest they should take some time apart. 'The boys will be fine,' he had told her on Sunday. 'Because we will make sure they are.'

Ede closes her eyes as she rests her head back.

'Look at this,' Marjorie says, flapping a magazine in front of Ede's face. 'In America you can pay one hundred dollars to have a snail facial.'

'What on earth is that?' Ede asks.

'They get snails to slither all over your face and leave their mucus in the hope it will plump up your skin. Oh, for heaven's sake, I really have seen everything now. Whatever will they come up with next?' she mutters as Ede laughs. 'Can I get you anything?'

'No. I'm fine.'

'Cup of tea?'

'No. Thank you.'

'Water?'

'Marjorie!' Ede stops her.

'Well, I'll just go back to reading about my snails then, shall I?'

Ede smiles. 'You don't have to sit here with me.'

'Nonsense. What else am I going to do?' Marjorie shifts on the plastic seat beside her. 'Besides . . .' She hesitates. 'I promised Jennie.'

Ede nods, tears threatening as they do every time her granddaughter is mentioned. Her heart sinks at the memory of Jennie, the last time she managed to visit ten days earlier.

It isn't easy when the journey is so long. Her granddaughter is on remand in a prison called Bronzefield that Ede hadn't even heard of before a month ago. It is in Surrey, an hour or so up the M3, and never mind the fact she has to get the ferry across first.

But what else can she expect when Jennie took four people hostage at gun point? When a man was killed. Ede feels sick every time she thinks back to that day. A month hasn't changed the impact of its memory. She wonders if time will ever heal it.

The fallout is unimaginable. A life has been taken, leaving a mother without her son, and a wife who is carrying a child without her husband at her side. A little baby who will be born into the world never having the chance to know its father.

That is something Ede will never be able to come to terms with and yet it is Jennie who is her priority. Her girl, whose life has been for ever changed. Whose life was for ever changed twenty-five years ago, and yet Ede knew nothing of it.

'You mustn't blame yourself, Gran.' Jennie had looked broken ten days earlier. 'You need to promise me you never will.'

It might seem a funny request when Ede knew nothing of it, but anyone who understands the love they share wouldn't question it. They also wouldn't be surprised to hear Ede reply that of course she blames herself.

'I need you to tell me everything the solicitor is discussing with you,' she had said to Jennie. 'Prepare me for what lies ahead and don't think of keeping anything from me. Because I *will* find out.'

Her hands were shaking underneath the table. She was trying not to get upset. She wanted Jennie to think she was being strong and capable. Ede liked to imagine she could sort this whole sorry mess out for her. She didn't fall apart until she got outside, and Marjorie caught her in her arms.

'I don't know for sure,' Jennie told her. 'But I pleaded guilty from the start and so they'll take that into account. It could reduce my sentence by a third.'

There is no mandatory sentence. It could be anything

from two years upwards, Jennie has told her. *As if it will only be two years,* Ede thinks, though they can but pray.

'They take other factors into account too,' Jennie went on, all positivity that Ede knew must only be for her sake. 'My otherwise good character, the fact I didn't intend to cause any physical harm – though, well, as you know, that might not be as easy to prove.'

'And the others?' Ede had questioned. 'The ones who were in there with you.' She could not bring herself to call them hostages. 'What will they say?'

'I don't know. Hopefully, that it was the accident it was.'

'And Liv Hamilton?' Ede had eventually asked.

She could see Jennie deflate at the mention of the woman's name. A flash of pain crossed her face. She hadn't wanted to talk about Jacob Hamilton on this visit, not after the last time when Jennie was inconsolable about what had happened to him.

Ede understood what a mix of emotions Jennie must be going through. A man who had made her life a misery – of course there had to be a part of her that wanted to cause him harm. But to take his life? Well, Jennie isn't that person.

So Ede had moved the subject on, asking, 'I mean, what does your solicitor think she might say? Anything that could go against you?'

'She could make a personal statement about Jacob,' Jennie admitted. 'About how his death has affected their family. So yes, I guess that could go against me,' she added quietly. 'You know, with her being pregnant.'

'Oh dear,' Ede had sighed.

'Gran, what are you thinking?'

Ede's thoughts were a whole heap of a mess. She was thinking about Rafferty Jones and how she remembered the little boy and his parents. Such a loving family. So tragic. She was thinking that she couldn't forgive those four people for what they did to him, nor for the way they used to torment her Jennie.

She was also wondering what she would have done if Jennie had told her at the time that she was being bullied. Walked round to their houses and threatened the evil kids? Threatened their parents?

Or what would she have done six weeks ago if her granddaughter had finally spilt the rage she'd been carrying inside her all this time? Ede would have wanted to exact some kind of revenge. At least in her head. She'd have imagined Daniel's writing career drying up, and Eleanor Lombard's husband leaving her. Hannah Parish paying in some way that Ede couldn't put a finger on.

But she would never have wanted a man to die. And Jennie hadn't either. She can see the anguish tormenting her granddaughter. It is one more thing Jennie will have to live with for ever.

And Ede was also thinking that she knew Liv Hamilton would do whatever she must to redress her husband's death, and that it would be to Jennie's detriment.

'Oh dear,' she groans now to Marjorie. She cannot get comfortable.

'Ede, are you okay?' her neighbour questions.

'Yes. You must stop fussing.'

Marjorie is frowning. 'You don't look right. Shall I get a nurse?'

'No. No nurse. I'm okay. Did you see Plum this morning?'

'Of course I did, she ate all the food.'

Ede nods as Marjorie strokes her hand. 'What would I do without you?' she murmurs.

'You'd have to get a bus back from the hospital for a start.' Ede laughs.

'How long are we going be here for anyway? I told Ray he was going to have to put his own chicken in the oven.'

'We'll be able to leave by 4. 5 at the latest.'

'And you're staying with me tonight. This treatment, it's going to knock you out.'

'It might do,' Ede admits. 'But it's worth it, isn't it?'

'Absolutely.' Marjorie nods. 'One hundred percent.' Her neighbour smiles.

'I won't leave Jennie even one day too soon now.' Ede smiles in return as she closes her eyes again and leans her head back against the hospital chair.

'There's the heart.' The midwife smiles at Liv. 'Can you see?' She points her finger at the screen as the beat gallops loudly.

'I can see,' Liv says as she stares at the image on the monitor. 'So, it's healthy?'

'As far as we can tell everything is progressing exactly as it should.'

Liv smiles to herself now, relaxing back on the bed. 'And you can't tell its sex?'

'Not until twenty weeks.'

'Do you want to know?' Joyce asks in a whisper. She is squeezing Liv's hand as she also stares at the picture. Liv's mother had wanted to be the one to come to the first scan.

'Don't you think it should be me?' she had said. 'Rather than getting poor Joyce to come all this way.'

Liv hasn't told her parents yet what she's spoken to Joyce about. She's found a small house half an hour's drive from Wimbledon and put down a deposit. It's a twelve-month rental that'll be vacant by the end of May and will be perfect for Joyce to move in to. She wants her mother-in-law close. Already she knows that Joyce is the one she'll turn to for help. Her own mum may be physically more capable, but she still rushes around between appointments, planning holidays abroad over the next year. She doesn't intend to be on hand for Liv, not really, and Liv is okay with that.

'I don't know if I'll find out,' Liv says. 'What do you think we should do?'

'Oh, well, in my day we didn't have the choice. But I guess things are different now, aren't they? People are buying all that colour co-ordinated nursery furniture and what have you.'

'I don't think I will,' Liv says. 'It'll be nice to have a surprise.'

Joyce smiles. Neither of them can tear their eyes away from the little peanut shape on the screen in front of them. 'I wish Jacob could see this,' she says.

Liv clears her throat. 'Could you give us a minute?' she says to the midwife. She doesn't know what she wants to say when it is just the two of them, but this moment feels too personal to share with a stranger.

'I don't mean to upset you, love,' Joyce says.

'You're not upsetting me.'

'Oh dear, I am. You're crying.'

'Well, it's bittersweet, isn't it? And it's always going to be like this, so I suppose it's something we have to get used to.'

'He would have made a lovely dad, you know,' Joyce murmurs. 'Don't you think?'

'I think he would,' Liv tells her. What else is she supposed to say to his mother? Or to herself for that matter. It is what she will be saying to their child in the years to come, after all. Liv has no choice but to shower their baby with comforting stories about their father.

Like how he was funny, and he could make her laugh out loud in a way no one else ever had before. And how incredibly handsome he was. Even up to the last time Liv saw him when he kissed her goodbye and walked out of their home that Sunday evening one month earlier, he still had the ability to make her stomach flip. And how he did things for her like opening doors and putting the bins out every week, and how he always offered to cook but never did because he was terrible at it. And that he would iron her clothes if they were going out for an evening, while she was in the bath.

There are so many stories she can pass on to their baby that mean she doesn't have to think about the others. No one is all bad. Jacob certainly wasn't.

Joyce doesn't know the extent to which Liv had been questioning her husband that day, and how quick she was to believe he was having an affair. Only Katy saw her expose the rawness of their marriage and Liv tells herself that anyone would have done the same in her position, if they were faced with the fact their husband was lying to them.

She isn't sure what to make of what she now knows about Jacob's past. Sometimes she and Joyce wonder if the others are using him as a scapegoat. Other times she believes, deep down, they are telling the truth.

Liv has been asked if she wants to make a personal statement about her husband for the prosecution.

'It could go in your favour, help secure a longer sentence for Ms Hogan,' the solicitor told her. It would be easy to show how much his death has affected her when she's carrying his unborn child.

'Joyce,' she says now. 'Have you been thinking about that personal statement?'

'Oh, well, dear, yes. I suppose I have given it some thought.'

'What do you think we should do?'

She watches her mother-in-law intently, biting her lip as she continues to study the picture on the scan. The books say she might be able to feel the baby in another three to four weeks.

'I'll do whatever you think is best,' Joyce says, eventually turning to look at her.

Liv has been thinking about this a lot. About Jennie Hogan, whose actions have taken her husband from her.

And then about the other three people inside the café who have all said that Jennie didn't intend to hurt anyone. And how the gunshot was an accident when someone lurched towards her to grab the gun.

Liv has been thinking about the stories that have been told about her husband, and how he cajoled the boy called Rafferty Jones to go to the quarry. How he tried to tie him up to a tree and how the boy was so scared he fell backwards over a sheer drop.

She shudders at the thought of it. Liv wasn't there. She doesn't know what really happened. All she can do is try to reconcile that version of Jake with the Jacob she knew. Stand by her husband and make a personal statement about the good man he was. Doesn't she owe him this much?

She is desperate to do the right thing. At her core this is what makes Liv the person she is. But still she keeps coming back to the niggling idea that, while this is who *she* is, it is not the person her husband was.

Eventually she says to Joyce, 'I don't think we should make one.'

Joyce nods. 'I agree,' she says.

Liv breathes a little lighter. It is the right thing. Jennie Hogan will pay for what she did that day, but Liv will not make it worse for her.

'I didn't know whether you would see me.' Hannah is sitting opposite Jennie Hogan. She hasn't seen her in the flesh since they left school at sixteen.

'I didn't think you would come,' Jennie replies.

Hannah isn't sure she would have recognised Jennie if she'd bumped into her in the street, not if she hadn't seen her photo splashed across the papers. She only did the moment Jennie walked out of The Boatyard, handcuffed to a police officer, because she was expecting to see her.

But if Hannah had been the one to find the note that had been pushed through their letterbox, instead of Connie, and she had been the one to go to the marina at 7 a.m. as requested, she isn't certain she would have realised it was Jennie standing behind the counter that morning. The others hadn't after all. Not until it was too late.

Hannah still wakes in the middle of the night, skin flushed with heat and dripping with sweat from a nightmare. 'It's nothing new,' she's told Connie. Her sister knows she's had nightmares since they were teenagers, just not the extent of them. Over the years they have come out in different ways. The dream that has been most frequent is of Abbie slipping over a precipice, Hannah reaching out a hand to save her but never being able to.

She isn't sure why she replaces Raff with Abbie in her dreams. Or why they don't take place in Bluestone Quarry. Or even why she always tries to reach out for Abbie when in reality she was immobile the moment Raff went over.

Maybe it's because of the inordinate amount of responsibility she has always felt for the girl. Maybe it's that Hannah feels responsible for Raff's death too.

Now she feels an added responsibility, for the fact her sister was at The Boatyard instead of her.

Connie has grown tired of telling Hannah what happened that day, but Hannah has wanted every detail, every moment relived, from the letter she had found on her doormat a week earlier.

'Why didn't you give it to me?' Hannah challenged her.

'Honestly, I didn't see your name on the front. I thought it was an early birthday card,' Connie said. 'Then I read it and—' She broke off. 'I didn't know what I was walking into,' she admitted. 'But it said it was from Eleanor, and after everything you've told me I just didn't trust her.'

'You didn't trust me to deal with her,' Hannah stated.

'No. That's not what I meant.' Connie looked up, but there was a sheepish tell in her expression. 'I never liked her when you were friends as kids,' she said. 'I had no idea why you hung about with her. When you told me everything that happened, you said yourself you were under her spell.'

'I was fourteen,' Hannah cried. 'I'm thirty-nine now. I wasn't going to be under her spell still.'

'I didn't want to take that chance. Jesus, Hannah, look at yourself. Your whole life is dedicated to trying to make up for what you did. You think by saving one kid at a time you can chip away at your misplaced guilt. But you never feel any different. It's drowning you. You don't want to live your life to its fullest, or meet anyone, or even have fun,' she said. 'And I hate seeing you withering away the way you are.'

'That's not true.'

'Yes. It is all true. And you know it.'

Hannah felt her cheeks burning. 'I still would have been able to handle Eleanor.'

'I didn't want you to see her,' Connie told her. 'And I didn't want you to have to handle her, because you didn't need all that coming up again. I thought I could find out what she wanted to talk about and figure it hopefully wasn't all that bad. And I did *not* want you missing your interview for it.'

'I thought you were pissed off I hadn't taken the day off,' Hannah admitted.

'You're kidding, right?'

Hannah had smiled. 'What's Eleanor like now?' she'd asked Connie.

'A mother,' she'd replied. 'That's pretty much how I'd sum her up. Other than that, I don't know, Han. I saw her in her worst moments.'

'And Jennie?'

'Angry you weren't there. Angry at me because of it. Angry at the world.'

'She has every right to be,' Hannah said as Connie got up, saying she was going to finally open that bottle of Chablis she'd bought for her birthday.

She had stopped in the doorway. 'You know I would do it again for you?' Connie said.

'I know,' Hannah had told her.

'I'm sorry I wasn't there,' Hannah says to Jennie now. 'I should have been.'

Jennie raises her eyes questioningly. 'You're sorry?' she says, mockingly. 'For not being held at gunpoint?'

'Well, I'd rather it was me and not my sister. But also, I imagine you probably had things you wanted to say to me. You can say them now,' she adds. 'Ask me anything.'

'And you'll be honest?' Jennie tries.

'Yes,' Hannah tells her as she inhales a tight breath at the thought of what is coming.

Jennie hesitates a moment, as if considering what she wants to know. 'Why didn't you ever stand up to Eleanor?'

'I thought if I did, I would lose her as a friend,' Hannah answers truthfully. 'And being on the right side of her was easier when everyone else seemed to love her so much.'

'No one loved her. They were just scared of her.'

'I know. I was too. I was scared I'd be ostracised.'

'The way I was?'

Hannah pauses, keeps looking at Jennie. 'Yes,' she says. 'Like you were.'

'I thought you were my friend.'

'I was. I really liked you, Jennie. But I was thirteen when we drifted apart and it was because I needed more friends, girls who went out and did stuff and had a laugh. Believe me, I know how shallow that sounds but it's the way it is at that age. I see it all the time with girls today.'

'You didn't need to be my friend,' Jennie tells her. 'You just needed to speak out. Once. You needed to tell her to back off. You needed to say that chasing Raff through the woods when he was so scared was wrong. You *needed* to tell someone the truth about what happened that day.'

'I know,' Hannah admits. 'I know all of that.'

'Counselling teenagers doesn't make up for any of it. Not when you could have said something at any point over the last twenty-five years.'

'I know.'

'But at the end of the day you chose getting away with it over coming clean.'

'If it was only me, I would have said something,' Hannah admits. 'But it wasn't. It was three other lives, and we'd made a pact. And I didn't know how I could betray that.'

Hannah sees the way Jennie's eyes darken at this. The fact that the four of them colluded with each other to keep such a dreadful secret. She remembers it so well, walking away from the others knowing she didn't want anything to do with any of them ever again.

Two weeks ago, she'd sat in a coffee shop opposite

Eleanor and Daniel, and even though the years showed through the lines on their faces, and the colour of their hair, in another more haunting way it felt like no time had passed at all. They'd agreed to meet just the once. Sitting down with their coffees, they'd uttered regret that Jacob – or Jake, as they'd always known him – had died. They'd spoken about what happened that day at The Boathouse. And also what happened all those years ago at the quarry. Two people dead. Because of them.

After two hours they'd walked away, and Hannah realised that if anything she felt worse than she had done before. For three nights following their meet-up, she'd dreamt of her sister being held at gunpoint. Only she was the one holding the gun. She'd had the same dream again last night.

'It was wrong,' Jennie hisses.

'I know. But it's also the truth. I would have said something if it was only me who would have had to deal with the consequences.

'I don't ever expect you to forgive me,' Hannah goes on when Jennie doesn't respond. 'I'll never ask for that. But I want to be here for you, Jennie. I want to try and make it up to you if it isn't too late. In whatever way I can.'

Jennie looks away and when she speaks it's not what Hannah expects. 'Do you think anyone will forgive me?' Her tone is abrupt and yet Hannah can tell she needs an answer.

'Yes,' Hannah urges. 'I know you didn't mean to hurt anyone. The others know that too.'

Jennie's eyes well up with tears as she bites her lip. When she turns back to Hannah she says, quietly, 'I have to live with the decisions I made for the rest of my life too. Now I have to live with the fact someone else ended up dead because of me. I'm no different from any of you.'

Hannah shakes her head. She didn't come here for an apology. As far as she is concerned Jennie has nothing to apologise for, even if she's the only one who thinks that.

'I do regret that, you know.'

'I know,' Hannah tells her.

Jennie's pain is palpable. Hannah feels it deep in her own heart. And it hits her how they aren't that dissimilar either. Neither of them has many people in their lives who they can turn to. Both of them have only one person who is their world.

Hannah wants to change that if she can. 'I was thinking that I can be there to look out for your gran,' she suggests, moving the conversation on. 'I can bring her here if you would like me to? Just say what you think she might need.'

Jennie seems to consider what Hannah is offering. When she finally answers, she says, 'You can make sure she keeps living.'

'Of course I will.' Hannah feels a lump in her throat. She knows a little about Ede Hogan and that she's going through treatment for cancer, or at least that's what she believes it to be. 'I'll do that,' she says, making a promise they both must know she cannot keep.

Eventually, Hannah gets up to leave. 'I don't expect you to want me to, but would it be okay if I visited you again?'

'I don't need friends,' Jennie says quickly.

Hannah shrugs. 'I could do with one.'

Jennie regards her, looking away again with a tell-tale glisten of tears still in her eyes. 'Fine,' she says eventually. 'Fine, if that's what you want.'

Hannah nods and is about to take a step away from the small visitor's table when Jennie stops her.

'You said I could ask you anything.'

Hannah cocks her head and nods.

'Did they tell me the truth?' Jennie asks. 'About what happened at the quarry?'

Hannah feels the blood drain from her face and hopes it hasn't taken the colour with it. Her mind flashes back to the day and how it had all happened so quickly before they ran away and made their pact never to talk of being there ever again.

She thinks back to two weeks ago and how she, Eleanor and Daniel broke their silence just that once.

It was Daniel who had said it. 'Only—' He had paused, hastily glancing at each of them in turn. 'It *was* an accident, wasn't it?'

Hannah had felt her throat constricting.

'Of course it was,' Eleanor had interrupted. 'We saw Raff stepping back.'

Hannah watched Daniel, his fingers clawing into the table. He was nodding but his face betrayed the fact he didn't entirely agree. 'I don't know if that's how I remember it. And I want to say it, just this once and then never again.' He'd shaken his head. 'I think Jacob pushed Raff.'

'No!' Eleanor was adamant. 'No, that isn't what happened.'

Daniel glanced at Hannah, desperate for her to give him

an answer, likely hoping for her to confirm what Eleanor said was true.

Only she wasn't sure. She never had been. And she'd pushed it to the back of her mind from that day on.

But Daniel's words raised one flicker of memory that has taunted her at times. *Had* she seen Jake's hand on Raff? *Had* Jake pushed him?

The truth was she wasn't sure, but then as Daniel voiced his doubts, Hannah felt the air spinning around her.

She'd clamped her eyes shut, not wanting any memory of that kind to burn into her eyelids, because over the years she'd convinced herself it wasn't true. Memory can play the harshest of tricks after all.

'I've tried to tell myself he didn't,' Daniel said.

'And he didn't.' Eleanor was firm.

Did she really believe that? Because if Jacob had pushed him, then their silence is more damning.

By then Daniel was nodding again, more vehemently this time. 'Yes, you're right,' he said, because perhaps all he needed was for one person to tell him he was wrong, and he could live with that. She was sure Daniel would never utter another word about it. Dredging up half-formed memories now that Jacob was dead would do no good.

Jennie is looking at her now, waiting.

Knowing, *believing*, that Jacob pushed Raff is so much worse. And Eleanor *had* been adamant this wasn't the case. It would be so easy for Hannah to take her word and tell Jennie that they'd told her the truth.

But she can't.

Not just for her own sanity, but because she cannot lie

to Jennie. And so, she says what she trusts to be true. 'I think they believed they were telling you the truth.' Hannah pauses. 'And all in honesty, it might be.'

'But?'

'But I don't know that it is. I think I've always believed deep down I saw Jacob push him.'

She watches as Jennie releases a breath she's been holding and a look of something crosses her face. Relief that she finally knows the truth? Hannah isn't sure, but what she does feel is relief seeping through her own veins that she has finally admitted the truth to herself.

Jacob pushed Rafferty Jones that day. He had been the one to kill him. She knew it then as much as she knows it now. They had all been too scared to do the right thing back then, but she isn't that young girl any longer. And, without even knowing it, perhaps Jacob Hamilton has finally paid the price.

# Acknowledgements

I loved writing *It Ends Here*, and so thank you, readers, for enabling me to carry on doing something I am so passionate about, and also, to all the wonderful bloggers who are so enthused by what they love, and who take the time to read, post and share the love for my books.

As always, heartfelt thanks go to Chris Bradford who has been my absolute rock, providing me with all things police-related through all of my books. He has helped me shape the story realistically and make it better. All mistakes are my own, and I have used artistic licence when needed, because, after all, this is a work of fiction.

I work with such wonderful teams. My agent, Nelle Andrew, who, by the time the book is published, will have been by my side for ten years helping me navigate the ups and downs of having a writing career. Your ideas are always spot on, even when they do mean a complete re-write! And Emily Griffin, who I have also been working with since my very first book, published in 2018. You are an amazing editor; always there at the end of the phone to help, with brilliant advice, and an ability to pick out exactly what is and isn't working.

Many thanks to the teams who bring my books to life at PRH and RML: Hana Sparkes, Issie Levin, Anna Tuck, Annie Peacock, Emma Grey Gelder, Jade Stratton, Alice Gomer, Emily Harvey, Alexandra Cliff and Nick Ash. And now I'm also incredibly lucky to be working with Anna Michels and the team at Sourcebooks to take this book to America.

Finally, to my amazing family who give me all the support and encouragement I need: who enabled me to start writing in the first place (John, that's you, my love); who have believed in me throughout my life (my lovely mum); and who give me the passion to keep doing something I love (Beth and Joseph, my brilliant children). I love you all.